THRILLER

Matthew James Publishing Ltd
Unit 46 Goyt Mill
Upper Hibbert Lane
Marple
SK6 7HX

www.matthewjamespublishing.com

ISBN: 978-1-910265-95-6

CONTENTS

CHAPTER ONE

THE BLACK TRANSIT wove down the single-track road, its headlights piercing through a torrent of rain that seemed unable to make up its mind whether to fall in a vertical or horizontal wave.

The crumbling stone dykes lining either side of the road provided a familiar indication that their meeting place was not far away and the vehicle's driver, a gap-toothed male with a vicious scar running down the left-hand side of his face, shot his passenger a sharp sideways glance. "No fuck-ups, Gregsy, we need the safe blown and emptied sharpish and we need to make sure it goes tae plan."

His colleague was by comparison fresh-faced, yet a slightly ruddy complexion hinted that he was already starting to face a battle with the demon drink to retain the gifts that had made him the most sought after peterman, or safe-blower, in Glasgow.

He nodded his ginger mop curtly by way of an answer, before adding after a short pause: "Don't it always, Jimmy? You just dae yer bit and leave the technical stuff tae me and we'll both be fine. The big man will be purring and before you know it we'll be counting oor wedge and on the way hame to a warm bed where big Betsy will nae doubt be hot and ready for you under the covers."

"Aye, it'll be a case of heavens to Betsy right enough!" quipped big Shug Fowler from the rear of the vehicle.

The one-liner elicited a chorus of rough mirth from the other three members of their team, who sat around the safe that was now the object of their desires and dreams. Located in the rear of the vehicle, it was held firm by rope to the van's side slats to stop it cannoning about and crushing anyone's limbs.

"Aye, with all that wedge yer gonna be bringin' hame tae her, Betsy will be ready to give you a roll the night, Jimmy, son!" shouted Bobby Simms through the vehicle's hatch.

Gregsy guffawed harshly but his laughter was slightly forced and betrayed his unease and tension at the knowledge that his looming performance would be given in front of one of Glasgow's most vicious crime lords, and the extra burden of expectancy was already causing a bead of sweat to squeeze its way out from his rapidly furrowing brow.

An uneasy silence dominated most of the journey from the Loch House post office, where they had efficiently and brutally dealt with the septuagenarian postmaster and his wheelchair-bound wife and relieved the premises of the receptacle that now sat in the rear of the vehicle.

And there it was: a metallic box, flush, if their information was correct, with a payload of almost £100K. Yet the brooding silence that filled the vehicle hinted that none of the crew was happy with their destination and the turning over of the cargo they had procured for a paltry percentage in return.

Simms was first to articulate this building resentment: "Look, boys, I dunno about you two in the front, but me and Shug here, well we reckons that 20% is nowhere near enough cut for the fruit of our soddin' labours. Fuck me, Jimmy, that's just five grand a heid. Why don't ye just pull over tae the side o' the road and let's discuss this aw before it's too late and we've lined McGrain's pockets again without him liftin' a bleedin' finger?"

Simms' confederate in the back of the van, Fowler, echoed his agreement: "Simmo's right, Jimmy. McGrain's takin' the piss ... again. If yous ask me, we hae two options. First, we either stop the motor right now, birl round and head for the hills, where we divvy up the wedge between us and scarper, but forever have tae be lookin' over our shoulders."

From the driver's seat, Jimmy Glavin had heard enough. "Whit, and leave us with a set of targets on our back and McGrain and his attack dugs pursuin' us fae here to eternity? Nae feckin' chance."

His head peering back round through the hatchway linking the front and rear of the vehicle, Gregsy snapped: "Awright, Shug, since yer such a bleedin' smart arse … whit's yer plan B?"

Fowler casually leant forward so that both of his elbows were sprawled across the top of the tethered safe and then his right arm slid down the far side of the metal box; and when it snapped back he smashed a baseball bat off the top of the safe, causing a brutal metallic ringing sound to echo around the back of the van. "It's pure and simple, peterman … we waits for McGrain and his monkeys to become trans-fixed by your safe-blowin' masterclass and then we baton the fuck oot o' them and make sure they is and never will be in any fit state to be chasin' us anywhere … capiche?"

Fowler's challenge hung in the air, but as time drew on the only answer he received was silence as the Transit continued to lurch on.

Then, as the stark lines of St Serf's derelict bell tower loomed increas-ingly large, Jimmy took the tight left into the lane that wound its way up the hill to the old ruined church a little bit more sharply than he should have.

His passengers in the rear were thrown from one side to the other in a manoeuvre that drew a volley of profanities. "Aye, ya bunch o' bastards, that wan was for Betsy!" he yelled, before dissolving into a grating peel of laughter that seemed to shift a chest full of mucus from within him.

Refocussing his eyes, Glavin stared ahead to the lightly wooded area to the left of the derelict place of worship's ruined graveyard, where the lights of three vehicles illuminated the night in a semi-arc of flickering light that pierced the hard rain continuing to fall relentlessly from the dark above.

Continuing to act almost as if nothing had happened, Jimmy, despite the fact he could feel three pairs of eyes burning into his skull, quickly turned the Transit around and reversed it up the track that led to the clearing at the heart of the birch wood. Then, as he brought the vehicle to a halt with a rasp of the handbrake, he at last turned round in the cabin and met his crew's scorching stares. "Okay, so let's go with plan B. Yer right, Shug, I've had aboot aw o' McGrain that I can take," said Glavin, patting the inside of his anorak where a bulge indicated the presence of a revolver.

Glavin swept the eyes of his team, silently challenging each one of them to make sure they were all on-message. "A guess we're aw tooled up anyways, but the timing's gonna be everything. So we play it all nice and easy until we are at the point of explosion and when I plunge the detonator, we take the three o' them out. That means, Simmo, that you and Shug need to make sure you are flankin' McGrain and his arse-lickers, 'cause I'm gonna be on the detonator just in front of them and Gregsy will just have got back behind the dyke after setting up the jam shot."

"So, are we aw good wi' this, boys?" he demanded.

"Too right, Jimmy," replied Simms, flashing a rotten-toothed smile, while Fowler grinned grimly, adding a simple thumbs up from the rear of the van and Gregsy gave a curt nod of his red head in the affirmative.

"Okay, so it's business as usual right up until the point of deto-nation and then we give McGrain and his boys whit they've been askin' for long and weary. Right, lads, get the safe on tae its runners and I'll get the doors open and then we can get this fuck'n thing done," concluded Glavin, before swinging the driver's door open and jumping out of the vehicle onto the squelching turf.

Chapter Two

FIFTY YARDS away under a 15-foot awning propped up by four wooden posts, a foreboding, dark figure stood in the middle of a gathering of three ghoulish silhouettes.

He was clad in a black ski anorak that was zipped up around his neck, with a dark beanie clamped firmly down over his head, and was repeatedly punching the balled fist of his leather-sheathed right hand into the opened palm of his left, in a grizzly gesture of impatience.

His eyes taking in their grim welcoming committee, Gregsy grunted as he hoisted the runners' metallic handle in perfect sync with his three comrades and began to carry the safe towards McGrain.

After they had squelched their way over the greasy grass and gained the cover of the awning, the metal receptacle was placed in front of McGrain and his men. Jimmy Glavin stepped forward and met the penetrating dark gaze that was devouring his features with a keen, hawklike interest.

"You're 15 minutes late. I hope that doesn't mean there were any cock-ups?" asked McGrain with understated, yet still palpable menace.

Despite himself, Glavin scratched the scar on the left-hand side of his face with his right index finger, in a gesture that betrayed the fraught state of his nerves. "It's all gone accordin' tae plan, Mr McGrain. The auld postmaster took a dull yin tae persuade him tae play baw, but grandad and his missus are tied up nice and cosy, like. Aside fae his sare heid he'll be fine after a couple o' paracetamol and a goldie, nae doubt!" he finally answered, adding an unconvincing smile to try and inject some levity into the moment.

"How much?" rapped McGrain, ignoring Glavin's attempt at humour and snapping open the palm of his left hand towards the safe, as a drop of moisture slipped off his almost Roman beak.

Before Glavin could answer, Gregsy beat his gaffer to the punch: "100k in payroll, pensions and aw the other shit o' the day, Mr McGrain, and just waitin' to be sprung open and left winkin' at you nice and sweet!"

McGrain continued to stare straight at Glavin as if it had been he who had spoken and not the safe-blower. "Then it's show time, Jimmy." Ignoring the water that continued to cascade off their features, despite the cover, McGrain slowly inclined his gaze towards Gregsy. "You better be right, son. I hope for your sake you're as good at your joab as you are with yer gob. Now fuckin' spring it, peterman," he said, and with that McGrain and his lieutenants took a step back to the edge of the awning's cover, all the while their eyes never leaving the safe and its handlers.

Knowing the pressures he was working under, Gregsy wasted no time. "Okay, boys, first let's get the safe on its back, then we need tae dry it aff so there's no moisture around the lock or anywhere else on the door that can compromise oor little pyrotechnic show!"

With a series of grunts and groans, the four men eventually manoeuvred the safe onto its back and crouching down, Gregsy immediately produced a set of two cloths with which he began to wipe down the steel container with an almost manic energy.

He placed the Mini Maglite torch in his mouth, using it to cover every inch of the contraption in search of any stray droplet he might have missed, while paying particularly intense attention to the area around the lock.

Satisfied at last that the safe was moisture free, Gregsy stood up and waved the rest of his cronies away from the safe and, turning theatrically to McGrain, said: "Right, gents, what yer about tae witness is the simple beauty of a nitroglycerine method known as a 'jam shot'.

The purpose o' the jam shot is to blow the door open while leaving it still on its hinges. When blowin' a safe with nitroglycerine, the peterman also needs a mouldable substance tae create a funnel-like device. Historically, soap, like Fels Naptha, has been used for this purpose and ..." – Gregsy paused and fished out a knotted cellophane bag from his Berghaus inside pocket – "here's a bar of soap I've been hand-kneading for most o' our journey here in order that it has become extremely malleable wi' a consistency that will naw permit the nitro to leak through it."

Lowering his face to within inches of the safe door, Gregsy produced a cellophane strip about 8 inches by half an inch and placed it lengthwise into the space between the door and the doorframe. The soap, now fashioned into a cup in the shape of a funnel, was then manipulated around the cellophane by his dexterous fingers, to provide a channel for the flow of the nitroglycerine when it was introduced into the cup.

The concentration on his face clear for all to see, Gregsy was all too well aware that every moment of his labour was being watched avidly by his enraptured audience, as he placed the blasting cap tenderly into the soap cup and began to unroll wires that he extended back over a matter of yards.

At the full extension of the awning's cover, McGrain and his confederates huddled behind part of the broken perimeter dyke that they had taken as cover from the impending blast. Jimmy Glavin had already placed the battery hookup and quickly took the wires from Gregsy before attaching them to it.

Smiling angelically at his confederates, Gregsy returned to the safe, and hunkering back down produced a glass vial containing a syrupy liquid. He began to pour the nitroglycerine into the cup, intently scrutinising the rate at which the safe drank the nitro, all too aware of the need to maintain a continuous, unbroken flow of liquid all the way to the detonator.

Dragging in a deep breath, Gregsy waited for the crucial moment when approximately 1 ounce of the nitro had been consumed and a continuous river of the substance, from the last drop down inside the door all the way to the blasting cap, existed.

Nodding his head in silent appreciation that the moment had indeed arrived, Gregsy retreated to the far side of the stone dyke and eyeing McGrain, he turned his gaze towards Glavin and nodded at him to detonate.

Cowering behind the dyke, the sound of the blast was muffled, yet still its percussion reverberated through the rain-filled air. Gregsy was first to move, vaulting the wall and bounding the yards between him and the safe, desperate to inspect his work.

"Eu-fuckin'-reka!" he shouted into the night. The safe door teetered precariously, somehow still attached to the safe, but it was what Gregsy saw inside the steel repository that he liked the most.

Moments later, he felt company behind him and a leather-encased hand gripped his shoulder. "You did well, peterman," said McGrain.

Turning round to face McGrain, Gregsy's glance strayed over the crime lord's shoulders, the startled look in his eyes sending a shock-wave of concern through McGrain.

CHAPTER THREE

ONCE GLAVIN had slammed the detonator down, the subsequent explosion provided the green light that Fowler and Simms had been waiting for; it was the former who sprang into action first.

Almost as soon as the safe had been blown open, Fowler whipped the baseball bat from the sheath that had held it concealed snug under his waterproof and began to wind it up in a figure of eight motion that resembled some Teutonic knight from days of yore about to put a Saracen to the sword.

But here, just outside St Serf's graveyard in the rain-lashed night, it was one of McGrain's unsuspecting lieutenants who was to be his victim, and as the bearded hood caught the shocked look in his boss' angular face, he was alerted to his impending doom.

Yet black-beard was too late, and although he spat out a defiant "Bastard!" as he began a semi-defensive turn towards his attacker, it was as far as he got. The swish of the air as the blow arced his way enveloped him and three-and-a-half feet of solid ash exploded off the side of his head and dropped the gangland soldier unconscious with a dull thud on the sodden dirt.

But the combination of McGrain's startled stare and the time it had taken for Fowler to wield his weapon had alerted the second of the crime lord's underlings – a chisel-faced, ponytailed bruiser with a black tattoo of a spider at the top of his neck – to the imminent danger that was heading his way.

He had just enough time to face Simmo as the old military bayonet the latter always used as his personal insurance plan on a 'job' reached the apex of its deadly journey.

A rotten grin flashing across his face in anticipation of impending vengeance, Simmo screeched: "Suck on this, you fuckin' parasite!" His eyes shining bright with manic glee, he plunged the glinting blade downwards towards the inked-up enforcer.

Yet Simmo's would-be victim was too quick for him and from his overcoat pocket he had already drawn an ivory-handled, viciously curved blade that was now waiting to provide a deadly welcome.

The glee in Simmo's eyes suddenly dissipated and was replaced with sheer terror as his momentum meant that his body descended with all the force of his follow-through onto the waiting knife.

The ornate Damascus steel impaled Simms handle-deep and as he let out an agonised howl, Spider brutally twisted the embedded blade to make sure there would be no recovery for Glavin's crewman.

Writhing in agony, impaled on the metallic stake, Simms started to slide down as his assailant, poker-faced, pulled the blade free and rammed the sole of his boot into Simms' chest, sending him backwards onto the turf, clutching at his fatal wound and moaning in agony.

But Glavin had anticipated the ensuing stand-off and before anyone else could move, he pulled his revolver from his anorak and advanced barrel-first towards McGrain, who stared in wide-eyed disbelief as his former henchman now stood just 2 yards away with a Smith & Wesson Victory ready to spit lead into his cranium.

"I'd tell yer man to put his blade down, Tony. I'm afraid, as somebody once said, 'there's no use taking a knife to a gun-fight'. It's time we cashed in your chips, McGrain. Now get yer mits away from yer body and stack 'em on yer heid, nice 'n' easy, one at a time," ordered Glavin.

Doing as he was bid, McGrain slowly lifted his leather-sheathed hands onto his soaking beanie.

"What's the problem, Jimmy? No happy with your cut? Someone been whispering in your ear that you could be doin' better working for them? Do you really believe that?" snapped McGrain.

In the background, a slight squish on the soaked turf betrayed movement as Spider took a defensive step towards his boss, but as he did so, Shug Fowler stepped across his path with his baseball bat raised in front of him. "Take one more step, son, and I'll turn yer heid to pulp and Jimmy will fill yer boss full o' lead."

McGrain, the full reality of his desperate plight now all too apparent, attempted to parley: "Okay, so you're no' happy with the 20%? We can sort that no bother, Jimmy, but where's this gonna take you? You come out from under my umbrella and whose protection do you have then?" asked the crime lord, his eyes darting urgently towards Spider and then sweeping the area around the awning for any hope of an exit strategy.

There was none.

"Sorry, McGrain, but it's time for a change and I'm afraid I've already reached a wee understandin' with big Ronny Parlane and his boys about how we plan tae conduct business after your … sad demise," Glavin said and barked out a harsh laugh as he salivated over his impending moment of ultimate payback.

Standing in silence behind McGrain, Gregsy watched the nightmare play out in front of him as his brain did the logistics over the stick of verbal dynamite Glavin had just lobbed into the proceedings and found himself shaking his head.

"On yer knees, McGrain. Gregsy, keep him covered," ordered Glavin and then he turned towards Spider and directed the Smith & Wesson his way. "Place the knife on the deck, blade first, nice and slow … now hands on yer heid … good boy. Right, Shug, bring him over here and make him kneel doon beside his boss," he said, his words filled with biting spite.

"You'll never get away wi' this, Glavin … dae ye think that Pauline is gonna let yous ice her man and his team and naw come for ye …

no fuckin' chance, believe—" but before Spider could finish his show of defiance, Fowler smashed his baseball bat into the enforcer's gut and the hood dropped to his knees, gasping for breath.

"I don't give a fuck what that treacherous bitch thinks she might get up tae after her man has bought it, 'cause she's gonna have a shitstorm coming her way," said Glavin from behind the Smith & Wesson, as Fowler lined up McGrain and his right-hand man for their execution.

"I've got six bullets chambered and ready to put the two of you out yer misery and then me and the boys will be splitting 100k three ways and lookin' at startin' afresh with Parlane. Aah well, McGrain, look at it this way, at least yer gonna die on holy ground! There's some-thing poetic, don't ya think, about the man called the Widowmaker meeting his maker in a churchyard?" Then Glavin took a step back and trained the Victory on McGrain.

"Time to say adios, old amigo!" Glavin snarled and smiled ferally as the hammer of the S&W began to draw back.

Yet before his trigger finger had completed its lethal journey, a splinter of explosive light flashed from behind McGrain and Spider, and the high-velocity report of a semi-automatic rang out four times.

The first two shots exploded in Glavin's chest and before he had time to react, Fowler found his head had been enfiladed by the third and fourth projectiles from the Browning Hi-Power's 10-round maga-zine, lethal at a distance of up to 50 yards. The power that exploded through their bodies propelled Fowler through the air and smashed him into the stone dyke like a rag doll, dead before his punctured being had crashed against the ruined wall.

Glavin, although launched backwards, had been stopped in his tracks by one of the posts holding up the awning and now the surprise, shock and agony on his shell-shocked features were replaced by a futile rage at his own betrayal and impending demise.

As McGrain and his lieutenant turned Gregsy's way, their visages were filled with confusion and uncertainty. The peterman smiled almost beatifically but continued to keep his Browning Hi-Power trained on them. "Yous keep yer hands on yer pates and stay down on yer hunkers. I just needs to take care of some unfinished biz," he said, before walking past them. He stood over Fowler, examining his former comrade intently for any signs of life ... but there were none.

Then he walked over to the post where Glavin sat, half-propped-up against the wooden column, and squatted down besides him. Before Gregsy could say anything, his former gaffer spat: "Why?"

"Because you were doing to me exactly whit McGrain was daeing to you, Glavin. You undervalued me, disrespected me and treated me like some school wean who should've been grateful for every crumb you threw him fae the big table. Well, guess what, Glavin, I stopped wearin' shorts years ago. If it was'ne for this ..." – and Gregsy pointed at his red mop to underline his point – "that safe filled full o' dough would'ne be here."

His breathing starting to become shallow and rasping, Glavin whispered: "You think it's gonna be any better workin' for the Widowmaker?"

Gregsy smiled benignly. "Considerin' I just saved his and his right-hand man's lives from an act of dirty bawbag treachery, I think there is every chance we can live happily ever after, Jimmy. Now, if you dinnae mind, as you might say, I think it's time I said adios!" and at that Gregsy stood up and pumped two 9mm projectiles into Glavin.

"Fuck you, amigo," he spat and turned to face McGrain and Spider.

CHAPTER FOUR

THE LIGHT KNOCK on the door was met with a sharp retort – "Come in!" – and Community Constable Angus Thoroughgood walked into the sergeants' room at the double.

Sitting in one of the two grey moulded chairs just in front of him was a tousle-haired male with an unruly greying moustache that matched the two-tone of his thatch. Thoroughgood put the cop in his 50s and while he was assessing his colleague, he found a pair of sharp grey eyes doing the exact same thing to him.

On the other side of the desk, Sergeant Sam Storey observed the two cops through eyes that were amused, but also appraising. "Judging by the way you two are eyeing each other up, I think an introduction will, indeed, be needed. Would that be correct, gentlemen?"

"Aye, you could say that, sarge," replied the older cop, seated crossed-legged, the minute sway of his right foot indicating some slight agitation. Yet his moustache was soon twitching as a smile flashed across his sharp features and turning to Thoroughgood, he offered a welcoming handshake. "Good to meet you, young Thoroughgood … I've heard a lot about you!" he said and then gave a nervous laugh.

Not sure just what the senior cop meant, Thoroughgood loaded enough pressure into his handshake to receive a grimace from his older colleague. "Nice to meet you, Constable …?" he began, but before the question could hang in the air, Sergeant Storey came to the rescue.

"Angus, I'm pleased to introduce you to Constable Harry Currie. And there will be plenty of time for you two tae chew the fat …" – and he gave a short, harsh laugh – "because the reason you are both here is that you've been seconded to Community Policing and the bottom line is you're now paired up as the Community Cops for the Briarknock area." Storey paused to let the ripples of shock take effect and couldn't help a mischievous half-grin playing at the side of his thin lips.

"Whit?" was all Currie could manage by way of a reply, while Thoroughgood looked again at his new 'neeber' before letting out an incredulous "Really … er, sergeant?" as his eyebrows descended to their normal position from the Alpine heights they had just reached.

"Aye, I thought you'd both be delighted … but let's no' get carried away," drawled Storey sarcastically, as he flicked an unruly strand of hair back above his brow.

"I don't know why this should come as such a big surprise to the pair of you. You had a bloody good run in the divisional fast response vehicle Zulu Mike One, Harry, and with 4-years service left it was time to bring all your experience to bear in the community and also complement your more … er … youthful new partner here," concluded Storey.

"From whit I hear, Thoroughgood doesn't need anyone riding shotgun for him because he is Z Division's answer to Billy the Kid—" but before Currie could finish, Storey's right hand shot forward open-palmed and he fixed the senior cop with a blazing stare.

"Do I need to remind you, Constable Currie, that your little cameo as a waiter-cum-cabaret act on HMS Glasgow while you should have been elsewhere was the straw that broke the camel's back? As for you, Thoroughgood, you need plenty more experience on the beat and perhaps an older heid to help you gain it. Surely this is a match made in heaven, gentlemen, no?" concluded Storey.

The sergeant's sharp words were met with stony silence as both cops eyed each other awkwardly. The prospect of teaming up with a new partner who was from a completely different side of the policing scale and was almost 30 years his junior clearly did not enamour Currie.

And Thoroughgood couldn't help grimacing at the prospect of being saddled with some old dinosaur who was only interested in counting the days down until his '30' was in.

For his part, Storey seemed more interested in rolling up his perfectly folded white shirtsleeves than the thoughts of either of his two new Community Policing Department recruits.

A mischievous smirk on his face, the sergeant said: "Excellent, I'm glad you're both delighted to come on board and so enthusiastic about your new partnership. Now we've got that over and done with, we need to get to the bottom line and quick. Briarknock is in the middle of a housebreaking epidemic and it's particularly nasty. Your new community policing area is being terrorised by a gang of housebreakers known as …" – and Storey paused to apply metaphorical quotation marks before continuing – "'The Creepers'. These scumbags specialise in turning houses during the wee small hours and if they are disturbed they hand out a particularly vicious beating to anyone who is unlucky enough to stumble upon them or stupid enough to try and protect their property. Six weeks back, an 82-year-old widow was hospitalised with a fractured eye socket, while a fortnight ago a retired miner was left unconscious with a broken jaw. Surprise, surprise, no one is prepared to speak to us about The Creepers and that is where the job of the Community Bobby is so important. We need you up in Briarknock pounding the beat, being seen in the area's streets, showing the uniform. Listening and watching for any snippet of information that will be out there and we need you up there pronto," and at that Storey jerked his eyes in the direction of the door.

"Is that it, sarge?" asked Currie, his dark bushy eyebrows raised in incredulity.

"That is indeed it, my dear Currie. You never know, this job could provide you with a new lease of policing life and you with the opportunity to take a giant step towards the CID Aide you obviously covet, young Thoroughgood. So, as Confucius once say, the journey of 1,000 miles starts with the first step and by the time you get out that door you'll have taken half a dozen: now get a bloody move on!" snapped Storey, as another strand of unruly hair broke loose from above his brow.

Thoroughgood pushed his chair back and stood up. "Thank you, sergeant. We'll get cracking," he replied, and as he did so he was sure he could see a twinkle in his new gaffer's eye.

After a 10-minute wait at the bus stop just around the corner from Bayne Street HQ, a number 63 kindly came to the two CP cops' rescue. As they took their seats at the rear of the vehicle, Thoroughgood turned to Currie. "Look, I'll be honest with you, I knew I was up for a move into the CP for a while now and with all the problems the place is having with these Creeper bastards, the smart money was always on the Briarknock beat. I just didn't know you would be being parachuted in as my senior man … I take it you didn't either?"

"Not a fuckin' Scooby! So what do you know about The Creepers, young 'un?" asked Currie from behind a poker face.

"I did a bit of diggin' on that while I was still on Group Three and I think I may have someone who can help us out with the information we need. I busted a junkie burglar called Jeb Nicholas about a month back for a Section 57 and we had an interestin' conversation while he was in the holding cell waiting to get processed. It turns out that the 82-year-old widow with the fractured eye socket that old man Storey was telling us about is his great auntie and he hates The Creepers … so much that—"

Before he could finish his sentence, Currie couldn't help himself doing it for Thoroughgood: "He wants to tout to you?"

Smiling smugly, Thoroughgood looked at his watch before returning his gaze to the older cop. "He does indeed and we'll be meeting him at the rear of Stobhill Hospital in 30 minutes."

Narrowing his eyes, Currie inclined his head slightly. "Mmm, interesting," he said.

CHAPTER FIVE

"SO WHEREABOUTS EXACTLY are we meeting this ned … what did you call him again?" asked Currie, before taking a gulp of air.

"Jeb Nicholas is his name. Under the old clock tower," answered Thoroughgood flatly, as he continued to set a brisk pace that left his older colleague gasping for air and unable to respond.

As they snaked their way along the footpath, the rear entrance of the hospital's assortment of red-brick buildings began to dominate their view.

For many years, Stobhill had carried a stigma for being a hospital for paupers and in fact the birth certificates of any baby born there at the beginning of its life only recorded the address and not the name of the hospital. Yet Stobhill lay at the very heart of the community and the huge red-brick clock tower at its heart dominated the area for miles around: a minaret monument to the post-Victorian architecture of its creators, the renowned Glasgow architects Thomson & Sandilands, whose foundation stone had been laid by Lord Balfour of Burleigh, the then Secretary of State for Scotland, in September 1901.

"So what makes you think Nicholas will actually be there, Thoroughgood? Let's face it, how much trust can you place in any junkie? For fuck's sake, Thoroughgood, Jeb Nicholas, you'd be as well getting' Charlie Nicholas tae tout to you!" concluded Currie, before dissolving into a grating laugh that was accompanied by a shallow wheeze.

"His old aunt has been left concussed and with a smashed eye socket. Even junkies have some shred of humanity left in them … Harry," replied Thoroughgood, purposely using his venerable colleague's Christian name for the first time.

"We'll soon find out, boy. Remember, I've been in the job for 26 years, been there, done it all before. First things first, let's see if yer man actually shows," retorted the senior cop.

Thoroughgood kept his frustration at his colleague's attitude masked behind his best straight face, but despite the fact he'd only been in Currie's company for an hour, he was already getting a bad feeling about how his relationship with his new 'neeber' was going.

Deciding that silence would be golden, Thoroughgood put his right foot in front of his left and continued to force Currie, his pride under threat and the silver buttons of his tunic straining, to keep up the pace.

As they made their way through the flaking green-painted wrought iron gates, the horizon became dominated by the towering B-listed clock tower. In the cover of the arched garage doorway at the bottom of the Victorian edifice stood a male wearing a navy-blue Kappa tracksuit with a red New York Yankees baseball cap clamped down tight on an unruly dark mop that protruded from underneath it.

Nicholas had shown and Thoroughgood couldn't help himself sending a dig Currie's way: "Nice to see my faith in humanity being rewarded."

As they closed to within 20 yards of the tower, Thoroughgood watched as Nicholas slotted his hands into his tracky bottoms' pockets and shuffled uneasily from one foot to another.

"All right, Jeb," said Thoroughgood, smiling in reassurance and holding out his right hand in greeting. As Nicholas extended his own paw, a rotten smile also crept across his face when he saw that the cop's hand had been enclosing a Mars Bar. "Thought that might go down well with you, pal," said Thoroughgood before adding: "Now, let's take a wee turn round behind the garage for some privacy and see what you have for us, eh?"

"Nae bother, Mr Thoroughgood," replied Nicholas, his voice rough as gravel.

Thoroughgood quickly took a furtive squint at Currie to see how his little gesture had gone down with the old cop and the look of distaste on the old stager's sweat-streaked grey features gave him no cause for hope their partnership was one that might blossom.

They turned around the block and found a deserted archway that had clearly not been in use for years and Nicholas quickly drew into the darkness of the building's shade.

"I dinnae like to be oot in the daylight too long, especially no' wi' company like yerselves, Mr Thoroughgood ... er, nae disrespect tae yous, like," muttered Nicholas.

Before Thoroughgood could answer, Currie snapped: "Is that right, Dracula? No surprise there that scum like you would'nae want to be seen dead with the uniform of her Majesty's Police Service. But if you've dragged us up here to waste our time then I'll have your guts for garters. Now sing ..." he demanded.

Nicholas recoiled and his eyes darted towards Thoroughgood for help and reassurance. "Noo, hold oan a minute ... am here tae deal with Mr Thoroughgood, boss ... I dinnae know you fae Adam ..." Nicholas, his agitation clear, turned his right hand up, palm open in Currie's direction.

Gritting his teeth and trying hard to suppress his mounting anger, Thoroughgood stepped in front of Currie and smiled reassuringly at his would-be informant. "And so you are, Jeb, son. Let's just cut to the chase: you owe me for getting' that 57 binned, and we know what the price of that was. Give me what you've got on The Creepers and everything will be hunky dory," said Thoroughgood, before placing a calming hand on Nicholas' tracksuit-clad shoulder and giving it a friendly pat.

The junkie pulled out a crumpled piece of paper that looked remarkably like an old bookie's slip, thrust it in Thoroughgood's direction and opening a mouth of broken, decayed yellow teeth, rasped in an almost inaudible voice: "Oan that paper is the address I think yous'll find The Creepers holed up. Yer gonna need tae be cute, like, but if yous hit them at the right time they'll be like fish in a barrel. Just make sure yous go in team-handed. Whit they did tae ma Auntie Sandra and that old miner boy … it's naw right, I hope yous gie them a right good bleachin' intae the bargain," and as Thoroughgood took the crumpled slip, the junkie started off from out of the half-shade.

But before he could pass Thoroughgood, the young cop's right hand dropped and a balled fist half playfully buried itself in Nicholas' midriff. "Not so fast, Jeb. There were three motors done in Auchin-roan Road last night … you been busy?"

Nicholas half-gasped, but his furtive eyes switched from Thor-oughgood to Currie, who had taken a threatening step towards him, his jaw set grimly.

Recognising the hopelessness of his plight, Nicholas shrugged his shoulders. "No' guilty, Mr Thoroughgood, I promises you, but you might want tae chap number 44 Acreview Road and ask for the boy Kieran Busby. If I wiz yous, Mr Thoroughgood, I'd be lookin' to turn his midden this morn. Like I promised you that night back in Bayne Street, there'll be nae mair shitting in my own nest for Jeb Nicholas. Now if yous dinnae mind, I need to be getting ma meth-adone script …"

Smiling, Thoroughgood backed away and waved his informant forward. "Keep up the good work, Jeb, and you'll stay out of the tin pail. Just make sure you stay in touch," he concluded, keeping a sea-green stare on Nicholas' drawn, sallow features.

"Gracias, amigo," replied Nicholas and slinked off round the corner.

Turning towards Currie, Thoroughgood held his older colleague's cold, grey eyes for a moment. "Like the man says, I think it's time we headed for 44 Acreview," he said and without waiting for Currie to reply, Thoroughgood walked away.

CHAPTER SIX

FIFTEEN MINUTES LATER, Thoroughgood and Currie drew to a stop at the junction between Wallacebrook Road and Acreview and Thoroughgood drew his personal radio out of his breast pocket.

"Z325 Constable Thoroughgood to Zulu Control requesting a warrant check, over," he rapped.

"Go ahead Z325, who you after?" replied the precise tones of Madeleine, the Divisional Controller.

"Have you anything for a Kieran Busby, believed home address 44 Acreview Road, over?" he asked.

"Let you know asap, Z325," replied Madeleine crisply.

Checking his watch, Currie grimaced as he saw the hands hit 11 a.m. and leaning against the corner railings he unclipped his polyester police tie to let some air percolate down his tunic. "Look, Thoroughgood, I could murder a coffee and a bacon roll. We've been on the hoof now for an hour solid and I dare say this boy Busby's naw gonna be oot his scratcher until the middle of the afternoon anyway. As the old sayin' goes, an army marches on its stomach. Whit do you say we head up to St Luke's: they have a wee midweek coffee morning every Wednesday. It's just 10 minutes away and we could be hosed and fed and back at 44 Acreview and Busby will still be rollin' aboot in his baws. I'm parched, boy ..." concluded the by now clearly overheated Currie.

But before Thoroughgood could reply, his personal radio sprang into life. "Z325 Constable Thoroughgood, have you got the suspect there? We have a Warrant to Apprehend with warning signals for 'V'

Victor, 'W' Whisky and 'D' Delta. Proceed with extreme caution," warned Madeleine, a note of concern running through her words as she relayed the codes for violence, weapons and drugs.

Thoroughgood whipped his personal radio back out and replied casually: "Not yet, Zulu Control. Z327 Constable Currie and myself are just about to turn 44 Acreview for the suspect, acting on information received. Will keep you updated, over and out." Then he turned towards Currie and smiled. "Sorry, Harry, but I think the die has been cast and your roll and bacon will have to wait a while," and for a second time that morning Thoroughgood walked on with his senior man trailing reluctantly in his wake.

It may have been 11 a.m. on a sunny spring morning, but there were no signs of life at number 44 Acreview Road. Thoroughgood was surprised to find that Busby's home address was a semi-detached, roughcast council house occupying a corner slot on a relatively quiet side street off the main thoroughfare of Wallacebrook Road.

"Front door or back door: what do you want, Harry?" But before his neeber could answer, Thoroughgood did so for the older cop: "Look, why don't you chap the front door and do the needful and I'll get myself round the back just in case Busby tries to bolt for it," he suggested.

Fanning himself with his lid, Currie gave a half-smile. "Aye, I'll give you this, Thoroughgood, yer keen enough, son. Okay, you get in position and let's see what we can flush us oot." Then for the first time that morning he took the lead. He opened the gate at number 44 and walked down the path and up to the brown, paint-peeling door. Checking over his shoulder as Thoroughgood slinked round the back, Currie tried the doorbell, found it didn't work and then gave the classic 'polis' five-rap knock … and was met with silence.

The senior cop climbed impatiently onto the doorstep and endeavoured to peer through the square wire-meshed panel in the top half of the door but he could see nothing through it.

He stooped down and prized the letter box open with surprisingly long and slender fingers, but although the hallway was full of junk, there was no sign of life. Taking a deep breath, he hollered through the letter box. "Kieran Busby, it's the polis. I've gotta Warrant to Apprehend for you. I suggest you open the door or I'll take it off its hinges!" Then he stood back down off the doorstep and folded his arms.

Taking a glance towards the building's back green, a smile started to play under his greying moustache as he saw that Thoroughgood was awkwardly attempting to secrete himself behind a ragged privet hedge.

But Currie's attention was soon snapped back to the building's front door as the clear sound of steps coming from inside number 44 Acreview reached his ears and as it did, so Currie rubbed his hands together and said: "Come to Daddy."

CHAPTER SEVEN

AS HE ATTEMPTED to crouch down behind what was a poor and prickly excuse for a privet hedge, Thoroughgood could see that his cover was less than perfect. He scanned the backyard for somewhere better to hide, but the only thing he could see was what appeared to be a yellow plastic kids' Wendy house that had pride of place between the four black metallic washing poles in the corners of the back garden – and he wasn't about to use that as a hiding place.

Thoroughgood noticed Currie's amused glance from around the house's corner, but his attention was soon snapped back to the here and now by the sound of the front door opening and Thoroughgood wondered what kind of 'welcome' his new colleague was getting.

The front door had indeed opened and Currie now found himself face to face with a small, white-haired woman who was chewing furiously on he knew not what. Although he initially put her around her early 60s, the cop was already guessing she could be at least 10 years younger and with that reassessment Currie found himself startled by the realisation that she could indeed be around the same age as him.

Clearing his throat and his head of its disconcerting thoughts, Currie served up his opening gambit: "Aah, good morning, I'm looking for Kieran Busby, I believe he lives here …?"

The woman, who was barely over 5 foot, shifted from one foot to the other, her hands slotted in the front pockets of a light-blue floral pinny, her petite body almost vibrating with energy and her startling blue eyes burning with hate.

"Well, polis, ye can get yersel tae feck, there's no Kieran Busby living here and even if there wiz, I would'nae be lettin' you in tae have a mooch aboot for him," she snapped and with no attempt to conceal her contempt for Currie and the uniform he wore, spat a mouthful of what appeared to be chewing tobacco a foot away from the immaculately gleaming toes of his bulled boots.

Currie's grey eyebrows shot up as his features took on an almost wolfish look and he whipped out his official police issue notebook and the pencil that was attached to it. "Aye, is that so Missus …?" he asked and left the question hanging in the air and as it did so an uncomfortable silence drew out.

Her searing blue eyes boring into him, the woman finally decided to honour Currie with a reply: "It's May, May Busby."

Currie feigned a smile. "Well, it doesn't take Einstein to work out you will be Kieran's maw and the Voters' Roll has him still residing with you … so if he's not stopping with you, have you any idea where he is … Mrs Busby?" asked Currie conversationally, his eyes trained behind her as they took in the hallway, scanning for any signs of sudden movement.

"Last ah heard o' the wi' scroat he wiz doon in Easterhoose, holed up wi' his bidey-in, some wee junkie Scouse bitch," spat Mrs Busby, as Currie furiously scribbled down the information in his Strathclyde Police notebook.

Concluding his notes, Currie looked up, while at the same time inserting the pencil in its notebook clip and then re-holstering the journal in his right breast pocket; but as he did so, he took a step towards old May Busby and whispered into her ear: "Thank you for that, Mrs Busby, now get the fuck out of my way," and at that his right forearm shot out and knocked the diminutive, bristling ball of hatred back against the wall of her hallway just inside the door, pinioning her against it.

As soon as he'd done this, Currie shouted out: "Time to come out and play, Kieran—" but before he could continue, his voice was drowned out by a burst of profanity that would have made a drill sergeant blush.

Finally May Busby ended her tirade: "Ya dirty fuckin' polis scum, get oot o' ma hoose or ah'll …"

Continuing to pinion her to the wall with his forearm, Currie turned his cold, grey stare on her. "Or you'll what, old woman … call the polis?"

But while he might have had the top half of May Busby's body immobilised, the same could not be said of her welly-booted feet. As a gleam swept through her eyes, Currie became painfully aware of what was coming next and with all her power she booted him in the shin of his left leg.

The kick had its desired effect and Currie immediately recoiled, clutching his throbbing shin and raging: "You old hag, that's you done for polis assault and breach o' the peace," but May Busby was already halfway down her hallway and behind her Currie saw movement.

A shadowy figure wrapped in what appeared to be a quilt had shuffled into the hallway, where he was immediately met by May Busby's scorching broadside: "Ye lazy wee arse, whit ye been up tae noo?" Yet just as the recoiling figure was about to answer, he received an almighty clip to the side of his jaw from his maw.

"I told you this wiz yer last chance, ya little bugger, and ye promised me you had cleaned up yer act …" But just as May Busby was winding up for another crack at her dearly beloved son, Kieran Busby cast off his quilt and bolted into the house's rear room. As Currie limped down the hallway after him, he heard the sound of the backdoor opening then slamming shut.

From his semi-concealed position behind the woeful excuse for a hedge, Thoroughgood, who had heard the raised voices coming from inside 44 Acreview, watched in startled amazement as a male in his twenties bolted out of the backdoor, took a furtive look around the back garden then dived headlong through the flapping door of the Wendy house.

The surprise that had initially swept over Thoroughgood was now replaced by a desperate desire to burst out laughing, which only grew stronger as the backdoor opened and May Busby appeared with Currie standing, clearly fuming, behind her.

"I hope for your sake, Mrs Busby, that we get a hold of your boy or you'll be in the pokey for the weekend," he spat from over her shoulder, but as he did so Currie saw Thoroughgood emerge from behind the hedge.

Straightening himself up and brushing off various bits of twigs and leaves, the young cop flashed a smile towards the back door. "Aye, old May Busby, you're still a ball of fire, aren't you?"

As he realised he had been deliberately sent to the front door to run the gauntlet of May Busby's volcanic temper, Currie narrowed his eyes once again, this time at his neighbour, but Thoroughgood smiled amicably and strode over to the plastic Wendy house, which seemed to be moving slightly as a morning breeze stirred.

Folding his arms just to the right of the Wendy house, Thoroughgood asked conversationally: "So where do you suppose Kieran has gone, ma?"

"I dinnae hae a feckin' clue, polis, and even if ah did, after yous stitched me up for them kippers, yous wid be the last I'd be tellin' on ma ain flesh and blood. Anyways, where's the warrant for turnin' ma hoose and ma property?" spat May defiantly.

Thoroughgood barked out a harsh laugh. "Aye, you sold me a red herring and got done for a parcel o' kippers right enough, ma, but justice must be done." Then he stooped over the 4-foot Wendy house and said: "Well, this is one hoose I don't need a warrant to search," and at that he grabbed hold of the plastic tent-like awning and wrenched it off the ground. "Eh, voila," said Thoroughgood theatrically and there, sitting cross-legged on the grass with his head in his hands, was Kieran Busby.

Looking up, the thief and petty criminal groaned: "Shit!" His moon-shaped head appearing almost to be too big for his relatively small body, he looked over furtively at the seething presence of his mother, shook his head sheepishly and added: "Sorry, Ma."

Chapter Eight

BUSBY STARED at the clock on the graffiti-scrawled walls of the detention cell. He found he was in a strange state of limbo, waiting for the paperwork that would soon see him in front of the Sheriff Court, where his fate would ultimately be decided.

Sitting on the room's wooden bench, Busby thrust his overly large cranium forward until his right ear was level with the door's keyhole and strained to pick up any information from outside.

As he sat almost doubled over in his determination to find out what his fate would be, Busby failed to see the green eyes that were now peering through the door's meshed viewing window just above him and as such when the door opened it cracked nastily into his shoulder and he was thrown off the bench and onto the concrete floor that still smelt of that morning's disinfectant wash.

"Bastard," spat Busby, sprawled on his back, and as he attempted to sit upright he began to rub furiously at his right shoulder. "That's polis brutality! Yous cannae dae that tae me, I wanna brief, pronto," he demanded.

He found his words met with Thoroughgood's harsh smile. "You've been a silly boy, Kieran, don't make things any worse for yourself. There's a Warrant to Apprehend already out for you and then you decide to go tanning a few motors just around the corner from your own hoose! It was'ne the smartest move, was it, son? So a wee word of advice: don't go thinkin' you're going to go making any complaints against the police, otherwise Constable Currie and myself will be paying the Wallacebrook Housing Office a wee visit and letting them know about your maw harbouring a known fugitive and trying to help him escape the law … how long do you think she'll be staying in her midden if that happens … wee man?"

Busby's teeth locked in an almost feral grimace. "So you've got me bang tae rights for the warrant, but the motors … naw, am no wearin' that," he spat defiantly.

Hunkering down close enough to get a waft of his prisoner's stale sweat and fetid breath, Thoroughgood grabbed a fistful of black shell suit and snapped Busby to within inches of his taut features. "I suggest you shut the fuck up, Kieran, and start listening. How many Greens have we got lined up for Mr Busby, Constable Currie?" asked Thoroughgood, his head inclining slightly round over his right shoulder at the looming, almost baleful presence of his elder colleague.

"Well, Constable Thoroughgood, I'd say there were the three attempted openings of lockfast places – the OLPs – in Auchinroan Road, but I've got two more for attempted theft of a motor vehicle in Wallacebrook and then we've gotta couple of diggys done just round the corner in Briarknock Road. That's a decent wee roll-up for our wee Busby babe to be takin'," and at that, just to illustrate his point, Currie stepped forward, somewhat stiffly knelt down in front of Busby and fanned out the green sheets of paper that were the second part of the triplicate Crime Report Form all acts of criminality had to be recorded on.

Busby eyed the paperwork and then his gaze snapped towards Thoroughgood and Hardie. "I wiz in Easterhoose wi' ma bird, soes am alibied up and yous can wipe yer arse wi' these." He kicked out an Adidas-sheathed foot and booted the paperwork to the four corners of the room. "Am takin' fuck aw but the warrant … rozzers," snarled Busby angrily.

"Really?" asked Thoroughgood amicably enough, before the younger cop theatrically turned to his colleague for confirmation that this might not be such a good idea. "What do you think, Constable Currie, would you recommend that Mr Busby follows that course of action?"

"Och, am no' so sure about that, young Thoroughgood, after all, when the word starts filterin' around Barlinnie that Mr Busby here is one of The Creepers who's been handin' oot bleachins to defenceless old folk and putting them in the hospital, well I would be worried for Mr Busby's health … cause the folks in Bar-L don't take too kind to that sort of thing … if you're asking … in my experience type thing," smirked Currie, his neatly trimmed grey moustache twitching with growing amusement.

For the second time that morning Busby spat out a one-word profanity: "Bastards!"

"Nice to meet you too, Busby. Now are you takin' the roll-up and admitting the blame, or do you want to come out of the Big Hoose in a pine box after havin' yer throat slit in the laundry room?"

Busby's moon-like features quivered with anger but he knew that he was between a rock and a hard place: he had no option but to take the hit.

Finally, through gritted yellow teeth, he admitted: "Awright, awright, ah'll put ma hawnds up to the motors if it gies me a quiet life in Bar-L. But yous polis hae got to gie me yer word yer no gonna welsh on this wee deal and start whisperin' in certain ears, like?" Busby almost begged.

Thoroughgood appeared to ignore his words as he deliberately collected each of the Greens from the floor and then stood up and walked towards the room's entrance, where Currie was leaning nonchalantly against the doorway.

He slowly turned towards Busby and smiled beatifically. "You'll never know the answer to that, baw-jaws, until you take up residence in the Big Hoose, but if you don't spill for the OLPs you better tell old Ma that she needs to start planning your funeral." Thoroughgood slammed the door shut just as Busby launched himself at the door and his furious features appeared rammed up against the wire-meshed glass.

"You better hope ah never meets you on the street oan a dark night, Thoroughgood, ya smart-arsed fucker."

Taking a step back, Thoroughgood turned to Currie and quipped: "Our first roll-up and another satisfied customer!"

"Aye, just another day in paradise," smiled Currie, his sense of humour seemingly reawakened, as they both burst into a spontaneous round of laughter.

But their mirth was soon silenced as the fire doors that led to the front of Bayne Street Office burst open and a foreboding presence appeared just in front of them.

"Well, well, if it isn't 'Z' Division's man of the moment, Constable Angus Thoroughgood," said DI Ronan O'Toole, pale-blue shirt sleeves rolled up to the elbows and his shirt collar loosened so that a navy-blue tie hung loosely from around his neck.

Hands planted on his hips, O'Toole eyed Currie and Thoroughgood with interest and then working out that they were congratulating each other on an arrest, his shrewd brown orbs strayed towards the holding cell.

"Who've you got in there, lads?" asked O'Toole casually.

While the Detective Inspector's eyes rested on Currie as he waited for the answer, it was Thoroughgood who provided it: "Kieran Busby, sir, on a Warrant to Apprehend," replied the young cop with due deference.

O'Toole inclined his head in appreciation. "Good job. Once he's booked in you can send him through to CID so my boy DC Jimmy Lynch can put a few Greens to him for a set of OLPs," smiled O'Toole amicably.

"I'm afraid we've already done that and the bold boy has burst to them, sir," replied Thoroughgood.

O'Toole's previously friendly manner was instantly replaced with a harsh expression, his thin lips almost disappearing in on themselves.

O'Toole took a step forward menacingly and jabbed a finger into Thoroughgood's chest. "And who gave you permission to go doing that, Constable? Criminal investigation is the job of the Criminal Investigation Department, the clue is in the fuckin' title, Thoroughgood … understand me?" he snapped.

The young cop deliberately held O'Toole's stare for several seconds, but just as he was about to answer, Currie beat him to the punch: "Ah, listen gaffer, it was probably my fault as senior man. Look, we've just been paired together in the CP up in Briarknock and we got a tip-off that Busby was holed up at his maw's over in Acreview, hidin' out in a Wendy hoose on the back green, would you believe! Well, once we nabbed him I thought it would be a good idea to put a few Greens to him and see if we could get our new partnership off to a flyer … you know how it is, DI O'Toole?" finished Currie deferentially.

The Detective Inspector's eyes narrowed as his gaze flitted from Currie to Thoroughgood and back again, O'Toole evidently trying to make up his mind who was the monkey and who was the organ grinder in the 'new partnership'.

Then a slight smile tremored across his thin lips and O'Toole barked out a harsh laugh. "A bleedin' Wendy hoose! That's a belter, wait 'til I share that one with the boys!"

O'Toole took a pace towards Thoroughgood once again and, even though it meant he had to stretch, placed his arm around the young cop in an almost fatherly fashion, before nodding towards Currie. "Now look, boys, I know what it's like, I had a short spell as a CP sergeant out in Drumchapel a couple of years back and your gaffer will be on yer backs for instant results. So I'm quite willing to let you have your roll-up with Busby and good work it is too to get a hardened ned like that to burst to a sheaf of Greens. But you know what the rules are and I would appreciate it if you'd turn anything else you've got like this over to CID so we can do our job. After all, that is all any one of us is trying to do, lads … catch my drift?"

Thoroughgood, still enveloped in O'Toole's uncomfortable embrace, shifted uneasily before the DI, his point made, finally pulled his arm away.

But it was Currie who once again rode to the rescue. "Aye, nae bother, gaffer, we know the score and apologies for oversteppin' the mark, me an' the boy have been just a wee bitty keen, I have to admit," smiled Currie obsequiously.

"Excellent," laughed O'Toole, before adding with a slight emphasis: "Then we'll just file this in the dookit under a slight misunderstandin' and move on." He looked Thoroughgood's way once more. "You've obviously gotta nose for crime detection, Thoroughgood, and the best way to get a CID Aide is to make sure you keep the Detective Inspector happy. Clear?" asked O'Toole.

"As crystal, Detective Inspector O'Toole," answered Thoroughgood.

"First class, now don't be strangers, lads," quipped O'Toole, before he pirouetted neatly on his burgundy loafers' leather heels and headed back from whence he came.

"Nasty wee bastard that and one we don't want to be fallin' out with, young 'un. Let's just play it all by the rulebook from now on, son," advised Currie.

"Really … so CID can take all the credit and we get earache from old Storey … how does that work, Harry?" But before Currie could answer, a clipped voice broke over their conversation.

"Are you two still chunterin' on, sweet Jesus, what do you think this is, a bloody knittin' bee? Will you get Busby out of my bar and let me get the wee bastard processed," demanded Duty Inspector Dougald McGarry from behind a pair of half-moon pince-nez glasses.

CHAPTER NINE

THE BLACK MERCEDES-BENZ 560 SE pulled onto the kerb adjacent to the restaurant's gently ruffling red, white and green awnings as an early morning breeze swept down Alexandra Parade and a hawk-faced male opened the rear passenger-side door and sprang onto the pavement with an easy energy.

A powerful, brooding figure, ponytail swaying slightly in the gentle wind, followed him from around the front passenger side, and behind the wheel, the black-bearded driver nodded his head curtly and drove off.

Before McGrain had reached the entrance of the Trattoria Rossi, the glass-panelled door opened for him and there stood the welcoming presence of the restaurant's owner, Gianfranco Rossi, who bowed obsequiously, before snapping upright. "Good morning, Mr McGrain," he smiled from behind a mouthful of irritatingly white teeth.

"Good morning, Gianfranco. I hope you have the smoked salmon and scrambled eggs on this morning?" asked McGrain, the rough burr of his Glaswegian voice warning that any answer other than an affirmative would meet with disaster.

Instead, Rossi's perma-smile met him. "Of course, Signor McGrain, I have your booth seats waiting for you just as you like at the top of the Trattoria," said Rossi, dipping slightly and wiping his hands agitatedly on the front of the white apron that hung smoothly immaculate from his waist down.

"Good man," said McGrain and with a slight squeeze of the restaurateur's right elbow he walked over the gleaming black-and-white tiled floor towards the booth table at the innermost part of the restaurant and sat himself down precisely in the leather seat that faced the door some 50 feet opposite his position.

Located at the table to his right-hand side in a position that also allowed a full view of the door, Spider pushed the handle of his Glock 17 back under his jacket as Rossi arrived with two menus.

"Come on, Gianfranco, you know us well enough by now. I want the smoked salmon and scrambled eggs, nicely drizzled with lemon juice and an espresso on the side, and it'll be two full Englishes for the boys, plus two black coffees for them," smiled McGrain slightly impatiently.

"Of course, Signor McGrain, I … you know … just like to make sure you are happy," he explained nervously.

"I will be when you serve me my smoked-bloody-salmon just how I like it. Now we'll have the coffees pronto, Gianfranco," ordered McGrain.

Rossi smiled and bowed his understanding before shuffling away and spouting a slightly high-pitched volley of Italian across the glass serving counter and into the restaurant kitchen.

Leaning back against the padded ruby leather of the booth, McGrain let his legs stretch out across the passageway between his table and his pony-tailed lieutenant's. "You putting any money on him showin', Spider?" he called across to him.

Scratching his neck just above the tattoo of the spider that gave him his nickname, McGrain's enforcer-in-chief said: "The boy's no mug, Tony. He knows that he was lucky to escape St Serf's with his baws still attached and he knows how big this joab is. Where does he go if he's got cold feet? You warned him well enough that the polis is'ne an option, so I think he'll be here any minute now," concluded Spider with a reassuring check of his watch.

"And do you know why Gregsy will show, Spider, son?" asked McGrain amicably, then providing the answer before his henchman could reply: "One word … ego. People like our peterman have a weakness and that particular deficiency means they constantly need opportunities to prove they are what they believe themselves to be. That, Spider, son, is whit we are dealing with in Gregsy and why he will be here in …" – McGrain gave a quick glance up at the gold starburst wall clock diagonally opposite him before adding – "2 minutes."

Spider nodded his head in agreement. His jaw jutting as was his wont when he spoke, he replied: "Nevertheless, Tony, I've told big Fergus to take up a position across the Parade just in case things go pear-shaped and our ginger freend surprises us."

"Fair enough," replied McGrain, but his eyes were already wandering as the glass door swung open and a male in a white Planet Hollywood sweatshirt and black baseball cap entered, red curls popping out in an unruly fashion from underneath the hat.

"Excellent," smiled McGrain, his eyes remaining on the new arrival as Gregsy drew to a stop 2 yards away. "Smart boy!"

But before he could move, Spider sprang to his feet, deliberately letting his Glock reappear from under his jacket. He placed two powerful hands on top of Gregsy's shoulders. "Ye won't mind if I pat you down, wee man, just a small precaution after our last meeting …" smiled the enforcer menacingly.

"Go ahead, chief," replied Gregsy, refusing to meet either of their gazes from under his black baseball cap.

Spider completed the frisk with a playful but overly powerful punch to the safe-blower's stomach, before concluding "All good."

"Excellent, now why don't you sit down?" said McGrain, gesturing to the empty seat opposite him, in a tone that brooked no argument.

As Gregsy made himself comfortable, McGrain continued to soothe the peterman's clearly fraught nerves. "I've taken the liberty of ordering you a full English and black coffee. I don't know about you, pal, but I'm starvin'. We have a lot to get through, so it's better that we've got food for thought, eh?" quipped the crime lord as his mouth cracked in a smile at his own humorous effort.

No sooner had Gianfranco laid the coffees down than McGrain took the opportunity to make sure Gregsy was fully on board. "Do you know why you left St Serf's graveyard on your feet and naw in a body bag?"

His baseball cap had been dipped slightly so that his eyes didn't actually hold McGrain's piercing gaze, but now Gregsy had no choice but to lift his head to meet his would-be employer's intimidating stare. "Because I'm the only peterman in Scotland can blow this safe for yous … Mr McGrain," answered Gregsy, for once feeling slightly awkward as he blew his own trumpet.

"Correct, and now that you have managed to make this rendezvous without any screw -ups, I think we will be able to proceed to the meat of the business … after breakfast," added McGrain, just as Gianfranco arrived with his smoked salmon.

As the restaurateur stepped back, he was replaced by a far more menacing presence: black-beard's shadow filled the passageway between the two tables.

"It's all quiet outside, Mr McGrain," advised black-beard.

"Excellent," replied McGrain, having already swallowed his first mouthful of salmon and scrambled eggs. "Get yourself a table near the door and let Gianfranco fix you up, big man …"

Rossi nodded enthusiastically that he would see black-beard all right and the latter's eyes began to bulge with hunger at the two fry-ups that arrived for Gregsy and Spider. As the waiter made his way back towards the serving counter, McGrain's henchman set off in hot pursuit.

Looking across the booth, McGrain lifted his fork and jabbed it in Gregsy's direction. "Eat up, boy, cause it's the last free meal you'll be havin' on me."

Gregsy, his face rippled with a confused frown, didn't know whether to laugh or cry.

CHAPTER TEN

AFTER THE TABLE had been cleared with precise efficiency by Gianfranco and – at the insistence of McGrain – a fresh round of coffees served, the crime lord turned his full hooded gaze on Gregsy.

"Spider has something he wants to show you … James," said McGrain, surprising Gregsy with the use of his Christian name.

Before the safe-blower could turn towards McGrain's lieutenant, he felt the full effects of his arrival on the booth seat next him.

"Budge!" ordered Spider in a voice that brooked no argument.

Gregsy didn't know who to look at; he couldn't help but wonder if the stay of execution that he had been granted at St Serf's was about to come to an end.

As his mind spun, the peterman's attention was snapped back to the here and now by Spider suddenly ripping a savage curved blade out from his ski anorak and ramming it into the wooden table in front of him, leaving the glinting six-inch blade vibrating viciously in the punctured mahogany.

Observing the fear spreading across his prey's stricken features, McGrain smiled almost benignly before speaking in a conversational tone: "Observe, James, if you will, the elegance of the rhinoceros-horn ivory hilt, the lethal precision of the Damascus steel blade with its twin edges and marvel at the janbiya dagger …" said the crime lord, his words fading menacingly into silence as his dark eyes held Gregsy's.

Smiling thinly once again, McGrain continued in his Glaswegian burr: "You are wondering why I am showing you this magnificent piece of 19th-century Ottoman craftsmanship?"

Gregsy shifted in his seat nervously before responding: "Guess so," was the best he could manage.

McGrain leaned forward and stroked the blade's impressive ivory handle lovingly. "Be patient, my young friend, and you will have your answer, but first I think it's important to know the etymology of this fine piece … so, if you don't mind, just bear with me for the time being …" McGrain paused, his eyes sparkling with cruel delight, before he added: "Did you know that the derivation of the name janbiya comes from the Arabic 'janb', which means side, because the dagger is worn sheathed to the side of its wearer?" McGrain gave a short, sharp laugh and ripped the janbiya out of its wooden plinth.

Holding the ivory handle gently in his right hand, he deftly stroked it. "The most famous type of janbiya is a saifani or ivory handle with a dim, almost yellowish lustre. The more translucent ivory will turn yellow with age and this is called a saifani heart. But some of the ivory handles are also called asadi, when they turn greenish-yellow. When the handle becomes whiteish, it is referred to as zaraf, but there is also a handle called an albasali, with a colour that resembles a white onion. Is it not a thing of beauty, James? Just think of all the loving hours of work that have gone into carving this beautiful, ornate piece of craftsmanship."

Placing the blade back down reverently on the table in front of him, McGrain stopped to take a sip of his espresso, savoured the bitter richness of Gianfranco's house speciality, and swallowed.

Then from Gregsy's left-hand side Spider's deep voice rumbled back into life: "The beauty of the curved blade, peterman, is that it bends taewards an opponent so that yer man who's lucky enough to wield the janbiya does'nae need to angle his wrist and by doing so make it vulnerable tae attack. Soes as well as making himself less vulnerable it also makes the art o' knife fightin' that much more comfortable and the janbiya mair lethal as a stabbin' weapon, far more so than straight-bladed knives."

Gregsy remained staring dumbfounded for several more seconds before finally finding his voice: "Okay, I gets the message. I crossed yous back at the graveyard and now yous are makin' the point that I need to produce big time and if I dinnae then … well … but what has some fancy Arab dagger got tae to do with the price o' bread?" stammered the safe-blower, his eyes wide with fear.

McGrain leaned back in his booth seat and sighed. "The janbiya, my friend, is a symbol of what binds the three of us together. Would you believe, James, that three Glasgow boys all found themselves serving under the banner of the French Foreign Legion?" asked the crime lord.

Gregsy couldn't help himself: "Yer havin' a laugh, McGrain …" he half-asked, half-stated.

But before he could finish his statement of disbelief, McGrain had ripped the glinting blade from the table and jammed its merciless Damascus steel against Gregsy's throat. "I jest not, mon ami, and before we are finished with you, James, I can promise you that you will know and respect the meaning of La Légion Étrangère's motto, 'Honneur et Fidélité', or you will die learning that lesson, mon brave."

CHAPTER ELEVEN

AS THE JANBIYA pressed viciously against the skin of his throat, Gregsy's breath came sharply and his eyes tilted upwards. To his relief, the agonising silence was punctured by the sound of a phone ringing. McGrain withdrew the janbiya and fished out his brick-like mobile phone from an inside jacket pocket.

Pressing the phone to his mouth and ear, McGrain turned sideways, covering his mouth with the left hand that still held the janbiya, and answered with a curt "Yes?"

Although he strained his ears as best he could, Gregsy could only make out the animated manner in which the male on the other end of the mobile was talking … frustratingly, the content of his delivery was beyond him; but there was no doubt about the impact it was having on McGrain.

"All right, thanks for the heads-up. We will be out of the restaurant pronto. Good work," was the crime lord's succinct summary.

Putting the mobile away, McGrain grimaced towards Spider. "We've got maybe 5 minutes to get out of here before the cops hit the place," he snapped.

McGrain's right-hand man immediately shot out a massive calloused hand and filled it with Gregsy's sweatshirt. "I told you, boss, we could'ne be trustin' this wee scroat!" Spider whipped out his Glock. "I say we end the bastard out the back and leave a present for the boys in blue to discover," he spat furiously.

McGrain's index finger rubbed his stubbled chin and staring straight at Gregsy, he appeared to give the suggestion some serious consideration. "Well?" was all he said.

"Look … I swear on ma maw's grave I've naw been singin' tae the filth, no way, Tony. Yous gied me a second chance and I've come here in guid faith determined tae take it. I'm good … I promise yous."

McGrain stared at Gregsy's features almost as if he could gain access to his very soul, but before he could reach a decision the sound of the first siren penetrated the restaurant.

"Fuckin' great," raged Spider just as the brutish form of black-beard started to make his way back up the passageway between the tables.

"It's the polis, Tony, two marked vehicles and a CID Escort. Someone has dobbed us in!" he said.

But McGrain had already sprung to his feet. "Is the Merc out the back, Ferg?"

Black-beard nodded in the affirmative and McGrain snapped: "This will have to wait for another day. Get out there and make sure we ain't surrounded and have the motor turning over. Come here, you wee bastard," he spat in Gregsy's direction and hauled the peterman off his feet and dragged him in black-beard's wake towards the rear entrance. As he did so, he turned momentarily towards Spider. "Cover us from the back door until we're in the motor and then join us sharpish. Gianfranco, lock your front door and put the 'closed' sign up," he shouted back towards the startled restaurateur, who had been watching the drama unfold inside his premises with undisguised fascination.

"Si, Signor McGrain," he replied and shuttled towards the entrance; but before he could get there, the door smashed open, narrowly missing the startled Italian.

There standing in the doorway, a Smith & Wesson held in a two-handed grip in front of him, was DI Sean O'Toole. "Where's McGrain?" he shouted and as he spoke another plain-clothes cop flanked him, similarly tooled up.

"Signor, I no understand, who you say?" stammered Gianfranco, playing dumb.

But O'Toole, two uniformed cops following behind him, brushed past Gianfranco almost before he had finished speaking. His revolver swept out in front of him, he paced forward, covering every angle of the restaurant with its barrel as he made his way towards the rear of the Trattoria, while DC Jimmy Lynch, a stocky individual who almost bristled with restless energy, followed in his footsteps.

Reaching the two tables previously occupied by McGrain and his confederates, O'Toole's eyes clamped on the damming evidence of the espresso and coffee cups that the restaurateur had not had time to clear.

Turning to Lynch, he snapped: "Bring our greasy I-Tie friend here, Jimmy boy … seems he's been spinnin' us a fanny." The DI turned to the two uniformed cops flanking him. "Right, boys, out the back, secure the rear exit and make sure there are no surprises waiting for us."

But as the first uniformed officer made his way to the exit, a creak from the door alerted the cops to the fact they were not alone.

Sighting up the advancing copper, Spider grimaced. "Shit," he growled, for he was about to make a decision that could have monumental ramifications for his crew.

There in that split second he knew that he had to buy time for his mates to make their getaway; yet to shoot a cop would make, in the blink of that same second, McGrain and his troupe the most wanted men on the streets of Scotland, not to mention the rest of the UK.

He glanced over his shoulder to see that black-beard was gunning the engine and that McGrain had Gregsy in the back passenger seat of the Merc and was manically waving him into the vehicle. Quickly turning back towards the imminent arrival of the copper, who he saw almost laughably was brandishing a wooden baton that looked like it belonged to the Middle Ages rather than the final decade of the 20th century, Spider's index finger began to tickle the Glock's trigger.

"Legio patria nostra," he spat through a feral grin and proceeded to unload the Glock's 9x19mm Parabellum cartridge magazine into the restaurant.

Spider shot high, intending his bullets to warn rather than kill and watched with professional delight as the spherical light saucers that hung from the ceiling began to shatter one after another, sending shards of glass and plastic splintering through the air.

The monkey suit who had been coming his way was first to be enfiladed by the shards and one jagged skelf buried itself viciously in his left eye. "Jesus Christ," the cop howled in agony before dropping down on his knees, his right hand pawing nervously at the fragment.

Behind him, the first plain-clothes officer dived down under a table, turning it onto its side as if the fake mahogany would offer any protection against the Glock's deadly payload.

Following in his wake, a stockier individual with a grim face was now sighting the enforcer down the barrel of a Smith & Wesson and Spider decided he had no option but to shoot to kill.

He pulled the trigger once again and DC Jimmy Lynch was propelled back against the Trattoria's front window as Spider whispered: "Français par le sang versé," the motto of the French Foreign Legion: 'French by blood spilled.'

O'Toole, his eyes bulging, watched his number two land sprawled and bloody on the black-and-white tiled floor, but to his relief Lynch clutched his left shoulder … he was only winged and through clenched teeth he shouted "Bastard!"

Then, to O'Toole's disbelief, he promptly but shakily regained his feet and proceeded to empty the contents of his Smith & Wesson at the rear door, all the while advancing towards the DI and beyond.

His head turning back and forth as if he was a spectator at Centre Court, the DI followed in his slipstream and saw that all that was left of Rossi's rear exit was a splintered door that swayed broken and half-ajar in a stinging draft.

O'Toole levelled his S&W at the door and nodded to the winged Lynch to boot it open. As the door sprang wide, the DI advanced through the splintered frame, sweeping the restaurant's back alley with his gun … but there was nothing there.

Yet as he noticed an oily patch on the tarmac of the roadway, the air was penetrated by the sound of screeching rubber and turning to his left he saw a black Mercedes shooting out of the service road almost on two wheels.

CHAPTER TWELVE

"THIS IS FECK'N MADNESS, McGrain," spluttered Gregsy, sat rammed into the backseat between the crime lord and the rear passenger side door.

"Shut up, arsehole!" spat McGrain, his right hand jamming a Browning Nine Millimeter into the peterman's side. His eyes locked onto the driver's rear-view mirror, he snapped: "Well, Ferg?"

"Nothing, gaffer, there was no one in the alley when we turned out, the useless bastards hadn't even put anyone on the rear of the premises. Plus, from what I saw as we took the corner intae Ally Parade, the two jam sandwiches and the CID Escort are all sittin' with the lights flashin' but nae wan hame ... so they've all gone firin' hell for leather intae Rossi's ... Strathclyde fuckin' Polis ... mair like the Keystone Cops if you ask me!" He barked out a harsh laugh to underline the contempt he felt towards the erstwhile forces of law and order that had made such a botch of their bust.

Despite the derision of his driver, McGrain nervously dipped down and squinted out of his passenger window, scanning the vista to his left and also the skies above him ... all was quiet.

"It's hard to believe they didn't put someone round the back, but it's a lesson to us, boys. We've become complacent – that's something we should have been covering. I think it also suggests that their tip-off was very last minute ... the question remains ..." – and McGrain let his words trail into silence for a moment before he completed the sentence – "just where did that tip-off come from?"

Still trying to recollect his breath from his sprint out the back of Rossi's and into the Merc, Spider attempted to sit himself upright, now that the brute force of gravity brought to bear by black-beard's handbrake turn out of the alleyway had relented.

But swivelling round so that his intimidating visage could focus squarely on Gregsy, he said: "There's only one answer to that, Tony, and he's sittin' right next tae you. I says we smoke him."

But Gregsy was determined to plead his innocence. "Come on, Spider, listen tae yer boss: like Tony says, the tip-off was so late that they could'ne dae the turn properly. I was in Rossi's long enough tae put away a full fry-up and a couple o' coffees, so if it had been me and I'd tipped the filth aff before I arrived, why did they come rushin' in like a bleedin' herd o' bulls in a china-friggin'-shop, all arse for elbow?" His case made, Gregsy couldn't help a slight smirk developing across his ruddy coupon, such was the confidence he felt in his self-defence.

The wind taken out of his sails, a look of irritated confusion enveloped Spider. "I still say we ice you for that business at St Serf's," he muttered, then his eyes locked on McGrain's hooded gaze.

"However, our young friend has a point, Spider. Now why don't you tell me what happened back at Rossi's?" asked McGrain, re-holstering his handgun.

"Okay, Tony, I winged wan o' the bastards, a copper in plain clothes, but that did'nae stop him chargin' me all guns blazin' as I scarpered oot the back. Aye, he wiz still alive and feck'n' dangerous … nae doubts," concluded Spider.

From the driver's seat, Fergus soon added his rumbling thunder: "Look, gaffer, I checked the rear-view mirror as we turned the corner and there wiz'nae wan o' them pokin' his nose oot when we made the turn. We're in the clear and we can get doon the road and get this fuckin' job done and then piss aff intae the sun, nae bother like."

As they drove down Alexandra Parade, black-beard continued to monitor his rear-view mirror but apart from the usual street life, all was as it should be and the blazing lights of the three cop cars stationary and wedged outside Rossi's became obscured by the normal traffic of a Friday morning in the East End's most salubrious street.

"Aye, we's good, Tony, nothin' doin'," concluded Fergus, smiling in satisfaction at their getaway.

But McGrain was busy slipping a cellophane wrap out of his jacket pocket, one full of white powder, and he deftly poured out a line onto a plastic bank card before taking a hungry snort. He sat back in the Merc's rear seat and let the cocaine rush hit him.

"Aaah," he sighed in satisfaction and leant forward and handed the cellophane bag to Spider, who quickly followed suit, before turning slyly to black-beard and smirking: "Pity yous otherwise engaged, big man, it's quality Charlie."

The Merc drew to a crawl before coming to a standstill behind a service bus that had pulled in at a stop. An assorted group of shell-suited worthies gossiping outside a newsagent's noticed what was going on in the Merc and one of the junkies approached the front passenger door and chapped it with a couple of ink-stained fingers.

"Here, mate, yous bein' naughty in yer motor there? Gonna gie us a wee share o' yer Charlie?" asked the Ned, grinning wickedly through yellowed teeth.

Spider pressed the window button and the electric pane drew down; through the space it now left, his Glock snapped out and he rammed it against the white-baseball-capped youth's cranium. "Say one more word, junkie, and you'll be in oblivion sooner than yer hopin' for … awright!"

Gregsy took in the scene in disbelief and couldn't help himself articulating his surprise. "Is that … well … er … wise?" he asked and immediately regretted it.

McGrain, his eyes narrowing in irritation, turned sharply on him. "What you need to be askin' yourself … James … is what's going to keep you breathing … and stupid questions like that aren't gonna help you in that respect … are they?"

Outside the Merc, the junkie drew away while his mates started to slink off in sheer terror, seeing the Glock that Spider was still training on them out of the passenger window.

They sat back, and with Alexandra Park looming to their left, McGrain waxed historical. "Did you know that Alexandra Park was opened in 1870 and named after Princess Alexandra of Denmark, the future wife of Edward VII, who, young James, was a major league shagger and also liked a large cigar?" and at that the Merc rocked with laughter. Such was the brightness of their smiles, the motor could have been powered by their wattage – and even Gregsy managed a chuckle; but their mirth was short-lived, as a set of flashing lights lit up black-beard's rear-view mirror.

In the cop car, O'Toole levelled the accelerator to the Escort's floor, his grey eyes sparkling with rage. "A fuckin' Escort, I mean, whit chance do you have? It's like trying to chase a fuckin' Formula One racing car in a Reliant bleedin' Robin!" Then, almost guiltily, he snatched a sideways glance at his wounded neeber, Jimmy Lynch.

His right hand clutching his bloodied left shoulder, the young DC held the Escort's radio transmitter in his left paw and barked out an update to AS control: "'Z' Division CID, DI O'Toole and DC Lynch in pursuit of a black Mercedes, no registration at this stage, believed four up. Suspects armed. Request airborne support and all available uniform vehicles to head for the Edinburgh Road end of Alexandra Parade," he barked, nobly refusing to intimate news of his own injury such was his manic determination to apprehend McGrain and his minions.

"Proceed with extreme caution, DC Lynch. There is no airborne support available at this stage, Hotel Mike 40 is engaged in a missing person search for a child in 'K' Kilo division. Please also note that the nearest armed response vehicle is coming from Loch Lomondside. Will do our best to get you uniform support from division, repeat, don't be a hero," advised the Force HQ controller in her nasally feminine tones.

"Fuckin' great, gaffer, looks like it's us and the bleedin' wooden tops," spat Lynch, in reference to the single Bayne Street patrol car that followed in their wake.

"Aye, you're right there, Jimmy boy, it's a bleedin' bugger's mess. We've already lost one of them to the Glasgow Royal Infirmary with a punctured eyeball. You sure we should'nae back down and get you to the quacks asap?" asked O'Toole, his concern for his colleague clear.

"No fuckin' chance, gaffer, I want the pony-tailed bastard who drilled me and I wanna pop at him with my right hand before they stitches me up," raged Lynch defiantly.

"That's the spirit, Jimmy boy," replied O'Toole through gritted teeth, meanwhile surging into a gap in the oncoming lane as he gave the CID motor full throttle.

As the delivery van in front of them finally reacted to the Escort's screaming siren and flashing lights and pulled lamely to the side of the road, O'Toole at last had a clear sighting of the Merc, which was still waiting behind the service bus as the queue at the bus stop slowly got on board.

Checking his rear-view mirror, black-beard broadcast the good news: "Here they come, it's the unmarked CID motor from outside Rossi's, so that means we've got some very mad, as well as injured pigs comin' after us. Aye, and there's wan marked motor behind him, Tony; what you want me tae do?" asked Fergus.

McGrain laughed out loud and then to the amazement of everyone in the Merc he opened his passenger-side rear door and shouted at the group of neds: "Lookin' for some good gear, boys … come and get it!"

He fished out a sheaf of cellophane wraps and proceeded to lob them back over the roof of the Merc and all across the roadway.

The effect was immediate. "Ya fuckin' dancer!" shouted the ned with the white baseball cap and he sprinted round the back of the Merc with his crew of assorted pond life in hot pursuit.

Some 100 yards away, O'Toole stared wide-eyed in disbelief as the group of neds started hunkering down on the roadway, desperately trying to pick up the cellophane pouches while the traffic on the other side of the road ground to a halt and bedlam erupted.

Inside the Merc, McGrain bellowed: "Get us the fuck out of here, Fergus!" Black-beard swerved around the bus and shot back in, just before an Arnold Clark delivery van could collide with them.

Oblivious to all and sundry, the neds continued to clear the road of the cellophane wraps like a bunch of demented pigeons pecking at crumbs, while the CID Escort drew to a stop 20 yards away. "Dirty fuckin' bastard!" raged O'Toole.

Chapter Thirteen

THOROUGHGOOD SAT on an upturned crate and sipped tomato soup from a paper cup while Currie checked his watch for the umpteenth time, before taking a hungry bite from a sausage roll he'd deftly half-wrapped in a paper napkin, taking great care not to get any flakes of pastry on his uniform.

Standing in the doorway that led to the front of Brown's Bakery, the outsize figure of the owner, Linda Brown, leaned against one side of the frame, her florid features sweat-streaked from the heat generated by the shop's ovens. "I'm tellin' you, boys, I guarantee you he'll be here in the next 10 minutes. So if I was you, Constable Thoroughgood, I'd get my coat and hat on sharpish. I'm sure you'll look quite fetchin' in them!" she concluded with a chortle.

Thoroughgood took another sip of soup from his cup and through gritted teeth delivered the question he was desperate to avoid asking: "What makes you so sure it's Nicholas?"

Folding her fleshy forearms in front of her, Linda answered in a tone that brooked no argument: "'Cause I've known Jeb Nicholas boy and junkie for 15 years. He dipped the OAP's handbag last week and I'll tell you why he is sniffing about here on a Thursday morning, because he knows this is the first place a lot of the old dears come when they've drawn their pension. So he slopes in here eyeing them up like a wild dingo and then when he sees the colour of their money he bumps them and makes off with a week's pension. That's two he's done in the last fortnight and he's so out of his face he doesn't even bother to try and disguise himself," finished Linda, her flushed features reddening even more with her broiling anger.

From behind her left shoulder, the sharp features of her assistant, Mags, popped out. "It's a disgrace and all you coppers can do is sit in oor back shop filling yourselves with soup and sausage rolls. I heard Nicholas thinks he's done a deal with yous, is touting to you and claiming he's untouchable," she concluded, her darting grey eyes magnified alarmingly by her thick horn-rimmed National Health glasses.

Knowing what was coming next, Thoroughgood met Currie's 'I-told-you-so' look square on and tried not to flinch; but when the old stager opened his mouth, his words took Thoroughgood by surprise. "Aah, now listen, ladies, there is no one who is untouchable on the Briarknock estate and if there were, do you think we would be sitting here about to do our Batman and Robin act?" Currie said and levelled his gaze at the indignant bakers, inviting a reply.

Linda shuffled awkwardly in the doorway between the front and back of the premises, but before she could say anything else Mags beat her to the verbal punch: "Aye, well, it's a bleedin' disgrace regardless and it's costin' us customers, so let's hope the junkie scumbag thinks he's on a hat-trick—"

But before she could continue her tirade, Linda intervened: "That's why the officers are here, Mags, and we're happy to have them, so why don't you take the mail from the postman who has just walked into the front of the shop," she said, before rolling her eyes to the heavens as her almost feral colleague returned to the serving counter.

Eyeing the clothes pegs on the wall to his left, Thoroughgood shrugged his shoulders, then jumped up from the crate and pulled the baker's hat and coat from the pegs and did his best quick-change routine. It was so hot that it was almost a relief to whip off his already unbuttoned black woollen tunic and snap his polyester police tie from his neck, before opening the top button of his shirt and tossing his garments back onto the crate. Then he pulled the baker's coat on and buttoned it up before slapping the white hat onto his head and holding his hands out in front of him.

"Eh, voila!" said the young cop.

"Very fetching," drawled Currie, before adding: "Aye, well, I suppose I better take up my position round the front in Brushknowes Road. You quite happy with what you're doing?" he asked Thoroughgood and received a curt nod from his younger colleague, who made his way wordlessly through to the serving counter.

Materialising behind him, the figure of Linda Brown loomed large. "What I suggest you do is get to work cleaning the shelves, that way you're busy, but you're not facing anyone who is likely to tumble as to your real identity," suggested the baker, and then she handed Thoroughgood a bucket of hot soapy water and a sponge, before adding: "The tools of the trade!" and at that the front of Brown's Bakery was filled with twin peels of feminine laughter.

As his cellophane-wrapped hands delicately removed some pan loaves from the top shelf before starting his cleaning operation, Thoroughgood saw the shop clock was reading 9.53 a.m. Given that the previous two robberies had been done before 10 a.m., Nicholas' appearance would surely be imminent – if he was indeed to show. The problem was that for him to be drawn to the baker's, there needed to be prey for him to track and at this precise moment the shop was empty.

As he chewed that over, Thoroughgood's jaw locked with the knowledge that he had been played and that Currie's reservations had indeed been proven accurate.

Yet he took some consolation from the fact that the address the junkie had given them for The Creepers up in Torrybrook Road had checked out on the Voters' Roll. As he took a shred of comfort from that knowledge, he felt a light tap on his shoulder. "I think it's show time!" Linda whispered in his ear.

Turning round to face the counter, but keeping his head dipped so that the hat shaded his eyes and most of his face, Thoroughgood saw that an elderly lady with a walking stick had just managed, with some difficulty, to open the shop door. As she did so, Thoroughgood observed the navy-blue Kappa tracksuit and red New York Yankees baseball cap of a familiar figure loping across the road and then leaning nonchalantly against the postbox 10 yards away from the baker's entrance. Nicholas had arrived, hungry for his breakfast.

Taking another quick glance across the street, Thoroughgood could see Currie had made his way out of the tenement close he had originally concealed himself in and was now crouching down behind the hedgerow that ran out from it.

Gritting his teeth, Thoroughgood knew that timing would be everything and that the balancing act between catching Nicholas in the act and avoiding any hurt to the old lady was going to be a difficult one to pull off.

CHAPTER FOURTEEN

"NICE TO SEE THE SUN out this morning, Jeanie. You after the usual?" asked Linda Brown, flashing a welcoming smile.

The elderly lady hooked her walking stick across the serving counter and placed her handbag on top of it before looking up to deliver her reply. "Aye, that would be just fine, Linda, a couple of your nice fresh morning rolls, buttered, please, and I'll treat myself to an Empire biscuit for elevenses today. It's nice to be nice to yourself: after all, someone's got to," said Jeanie, the sparkle in her grey eyes underlining that despite her octogenarian status she was very much still 'all there', her cackle resembling an old unoiled barn door creaking open.

Thoroughgood continued to work hard at his cleaning duties but his industry had not gone unnoticed and Jeanie's shrill tones sprang into life again: "Aye, ah see you've got yer helper this morning, he's a busy big boy!" she chirped, a twinkle now clear in those lively grey eyes.

"He's YTS, Jeanie, but young Angus seems to be a quick learner all right, I'll give him that," agreed Linda.

She handed over Jeanie's rolls and Empire biscuit in two separate paper bags, but as Thoroughgood half-turned to smile at the elderly lady, Mags' machinegun delivery erupted: "Aye. I'm glad he can clean a shelf, 'cause that's aw he's about good for."

Fishing in her handbag for her purse, old Jeanie eventually managed to come up with the right change and as she handed it over to Linda, she flashed a surprisingly mischievous smile Thoroughgood's way and said: "Maybe so, but I'm sure he gives you something nicer to look at than anything back in yer gable end, Mags Smith!"

For once, Mags was silenced and as Linda handed old Jeanie her change she smirked at her assistant and it wasn't long before a huge grin split her scarlet features.

Waving her walking stick in the air, old Jeanie turned for the door, but over her shoulder her parting shot reached their ears: "You'd dae well to remember, Mags, that it's always nice to be nice," and at that Jeanie toddled towards the door and out of the baker's shop, her walking stick waving almost comically in the air above her head.

In the background, Linda erupted into a bawdy laugh. "Well, is that right, Mags Smith, are you appreciative of our new colleague's athletic presence?"

"Is that whit ye call it?" snapped Mags and stormed off into the back shop, but Thoroughgood's attention was already trained through the baker's window, where Jeanie was about to draw level with the wolfish presence of Jeb Nicholas.

From his baker's coat pocket, Thoroughgood fished out his personal radio and barked out an assistance call: "Constable Thoroughgood requesting assistance to the outside of Brown's Bakery in Brushknowes Road, Code 63 in progress, repeat, Code 63 in progress."

Without waiting for a reply, he clipped the radio back onto his belt underneath the baker's coat and vaulted over the counter. A round of appreciative applause erupted behind him and big Linda shouted: "Go get him, Floyd!"

Nicholas' glazed eyes were only interested in one thing and as Jeanie drew level with him, he lunged for her brown leather handbag; but as he clamped grubby hands around it and attempted to rip it free, the feisty octogenarian slashed her walking stick across her body with surprisingly ferocious force and the wooden walking aid cracked off Nicholas' red baseball-capped bonce.

"Think yer gonna rob old Jeanie Watts, junkie scum ... get tae!" spat Jeanie and as Nicholas stumbled from the whiplash of the first blow, Jeanie started to wield her walking stick like some demented miniature version of the Grim Reaper, raining blows down on the hapless and clearly shell-shocked junkie.

Nicholas let out a whelp, before making a second lunge for Jeanie's bag. "Ya mad old hag, just gie us yer bag and ah'll be aff!"

This time the strain of Jeanie's earlier efforts seemed to have taken its toll and the force of Nicholas' lunge knocked her backwards so that she started to lose her footing. He wrenched the bag triumphantly from her arm just as the white overalls of a baker came bounding into his view.

Sprinting out from the shop, Thoroughgood closed the 10 yards between him and the attempted robbery just in time to catch old Jeanie as she started her descent towards the pavement and as his arms quickly enveloped the OAP, Nicholas enjoyed his moment of triumph. "Aye, baker's boy, yous take good care o' the old boot ..." he hissed, just as a startled look of recognition started to spread across his jaundiced features.

But there was an even bigger shock in store for the junkie, as Harry Currie's brown wooden baton started it's descent at full throttle onto the top of his shoulders. Nicholas recoiled with such violent shock that he dropped the treasured leather handbag, blurting out "Bastard," as he half-turned to see who his assailant was. As he did so, Currie aimed a size 10 Doc Marten at the robber's privates with all his might and Nicholas went down like the Titanic.

"Gotcha," said the senior cop.

Helping Old Jeanie to her feet, Thoroughgood looked down at the writhing figure of Nicholas, who was clutching feverishly at his groin and filling the air with a series of agonised expletives.

From behind him, the baker's door opened and Linda and Mags sallied out. "Are you all right, Jeanie? You did yourself proud, old girl!" said Linda.

"Aye, ye did'nae dae so bad yourselves, boys," said Mags appreciatively towards the two cops.

"Well, thank you, ladies! Now would you mind taking Jeanie into the back shop while we deal with this piece of vermin?" asked Currie from behind a broadening smile.

"Of course, it'll be our pleasure, Constable Currie," said Linda, before adding: "There'll be a hot coffee waiting on you boys when you're finished."

His face taut with anger, Thoroughgood ignored the pleasantries going on around him and grabbed Nicholas by the scruff of the neck. He hauled the gasping junkie onto his feet before smashing him against the postbox. "I gave you a chance, Nicholas, and you threw it back in my face, you treacherous weasel, and now you're headin' for the tin pail," he spat.

As he stared into Thoroughgood's blazing green eyes, Nicholas, knowing that any attempt at sweet talk was futile, shrugged, before replying: "Fair enoughski, boss," just as a marked police Transit turned the corner.

CHAPTER FIFTEEN

THOROUGHGOOD STOOD at the bar in Bonham's and stared forlornly into the glass panel behind the gantry, studying his reflection.

The white of his uniform shirt showed through the unzipped black Harrington he wore carelessly half-open, his black hair still smoothed down on his head from the 8 hours it had spent with a police hat crammed down on top of it.

Finishing a mouthful of Stella he muttered to himself: "You're a mug, Thoroughgood." He placed the half-emptied pint pot on the marble-topped counter and slouched his jaw down onto the open palm of his left hand as the day's action repeated in his head.

He'd been played and what Thoroughgood couldn't make his mind up over was whether that painful reality, or the fact old Harry Currie had been right all along, was worse.

The bottom line was that he'd also been taught an invaluable lesson about the trustworthiness of junkies as informants. It had been all very well using Collins as a tout to help infiltrate Dawson and his cronies, but Thoroughgood had to admit that the threat of extreme violence combined with the streetwise approach of Numan, Malcolm and Hardie had been the real driver behind the grass working for them: not any ability of his to make the Cat dance to his tune.

Now, as a community cop, he was very much on his own, with enough experience to be trusted on his beat but still not enough, it seemed, to be able to decide whether a junkie's motives for providing information were meaningful or just a quick fix for freedom to continue to feed his addiction in any way he could.

Yet while Currie had initially looked like being a stultifying presence who would hold him back and drag him down at every cut and turn, Thoroughgood was forced to admit that the old boy was indeed a wise old head and one whose understated sense of humour had started to come increasingly to the fore.

Shaking his head to himself, Thoroughgood inwardly admitted that by assuming that Currie had no more than a series of moans and endless refrains of 'I told you so' to contribute, he in turn had been badly guilty of both arrogance and ignorance. What was now glaringly apparent was that his senior cop had a huge depth of experience to draw upon, if Thoroughgood would only give him the chance to bring it to bear and not blunder on, driven by his own obsession to gain a CID Aide.

Checking the wall clock over his left shoulder, he saw it was almost 5.30 p.m. and taking another mouthful of lager, Thoroughgood tried not to watch the entrance for her appearance.

He needn't have worried, for within moments the glass-frosted front door of Bonham's opened and in walked Celine, her afro tresses crisp precision and a halter neck leopard-skin top that only she would have dared wear at that time of day immediately making every man seated or standing in Bonham's look her way.

'Just as she liked it,' thought Thoroughgood, both amused and jealous.

But in her wake followed the assured presence of a sandy-haired, 6-foot-plus male whose watchful, slate-grey eyes swept the bar panoramically before seeking out Thoroughgood himself; and then clearly carrying out a threat assessment when they met his own sea-green gaze.

Celine pursed a slight smile and moved across the bar with the effortless feline grace of a panther, where Thoroughgood met her with a quick kiss of those mesmeric lips. As he did so, he couldn't help himself keeping an eye on the silent brooding presence that stood in her wake.

"Hi, Gus, another good day at the office?" she asked, breaking into a cute laugh.

"I've had better," he replied, looking past her at her silent friend and forcing Celine to end the developing awkwardness with an introduction.

"This is Declan Meechan, Gus, my new boss at Vesuvius, the new bar and club at—"

But before she could finish her sentence, Thoroughgood did so for her: "The bottom of Byres Road."

Meechan extended a paw and met Thoroughgood's handshake with a crisp, precise grasp, which the cop thought was a bit like the man himself: immaculate, grey double-breasted suit, red and white striped club tie, not a strand of his sandy reddish mullet out of place: all business.

"Pleased to meet you," said Meechan, allowing a tepid smile to flick over his poker face.

Replying with an emotionless "Likewise," Thoroughgood immediately decided he didn't like Meechan; and, more worryingly, that he was the last man he could trust around the woman he had fallen for.

"So, what you both drinking?" he asked, offering as little encouragement in his voice as he could – but Meechan refused to receive the subliminal message that he was unwelcome.

Instead, he laughed: "I think champagne is called for: after all, Celine has something to celebrate, it's not every day that you're made manageress of the West End's newest cocktail bar!" Then he waved a pale hand and managed to catch the attention of the chargehand, Jim, a shaven-haired individual from Partick, who Thoroughgood always thought seemed to nurse an outsize chip on his shoulder that the world had never dealt him a fair hand of cards.

"What can I get you, my friend?" asked the barman.

"Well, we're here to celebrate, so let's do it properly," joked Meechan and Thoroughgood noticed that he had slipped a proprietorial hand around Celine's back.

More annoyingly, Thoroughgood could see that Meechan had noticed his surveillance.

"Do you have any Dom Pérignon, bartender?" asked Meechan. He turned to smile serenely at Celine before letting his lifeless grey eyes flicker Thoroughgood's way. "After all, if it was good enough for the wedding of Lady Di and Prince Charles, I think it will more than do for our little celebration!" he quipped.

"How very … romantic," said Thoroughgood amicably, but inside he seethed.

Chapter Sixteen

FROM THE OTHER SIDE of the bar, the champagne cork had popped and Jim proceeded to pour the Dom Pérignon into three glasses. As the barman did so, he couldn't stop himself from letting his captive audience know just how knowledgeable he was.

Sweeping the three of them with a knowing gaze, which lingered just a bit too long on Celine, Jim smiled sweetly and said: "Well, folks, did you know that Dom Pérignon was named after a Benedictine monk of the same name?"

Thoroughgood couldn't help himself quipping: "Smart boy, James, amazing how appearances can be deceptive." It was a leaden rejoinder, one that smacked of arrogance and he immediately regretted it, as he noticed the prickly bartender's jaw set.

It also brought an admonishment from Celine: "Gus, that's unfair of you!" Then she turned to Meechan. "So, Declan, the question is, did you know that Dom Pérignon champagne was named after a Benedictine monk?"

Meechan smiled serenely and let his cool grey gaze meet the bartender's fuming features. "That's pretty impressive, Jim, if I may call you by your Christian name?" He received a curt nod in the affirmative before he continued amicably: "But did you know that although Dom Pérignon was an important pioneer of Champagne wine, contrary to popular myth he did not discover the champagne method for making sparkling wines?" concluded Meechan through a thin smile.

Thoroughgood drained the last of his Stella and set the pint pot back down on the counter. Before he could stop himself, he snapped:

"I repeat my previous comment, oh how appearances can be deceptive! So why don't you elaborate, Mr Meechan, and put us all out of our misery?" His ill-advised comments immediately drew a reproving glance from Celine and as Jim handed out the champagne glasses, Thoroughgood noticed that as well as being the last to receive his, the glass coming his way failed to complete its journey and remained opposite him – at the other side of the marble bar top.

His inconsiderate comment had also played right into Meechan's hands. "Since you've asked … Angus … I will indeed … elaborate!" Thoroughgood found anger surge fresh within him as an amused sparkle flickered through Meechan's eyes, which now rested on Celine, who in turn held his gaze for just a shade too long.

"Dom Pérignon was indeed, as Jim has just helpfully informed us, a Benedictine monk, but he wasn't just any Benedictine monk: he was cellar master at the Benedictine abbey in Hautvillers. He was an expert at perfecting the art of producing clear white wines from black grapes by clever manipulation of the presses and also in enhancing the tendency of Champagne wines to retain their natural sugar in order to induce secondary fermentation in the spring." Meechan paused momentarily to ensure he had his audience's attention before continuing. "Thus deciding when to bottle these wines in order to capture the trademark bubbles that sets champagne apart from all other wines." He tilted his head slightly as if in appreciation of the great man's efforts and then took a sip from his glass.

"Mmm," he said appreciatively and placed the champagne back down on the bar top. "But while he didn't discover the champagne method, he did introduce corks which were fastened to the bottles with hemp string soaked in oil in order to help his wine stay fresh and keep their sparkle. Monsieur Pérignon also used thicker glass to bottle his sparkling wines, as they were somewhat prone to exploding back in the late 17th century." Concluding his monologue, Meechan rewarded himself with another sip of the Dom Pérignon.

As he did so, Thoroughgood couldn't help himself from observing Celine in an almost detached fashion, like he was in an out-of-body state.

The bottom line was that Meechan was super-slick and she loved it.

Celine wasn't the only one who was impressed by Meechan's words of wine wisdom and from across the bar Jim said: "An ace beats a king every time, Mr …" he let his enquiry hang in the air.

Meechan finished his drink and placed the champagne glass back down on the bar. "It's Meechan, but call me Declan; and here, take my card. Why don't you give me a bell, we're looking for staff who actually take an interest in their job," he laughed.

Sitting next to him, her pencil-skirt-sheathed legs mesmerically crossed, Celine purred: "But Declan, shouldn't that be a job for your new manageress?" and this time they both laughed in unison as Thoroughgood began to feel physically sick.

"So if you two wine buffs are such experts, can you tell me which vintage of Dom Pérignon was used at Charles and Di's wedding?" asked Thoroughgood, confident that he would catch the smug Meechan out.

But before he could answer, Jim piped up: "It was 1961, I believe."

The barman's answer immediately drew an approving round of applause from Meechan, who gazed down on Celine, and asked: "Well, Celine, isn't it about time you hired your first member of staff?"

Her slender coffee-coloured fingers cradling the side of her jaw, she smiled coquettishly at Meechan before turning to the bartender. "Well, Jim, how would you like to come and work for us at Vesuvius? I could do with a chargehand with your type of knowledge if we are going to make the cocktail bar the place to drink in the West End."

Thoroughgood, shifting awkwardly on his barstool behind her, felt like he didn't exist and as the barman flicked him a smug smile it was all he could do not to get up and walk out.

But just then the sound of a phone ringing interrupted their conversation and Meechan fished out a black Nokia, checked the caller screen and smiled apologetically at Celine. "Sorry, but I need to take this," he said and with that he apologetically let his left hand stray onto her shoulder before answering his mobile. "Hi Jimmy, apologies, I've been in a meeting." Then Meechan shot Thoroughgood a furtive glance before he turned and walked towards the bar's door.

Turning back round towards him, it seemed that Celine had remembered Thoroughgood was still in the bar for the first time in the last 10 minutes. "Wasn't that fascinating," she gushed and then turned to Jim. "Well done, you! Can you make it down to Vesuvius tomorrow morning at 9.30 and we can get you sorted, and, if you don't mind, I'll call you James, I think that sounds bit more appropriate for the assistant manager's position!"

The smile that lit up Jim's grim features almost shocked Thoroughgood such was its intensity, as the barman said: "It will be my pleasure … boss!"

"And don't you forget it!" quipped Celine and they both laughed, while Thoroughgood, once again, sat in awkward silence.

CHAPTER SEVENTEEN

FOR THOROUGHGOOD, the champagne had undoubtedly lost its sparkle and what he'd hoped would be a quiet drink with his girlfriend had turned into a disaster that only served to magnify just how fragile his relationship with Celine was.

For the uncomfortable truth was that he did not trust her and he certainly didn't trust the almost serpentine Meechan, who already seemed to be alarmingly familiar with Celine in a manner that was more predatory than businesslike.

Yet there was no doubt that Meechan was a shrewd operator and his mixture of patronising, all-knowing conversation and the nous he had employed to use Jim the barman to empower Celine and allow her to hire her first member of staff was all clearly designed to weasel his way into her affections.

While admitting to himself that after the business with Nicholas he was unlikely to be anything like good company, Thoroughgood felt like this little episode had all too graphically illustrated the need to have Meechan checked out good and proper via Divisional and Force Intelligence channels, for the club boss' condescending, super-smooth manner wasn't the only thing that jarred with him.

When the 'businessman' had answered his phone, he had greeted his caller as 'Jimmy' and in his whirl of paranoia and dislike, Thoroughgood couldn't help himself wondering, given Meechan's line of business and its West End location, if the Jimmy on the other end of the line was Jimmy Gray, the Partick hoodlum made-good who now ran the West End and owned almost all of its top entertainment venues.

As these thoughts swirled around his head, Thoroughgood realised that he had fallen into an obdurate and painful silence and that her conversation finished with Jim, Celine was now staring at him from the barstool opposite and waving her hand in front of his face.

"Earth to Gus, come in, are you still with us?" she asked, smiling the smile that he knew would always make him melt.

Thoroughgood shrugged his shoulders awkwardly. "Look, Celine, I'm sorry, but I think this was probably a bad idea, me coming out, after the shift I've had. Just because I'm on a bit of a downer after a bad day on the job doesn't mean I should be ruining your good news for you," he said.

A look of tender concern crept across her golden features and she took a breath of air through that cute little nose of hers. Thoroughgood couldn't help reaching across and stroking her cheek tenderly with the back of his hand and to his delight she reached up and cradled it.

"What happened to you today, Gus?" she asked in that smoky, bourbon-laced voice that sent a shiver down his spine.

Thoroughgood's left hand massaged his forehead involuntarily before he answered. "I guess I had a wake-up call and one that led to an old lady getting a very nasty fright that could have been a whole lot worse, and all because I trusted someone I shouldn't have."

The minute the words had escaped his mouth, Thoroughgood wished a hole would open up and draw him down into its black depths.

Elton John's 'Sacrifice' provided an ironic soundtrack to their moment of mounting drama as a look of puzzlement enveloped Celine's previously serene features: but then a trace of anger blazed through her chocolate-brown eyes.

"You trusted someone you shouldn't have? Why can't I help myself thinking that comment has a double meaning aimed at me? Look, Gus, this is all a game and if I'm going to make anything of myself in this business I need to play to my strengths," she said, then stopped and took a drink of champagne, her eyes monitoring him from above the glass. "Basically, you're jealous, Gus Thoroughgood, aren't you?"

But before he could answer, Meechan timed his return to the bar with pristine perfection.

"Sorry about that, but when your boss calls, you run!" he quipped.

"But who would that boss be, Mr Meechan? A certain Jimmy Gray, perhaps?" asked Thoroughgood, locking his eyes on Meechan's.

"Look, it's Declan. Yes, I work for the West End's most successful restaurateur and bar owner, there's no shame in that, is there … Mister Thoroughgood?" replied Meechan, allowing a short pause before prefixing Thoroughgood's name with the title, which he then drew out with dripping sarcasm.

"No … Declan … there is nothing wrong with that legitimate side of Gray's business empire. What is wrong with it is the drug and enforcement money he uses to finance it. It's dirty money laundered clean through the cash registers and accounts of venues like your club. What did you call it … The Volcano?"

Thoroughgood's barb had hit its target and Meechan, his anger building, took a threatening step towards him, towering over the seated Thoroughgood, who turned slightly to face him. "I'd be very careful about throwing accusations around you can't substantiate," hissed Meechan, his slate-grey eyes burning.

"Can't substantiate? You're having a laugh, Meechan, either that or your righteous indignation is all for Celine's benefit?" asked Thoroughgood, trying to keep his voice even and his own anger from spilling over into something nasty.

But although he continued to loom large above Thoroughgood, Meechan switched his attention to Celine, checking the impact the confrontation was having on her. Although his rage remained in check, Thoroughgood could see that Meechan's jaw was set with the intensity of the battle to retain his self-control.

Remaining perched on his barstool, Thoroughgood reached for his glass and raised it in mock toast. "Here's to Dom soddin' Pérignon," he said and drained the champagne.

Then the cop stood up, and closing the slight gap between him and Meechan, Thoroughgood brought his face to within an inch of the club boss. "Now get the fuck out my way, Meechan," he spat.

For a moment Meechan held his ground. Then an insincere smile enveloped his face and he turned sideways and beckoned Thoroughgood past him with the sweep of an outstretched arm and an open palm.

As he walked out of Bonham's and felt the fresh air coolly washing over him, Thoroughgood found a maelstrom of emotion crashing through him and zipping up his Harrington he took a deep breath. Before he could take a step, a familiar honey-soaked voice called out from behind him: "What now, Gus?"

Just as Thoroughgood was about to turn her way, he caught sight of DI Ronan O'Toole and his lapdog DC Jimmy Lynch, his left arm heavily swathed in bandage, exiting the black wooden doors of Tennent's Bar across the road opposite them and, as they attempted to negotiate the Byres Road traffic, Thoroughgood could see that the DI's keen gaze had already taken in the mini-drama now playing outside Bonham's entrance.

Before he could help himself, Thoroughgood cursed: "Fuck it!" just as he started to turn back towards Celine, but by the time they faced each other the look of shock that had initially enveloped her silken features had already begun to give way to a mounting fury.

"What the hell do you mean 'fuck it'?" she demanded, but before he could reply Celine did so for him: "In fact, don't bother answering that, ever since I've met you, Gus Thoroughgood, it's been all about you, all about the job that dominates your life and that you expect to take precedence over everyone else's life. Well, guess what, just because I don't have a bloody degree from Glasgow Uni doesn't mean I don't have ambitions of my own too and that I'm not aiming to make the most of my life—"

Before she could complete her tirade, a familiar Glaswegian voice interrupted their exchange of pleasantries. "Everything all right, Constable Thoroughgood? Your young lady here is looking a little upset," said Detective Inspector Ronan O'Toole, in an almost paternal show of interest.

Jimmy Lynch was less sympathetic to the travails of Thoroughgood's love life. "Well, blow me, Thoroughgood, I never thought you had it in you! If you want to hold on to a beauty like this gorgeous creature you really need to treat her a bit better than having a stand-up outside a Byres Road bar," advised Lynch, his delight at Thoroughgood's predicament glaringly obvious, but brought to an abrupt end when a wince caused by his wounded shoulder whip-cracked across his taut features.

As his green eyes darted from O'Toole's unconvincing concern to Lynch's leering delight and back to Celine, Thoroughgood blustered: "You've got the wrong end of the stick, Celine ... I ... I meant ... er ..." but his attempted explanation petered out into silence at the realisation the verbal hole he had just dug himself was already man-size.

"Why don't you just save it for someone who gives a damn," snapped Celine and as she turned back towards Bonham's entrance, the door opened with all-too-perfect timing and there stood Meechan.

"Is everything all right, Celine?" he asked, touchingly concerned.

"It is now," replied Celine, and as she joined him in the doorway a dagger shot through Thoroughgood's heart when her right hand reached out and squeezed Meechan's wrist.

While Meechan surveyed Thoroughgood in triumph, Celine didn't even turn around, but her words still reached him clearly: "Gus Thoroughgood has just left the building ... let's go back in and enjoy the rest of the champagne ... Declan," she said, almost purring Meechan's Christian name.

Then Celine disappeared inside the pub, but just as she did so, Meechan's eyes flitted towards O'Toole and Lynch. "I think your colleague could do with a pint, DI O'Toole … and a shoulder or two to cry on," he sneered, before nodding to O'Toole, who smirked his acknowledgement.

And with that he followed Celine back into Bonham's.

Chapter Eighteen

THE MERC HAD BEEN replaced by a green Transit van, which now sped down the M74 with black-beard once again at the wheel. McGrain sat studying a map in stony silence in the front passenger seat and Spider watched Gregsy, like a hawk, in the vehicle's rear.

As he sat fidgeting on a bench seat, the peterman couldn't help himself giving vent to the events of the previous few hours, which had now taken on a surreal sheen.

"I knows you've had the job planned for a gid few weeks, but is this the right time tae go for it ..." – Gregsy hesitated before using the crime lord's first name – "Tony?" He waited anxiously to see whether McGrain took offense.

From the Transit's front cabin the rustle of paper indicated that McGrain was folding the map up and he almost immediately climbed through the cabin, back into the panel-enclosed rear of the van and sat down next to Spider on the bench opposite Gregsy.

"I would say that the events of this morning make today the perfect time for our little jaunt south. Put simply, James, if ever there was a good time for us to disappear then that time is now. The only way we have managed to remain at liberty is by staying one step ahead of the polis and that has been done by planning, always having the next move laid out and every eventuality covered; that is all part of what we learned in La Légion," said McGrain, leaning back against the Transit's metallic walls.

That was something that Gregsy had to admit he couldn't argue with. As soon as they left Alexandra Parade they had made for the quiet winding roads that ultimately led to the grounds of Gartloch Hospital; but they had turned off before that, to go towards the Bishop's Loch, where it had long been rumoured the medieval residence of the Archbishop of Glasgow lay somewhere broken, fragmented and now swallowed whole by mother nature.

It was in the woodland near to the loch, where the Victorian turrets of the nearby hospital could still just be made out, that they had swopped the Merc for the Transit at a wooden hut with a lean-to garage that was obviously a safe house for the crime lord and his minions.

They had also picked up three large kitbags that were quite clearly remnants from McGrain and his cohorts' time in the Legion and now 5 hours later, as Gregsy found himself eyeing the green canvas holdalls, the safe-blower could just make out 'Légion Étrangère' printed in almost illegible gold lettering, so faded was it. As he stared at the kitbags, Gregsy gave an involuntary shake of his head, his brain struggling again to compute the implications of the journey he was on.

But McGrain had watched the direction of Gregsy's gaze and immediately moved to refocus the newest member of his team's mind on what was important.

"Don't you want to know where we're going, James?" he asked conversationally.

Gregsy smiled at McGrain's offer, for it was proof that the crime lord now trusted him. "Well, I guess it ain't a trip to the seaside!" he said.

He was immediately met by a harsh peel of laughter from Spider, who quipped: "Ah would'ne be so sure o' that, wee man."

This time it was McGrain who laughed. He unfolded the map he had previously been scouring and flattened it out on the van floor in front of Gregsy. "We are indeed on a trip to the seaside. Ever heard of the village of Heysham in Lancashire?" he asked, pointing to the map.

"Nope, can't say I have," replied Gregsy flatly.

"It's a very interesting place, with Viking burial grounds, the only sea cliffs in Lancashire and a busy wee port that could take you to Ireland or the Isle of Wight, whichever took your fancy. But we have another reason for finding Heysham interesting ..." McGrain let his words trail into silence.

Sitting on hands curled around the van's bench, Gregsy was enthralled. "Which is?"

"The NatWest bank and, more importantly, the three mill in payroll that will be inside the vault shortly, waiting to be removed by those with a little specialist knowledge," said McGrain matter-of-factly, before smiling reassuringly at Gregsy.

The peterman's reply was a long, slow whistle.

This time it was Spider who took up the story. "Aye, you would'ne think a bank in a little seaside village would be holding that kind of wedge but wi' it also being a port, the local NatWest branch is where the Port Authority and ferry companies deposit their payroll. We have the inside track on aw that thanks tae Ferg's sister, Senga, who works as a cleaner there ... and less than 3 hours fae Glasgow, waitin' tae be picked like a ripe plum. Aye, it's a thing o' fuckin' beauty if you ask me!" he concluded triumphantly.

As Spider was finishing his monologue, McGrain helpfully circled the map on the floor beneath them. "There we are: Heysham, just around 30 miles away. Your wee sis has been very helpful indeed, Spider. The bottom line is that we will be staying tonight in the village at The Royal Hotel and tomorrow, after we've had a good scout about and cased the bank, thanks to our insider we will be staying overnight in the bank itself, but the detail can wait. Right now, it's time for some coffee and some grub. That's Killington Lake services just coming up, Fergus, make sure you take the turn-off, 'cause my belly thinks my throat has been cut!"

But Gregsy couldn't help his curiosity getting the better of him: "Okay, so you've got a tout inside, but how we gonna overcome the security?"

"That'll be no problem because sweet little Senga will be leaving the backdoor unlocked and also have helpfully turned off the alarm when she finishes her night-time cleaning round. Then we'll be spending the night playing pool in the staffroom while we wait for the manager to turn up with the keys in the morning, like he's done every day for the last 3 years, without fail, at 9 a.m. sharp," said McGrain.

"Sweet," said Gregsy, and the Transit filled with the sound of their laughter.

CHAPTER NINETEEN

WITHIN AN HOUR, the empty plates that lay strewn across the Roadchef's chipped enamel table provided ample proof that four mixed grills had been devoured. Even so, Gregsy couldn't help himself from toying with his coffee cup as worry gnawed away inside his head.

"Do you think we're really in the clear, boss?" he eventually piped up.

"I didn't see anyone following us down the road, so why would you think otherwise, James? There were no cop cars on the motorway, were there? That's the problem with the polis, they are so provincial, one force doesn't know what the others on its borders are up to. So relax, everything is good, all we need to do is get ourselves down to Heysham, get a couple of beers, a decent night's kip and in the morning we'll start to familiarise ourselves with the bank, the village and the road layout. All of which I have the plans for in here," said McGrain, patting his jacket pocket, before adding: "Like I say, son, all I need you to do is relax!"

"Aye, why don't you fuck aff and play the puggy for a minute, wee man, and let the adults talk!" quipped Spider and was met with a hearty laugh from Fergus that reminded Gregsy he was still very much the junior member of the crew.

Despite himself, Gregsy found his gaze wandering to the amusement arcade situated in the service station's foyer just along from the Roadchef, his red-tousled mop flicking in its direction.

As his gaze returned to his comrades, Gregsy realised that his quick glance had been surveilled by three sets of eyes and he raised his hands in open-palmed admission that the prospect of a quick punt on the fruit machines was one he found mighty attractive. "Don't mind if I do …" he murmured. Then a frown of uncertainty slipped across his pale features, as the possibility that indulging his great weakness would mean he might miss something of importance began to trouble him.

But McGrain immediately provided reassurance: "Look, son, you're naw gonna be cut from anything. You're here to make sure there are no problems with the safe: the rest is our headache. We need 20 minutes to go over a few nuts and bolts then we'll be good as gold and ready to get going again. So, off you go and rattle the puggy."

Gregsy was already easing his way out of the booth before McGrain had finished his sentence and as his denim-clad back exited the Road-chef, Spider was first to speak: "What do ya reckon, Tony, can we trust him? I'm still no' 100 per cent he was'nae behind that feckin' polis raid," he said, his agitation emphasised by a quick yank he administered to his ponytail.

"You would'nae trust yer granny to make ye a plate o' mince an' totties, would you, Spider, son?" quipped black-beard and the table shook with laughter.

"Aye, Fergus has a point, Spider, but what matters now is Heysham. The peterman is only along for one thing and once we are clear, he becomes excess to requirements and we may or may not remove any concerns you have over him once and for all. Bottom line is James Greg is the best in the business at what he does and in any case, if Senga has been servicing the bank manager the way you assure me she has, then his pillow talk may mean we don't even need to rely on our peterman when push comes to shove. Now, let's finish these coffees and hit the road," concluded McGrain.

"Sounds gid tae me, Tony, I'm just gonna take me a leak," grunted Fergus and at that he stood, and, pulling up his trousers by the waist band, added for good measure: "Aye, it's time tae syphon the python!"

McGrain waved a disgusted hand at his minion while Spider chirped: "First you'll need tae find it, big man!" and received a one-finger salute for his trouble before black-beard strode off.

As Fergus' bear-like figure passed the amusement arcade, he ambled over to Gregsy and rapped the peterman on the back with a powerful paw. "Awright, wee man? Won anythin' yet?"

Gregsy just about jumped out of his skin. "Fuck's sake, Fergus … am no likely tae win anything with you scarin' the livin'-bejesus oot oh me, now am I? Is that us good to go, then?"

"Cool yer jets, boy … am a way for a quick slash. Tony and Spider are just finishing up and then they'll get us here in the foyer in 5 minutes, if that's awright with you, peterman?" concluded black-beard.

"Just grand," mumbled Gregsy, but his eyes were already boring back in on the puggy.

As Fergus made his way across the foyer and into the urinals, a smile of splintered, stained teeth attempted to light up the still black of his beard. He whistled 'The Fields of Athenry' tunelessly to himself as he let his mind project forward to the business that awaited them in sleepy Heysham town.

Pulling his manhood out and proceeding to unleash its contents on the urinal, Fergus couldn't help humming his relish at the job he was about to help perpetrate and by doing so, hopefully reach out and secure the mirage of security that, whatever turn, heist or drug deal he had been involved in before, had always been maddeningly out of reach.

His mind started to conjure up a vision of his Sadie, all knowing smiles, chestnut tresses and cleavage, pulling ice cold pints of San Miguel in the Magaluf bar he'd already put a four-figure deposit down on.

That warming thought put a glow of almost infant-like happiness into black-beard, but as he zipped up and turned around, Fergus just had time to notice that the cubicle door opposite his urinal had swung open and a male wearing a Jaxon & James Detroit trilby and a Donegal two-piece suit that made him look like an extra from a Madness tribute act was there, standing still as a statue.

In his two cupped hands, the Suggs wannabe cradled what Fergus dimly recognised was a silencer-fitted Luger.

Then its deadly payload enfiladed him.

Desperately throwing his huge arms up to try and ward off the murderous projectiles, Fergus felt the bullets penetrate his flesh and shouted desperately: "Whit the fuck ..." but by the time the last of the words had left his mouth he had already hit the tiles with a thud and groan. As his orbs started to glaze and Sadie's saucy features flashed before his mind's eye one last time, his gaze momentarily returned to the here and now.

Standing above him, the male in the sharp claret two-piece suit removed his shades and tipped his trilby in mock salute, then hunkered down, pressed the Luger's silencer to Fergus' forehead. "Bonsoir, Beau fuckin' Geste!" he said, sending black-beard to his maker once and for all.

CHAPTER TWENTY

Grabbing black-beard by his outsize shoulders, the Suggs looka-like quickly span him round and dragged him back into the cubicle he'd just used to spring his deadly ambush, propping him up on the toilet seat in a macabre act of personal amusement.

He had been lucky in that the toilets had been momentarily empty and now he had to cash in on his almost eerie piece of good fortune and finish the job he had come to execute.

Re-holstering the Luger inside his Ben Sherman two-piece and smoothing out the claret folds of the tweed, Suggs pulled the cubicle door shut behind him and strode purposely out of the toilet in search of the rest of his prey.

Scanning the foyer through his shades, he quickly focussed in on the amusement arcade; but there was nothing there to interest Suggs, just some ginger-haired loser playing a fruit machine and a few kids on the Space Invaders.

Then his gaze reached his confederate, a stocky individual whose head was covered by the hood of a large Fred Perry fishtail parka, who was leaning against the side of the entrance to the Roadchef and scanning the interior of the restaurant for any signs of their targets.

Suggs' cobalt-grey eyes bored in on his confederate and he was rewarded when the navy-blue hood turned his way and inside it the pale features of Ronnie Parlane grinned. Ronnie then flicked a quick thumbs up followed by a serious of hand signals that confirmed that their two victims were within and seated at the far window.

Suggs didn't need a second invitation and joined Parlane in the doorway, taking up a position opposite, some 10 feet from his leader.

Smiling cruelly from under the hood of his parka, Parlane said in a voice that was just audible over the passing pedestrian traffic: "Show time, Johnstone," and waved his sidekick forward.

Making their way with immaculate timing that saw them slip through the bustling grillhouse almost in step, the two of them began to close the pincers of their trap. Sitting in a window booth at the far side of the restaurant, their prey continued an avid conversation, oblivious to the threat.

"Time we got going," said McGrain, dabbing the remnants of a coffee moustache from above his lips.

"Aye, if we dinnae get moving soon, that Gregsy will have spent aw his bleedin' pocket money!" joked Spider and McGrain smiled his appreciation.

Just 3 feet away from them, a young, blonde waitress was clearing up the remnants of a messy family meal. As she reached across to grab the last plate, an empty milkshake glass tumbled off the table, smashing off the tiled floor with a sharp crack.

Sat opposite this scene of domestic disaster, McGrain, who had moments before been admiring the waitress' shapely derrière, leapt suddenly from his booth and hunkered down next to the girl, who, up close and personal, proved to be an attractive, tanned 20-some-thing-year-old. "Here, let me help you, miss," smiled McGrain just as a thud came from the seat he had just vacated.

Realisation instantly dawned on McGrain, but if he needed any more confirmation it came in the shape of Spider throwing himself to the ground between the two rows of tables as a second bullet shattered the coffee cup he had just placed down on their table.

The young waitress was the first to start screaming and McGrain instantly clutched her to him. "It's gonna be okay, sweetheart," he whispered reassuringly and hauled her down to the floor. As he did so, the previous hum of conversation, metallic sounds of cutlery clinking and bustle of restaurant staff were replaced by a cacophony of screams and panic-stricken shouting as bedlam erupted in the Roadchef.

Behind Spider at the far end of the row of tables parallel to theirs stood a male in a black trilby and a claret Donegal suit. Smiling viciously from behind black plastic shades, he advanced, his hand spitting death down the barrel of his shooter.

McGrain pushed the waitress under the table and, ignoring the shattered shards from the smashed milkshake glass cutting into his skin, drew a Glock from inside his jacket.

But as he attempted to sight his tormentor, another salvo of lead ripped through the table and exploded in the seat behind him, splintering wooden shards and spitting out stuffing into the air all around him.

Across the passageway, Spider wasn't faring much better. Parlane flicked his hood down from around his head and taunted his quarry. "How fuckin' ironic, Spider is caught in the web," he sneered and pausing momentarily behind a fiendish grin to savour the final righting of an ancient wrong.

Re-sighting his Browning, he started to unload lead-filled payback the former Legionnaire's way.

Spider felt a stab of scorching pain erupt in his left hand as a bullet scythed through his paw. Trying to ignore it, he gritted his teeth and in one dynamic movement of extreme explosive power, grabbed the legs of his table and ripped it onto its side, before booting it with the soles of both feet down the passageway towards the sneering Parlane.

Spider gave a warning nod to his mate and lunged diagonally past him and into the cover of the table and chairs immediately behind McGrain and the blonde waitress, who he could see was sobbing uncontrollably under her table.

His comrade's counterattack was the signal for McGrain to return fire … with interest. From his position, belly down on the linoleum, he started to unleash 9mm Parabellums Johnstone's way.

Standing as he was at the end of the passageway, the trilby sporting assassin was a far easier target than the ducking, diving, ultimately prone McGrain had been and while he missed with his first bullet, the second exploded into a shoulder of Donegal tweed and sent the hit man staggering backwards.

In the throes of fresh agony, Johnstone forgot to take evading action and as he staggered between the lines of tables, McGrain opened up with four more projectiles from his Glock that had his would-be killer toppling back over another table, sending cutlery and crockery flying as the air was filled by a fresh round of screaming and cries for help.

McGrain smiled Spider's way and quipped: "I think we should stop eatin' out, big man, 'cause every time we do grab a bite some bastard seems tae want to serve us up a lead sandwich," and received a wink for his reply.

As Johnstone's trilby rolled down towards him, Spider shot out his right hand and quickly grabbed it before placing it daintily on top of his head and sending a taunting grin in Parlane's direction.

Having seen what had befallen his mate some 20 yards away, Parlane desperately fought to keep his rage in check and his brain in gear. As McGrain and Spider turned their attention to him, he dove behind a cleaning trolley for cover, just before McGrain rolled across the passageway, covered by a hail of lead from his sidekick, getting closer and closer to the pinned Parlane.

The hunter was now well and truly the hunted.

Chapter Twenty-One

STEALING A QUICK GLANCE around the service trolley, Parlane could see that his only option was to make a run for it; but he also knew that any movement away from the cover he currently cowered behind would almost certainly leave him riddled with lead.

To his relief, the solution to his predicament came into view with almost perfect timing as the red overalls of a Parcel Force van driver caught his eye. The bald 40-something-year-old, whose sweat-stained, lobster-pink complexion was reddening by the second, was attempting to crawl his way out of the firestorm he'd been caught up in, just some few yards from where Parlane was hunkered down.

Nearby, a surge of rage coursed through Spider's veins. "Where the fuck is that weasel? I fuckin' knew it, he's set us up and tipped off Parlane and his scum. Any fuckin' money the wee shit's put a bullet in Ferg's heid while he's been on the khazi."

McGrain's grim features inclined in a vicious shake of his head in recognition that his sidekick may well be right, but their attention was soon snapped back to the present.

This time it was Parlane's turn to send a delivery to his tormentors. He propelled the cleaning trolley back down the passageway at them with all his power and unleashed a salvo of 9mm projectiles in their direction as he dived towards the driver, grabbed him by the back of his polo shirt and pulled him towards his own body while pressing the Browning into his head.

The Parcel Force man shook uncontrollably with fear and his eyes were like golf balls, such was the terror that now took hold of him.

"Please, mister, lemme go, I've three kids and a missus," he pleaded in the dull burr of a Cumbrian accent.

"Save me the sob story, bud. Do as you're told and you'll be right as rain," snapped Parlane, before he began to force the van driver slowly to his feet. As he did so, he made sure that Mr Parcel Force's torso was now providing him with a human shield.

"Whit you daein'? Lemme go!" pleaded the driver once again.

But Parlane increased the pressure of his Browning into the side of his victim's cranium. "Shut the fuck up, shit for brains. Do as yer told and maybe you'll see yer missus and three brats again," he rapped.

Peering over the driver's heaving shoulders, Parlane kept the pressure of the Browning firmly against his captive's head, took in the positions of his pursuers and started to retreat.

"Let me out of here or you'll have the blood o' an innocent man on yer hands, McGrain, and that's something even a piece of Fenian shit like yourself would'ne be wantin' tae confess to down the pineapple," spat Parlane.

The frown that enveloped McGrain's hawklike features confirmed he was right.

And while Parlane had a hostage acting as a human shield, he would also be able to discharge his Browning from a position of relative safety, which meant McGrain and Spider had to stay down.

McGrain's darting eyes devoured the scene in front of him. As he focussed all his attention in that brief pause, he for the first time noticed that an alarm was blaring and that the clock was very much ticking in terms of the arrival of the law.

"Where's Fergus?" he asked.

Parlane feigned surprise. "What? A smart boy like yersel cannae work out that when one of his boys does'ne make it oot the bog he's pan breed?" he said and gave a short barked laugh from behind the quaking, sweating figure of his human shield, all the while continuing to back off.

But it was Spider who gave Parlane his answer: "That'll make him aboot as dead as yer mate back there," he said, pointing his thumb back over his shoulder. "I love his fuckin' trilby, mind," he quipped, flicking the brim of the hat in a gesture he hoped would goad Parlane into a mistake.

Gritting his teeth, Parlane kept back-pedalling, his right arm locked around the driver's neck so tightly that he began to cough and splutter.

Yards away, McGrain and Spider had split up and were approaching their quarry from opposite sides, taking care not to present Parlane with a clear target.

Both of them knew that the minute he reached the foyer, Parlane would throw his human shield off and try to make good his escape at the first exit to hand and once he got outside the motorway services he would no doubt be able to melt into the hysterical hordes who had charged out of the premises as the gun battle had exploded.

As Parlane approached the entranceway, he allowed himself a quick smile: he was almost there. Leaning forwards so that his mouth was less than an inch away from the driver's left ear, he said: "You've done well, bud, and now am gonna let you go … awrabest," and at that he released his armlock, drew off and rammed a Doc Marten into the driver's derrière, sending him flying back into the restaurant.

Parlane turned and ran towards the thrumming, confused masses and attempted to lose himself in the crowd of people desperately making for the exits.

Reaching the Roadchef's entrance, McGrain and his lieutenant stopped and tried to sight their quarry, but the only evidence that Parlane had been there was his discarded Fred Perry parka lying in a crumpled heap just outside the amusement arcade.

"Bastard's gottaway," cursed Spider.

Fifty yards away, Parlane deftly rounded a grossly overweight female in a tent-like knitted cardigan, whose attempt at a run to safety was more like a waddle, and started to parallel her route to the services' exit.

As he did so, he stole a quick glance across his shoulder and saw with satisfaction that his pursuers were frantically trying to locate his presence, but with his fishtail discarded and the red, white and blue Ben Sherman gingham shirt he now wore helping him dissolve into the crowd, Parlane was confident he would slip out undetected.

He was wrong.

Fingering a large drop-down circlet earring, the startled brunette eyed Parlane with concern. "Whit the feck you up tae?" she asked, in a Glaswegian accent that suggested she was probably on the way back up the M74 from a holiday in the nearby Lake District.

Parlane attempted to overcome his instant revulsion for the panic-stricken, corpulent woman by returning an unconvincing smile. "Sorry doll, in a rush, like," he said and quickly broke into double time.

But the distraction of the female had indeed been fatal and as he returned his gaze towards the roadside services' front door, Parlane had just enough time to see the balled fist that was winging its way towards his jaw.

He went down like Frank Bruno.

Lying flat on his back, Parlane blinked furiously and tried to fish out the Browning he had rammed down the waistband of his jeans under the folds of his gingham shirt. It was a futile move and the pressure of a desert boot ramming onto his right hand and trapping it against his midriff confirmed the hopelessness of his position.

"Yer fucked, Parlane," smiled Gregsy from under his unruly mop.

"Ya wee ginger bastard, whit the fuck you done wi' Glavin and his boys?" snapped the enraged Parlane, the fury in his features, even from a prone position, scorching.

"You'll never know, Parlane," replied Gregsy amicably, and then he whipped out his semi-automatic and placed its barrel against his captive's forehead.

But this manoeuvre drew a scream from the large woman and swiftly a circle cleared around this fresh drama.

"You snivelling little arsewipe, go on then, tell me why you betrayed us? You don't have a fuckin' Scooby whit you've got yourself mixed up in, do you? McGrain's a card-carrying member of the RA and a polis fuckin' tout into the bargain. Explain that one away, Gregsy," demanded Parlane.

For a second, a look of confusion spread across the peterman's freckled features, but before he could say anything else he felt a powerful hand clamp onto his shoulder.

"Good work, James," said McGrain, before adding: "I knew we could trust you, but this isn't the place or the time to let Mr Parlane have his just desserts. Can't you hear the alarm, you oblivious to our audience, son? Naw, it's time we were off. Get him up," ordered McGrain and at that Spider materialised at the other side of their captive.

"Aye, put yer hardware away, wee man, we need tae be in the wind, fast. Don't worry, baw jaws will get his soon enough," said McGrain's lieutenant and hauled Parlane onto his feet, while in the process ripping his hand clear of his waistband and causing the Browning it had been clamped around to fall on the floor.

McGrain quickly retrieved and pocketed the firearm. "Aye, I'm certain we can find some use for Mr Parlane … I'm just not sure what," he said, but as his dark eyes bored into his captive's crumpled features, Gregsy was left in no doubt that something nasty awaited McGrain's rival.

Spider whipped a length of cord from his anorak pocket and proceeded to bind Parlane's wrists in it until the pressure threatened to cut off the circulation and then he threw his anorak over the captive's hands. They stepped out of the services and Spider propelled his prey through the car park, McGrain silently shadowing their process to the right, his hand clamped on the hardware inside his jacket.

As he followed in their footsteps, negotiating a path through knots of punters ghoulishly waiting for the emergency services to arrive in the car park, he noticed that the crowds were eyeing the four men nervously and cowering away from them, and a growing dread that he had become mixed up in something that had a whole vortex of subplots swirling just below the surface began to take hold of Gregsy.

CHAPTER TWENTY-TWO

THE RED VAUXHALL Astra snaked its way through grey streets bathed black by darkness and void of life, before turning into the rear entrance of Briarknock Primary's imposing brick edifice.

As they pulled up level with the janny's office, Thoroughgood brought the vehicle to a stop under a security spotlight, rolled down his window and, leaning out, flashed his warrant card at the office window, which was being manned by an elderly white-haired man, with silver-rimmed glasses, who was clad in a blue boiler suit.

"Awright, Tony? Polis, just in to use your staff car park before we go for a wee wander. All quiet overnight, mate?" asked Thoroughgood, as Currie smiled benignly from the passenger seat.

"Aye, it wiz all quiet on the western front all right! You boys are out early this morning," said Tony, looking at his watch for confirmation that it had indeed just turned 6 a.m.

"Early bird catches the worm and all that, Tony," quipped Currie from across the Astra cabin, and with a wink Thoroughgood slipped the van into first and wound his way around the back of the school into the teacher's car park, where the vehicle drew to a stop under the shadow of a large lonely Beech tree.

Turning off the ignition, Thoroughgood gratefully took the coffee handed to him by his senior man while Currie rolled down his passenger window, took a draught of his own and placed his left arm along the window rim of the door.

"Aah, that's better. Bit unfortunate O'Toole stumbling across your little spat the other night, it's the talk of the station thanks to that wee shit Lynch. Pity that bullet hadn't been a bit more accurate," said Currie with surprising vehemence.

Thoroughgood eyed his neeber sideways in surprise. "Really?"

"Really," replied Currie. "It's a problem for you though, son, yer bird mixed up with someone like Meechan. Are you serious about her, Gus?" he asked, turning his full attention towards his younger colleague.

Thoroughgood shrugged his shoulders. "The problem is we've been through a lot with the Dawson business, but I still don't feel like I really know Celine and she mixes in a world that … well, I wish she wouldn't … It's a bit of a mess really, Harry," he admitted finally.

"It is indeed and one you need to be very careful about, because O'Toole is a senior officer and Meechan has form. So if the good DI decides to make any official observations on paper you could find yourself getting whacked for …" – Currie paused to provide imaginary quotation marks with the middle fingers of either hand before recounting parrot-fashion from the Police Procedure Manual – "Associating with persons of immoral and unlawful means that a current service police officer should not form a relationship with," he concluded.

"You think I don't know that?" snapped Thoroughgood and was met with a reproving raise of Currie's lush grey eyebrows. "But you know what I found really interesting?"

"Surprise me," smirked Currie.

"I got the impression that the good DI was more than familiar with Meechan. Now how would that be?" asked Thoroughgood.

Currie swirled the remnants of his coffee around the bottom of the card cup and then looked up and met his younger colleague's enquiring gaze. "It's not so much of a surprise when you know that O'Toole was uniform sergeant at the Marine over in Partick on Group Two shift for nearly 3 years before he got his bump up to DI. So he would have had plenty of time to come across some young hoodlum on the way up through Jimmy Gray's ranks. It's not beyond the bounds of possibility that Meechan has even touted to our esteemed Detective Inspector," concluded Currie with a rueful shake of his head.

After swallowing a mouthful of coffee, Thoroughgood clicked the plastic lid back on the drinking carton and glancing at the vehicle's dash clock, before saying: "Interesting, but that's all something that will need to be saved for later. Come on, Harry, time we got ourselves set up at the Observation Point. How long will it take us to make our way there on foot?"

But Currie had already rolled up his window and jumped out of the passenger door, whipping out a black rucksack that contained the equipment they would need to conduct a surveillance operation on the address Nicholas had supplied for 'The Creepers'. Swinging it over the tartan-clad shoulder of his lumberjack jacket, he said: "10 mins, max. Sergeant Storey has stuck his neck out for us and we need to make sure we are on-site nice and early for the 0630 hours check-in."

They made their way along faceless streets lined by three-story seventies housing, intermittently daubed in graffiti, with verandas boasting an assortment of washing and other domestic debris that provided an interesting social commentary on the scheme's inhabitants.

"So tell me, why didn't we have someone manning the OP overnight?" asked Thoroughgood.

Currie shrugged his shoulders. "Should have been Stuart Mulgrew and Johnnie O'Brien from Two Group but they got taken off their beat for the night and ended up driving a panda after the flu took out half of the shift. Shit happens!" concluded Currie balefully.

"Far from ideal though," replied Thoroughgood, just as a postman passed by on the opposite side of the street, which prompted Currie to check his watch nervously and double his stride.

Two minutes later he drew to a stop at the top of a street that trailed down a slight hill and unbuttoned his padded lumberjack shirt, wafting some fresh air around his neck.

"You got the keys okay?" asked Currie conversationally.

Thoroughgood fished them out and opened his palm to reveal a set of three keys on the dark-green plastic key fob of the Glasgow City Housing Department. "The gaffer's done us proud with the keys to number 10," he laughed and then they both made their way down Torrybrook Road as the dawning of the day gathered pace.

Five minutes later and Thoroughgood inserted the main key and opened the grey, paint-peeled door of flat 3/1 10 Torrybrook Road before standing back and beckoning his senior man in with a not-so-respectful sweep of his left arm.

Currie flashed a mock grimace. "For what we are about to receive, may the good Lord make us thoroughly grateful," he said and brushed past Thoroughgood into a carpetless hall, the bare floorboards of which were peppered with old scrumpled-up newspaper.

Halfway along the hall, Currie stopped abruptly and flicked a light switch on. Thankfully, the bulb that hung starkly from the ceiling burst into life. "Excellent," said Currie and turned into a side room to his right, which Thoroughgood guessed was the toilet.

As he shut the front door and proceeded to enter the flat, he heard Currie's outraged voice filling the hallway again. "Aye, a bloody well knew it … there's no fuckin' bog roll," raged the senior man, but as Thoroughgood leaned against the toilet doorway, Currie swung the rucksack he'd been carrying over his left shoulder and ripped a lime-green roll of Andrex out.

Smiling triumphantly, he brandished the toilet roll above his head. "Aye, I've learned from bitter experience that you should never go on an OP without taking yer own." Shaking his head in amusement, Thoroughgood met Currie's twinkling gaze and they both burst into laughter.

Making their way into the flat's main room, the lounge, basking in the half-light from the hallway, boasted a burst, fag-burned black leather settee that looked like it had done well to survive the seventies, never mind reach the nineties, and two wooden table chairs, one upturned, the other tilted against a wall.

Although another light bulb hung from the ceiling, this time they left it in darkness and grabbing the upturned chair, Thoroughgood took it over to the window just inside the veranda and set it down before settling on it.

He carefully pulled the hideous brown and orange drapes that were blocking out most of the day's breaking light partially open and surveyed the street outside.

From behind him, he heard Currie's glum tones: "What do you see, lad?"

His eyes devouring the second-floor veranda opposite their position, Thoroughgood could only answer "Sweet FA." Currie drew up the other chair and, placing his rucksack on his knees, drew out a thermos and two plastic cups.

A discarded clothes horse lay partially upended on the veranda itself, while thick black curtains meant there would be nothing interesting to see anytime soon.

"Aye, it's a far cry from your work with the Unit, I'll bet. Stakeouts ain't what Hollywood makes them out to be, lad. Here, help yourself," said Currie, handing his junior partner a plastic cup filled with coffee and then with amazing dexterity producing a set of foil-wrapped sandwiches. "Aye, looks like it's corn beef and Branston … fancy a sarnie?"

Thoroughgood obliged and after devouring Currie's wife's masterpiece he washed it down with his partner's homebrew. "Aye, it's a far cry from the film Stakeout all right. I don't see much chance of Madeleine Stowe pulling the curtains back!" he said.

But Currie remained silent because the senior man was peering through the crack between the drapes, his attention completely focussed on the building opposite.

"Maybe not, but we have our first sign of pond life. I'd say that one of the brothers grim has just come home from his night's work," said Currie.

Thoroughgood stood up and quickly hovered above Currie's shoulder, twitching the curtain another couple of inches open. "You beauty, that's Albert Stringer all right. Game on!"

CHAPTER TWENTY-THREE

CHECKING LEFT AND RIGHT over his shoulders, Stringer was on red alert for any unwanted attention and the reason for that was presumably what appeared to be a video recorder he was carrying in front of him, in gloved hands.

From behind the drapes, Thoroughgood momentarily checked the Divisional Intelligence bulletin he had brought with him and the mugshots of Albert Stringer and his two brothers Frankie and Johnnie.

Five foot seven, dark-haired and wearing oval, wire glasses, with a lazy left eye that gave the housebreaker an eerie look, it all matched up perfectly with the evidence of his own eyes.

By the time he had returned his gaze across the street, Stringer was already halfway into the close and his disappearance was met with a groan from the irate Currie who had been unable to get his surveillance camera set up in time to snap the cat burglar.

"Shite," spat Currie as Stringer disappeared from sight. "I suggest we keep that little episode to ourselves. Storey is expecting me to call in at 0700 hours and what the gaffer doesn't know won't hurt him."

"Fair enough," agreed Thoroughgood, before adding: "Maybe we should have concentrated on setting up before bringing out the Branston!"

"Indeed," agreed Currie, finally snapping the tripod legs to attention and slotting the surveillance camera into its secure holder.

Thoroughgood checked his Timex and saw the hands were now pointing to quarter to seven. "So if Albert has just come in, then where are Frankie and Johnnie?" he asked.

"Maybe they're lying stoned in their midden?" asked Currie sarcastically.

"No chance. If Albert has been out on the rob and returned home with a video then they've done a turn somewhere; and we know they don't work alone, it's a team job, so where are the other two …?" asked Thoroughgood, letting his words fade away.

From the street outside, the thrumming of a diesel engine filled the airwaves. "Taxi?" asked Thoroughgood.

But Currie remained silent as he continued to sight the street through his camera's eye, until at last the word "Interesting," escaped from under his grey moustache.

"What you got?" asked Thoroughgood, now standing behind Currie's shoulder.

"A black Nissan Homy, two up in the cabin. You got the mugshots for Frankie and Johnnie?" asked Currie.

"Yep," said Thoroughgood, snatching the Intelligence bulletin rogues' gallery sheet up. "Pretty similar to big brother Albert."

"Driver's got gloves on," said Currie, before continuing: "Parking just up from number 13."

But from behind his colleague, Thoroughgood's attention had been drawn back to the close. "And here comes Albert to welcome them."

Sure enough, Stringer senior had come back out of number 13's front door and under his arm was tucked the video recorder he had taken in with him.

Stringer continued to glance around nervously for any unwanted attention before he made his way to the Nissan's driver-side door and started to engage in what was clearly a heated conversation, punctuated by regular finger pointing.

"Jeez, someone ain't happy!" exclaimed Thoroughgood, as Albert clenched his right fist and shook it at one of his brothers.

"What do you make of that, lad?" asked Currie.

"I dunno, but one thing's for sure, The Creepers are bloody confident they're safe up here and no one is gonna be firing them in anytime soon. Just shows how scared the people of Briarknock are of these evil little bastards," said Thoroughgood.

Stringer had now pushed the video recorder in through the Homy's driver-side window and the constant clicking of Currie's surveillance camera confirmed that when 0700 hours came, Sergeant Storey would be met with a full and comprehensive report, all of which would be backed up by substantial photographic evidence.

Thoroughgood had seen enough. "We could put out an assistance call and be down there and after them no bother, Harry. Christ, man, we've surely got enough already in our first 15 minutes to get them banged up and I'd bet my old granny that Homy is loaded with knock-off from their night's work."

"Let's just hold our horses, lad. We will include the van regy and description in our report and get a watch put out for it and that way we can have it tracked to wherever the Stringers' have their stash. If we go breengin' right in here, there is every chance we will lose the van, which they will ditch after removing their stash, and maybe you do get Albert ... but what for? One crappy VCR he will have ditched in a hedge before you huckle him and then what are we left with?" asked Currie from behind a knowing look.

Thoroughgood's frustration and anger showed in his gritted teeth but he held his tongue as Currie continued: "It's obvious that with Albert handing the VCR back there has been some, er ... cock-up: let's face it, he doesn't look too happy, he should never have had to bring back hot goods to number 13. But if we are patient then we can get The Creepers, their safe house and everything else that will help us get them bang to rights and make sure they go down for a long stretch."

Currie had barely finished his summation when the Homy jolted out from the kerb and sped down Torrybrook Road, leaving Albert Stringer, his gloved hands planted on either hip, clearly fuming.

"You got the regy number?" asked Currie, but as he glanced over at his partner he could see that Thoroughgood was feverishly updating the OP logbook.

"Oh, oh," said Currie in a worried tone.

"What is it?" asked Thoroughgood, looking up from his journal update.

"Uncle Albert is staring right up at us. Fuck me, he's a suspicious prick," said Currie.

Chapter Twenty-Four

CURRIE AND THOROUGHGOOD pulled back from the crack in the curtains, for now it was Stringer who, thoughtfully nibbling on the zipper of his navy-blue Adidas festival cagoule, continued to surveil their position at number 10.

After what seemed an eternity, Stringer dragged his eyes from their flat window. His head flicked to his right and he appeared to be listening to some noise that was percolating through the early morning air.

After a few seconds, Stringer shoved his hands into the front pockets of his cagoule and started to walk along the pavement, making his way briskly past the front door of number 13.

"What's the bugger up to?" asked Currie.

"Something's spooked him I'd say, Harry ... shit!" exclaimed Thoroughgood as it became clear just why Stringer had got on his metaphorical bike.

Because meandering down Torrybrook Road was the unsightly rectangular shape of a maroon Peugeot and behind its wheel sat DI Ronan O'Toole.

"Holy Mother of Kazan! That's all we bleedin' need," groaned Currie, rifling his right paw through his greying strands.

"It sure is and he's onto Stringer, look, he's windin' down the driver's window, ready to give him a tug," said Thoroughgood, his features showing his fascination with the events about to play out down on the street below.

"Surely Stringer's got to take to his heels?" asked Currie.

"What for? He's clean, isn't he? And right now there are no warrants out for him, all we have are two uncorroborated witness descriptions which could just as easily apply to either of his brothers as Albert. I checked the witness statements of the old boy and Nicholas' great auntie and neither mention anything about a scally eye," concluded Thoroughgood.

While Stringer was hardly hanging about, his walk remained steady and unpanicked even as the CID Peugeot drew level with him. O'Toole's right hand reached out of the car window and gave the arm of Stringer's cagoule a light tug, upon which he ground to a stop.

"Christ, what I'd give for some listening equipment," groaned Currie in frustration.

Stringer hunkered down until his face was level with O'Toole's window and the two began to engage in a conversation, while from the other side of the motor DC Jimmy Lynch gingerly got out from the passenger's side.

"You've got to be havin' a laugh, what's that mad bastard Lynch wantin' … a bleeding Victoria Cross … it's pathetic," spat Currie, while Thoroughgood once again eyed his senior man, surprised at the enmity he bore the DC.

Lynch walked around the front of the Peugeot and pulled back the jacket of his grey two-piece Slater's double-breaster. Clearly whatever was inside the jacket was enough to convince Stringer that his best move was to get into the back of the Peugeot.

"Lynch's tooled up; mind you, a Smith & Wesson be as much use to him as a chocolate teapot considering he's left-handed," said Currie spitefully.

Regardless of Lynch's wounded shoulder, Stringer did as he was clearly bid and opened the rear driver-side door before sliding along the back seat as Lynch carefully slotted himself in behind O'Toole.

"This is nothing short of a disaster," said Thoroughgood, as he and Currie watched the CID motor drive out of Torrybrook.

"Aye, yer damn tootin'," agreed Currie, before continuing: "The gaffer will have to be put in the picture and it's gonna get messy, we've just been conducting a surveillance op on a person of interest to O'Toole who hasn't a Scooby what we've been up to and what we've seen. Christ, he'll hit the roof when that all comes out. It'll be outright war between the CID and Community Policing and I know who my money will be on," concluded the consternated Currie.

"What if the gaffer could be persuaded that it might be in all of our interests to keep quiet about our little op and what we've seen? Unless they've got new evidence or turned up another witness there is every chance Stringer will walk once they've kept him for the 6 hours of his Section Two detention. I don't see any need to blow things to kingdom come just because O'Toole has been on a fishing trip ... problem is, can we trust Sergeant Storey to see it that way?" asked Thoroughgood.

Currie had turned his chair sideways and jammed it on two legs against the wall behind. He started to swing gently back and forth. "It's a 50/50 on that one. Old Uncle Sam hates O'Toole and his lapdog as much as anyone else at Bayne Street but you know what it's like between CID and uniform. We're just a bunch of wooden tops while O'Toole and his wounded hero boy bloody wonder think they're Glasgow's version of The Sweeney. If we are going to sit on what we've seen here this morning and save it for a rainy day when the CP might actually get credit for the job we do, then we're going to have to be mighty careful."

"In that case, why don't we get back to Bayne Street pronto, because you can imagine what Storey is gonna be thinkin' when he sees O'Toole and Lynch arriving at the charge bar with the very same ned that we're s'posed to be conducting surveillance on?" asked Thoroughgood.

Shrugging his shoulders, "I shudder to think," was the best Currie could come up with.

* * *

By the time they arrived back at Bayne Street, O'Toole's maroon Peugeot was nestled safely in a parking bay in the secure car park at the rear of the Police Office and Thoroughgood and Currie almost sprinted in through the rear doors.

As they made their way through the charge bar, DC Jimmy Lynch's familiar grating voice harangued them: "Well, well, if it ain't Bayne Street's answer to Cagney and Lacey! What you CP boys been up to, all dressed up in plain clothes? Doin' fuck all but sleepin' somewhere in the back of a van, I'll bet, while CID goes out and huckles the most wanted man in the Division."

"You disrespectful little whelp. I was on the book when you were still in shorts at primary school," raged Currie and launched himself towards the charge bar as Lynch's barb proved too much for the veteran cop, who despite the detective's recent injury, was intent on laying hands on Lynch.

But before he could make his way through the 2-foot passage between the charge bar and it's adjoining wall, Thoroughgood clamped a restraining hand on his senior man.

"Come on, Harry, he ain't worth it. I'm sure DC Lynch was just having a laugh and meant no disrespect," he said, but by this time, members of the Group Three bar staff who were manning the police station had started to gather in the central area between the public and charge bars to feast on the developing confrontation.

In the background of the gathering crowd, Thoroughgood noticed a familiar face, one he had not seen for almost 18 months. As his eyes locked on her darkly alluring features, a smile swept across the face of the WPC; but Thoroughgood's attention was firmly snapped back to the baiting of his partner, who was still bridling furiously at the sneering Lynch and threatening to break Thoroughgood's restraining grip.

While he may have been able to stop Currie doing anything rash physically that he may have regretted, he could not stop his partner's mouth going into overdrive.

"You glory huntin' little bawbag … tell me why you're in at your work when your nursin' a firearms injury? I'll tell you why, because you would sell yer fuckin' granny to make sure you got a pat on the back from O'Toole and a recommendation for your stripes. Tell me why you're packin' heat when you're left-handed and wouldn't be able to draw a bleeding tissue, never mind a Smith & Wesson with that winged shoulder?" raged Currie.

Thoroughgood gave a silent groan and as the look of surprise that had engulfed Lynch's milky white features turned to one of suspicion, Thoroughgood attempted to pull his senior man back from jumping into the hole he had begun to dig for himself.

"Come on, Harry, we have a report to make to Sergeant Storey and you know he doesn't like to be kept waiting," he said.

Currie had finally realised he had gone too far and was starting to back-pedal from the charge bar. The problem now was that Lynch, his suspicions pricked by Currie's rage-fuelled, ill-considered words, was on the offensive.

"You old has-been, what do you mean packin' heat? The only way you'd know I was carrying hardware was if you were perched up somewhere watchin' us snaffle Stringer … that's it, you useless old bastard, that's why you two fuckwits are out on plainers. You were on an OP point conducting a surveillance operation on The Creepers. I fuckin' well don't believe it … wait 'til DI O'Toole hears this. He'll have yer guts for bleedin' garters, old man … you're finished and the whole of the CP will be too, he'll shut you doon and make sure you're all back on the shift by the morra morning."

CHAPTER TWENTY-FIVE

STOREY SAT STILL as stone on the other side of his desk, his hands clasped in front of him as he listened to Thoroughgood and Currie's debrief, which had just reached the point where O'Toole and Lynch had huckled Stringer on the street.

"Well, there's nothing like perfect timing, is there, gents?" said Storey, before adding: "Trust Strathclyde Polis' answer to Serpico and his pet Rottweiler to steal a collar from us and nick the glory. Ah well, you did well, I think it was a good call to stay your hand and wait until we can locate the van, if we play this right we can get the whole CP out, cover all points and make sure we have The Creepers, their safe houses, the whole shootin' match snaffled in one fell swoop. It might be the turn's worthy of a nice little snap with the local rag and how well would that go down with the Divisional Commander?" purred the sergeant, before he took a sip from a cup of his favourite Earl Grey breakfast tea. Wincing at the fact it was at least 5 minutes too cold, Storey added: "Still, it's all a bit delicate, you never know what O'Toole will pummel out of Stringer, while of course details of your little surveillance operation will have to be kept hush hush as far as our dear colleagues in the Sid are concerned."

At that point, Currie cleared his throat nervously and by doing so alerted his gaffer to the fact that he had not heard the full report. Storey's eyes started to widen as his experience warned him that the serious stuff was still to come.

"Well … why do I get the feeling there is something you don't want to tell me that I bloody well need to know … now?" rapped the sergeant.

Thoroughgood watched his senior man and for once was inwardly relieved that he was the junior officer in the partnership as Currie shifted uncomfortably in his chair before he finally started to talk: "Well, er, Sergeant Storey, I might have inadvertently let it slip that we were on a watch …"

But before he could get any further, Storey's patience burst its dam. "And tell me how the hell you managed that, Harry?" he demanded.

Currie's flustered gaze turned to Thoroughgood and was met with a grimace from his junior man. He took a deep breath and got to the meat and two veg of it: "We noticed that Lynch was packing. He flashed his double-breaster open to warn Stringer not to try any funny business before he got into the CID Peugeot and surprise, surprise, Albert does exactly as he was bid without a whimper."

"Bollocks," snapped Storey, his right hand pushing an unruly strand of hair back onto the top of his head. "The devil's certainly in the detail. Rumour has had it along the command corridor that O'Toole has been authorising the routine carrying of firearms among his CID officers and your little comment will have touched a nerve as well as underlined the fact that you were tucked up somewhere nice and cosy watchin' the detectives, never mind The Creepers' comings and goings. One thing's for sure, you can bet your bottom dollar that the Detective Inspector is currently being briefed by his lapdog. Aye, it's just as well the DI's room does'nae have any wallpaper, 'cause I'm sure O'Toole would have it peeling off with that tongue of his." Storey took a breath and scanned the faces of his two subordinates, who remained seated as an awkward silence drew out.

Finally Thoroughgood spoke up: "You know what will happen when O'Toole comes calling, gaffer. If we burst to all of this and he knows exactly what we were up to, he will use this as a lever to try and take control of all CP plain-clothes operations and that will be just the start. But what if we come up with an alternative reason for our visit to Torrybrook Road?"

"That's all fine and dandy, Gus, but what possible reason could two CP officers have for being in plain clothes at 0630 hours on a Saturday morning?" asked Storey.

"I'm sorry gaffer, I've made a complete arse of it," groaned Currie, his shoulders hunching. "There's no way out of this, O'Toole will be burstin' through yer door any minute now and he will have us well and truly busted and it's aw ma fault."

"Not so fast, Harry," said Thoroughgood, and he pointed the index finger of his right hand to a pile of paperwork sitting on the in-tray of Storey's three-tier desk tray. "Is that the outstanding warrant list for Zulu Alpha sub-division, gaffer?"

"It is," answered Storey from behind a taut face that began to show the first dawnings of realisation at where Thoroughgood was going.

"Surely there must be an urgent outstanding warrant for some ned living up in Torrybrook?" asked the young cop, before adding: "Isn't Thomas Leo Tobias, the sexual predator, a resident?"

For the first time during the conversation, a smile broke out across Storey's saturnine features. "He is indeed and I'm impressed by your local knowledge, young Thoroughgood. Aye, there's always a warrant out for Tobias," concluded Storey and started to rifle through the warrant pile for his get-out-of-jail card. "Peaches and cream! Here it is, a Warrant to Apprehend for assault and robbery. Dear old Tobias Leo has got a rent boy to lure some sad banker to a flat in the Red Road for a bit of hide the sausage and then ..." Storey stopped mid-sentence as he burst into a peel of uproarious laughter. He eventually regained his composure and continued: "And then he's jumped out a wardrobe and threatened to plunge said banker with one of his HIV-infected needles unless he pays up. Trouble for Tobias is that the rent boy got rumbled in a shakedown by the vice squad and has spilled the beans on Toby's nefarious activities and now, would you believe it, we have a warrant for his arrest that I would have been issuing you two outstanding officers with when you rolled up for early shift on Monday morning."

A long slow whistle escaped from under Currie's twitching silvery moustache before the senior cop exclaimed: "Eureka!"

"Aye, and just as well for you that yer neeber has struck gold with this one!" quipped Storey and the CP sergeants' room rocked with laughter.

Such was his relief that Storey jumped to his feet and kissed the warrant. As he did so, his office door flew open, rebounding off the adjoining wall and there, his rage volcanic, stood Detective Inspector Ronan O'Toole.

"Sergeant Storey ... can you please tell me what the fuck your boys were doing mounting a plainer op on a CID person of interest without me being notified?" rapped O'Toole, standing in his full hands-on-hips, trademark pose.

Storey had just about enough time to recover his composure and as he did so a smug grin crept back over his semi-florid features. "Of course I can, my dear Detective Inspector. Constables Currie and Thoroughgood were going about their duties and attempting to execute a lawful warrant, in fact an urgent Warrant to Apprehend for the miscreant Thomas Leo Tobias, who according to this ..." – Storey took a moment to brandish the paperwork theatrically in the air – "resides at 13 Torrybrook Road."

Despite himself, O'Toole's right hand shot out and grabbed the warrant and he began to scrutinise the minutiae of the paperwork. When he had finished devouring it, his shrewd eyes swept the three CP officers, his mistrust of the explanation he had been offered clear.

This time it was Thoroughgood who couldn't help himself. Keeping his features inscrutable, he filled the drawn-out silence: "We will be back out for Tobias on Monday, DI O'Toole, and I promise you, if we huckle him we'll bring him straight to your door for a shakedown."

It was an ill-considered remark delivered at the worst possible time. O'Toole's wafer-thin veneer of self-control shattered and he lunged at Thoroughgood, grabbing him by the lapel of his Harrington. His eyes locked on Thoroughgood's green gaze. "You jumped-up smart arse. I'm marking your card, all of you, if I find out different I will make it my mission to shut down all CP plainer ops and I promise you, Storey, if you've fucked me over, you'll remember this day for long and weary. Now get out of my way," and at that O'Toole rammed Thoroughgood back down onto his chair and stormed out of the CP sergeants' room.

Currie let out another long slow whistle and added: "Hurricane Ronan has left the building," but this time laughter didn't fill the room, as its three incumbents shared worried glances that confirmed they all knew O'Toole would be back.

Afterwards, the rest of the shift was spent completing a detailed report for Storey, which was amply illustrated by Currie's best efforts at becoming Strathclyde Police's answer to David Bailey.

But while they had attempted to finish their paperwork, concern over just what O'Toole and Lynch had got out of Stringer proved a constant distraction.

"That's 6 hours up," said Thoroughgood, eyeing the CP report writing room clock and adding: "If O'Toole has had Stringer in on a Section Two then he should be ready to walk if they don't have anything fresh to nail him with."

"Don't have anything fresh? If they don't, then I'm sure the good DI and his mutt will make something fresh up ... wouldn't you agree, Gus?" asked Currie bitingly.

But before Thoroughgood could answer, the writing room phone rang out and Currie quickly reached for the receiver. "Hi Andy, what can I do you for, mate?" he asked, a quizzical look spreading across his face.

Then Currie's eyebrows arched as he digested the news from the other end of the phone. "Albert Stringer has just walked free with his brief ... no charges were preferred? Well thank you, Andy, you were right, that is something I very much wanted to know," and with that he placed the phone back on its wall holder.

"Andy Jamieson, the CID clerk, is an old mate of mine and one who misses nothing in the CID corridor," smiled Currie.

"Very good! Well, there's our answer: it was nothing more than a fishing exercise. Let's get the report and our news along to Storey. With a bit of luck, that little titbit is exactly what we need to persuade him to keep the OP going on the q.t.," said Thoroughgood.

CHAPTER TWENTY-SIX

RELIEVED THAT a difficult shift had been completed without it turning into a disaster, Thoroughgood placed his personal radio holder in the top shelf of his locker and then did the same with his notebook, before taking his baton and its holster off and placing them in the bottom of the 5-foot metallic receptacle.

For a moment he looked at the picture of himself and his grandfather holding the Strathclyde Police squash championship trophy that he kept stuck to the inside of the locker and felt a pang of guilt that he hadn't been to see the old boy for several weeks. He found himself silently muttering the words "Sorry, old fella," to himself and resolved to right that wrong.

He pulled his Harrington out of the cabinet, slammed the badly dented door shut and then locked it, remembering how he had been the last probationer to be given a locker and how it had been in such bad shape compared to the rest of the gleaming lockers detailed to the other new recruits at Bayne Street that it had left him feeling well and truly like the runt of the litter.

Another one of Rentoul's little welcome tricks.

As he headed out of the top-floor locker room and descended divisional HQ's three-storey staircase, Thoroughgood found himself starting to replay the events of the day and wishing yet again that his smart mouth had not betrayed him with the ill-considered barb he had fired at O'Toole.

Before he knew it, Thoroughgood was in the car park turning the key in the door of his white MG Metro when a familiar voice punctured his thoughts.

"Hi Gus, are you still staying in Hyndland?" asked Emma McCabe, whose presence in the uniform bar had given him such a surprise an hour or so ago.

Looking up over the MG's white metallic roof, Thoroughgood was met by a smile that sent a tingle down his spine and for a moment that stretched just a shade too long he held her delicious blue-green-flecked gaze, before replying awkwardly: "Hi Emma, what brings you all the way from 'P' division to the Wild West?"

"I'm meeting a friend in Byres Road later on for some shopping. When I saw you I wondered if you could save me a taxi fare?" she enquired artfully from behind a wide-eyed smile framed by full lips that Thoroughgood remembered warmly sampling all those months back on the final night of their probationary course.

"Of course I can, jump in," he said, his eyes sparkling with pleasure.

"I heard you had a bit of a time of it on your shift out at Lennox Hill. I wondered if you'd still be in the job but never saw your resignation pic in 'The Bulletin' …" said Emma, perhaps regretting that she had said too much, too quickly.

Thoroughgood, his mind replaying the scenes of their lovemaking that night way back when, only just managed to snap himself back to the present, and angling his head he squinted a glance Emma's way.

"Have you got time for a coffee at the Grosvenor Cafe?" he asked hopefully.

Emma's smile was answer enough and 15 minutes later they were walking over Ashton Lane's cobbles before taking a seat in the cafe that had been one of Thoroughgood's favourite university whistle-stops.

As their eyes met and held across the table, Thoroughgood found himself beaten to the verbal punch: "So how have you been?" asked Emma in her velvet tones.

"A hell of a lot better than I was 16 months back!" quipped Thoroughgood, smiling his thanks at the waitress who had just laid down their two coffees. In the background, the guitar intro to Tears For Fears' 'The Hurting' sprang into life.

Emma couldn't help herself reacting to the familiar tune and Kurt Smith/Roland Orzabal's tortured vocals, and her eyes looked up and located the speaker at the end of the aisle. When she turned back to look at the man who sat opposite her, she found his emerald gaze had remained locked on her.

He smiled. "Yeah, it's been a mad world all right, since the last time we were …" – he stopped himself – "sorry … met," concluded Thoroughgood awkwardly.

Emma flashed her delicious smile and raised an eyebrow in that way that had always done something funny to him. Thoroughgood had to give himself a jolt in order to snap his eyes from hers, re-locating his stare uncomfortably on his white ceramic coffee cup. "I heard you'd been seeing someone from outside the job? That she was mixed up in that whole business with Dawson and your …"

This time Emma struggled to finish her sentence and Thoroughgood was happy to help. "Colleagues, is the word I think you are looking for, but it is one I would use in the loosest sense of the word!" he laughed and as he did so, Thoroughgood felt the warmth from her slender fingers stroking the back of his hand.

The lyrics from 'Pale Shelter' provided an ironic backdrop as Orzabal asked: "How can I be sure when you don't give me love?"

Emma's fingers remained on the back of his hand and Thoroughgood was in no hurry to remove them. "Celine is her name and yeah, it was all a bit messy but we came out the other side okay in the end."

The mention of Celine's name seemed to bring Emma a pang of guilt and she pulled her hand back over the enamel table surface. "'We' came through it okay?" she asked, before adding: "So does that mean there is still a 'we'?"

Despite himself, Thoroughgood's right hand rifled through his black mullet and his eyebrows raised involuntarily in an admission that he was anything but certain about the answer to her question.

Eventually, he admitted the truth: "'I dunno' is the best answer I can give you, Emma," he replied.

She pursed her lips and then sipped daintily from her coffee cup, placing it down on its white saucer with barely a sound and then turned her mesmeric eyes his way. Emma smiled that smile that Thoroughgood knew would always mean there was a place in his heart for her.

The warmth in her smile, tinged with a sadness that hinted of memories that had never faded, scorched him.

"I know you got my letter through internal mail, Gus," said Emma and deliberately let a silence draw out.

Thoroughgood winced before eventually responding: "I guess McNab couldn't help himself blabbing when you bumped into him at the Sheriff Court?"

"Aha. So you will also know my mother has passed?" she asked.

"I'm sorry for your loss, Emma, really I am, but it was your decision to call a halt to things so you could be there for her when all I wanted was to be there for you ..." concluded Thoroughgood, before seeking solace once again in his coffee cup.

Draining the vessel, Thoroughgood looked up and caught Emma watching him. "How was it at the end? I mean, I hope she passed ... Christ ... well, you know what I mean, Emma."

"Mum died in Strathcarron Hospice. To be honest, it was horrific. I don't think Dad and I could have gotten through it if it hadn't been for the nursing staff there, they were ... well ... immense."

This time as 'Watch Me Bleed' filled the cafe's airwaves, Thoroughgood reached out and took hold of Emma's hand. "I'm so sorry, really I am, Emma, it's just such a pity," he mumbled almost incoherently.

"What's such a pity, Gus? My mum dying … or what never happened between us?" she asked.

Thoroughgood leaned back in his booth seat, held Emma's gaze and shook his head. He had no answer to her question.

CHAPTER TWENTY-SEVEN

THE GREEN TRANSIT pulled to a stop in the lay-by. Spider pulled on the handbrake and winced as the hand that had been grazed by one of Parlane's bullets burned with pain through the red-stained bandage wrapped around his wound.

He took a deep breath and slowly allowed himself to relax, their hurried escape through side roads seemingly successful – there had not been any sign of police on their tail, as they had managed to get the hell out of the the services just in time. Now, in this isolated spot on the coast, they could enjoy time to shoot the breeze.

Across the bay, the slate grey of the sky and the cobalt of the sea were so alike that they almost merged into one on the horizon.

His window down, even up on the hill Spider could nearly taste the ocean's salt spray, as the sound of the waves rhythmically spending themselves on the bay below assailed his ears with soothing repetition.

In the passenger seat, McGrain stared out, apparently transfixed by the view, the only clue that he had more than some sightseeing on his mind being the Glock 17 that he held nonchalantly in his right hand lying across his lap.

"So what should we do with you, Mr Parlane?" he asked conversationally and slowly turned around to peer into the rear of the vehicle, where his would-be killer now sat captive with his wrists and ankles bound out in front of him, eyeing the semi-automatic on top of Gregsy's right knee with a keen concern.

McGrain climbed through the van hatch and plonked himself down next to Gregsy. "Do you know where we are, Ronnie?" he asked.

R J MITCHELL

"I don't give a fuck where we are, McGrain, and I ain't interested in playing any games with you. Now if yer gonna finish me then get it done, 'cause Ronnie Parlane will beg tae no man for his life," he rapped, a nasty welt on the right side of his face evidence of the blow that had felled him.

"Now, now, Ronnie, let's not be so rash. What about you, James? Have you any suggestions?" asked McGrain, shifting sideways to glance Gregsy's way.

The peterman shrugged. "If he lives, what are we gonna do with him, Tony?"

McGrain smiled sweetly. "And there, in a nutshell, you have it. If we spare you the imaginative death you so richly deserve for Fergus' untimely departure and your botched and amateurish efforts at a hit on me ... then what next for Ronnie Parlane?" asked McGrain.

But Parlane refused to play ball and instead retreated into silence while the hatred written on his face blazed from across the other side of the van.

"Unfortunately or fortunately ... whichever way you look at it ... Fergus' death has, ironically enough, given you a shot – pardon the pun – at redemption," smiled McGrain.

Sitting next to him, Gregsy appeared unable to comprehend what the crime lord was talking about. But Parlane had had enough of what he assumed was just cruel taunting prior to his imminent demise.

"For fuck's sake, McGrain, just get it done. I've lost and that's it. I ain't scared to die, so if yer gonna ice me, be done with it, man," raged Parlane.

McGrain laughed. "What a strange man you are, Ronnie Parlane. You disappoint me with your lack of imagination. Can't you see what I am suggesting?"

"So why don't ye spell it oot for me then, smart arse," demanded Parlane.

"Put simply, we are, thanks to your clumsy intervention, a man down prior to going on a turn that needs quatre hommes. It is too short notice to pull in anyone as a replacement and you, my dear Parlane,

129

inconveniently or otherwise, have expertise in the field required that would help us get the job done …" McGrain let the bizarre enormity of what he had just said ripple around the van.

From the vehicle's cabin, Spider was first to articulate his revulsion: "Come on, Tony, ye cannae be serious, like? For fuck's sake, even Parlane can see there is only one endin' for him."

Again McGrain turned sideways to invite Gregsy's comment. "And your thoughts on this novel solution to our problem are just what, James?" he asked, a tremor of anger at Spider's blunt opposition flickering through his pronounced Glaswegian accent.

"How can you trust a man who has just killed one of your best mates and was hell-bent on putting you in your box intae the bargain, Tony?"

McGrain's harsh laugh once again filled the rear of the van. "Aah, the issue of trust is at the heart of it once again. But there we have it, the crux of the matter. The bottom line, Parlane, then, would appear to be how much you want to prolong your life and just what you're prepared to do to stay on God's green earth?" McGrain took a deep breath and placed the Glock back on his lap.

"Now, if you don't mind, I need your answer within 10 seconds … starting now." With that, a look of total bewilderment swept over Parlane's pale features and McGrain started to countdown: "10 … 9 … 8 … 7 … 6 …"

Two feet opposite, Parlane gritted his teeth and then butted the back of his head off the van's metallic wall; but when his eyes rested back on McGrain, he saw that his nemesis was already fitting a silencer to his Glock as he continued his countdown.

"4 … 3 …"

The offer of a shot at survival, however unbelievable and surreal it seemed, was too much. "Awright, awright, am fuckin' well in," he shouted across the van.

McGrain, smiling serenely, ignored the "You gotta be fuckin' kiddin,'" that came from Spider, and said: "At last, common sense has prevailed."

CHAPTER TWENTY-EIGHT

FIFTEEN MINUTES LATER, the Transit entered the sleepy Lancashire port of Heysham with Spider at the wheel. The foreboding silence that hung to him made it clear to McGrain that his decision to grant Parlane his life and then incorporate him within their crew was something that his henchman was still struggling to get his head around.

"How's the hand?" asked McGrain, attempting conversation.

"It's a graze. As long as I keep it clean and freshly bandaged I think I'll get by until we're done." He paused. "What the fuck have you done, Tony?" he finally snapped, his anger and confusion at McGrain's clemency towards the man who had sanctioned Fergus' execution and been hell-bent on carrying out their own destruction crystal clear.

"Don't you remember Sergeant Lafayette telling us repeatedly that no one is expendable: 'personne n'est consommable', as he liked to say?" asked McGrain from behind his best poker face.

"Naturellement," responded Spider, sarcastically slipping into the French of La Légion. He shook his head angrily at himself and lowering his voice until it could barely be heard above the throaty groaning of the vehicle's diesel engine, said: "Look, I admit you were right over Gregsy but this is ... is too fuckin' much. Fergus was our comrade and now we welcome his murderer into our ranks with open arms ... it ain't right, whatever you got planned, Tony."

McGrain sat facing his confederate and in an act of rapprochement reached out his left hand and patted Spider on his arm reassuringly. "I have one question for you, Spider ... have I ever let you down?"

A dark frown was the only answer McGrain received, but undeterred he continued: "Look, I need you to trust me on this." He paused, then switched his attention to directions. "Aah, that's us into Heysham Road now. We need to get into Hillmount Avenue, which runs parallel to it, and then we are looking for Sugham Lane, if you take the right turning there …" McGrain pushed the town map from his lap up onto the dashboard and traced their route with his right index finger as Spider dropped down into second gear and indicated right.

"Easy does it, just slow her down," said McGrain and then pointed 100 yards to his left at an opening in the row of suburban semis. "There … don't that look like a lane to you, mon ami?" Spider drew the vehicle to a stop.

Slipping back through the hatchway, McGrain once again sat down next to Gregsy. "All right, we're here and this, my friend, is where you start to show me that I didn't fuck up when I decided not to have your brains blown out."

Across the van, Parlane gave McGrain a look of pure loathing, but said nothing.

"We need a recce done and you are just the man to carry it out for us. So we'll be going for a little dander, three up, while Spider brings the van round onto the main street." Shouting back through to the driver's cabin, McGrain added: "No offence, Spider, but your wounded paw could attract unwanted attention." He turned to look at the bound Parlane. "Now, before I have Gregsy untie you, I need your word, Mr Parlane, that you will do nothing bloody stupid, because if you do, not only will it fuck things up for us, it will ensure that your demise is imminent; and who wins out of that?" asked McGrain amicably.

"All right, all right, what d'ya want me to do?" asked Parlane, resigned to the inevitable.

"I need you to get this 50 franc note changed into pounds and while you are doing so, I want you to make yourself aware of every

CCTV camera position, the potential location of the panic button, any other security arrangements, how many tellers are serving and anything else that may be of interest to us. Just do exactly as I ask you and make sure that when you come out of the bank you are in a position to answer every question that you can think I would want to ask. But first, put this baseball cap on and pull it down tight, because I don't want that gash above your eye attracting unneeded interest," concluded McGrain, flashing his cruel, thin smile and leaning forward to place the note inside the chest pocket of his captive's gingham shirt. Then he fitted the cap snug over his former foe's head, before administering a reassuring pat on the pocket.

Parlane nodded that he was ready to go and Gregsy duly undid his binds. Two minutes later, as they walked up the lane, the noise of the Transit's diesel engine fading away confirmed that Spider was on his way around to the front.

As they drew level with three bins placed against a white roughcast wall, McGrain paused to take in everything he could in relation to the rear of the bank and checked it off mentally against the info he already had from Senga. "There we go, the rear entrance in off the lane and the flat-roofed extension at the back where the staff pool table is located," he muttered.

"One security camera at the rear mounted on the edge of the flat roof, Tony," chipped in Gregsy.

"Got it, James, thank you," replied McGrain, before Parlane surprised them both with his first meaningful contribution.

"These bollards are a pain in the arse. The lane would have provided a nice quick exit from the main road, be handy if they could be busted aff," he suggested.

"A reasonable point, Parlane, but one we are unlikely to have the time or the capability to overcome. Now here we are, it's time you spent a penny," smiled McGrain, before adding: "We will be waiting for you in the van, and remember, don't try and be a smart arse," he finished, his veneer of friendliness immediately replaced by a grim menace.

Parlane's checked shirt disappeared through the front door of the NatWest, which was little more than a conversion of two semi-detached houses into an office premises.

They waited for a gap in the traffic to open before crossing the road and making their way towards the green Transit that had now pulled up on the opposite side of the road, Gregsy couldn't help himself giving vent to his own scepticism over McGrain's call on Parlane. "I'm sorry, Tony, I just don't feckin' get it … Aah mean we've got all the inside info we need fae Senga and the whole idea o' that is that we walk in through an unlocked rear door … so why is shit-for-brains in doing a recce? For Chrissakes, Parlane's just had one of your oldest mates bleached and he's gonna take the first chance he gets to put you in the ground wi' him …" concluded Gregsy, shaking his head in complete bafflement.

McGrain held his right hand up. "If you think the slate is wiped clean with Parlane and me because he has agreed to help us then think again, Jamesy boy. Right now, Parlane's ugly mug will be all over the bank's CCTV film footage and when that is played back after we've been in, cleaned the gaff out and it's been turned back on again, then it will clearly show our fearsome Scottish villain casing the joint up," said McGrain mildly, as he pressed the button of the pedestrian crossing.

"No shit!" exclaimed Gregsy in wide-eyed admiration. Then a look of consternation creased his features. "But what if he dobs us in now? How can you trust him?" he asked.

"Whatever Parlane is, he's no snitch. No, I know we can trust him not to turn to the authorities. He wants to take us out himself, not rat." Then as they started to cross Heysham Road, McGrain continued: "Sadly for Parlane, that won't happen. He will not live to see Scotland again and when his body is found riddled with lead the only real conclusion the authorities will be able to arrive at is that his team have turned against him. Right now, although he does not know it, Ronnie Parlane is alibiing us up to the hilt … comprendy?"

A brilliant smile broke across Gregsy's ruddy features and he said: "That's quality, Tony, fuckin' quality!"

CHAPTER TWENTY-NINE

THE GREEN TRANSIT drew into the car park at the rear of the whitewashed walls of the town's 18th-century Royal Oak Hotel with Parlane once more seated in the rear opposite Gregsy, the silence in the back of the vehicle mirrored by the frosty still that enveloped the driver's cabin.

Parlane's return to the vehicle had gone off without a hitch and the report he had supplied in relation to the front of the bank and its apparent security measures was tersely delivered but nonetheless impressively comprehensive.

Now, as he vaulted out of the van and opened its rear doors, McGrain eyed his former rival with steely authority. "All right, gents, it's time we got ourselves inside. Gregsy, you will be sharing with our new friend here and making sure that he doesn't have any second thoughts. I will have food delivered to your room. Spider and myself will be next door but we are expecting a visitor down in the bar shortly. So, once we have checked in, you make yourselves nice and comfortable and I'm sure I can have refreshments delivered your way tout de suite!" he smiled.

But Parlane was far from happy. "Whit's wrang, McGrain, you scared I might do a runner? Fuck's sake, man, I had every chance tae dob you in back at the NatWest, so am no bloody likely to change my mind now, am I?"

McGrain's lips almost creased into a smile but instead something more akin to a grimace crossed his thin features. "I think we have established that you know where your best interests lie, Parlane. I'm afraid this has nothing to do with you but instead about meeting someone who is vital to our chances of pulling this job off. Now, if you don't mind, you'll wait here until I have the rooms sorted and then you will be looked after well enough."

"So whit's for dinner, McGrain? I could murder a balti an' I wid'ne mind sniffin' some skirt, like?" snapped Parlane, his pale features twisted into a sneer.

"Truly?" asked McGrain, shaking his head ruefully before continuing: "I'm afraid all of that can be done on your own time, my friend, after we're done. Tonight you'll be dining in," and at that McGrain slammed the van door shut, still wincing at Parlane's Neanderthal tendencies.

An hour later, McGrain and Spider sat under the bar's oak beams, facing each other across a wooden table. McGrain, as always with his back to the wall, nestled into a large red velvet bench seat that resembled a church pew.

"So tell me, Tony ... how you gonna break the news to Senga that her brother has been iced and his murderer is upstairs and now working as part of our team?" demanded Spider, before necking the remainder of his pint of Carlsberg.

McGrain pressed his body into the high back of the seat and groaned. "Look, Spider, Ferg realised full well the risks involved in our way of life and he has paid the ultimate price for that. But you know how useful Parlane will be to us after the job is done in terms of laying a false trail, dead or alive. I don't think even you can dispute his arrival in our clutches was something we had to turn to our advantage ... as for Senga, well, that's another fuckin' story."

"What do you mean?" snapped Spider.

"If we tell her the whole truth then I think we are setting ourselves up for a fuckin' disaster. Not only will she have to deal with the shock of the news her older brother is brown breed but to then try and explain to her we've taken on his killer, as you pointed out so eloquently, however useful he is and whatever his ultimate fate may be, is gonna be way too much for a 23-year-old girl to deal with. Who knows how she will blow and if it all goes pear-shaped then the turn itself will be at risk," concluded McGrain, taking a sip from a Gordon's and tonic.

"So what kind of damage limitation have you got in mind, Tony, 'cause you better get ready to spring it: Senga has just walked in the bleedin' door," said Spider.

Across the table McGrain muttered "Shit," through a forced grin, now flashed Senga's way.

As she walked through the heavy dark wooden door to The Royal Oak, a smile that was all teeth lit up her well-painted face. Spider stood up and blurted out: "Fuck me, it's Clare-bleedin'-Grogan!"

Her dark-brown hair was cut above the ear and heavily highlighted, while giant circular earrings dangled from her delicate ears and her bright-red lipstick, along with a mischievous, infectious girly smile, was enough to light up the darkest winter night.

"Hello Senga," smiled McGrain, providing a tepid handshake by way of an awkwardly restrained welcome, before Spider spouted: "Come here, ya wee darlin', how long's it been? Christ, you must have been back in first year of high school the last time I saw you," and at that the big man enveloped her in a bear-like embrace.

Senga's response was a giggle-laced reply: "Still got that mingin' ponytail, Spider, I see. Tell me how did the Foreign Legion allow you to keep it?"

The big man stroked his ponytail almost purring with delight. "That's for another time, ma petite chérie!"

McGrain attempted to bring some order to proceedings: "What can I get you to drink, Senga?"

"A brandy and Babycham wid be great, Tony. Where's ma big bruv?" she asked, smoothing down her outsized black-and-white checked shirt over her boogie stretch jeans.

"Oh, he's out and about, Senga, we're expecting him anytime now, but we need to make a start to this. Why don't you make yourself comfortable, I'll get your drink in and then we need to get down to it," said McGrain, catching Spider's uneasy glance at the line he had just spun her.

As McGrain lifted the silver tray of a Carlsberg, G&T and the brandy and Babycham, he caught the watchful eyes of the barman, a corpulent Lancastrian with a thick black goatee covering his jaw, assessing him and then flitting towards Spider and Senga in the corner.

"You awright, mate?" asked McGrain in emphasised, menacing Glaswegian tones.

His challenge startled the bar manager, whose furtive eyes returned back to his customer. "Never better, sir," he replied, but the message of threat had been received and understood.

And when McGrain added: "Let's just keep it that way, then," a nervous smile broke out between the folds of the barman's goatee.

Sitting down, McGrain laid down the drinks and waiting to make sure they all had a glass, he raised his Gordon's. "To getting' the job done!"

As Spider raised his wounded right hand, Senga spotted the blood-tinted bandage it was wrapped in. "You're hurt, Spider, does your wound need takin' a look at? I dunno if Ferg told you, but I've started work as an auxiliary nurse at the local hospital …" she said and dipped her head in a demure gesture that was laced with mischief.

It was an answer that brought a huge smile to Spider and he purred: "Is that right, pet? Maybees you can take a wee butcher's at it later?"

"What … you mean yer hand, big man?" she asked and broke into a tartish laugh that immediately started to grate on McGrain.

"Okay, that's probably a good move, but right now I need to know exactly what we are going to expect when we turn up at the rear of the NatWest tomorrow … so what you been up to, sweetheart, and don't disappoint me, 'cause Fergus has given you a big build-up!"

Senga just about managed to tear her eyes away from Spider. She took a quick sip from her drink and turned McGrain's way. "Mr Revie, the manager, is a randy old git but one wi' a big gob on him. He's also a creature of habit. His whole life's lived in a routine, everything is black an' white and as long as you treat him right he can be very generous ..." a sly smile twitched across her heavily made-up features in the direction of Spider, whose eyes were almost bulging across the rim of his pint pot.

"Okay, I think we get the picture, Senga. So why don't you tell us exactly what that routine is and more importantly how it's gonna fit in with our arrival at the back o' the branch at 11 p.m. the morro' night?" asked McGrain pragmatically.

"Awright, Tony, keep yer hair on," chirped Senga, playfully twirling her outsized hoop earrings, her gaze dancing towards Spider.

"So the routine is that the bank shuts at 6 p.m. on a Thursday and after old Revie has been around the office checking everything is shipshape and his cash is balanced and the rest of the staff are all away hame, well then Mr Bank Manager likes to have a bit o' fun with his favourite cleaner in his office. Tae be fair to the bald old prick, he's pretty generous in return. Then he pours himself a large scotch, finishes readin' his Financial Times and buggers aff hame to the missus for his hot pot: while the keys to the office remain snug in their closet just behind the huge mahogany desk that he seems to find so exciting when I'm sitting on it and flashing the wee black mini-skirt I always wear under my tabard on Thursday night," concluded Senga, breaking into her irritating laugh.

"That's all very good, darlin', but what I want to know is exactly what will be waiting for us when we arrive at the back door, if you don't mind ..." The look of impatience that had now spread across McGrain's hawklike features made it clear to Senga it was time to get to the bottom line.

"I finish up 'bout 10 p.m. on a Thursday night, because I have to make up for the time lost keeping old Revie happy. When I go,

I'll leave the latch off at the back door and of course the alarm switched off as well. I know exactly where the CCTV console is, 'cause Revie cannae stop boastin' about how he caught his chief clerk givin' wan o' the junior tellers a seeing too over the pool table! Anyway, I'll flick the switch aff and like I said make sure the alarm is also aff and you can waltz in and make yourselves comfortable," concluded Senga.

"So we are coming in through the staffroom, past the pool table …" McGrain paused and whipped out what turned out to be a hand-drawn floor plan of the bank. "Show me where the cleaner's room is and the cupboards we'll be waiting in for Revie's return the following morning," he demanded.

As the map flattened out, Senga leaned forward onto her forearms and scanned the paperwork before circling a section of the blueprint. "Just there, down the corridor to the left. But you're going to have aw night to familiarise yourself with the layout, Tony, and then you can expect Revie at 8 a.m. sharp the following morning with opening time at 9 a.m.," she said.

"Awmost an hour to get the keys to the safe aff him, keep any early arrivals quiet, empty the cash and get off oor mark. That's plenty!" said Spider, leaning back into his chair and clasping his hands behind his head as a large smile, which was directed Senga's way, broke across his dark features.

But McGrain had one other detail he wanted to firm up on. "So what's the bottom line, Senga, how much are we talkin' in your safe tomorrow morning when we get Revie to open up?"

"It's Friday morning and we have two big payrolls ready to be dished out and plenty of other small ones. Mr Revie likes to boast about how much he has in his safe every Thursday night, he calls it his 3-million-pound lottery and after we've finished on his desk he likes to fantasise about what he would do with me if he emptied the safe and did a runner!"

At that Spider barked out a harsh laugh that attracted the unwanted attention of the barman. Then he leaned forward and said: "Aye, well auld man Revie will get the chance to empty his safe of the three mill awright but then he's gonna have to watch it goin' oot the door in our kitbags!" As Senga burst into a bawdy laugh, even McGrain found himself smiling at the prospect.

"It'll be nae bother, Tony, honest," she said and flashed him a coquettish smile that sent Spider's temperature soaring.

CHAPTER THIRTY

UPSTAIRS, PARLANE lay back on one of the oak-beamed room's two single beds, his hands clasped behind his head and his eyes locked on the small colour TV that was perched on top of a cheap MFI unit in the corner, as Angus Deayton's smug features filled the screen at the beginning of an episode of 'Have I Got News For You'.

"I hate that prick Deayton," spat Parlane, propping himself up on one elbow to take a sip from the coffee cup handily located on the drawers at the side of his bed. As he did so the springs under him groaned and Parlane winced. "Like a fuckin' sandpit, I don't see me getting' a wink o' kip."

His denim-clad back to Parlane, Gregsy stared out of the bedroom window and down onto The Royal Oak's beer garden, already busy with patrons. Turning round, he glanced at the TV set. "Nah, the one that really gets on ma tits is that Merton tosser. Whit's that fuckin' hair all about, always flickin' it back like he thinks he's chocolate. Middle-class public schoolboy wankers the lot of them, but you know what, Parlane? Funny wankers," concluded Gregsy with a smirk of self-amusement, before he plonked himself down on an easy chair across the other side of the room.

"Maybees you find 'em funny, Gregsy, but I don't give a fuck 'bout what Edwina Currie thinks of eggs: I'll be havin' me a full English first thing in the mornin' and ma eggs'll be sunny side up, as per!" rapped Parlane with such surprising intensity that his roommate burst into laughter.

"Aye, yer no yokin'," replied Gregsy after he'd recovered himself.

But Parlane wasn't in the mood for the pun and looking Gregsy's way he said: "So tell me, Gregsy, what happened at St Serf's?"

It was the question that Gregsy had been waiting for ever since McGrain had ordered him to babysit their 'new colleague' and for a moment his eyes met Parlane's dark stare. "Shit is whit happened and people died," he answered flatly, pulling his handgun from inside his wrangler and laying it on his lap in front of him.

"I know that, peterman, 'cause I had an agreement with Glavin and that included a cut o' the post office job in 'turn for him comin' across and givin' McGrain the heave-ho and a bullet in the brains. One minute me and Johnstone are waitin' for Glavin and his boys to turn up, then instead there's a no-show and the jungle drums start beatin' that Glavin, Shug Fowler and Simmo have been iced by McGrain and his crew ... but you, Gregsy, live tae fight another day. And now here we are, yous a trusted member of the bastard's team ... that stinks, Gregsy ... almost as much as Edwina Currie and her pish about eggs. So why don't you tell me what happened at St Serf's?"

Gregsy ran his right hand through his thick red mop, reholstered his shooter and got out of the easy chair before hunkering down at the hotel room's minibar, opening the door. "Fancy a voddy, Parlane?" he asked.

"Now yer talkin'!" replied Parlane, his eyes twinkling with ravenous relish.

Gregsy removed two Smirnoff miniatures and lobbed one of them over to Parlane, who caught the small bottle with his right hand and almost in the one movement broke the seal and took a long greedy drink that left barely a trickle in the small bottle.

"Fuckin' needed that," he said and wiped his mouth with the back of his hand before adding: "Now, you wiz sayin' ..."

"Look, all I can tell you is that McGrain wanted the safe opened in front of him and when I was getting' tae work it all kicked aff behind me. Next thing I knows, Glavin and his boys are laid out cold and McGrain has made me an offer I cannae be refusin' if I don't want to be joining 'em, like ..." Gregsy took a sip of the Smirnoff, before adding: "Bit like yersel' in that respect, Parlane."

But Parlane refused to be deflected. "All a bit convenient, ain't it? The talk is that you had awready cut a deal wi' McGrain and that Glavin and his boys were never gonna be leavin' St Serf's in anythin' but their pine boxes. Speakin' o' which, what happened to their bodies? You just dinnae magic away three corpses with a click o' the fingas," concluded Parlane.

Gregsy shrugged his shoulders unconvincingly. "Look, I dunno, I wiz just happy to get oot o' there in one piece. Like you said, mate, I'm just the peterman here," he said and drained the contents of the miniature.

But Parlane was like a butcher's dog with a bone. "It all stinks. That McGrain is a sneaky wee shit, I tells ya. What about that botched polis raid on the Italian, then? We heard all about that ... Ask yersel' this, when have the polis ever raided a joint without coverin' the back door ... come on, Gregsy, everyone knows O'Toole's a bastard. You did'nae come up the Clyde in a bleedin' banana skin, di' ye?" demanded Parlane, anger sparking in his coarse voice.

"That's a crock o' shit, Parlane. If it wiz aw stage-managed, why has one o' the cops got a 9 millimetre in the shoulder? Naw, am no' buying that, next thing I know you'll be claimin' McGrain nabbed Shergar!" scoffed Gregsy.

"Look, aw I'm sayin' is that for long enough there have been rumours about McGrain being tight with O'Toole, so if he's on the rozzer's payroll and toutin' tae him then that would tell you everythin' you need tae know, peterman," said Parlane, arching his eyebrows to under-line his point.

But Gregsy was having none of it and shaking his head dismissively he said: "I know exactly whit yer trying to dae, Parlane. You're tryin' to unsettle me and get me to fuck this whole shootin' match up an' I can tell you that isnae gonna be happenin' anytime soon, mate."

Parlane's agitation was clear and he swung his legs over the side of the bed and stood up, flexing his shoulders backwards. "You little arse, you've been played, Gregsy. For fuck's sake, you think either you or me will be swanning off wi' our cut tae live happy ever after? No way, it's …" – and at that Parlane turned his right hand into a mock revolver, pointed it at Gregsy and dropped his thumb as if he had dropped the hammer – "night night for you and me the minute the joab is done."

Sat in the easy chair 3 yards away, Gregsy's taut features betrayed the fact that it was a thought that had already occurred to him … more than once.

CHAPTER THIRTY-ONE

THOROUGHGOOD PICKED his way over the rough surface of Ashton Lane, as always waiting to be ambushed by the combination of an uneven cobble and a lack of concentration that could mean disaster and embarrassment in equal measure were only a footstep away.

Even at 5.30 p.m. on a weekday, the centre of Glasgow's West End was starting to bustle with people looking for a good night out and it still amazed Thoroughgood that the area's transformation had only come about in the last few years.

In that not-so-distant past, the premises now occupied by upmarket bars and eateries had belonged to the famous optical engineering firm Barr & Stroud, an old coach house and a landscape gardener's yard.

The most famous resident of Ashton Lane had been Dr Marion Gilchrist, the first woman to graduate in medicine in Scotland and a redoubtable lady whose chauffeur's house and accompanying garage were usually garnished by her dark-green Wolseley landaulette. He wondered what she'd think if she could see the West End now.

But that was ancient history and right now what Thoroughgood was most interested in was a pint. Making his way upstairs to the bar of The Ubiquitous Chip, which had itself originally been an undertaker's stables, Thoroughgood grabbed the vacant barstool at the end of the bar, unfolded his Telegraph and scanned the sports pages, just as the familiar presence of Russell, the super-camp barman, placed a pint of his favourite Fürstenberg down in front of him.

"A tough day, Officer Thoroughgood, by the looks of it?" enquired Russell politely, in his almost louche accent.

Thoroughgood raised the pint pot in salute. "How can you tell?" he asked and half-emptied the glass before Russell had time to answer.

The barman smiled awkwardly but before he could make further enquiry, a middle-aged woman in a dark power suit commanded his attention. "Barman, over here," she called in a clipped tone that brooked no argument, and Russell shrugged sardonically before doing as he was bid.

Thoroughgood struggled to concentrate after his rendezvous with Emma. Even a hysterical editorial proclaiming 'Iron' Mike Tyson's tenth-round stoppage by James 'Buster' Douglas as the greatest shock ever witnessed in the noble art failed to keep his attention.

He'd heard nothing from Celine and had done nothing to change that situation, choosing to let the silence stretch in the stubborn belief that she would be the first to crack. Yet as time marched not-so-merrily on that appeared less and less likely to be the case anytime soon.

The continuing attempt to entrap The Creepers had also been anything but successful. O'Toole's huckling of Albert Stringer had sent him and his brothers to ground, and the sudden drop off in housebreakings did indeed seem to back up this theory. As a result, their OP point had become largely obsolete and Storey would surely bin the operation soon.

But right now Thoroughgood didn't want to think about any of that. Draining his glass, he signalled to Russell to pour him another pint of the house delicacy and wondered afresh what to do about Emma.

In the days that had passed since their coffee, he had only seen her once and that had been a fleeting glance and a meeting of eyes while she had been dealing with another failure to pay a taxi fare at the front bar in Bayne Street Divisional HQ.

The amount of time he was spending thinking about Emma was starting to cause Thoroughgood to feel increasingly guilty, yet the voice in his head seemed to be telling him to enjoy the journey.

As his inner angst mounted, Thoroughgood shook his head. The warming fire provided a pleasing, toasty glow from behind him, while the gentle hum of chatter left him undisturbed, even if he was in his own silent world of turmoil.

Checking his watch, he saw that it was 5.45 p.m. McNab would be at least another 15 minutes and as he shrugged his shoulders, Thoroughgood took temporary solace from his predicament with another large mouthful of golden Fürstenberg and placed the pint pot back where it had come from.

"Make a habit of drinking on your own, Angus?" asked a slightly sonorous voice from just behind him.

As he turned to face Meechan's iron-grey eyes, Thoroughgood didn't know what was making him angrier: the shattering of a moment of self-torture he was, in all honesty, revelling in, or Meechan's familiar use of his Christian name, not the shortened version that was his universal nom de guerre.

Thoroughgood held the new arrival's gaze momentarily and then turned back towards the Telegraph's sports pages. "I'm sorry … Dec … but I'm too busy right now to be bothered talking to you," he said caustically.

But Meechan was not easily deterred and he took up a position at the bar just to Thoroughgood's right so that his looming presence would not allow Thoroughgood any privacy worthy of the name. Taking another mouthful of lager, Thoroughgood sighed, put the glass back down and turned side-on to face his tormentor.

"What the fuck's your problem, Meechan?" he snapped, aware that, almost despite himself, his jaw had begun to set.

Meechan flashed a baleful smile back and leaned against the bar. "But it's not me who has the problem is it, Angus?"

The urge to jump off his barstool and crack a right hand off Meechan's square jaw in a manner that Iron Mike would have lisped his pride at was threatening to unhinge Thoroughgood, so powerful was it. But instead, he sought alternative employment for his right mitt and enclosed it around his Fürstenberg once again. "I didn't have a problem until you turned up, Meechan. So why don't you just say what you've gotta say and then get out of my face."

But Meechan's attention was already elsewhere and catching the attention of a barmaid, whose hair was dyed an almost luminous red, he said: "Two pints of Fürstenberg, please," and flashed a disposable smile.

"I choose who I drink with and you haven't had an invite," spat Thoroughgood, his eyes once again locking with Meechan's restless grey orbs.

"But I think you'll want to hear what I've got to say … Angus," said Meechan amicably enough, before adding "May I?" as he gestured to the empty barstool located a couple of feet away from Thoroughgood and got a shrug of the shoulders by way of an answer.

"Look, I don't want to be making an enemy of you and I think you would be foolish to be making an enemy of me," said Meechan, taking Thoroughgood completely by surprise.

Finishing his own pint, Thoroughgood quickly placed it down on his semi-soaked beer mat, still struggling to comprehend Meechan's peace offering. "And?" he asked.

"You and me, we aren't so different, Angus; maybe the opposite sides of the law but still on parallel lines, I'd say. But while maybe these lines are in black and white, in between there is a whole world of grey where we could maybe reach an understanding that could prove very helpful to both of us," concluded Meechan, stopping for a draft of lager and then placing the three-quarters-full pint glass back on its mat with a careful precision that immediately irritated Thoroughgood.

"Why don't you get to the point, Meechan, or should I be calling you Declan, since you're so keen to become my best mate?" asked the cop.

"Have you heard of a ... what should I call him ... yes ... how about a 'businessman' called Anthony McGrain?" asked Meechan equably.

"You mean the gangster Tony McGrain who's just had one of the North CID shot and made our esteemed Detective Inspector Ronan O'Toole look like an extra from the Keystone Cops?" asked Thoroughgood.

"The very same," smiled Meechan and then for good effect he let a short silence draw out to whet Thoroughgood's appetite. "But did you know that McGrain and O'Toole have an understanding and that the whole raid was a set-up?" he finished.

A foot to his left, Meechan's cobalt glare never leaving him, Thoroughgood nearly choked on his Fürstenberg.

CHAPTER THIRTY-TWO

THOROUGHGOOD GRABBED one of the pile of napkins and wiped away the foam that had been left smearing his jaw.

"I thought that would get your attention," said Meechan, the harshness of his Northern Irish accent slightly more pronounced than it had previously been, underlining the fact that he was all too well aware of the importance of the moment.

Thoroughgood nodded. "Go on."

"Did you know that you have something in common with DI O'Toole? That you are both graduates, although his degree is in psychology, whereas yours, Angus, I believe, is in medieval history, correct?" asked Meechan almost disinterestedly.

Despite himself, Thoroughgood recoiled slightly with surprise. "10 out of 10, Meechan, why don't you give yourself a gold star?" he asked flatly, before adding: "So …?"

"Just throwing in an interesting little piece of detail, but the point I'm making is that O'Toole is anything but what his name suggests he may be and his alliance with McGrain makes him someone that you would do well to avoid irritating," concluded Meechan, before taking a mouthful of Fürstenberg.

"While that's all fascinating and I thank you from the heart of my bottom for the warning, so what? If this is the extent of the understanding you're proposing between us then it's finished before it's begun, because right now all that amounts to is hearsay – gossip – and no more. Incidentally, how did you know I was going to be in the UB Chip or was it just coincidence you wandered in?" snapped Thoroughgood.

But the cop's show of irritation had gotten under Meechan's skin and for a moment his hooded gaze and self-restraint were displaced by a flash of anger. "Look, Thoroughgood, I make it my business to know exactly what is going on in Ashton Lane and who's about on my manor. I'm here to try and broker something that will benefit us both but if you can only indulge in petty barbs then I can see I'm wasting my time," and at that he drained his pint and slammed it down on the marble-topped bar, before turning towards the exit.

Behind him, Thoroughgood shook his head in a private admission that the importance of what Meechan had to say meant he must subdue his dislike for the Irishman. "All right, all right, you've my undivided attention, Meechan." As Meechan's silver-grey double-breaster turned back his way, the cop added: "Look, why don't you let me return the favour and throw in a bag of KP as a Brucie bonus?"

The tremor of a smile flickering across Meechan's normally emotionless features was all the answer Thoroughgood needed and he gestured to an empty table in the corner. "Let's re-locate?"

Meechan nodded his head in agreement and took up his new position. Moments later, the cop joined him and laid down the pints. Settling, he said: "Okay, no more bullshit, you've got my attention 100 per cent, but before you go any further, I want to know what you're expecting back in return for whatever is coming my way."

"Fair enough," replied Meechan, inclining his head and lifting his pint pot. "Sláinte," he said and they touched glasses.

"You already know that I work for Jimmy Gray and he has become, shall we say, a bit concerned with the Widowmaker's activities ... sorry, I assume you know McGrain's alias?" Receiving a nod of affirmation from across the table, Meechan continued: "The fact is that he seems to have access to information that is making him increasingly untouchable. Information we're assuming is coming from your revered colleague, Detective Inspector O'Toole. All of this is upsetting the balance of power in the world we operate in and when that happens the repercussions can surface in your world, if you follow me ..." said Meechan, letting his words drift off into silence.

"So what are you offering me? To help restore that ... balance ... and again, more importantly, what are you expecting back?" asked Thoroughgood flatly, a sense of foreboding starting to percolate through his body.

"I know it's not your patch but you may well have heard of a bloody little encounter that has cost three members of an Easter-house team their lives?" asked Meechan.

"You mean Jimmy Glavin and his wingmen, Shug Fowler and ... what was he called again? Simms ... Bobby Simms ... that's it?" replied Thoroughgood.

"Impressive! So you do take an interest in the outside world after all ... Gus!" said Meechan from behind an assessing grey gaze.

"So it's believed Glavin and his cronies have bought it but as far as I know there has been no sign of their bodies?"

"Exactly, and that is something I may well be able to help you with, for Glavin and his sidekicks are buried where most of the people who cross McGrain find themselves: in a place called The Blood Acre, his execution ground," concluded Meechan.

"The Blood Acre? It's all a bit melodramatic isn't it? It's almost like something from the pages of the Bible!" laughed Thoroughgood.

"And how well do you know your scriptures ... Gus?" asked Meechan.

"Not as well as my grandfather would like me to," Thoroughgood admitted.

"So a lucky strike then ... but nonetheless, an accurate one. The term is indeed taken from the good book and in fact Acts Chapter 1, verse 19 to be exact: the Blood Acre – in Aramaic it's called Akeldama – and for some reason it has become the name given to the place where McGrain puts his victims ... or at least parts of them," concluded McGrain.

Thoroughgood let out a long slow whistle and received a disapproving stare from the severe looking woman in the dark suit, her slightly greying hair tightly scraped back in a bun, who sat at the table to his left with a knot of other similarly clad companions of the same vintage. "Do you mind?" she snapped.

As Thoroughgood held his glass up in mock salute, Meechan helpfully said: "Lawyers from Jamieson & Sons down the bottom of Byres Road,"

Thoroughgood couldn't help a frown developing across his features at the little titbit that confirmed Meechan seemed to have his finger very much on the pulse of the West End, but recovering himself he returned his attention to the conversation in hand. "So you were saying … Akeldama in Aramaic, eh? Forgive the historian in me but what is the story behind that?" he asked.

Meechan raised his eyebrows slightly. "It's the plot of land that Judas bought with the 30 pieces of silver he earned from his betrayal of Christ!"

"Bloody hell," replied Thoroughgood.

CHAPTER THIRTY-THREE

A KNOWING SMILE broke Meechan's normally veiled gaze as he took in the look of wonderment that had enveloped the young cop's face.

"Clearly you don't know the good book as well as your grandfather would like! But to be fair, it's a chapter that is never really given much recognition. I suppose it isn't likely to be on any minister's playlist for a Sunday morning sermon! But just for the record, do you know what happened to Judas after his betrayal of Christ?" asked Meechan, stretching nonchalantly for his pint.

"I don't have a Scooby," replied Thoroughgood, shaking his head.

"After setting foot upon Akeldama ..." – Meechan paused to apply metaphorical quotation marks with the middle fingers of each hand – "Judas fell forward onto the ground and burst open so that his entrails poured out."

"Jeez ... I'm surprised they haven't made a film about it with Charlton Heston or Robert Powell playing the lead," quipped Thoroughgood and despite their unease in each other's company, they laughed in unison.

But it was Thoroughgood that brought their chorus of mirth to a halt. "So the bottom line is: do you know where the Blood Acre is and what lies in it, or should I say, who is interred in its sod?" he asked finally.

The wince that spread across Meechan's pale features was all the answer that Thoroughgood needed but cradling his jaw on his left hand, Meechan was keen to elaborate: "Unfortunately no, we don't

... just yet ... but I'm confident that I will have that ... what would you call it ... ah yes ... intelligence, some time in the not too distant future. But before I go any further, forgive me for asking the obvious question ... Gus ... but do you see the benefits of a reciprocal arrangement and, more importantly to me and to my boss, just what do you think you might be able to help us out with in terms of O'Toole? Make no mistake, if your corrupt senior colleague is brought down then the Widowmaker will come tumbling down with him and vice versa, of course. The best way to make that happen is to take out our two friends with an attack from more than one direction," concluded Meechan.

And the answer to that question, Thoroughgood had to admit, was a big fat nothing. His gaze catching the still untouched packet of KP nuts, he reached forward and started to rip them open, trying to stall for time, while the wheels of his mind turned desperately, attempting to locate a morsel of 'intelligence' that he could horse trade with Meechan for his dramatic revelations.

In the end, he had to admit defeat. Grimacing, Thoroughgood shook his head. "I'm afraid the answer to that, at this precise moment, is sweet FA: although word has it that the good DI is a ladies' man and is sailing a bit close to the wind with his current female friend, whoever that may be." He shrugged, almost embarrassed by his paltry offering.

Proffering the packet of KP nuts Meechan's way almost pathetically, he received a curt rebuttal, although that didn't stop him filling his mouth with a third of the packet.

Washing down the salted peanuts with another draft of Fürstenberg, Thoroughgood returned to the crux of their problem: "What if I could get my hands on a list of McGrain's associates? That might help you start to squeeze him. It would certainly let you know where the direction of any threat is coming from and just how close to home it is?" asked Thoroughgood hopefully, before adding: "The bottom line is I'm going to need time and a bit of help to make this work."

"But then I would imagine you would get plenty of that from your friends in the Unit who helped you bring Dawson and his minions down last year," said Meechan.

Their eyes locked, for Meechan had read his mind and again Thoroughgood found himself disconcerted by the level of Meechan's knowledge and the complete lack of doubt that pervaded those gun-metal-grey eyes.

But while Meechan didn't appear surprised that he had disconcerted Thoroughgood, he was keen to push another crust across the table.

"When you are having that conversation with your mates in the Unit, you might want to put this on the table. Word has reached us from across the Irish Sea that friend Tony is off somewhere down south on a job that he intends to help finance a bombing campaign the Provos have planned for England," and at that Meechan sat back and folded his arms, happy to watch the tremors of shock that broke out over Thoroughgood's taut features.

"Sweet Christ!" muttered Thoroughgood, his voice trembling in amazement at Meechan's final revelation. His right hand rifled involuntarily through his black mullet, emphasising his concern and triggering a cruel smile of satisfaction from his companion.

"This is dynamite, Meechan, and you're right, I need to be speaking to the right people to have it handled properly because if there is one thing that the Dawson business has taught me, it's that a uniform doesn't necessarily mean its wearer can be trusted. But the obvious question from your intelligence is that if McGrain is an IRA agent, what does that make O'Toole by association?"

Meechan raised his Fürstenberg in mock salute. "And all of that is exactly why I am sitting here spilling these golden beans your way, Constable Angus Thoroughgood. My boss Jimmy Gray watched the Dawson business develop and read the papers. We kept our ears to the ground and tried to find out just who was the architect of

Dawson's downfall and your name came to the fore and then of course, by chance, our paths crossed the other night through our mutual acquaintance ..." Meechan let his words trail off.

Again Thoroughgood's mind became a maelstrom of doubt, questions and suspicions, as he replayed Meechan's words, looking for any hidden meanings and wondering if Celine had been drawn into Meechan's world in order to help open an avenue of contact that had now been used to reach out to him.

Struggling to keep his business and personal life from messily overlapping, Thoroughgood desperately fought to stop himself from asking how Celine was.

But before he could make that mistake, Meechan again plunged the verbal detonator: "Okay, Gus, so I've furnished you with quite a bit of information that's of the highest value, to say the least. Although you may not be able to provide payback on it in return immediately, there is just one thing I want right now from you," he said, his Northern Irish accent again delivering the words with added bite.

Thoroughgood met his gaze again. "Which is?"

"Celine," said Meechan, and sat perfectly still, his grey eyes feasting on Thoroughgood's emotions.

CHAPTER THIRTY-FOUR

MEECHAN'S DEMAND, for that was what it was, rebounded around Thoroughgood's head like a scream waiting to get out and explode, but as he tried to get to grips with it, Meechan disinterestedly finished the last of his pint, pushed his chair back and stood up, all the time surveying the effects that his verbal hand grenade had had.

"Obviously it's a lot for you to think about and I am not stupid enough to expect your answer right here but you have a choice to make, Thoroughgood, one that just maybe has already been made for you," said Meechan, almost apologetically.

Looking up from his pint, Thoroughgood realised that the fingers of his right hand had gone white, such was the pressure with which they grasped the pot. "So that's what this is really about, Meechan? It has nothing to do with the forming of an understanding, has it? You've given me so much gold-plated info, you were expecting that to tip the balance by the time you got to what really matters. But by giving me intelligence – as you called it – of that quality you've left me with a question …" said Thoroughgood, stopping just short of the pay-off.

His hands clasped in front of him as he stood opposite Thoroughgood, calmly assured and in complete control, Meechan nodded his head slightly as if to say 'You think so,' but instead from behind an emotionless mask he asked: "Which is?"

"If you are the font of all knowledge, then why the hell do you need me?"

Meechan lifted his Barker-brogued foot and placed it on the spar of the chair opposite Thoroughgood, lowering his elbow onto the top strand of its wooden back, so that he was almost level with Thoroughgood's face. "I have barely scraped the surface, Thoroughgood, with what I know and what may be useful to you. But I recognise, as I said, that we have more in common than perhaps you would care to admit. It's clear we both have ambitions to make the most of the opportunities that our respective careers may offer us and by collaborating from time to time these opportunities are going to be considerably enhanced. What I don't want is to let something needless fracture these possibilities … because, Gus, I think Celine may well already have made your decision for you," and with that Meechan fished out a black business card and placed it on the table in front of Thoroughgood, before adding: "You can get me on these numbers when you have made your call. Enjoy the rest of your pint, my friend."

Meechan drew himself back up from the chair, buttoned up his double-breaster and with a final glance to assess how much of an impact his words had had, he turned and walked out of The Ubiquitous Chip confident that Thoroughgood was exactly where he wanted him.

* * * *

Staring into the bottom of his pint, Thoroughgood repeated Meechan's words of mass destruction over and over again, as emotions he had no control over pulled him this way and that.

Furiously shaking his head, he attempted to get himself in check. After all, hadn't his meeting with Emma rekindled old emotions that had now made him wonder if there was any point in continuing a relationship with Celine that contained so much conflict?

And now Meechan's offer had just reinforced that feeling.

The question that ricocheted loudest in his head, however, was: 'What does Celine have to say? You need to find her because only she can give you the answer.' It was the best advice anyone could have given him, because Thoroughgood realised that the internal fissure that Emma's arrival on the scene and Meechan's intervention had caused had left him incapable of seeing the wood for the trees.

Slamming his glass down on its coaster he sprang to his feet so abruptly that the knot of female lawyers who were now at least three bottles of Liebfraumilch to the better clasped admiring eyes on him, before a ripple of almost schoolgirl laughter swept over the previously peevish ladies. A forty-something blonde with a high white collar and sunglasses perched on a heavily lacquered Krystle Carrington-style bouffant, flashed Thoroughgood a predatory smile. "Hello, handsome, leaving so soon?"

But Thoroughgood was in no mood for pleasantries and as he stormed past their table he snapped: "Another time, darlin', maybe when you're sober!" and stalked off, leaving a chorus of outrage to erupt around their table.

Belmont Street was about a quarter of a mile away, as the crow flies, and grim-faced he picked his way in between embracing couples with eyes only for each other and drunken groups of boisterous students heading along Ashton Lane towards the Queen Margaret Union or the more straight-laced Glasgow University Union, both of which he had been a member of during his 4 years at Glasgow University.

Again Thoroughgood found himself marvelling at the fact that just 13 years earlier 'The Lane', as it was now known, had been a backwater, right until the closure of the Glasgow Subway had caused major refurbishment.

That redevelopment and the decision of the owner of the Ubiquitous Chip to relocate from Ruthven Lane was quickly followed by the creation of the Grosvenor Cafe. With the Cul de Sac crêperie also located in The Lane and a number of other bars thriving there, the ghost of Dr Gilchrist would be no doubt turning in her grave.

As he mulled on that, the thought struck Thoroughgood that surely a woman who had breached a bastion of male chauvinism and enjoyed being chauffeur-driven in a dark-green Wolseley landaulette would have enjoyed the finer things in life, and reaching that conclusion, despite himself, Thoroughgood couldn't help a smile flicker across his drawn features.

Yet his moment of mirth was fleeting as Meechan's taunting words replayed again inside his head: 'I think Celine may already have made your decision for you.' In his hurry to get out of Ashton lane, Thoroughgood's right foot slid off a cobble and he staggered, like a Saturday night drunk, almost but not quite regaining his balance before the ground came rushing up to meet him.

"Bloody hell, Gus, I know I'm a bit late, but you've made the most of it by the looks of it," said a familiar voice and as he got back onto his feet, Thoroughgood found himself face to face with McNab, a dark reefer coat pulled up tight around his neck and a flop of hair drooping down over his perma-tanned face, his right arm entwined around a diminutive, dark-haired woman.

"Well at least I don't have to ask what made you late, McNab!" he quipped and despite his inner angst a cheeky smile crept across Thoroughgood's previously taut features as he cast an admiring glance over McNab's new squeeze, before adding: "It's bad manners not to introduce me to your … young lady."

McNab cocked a proprietorial glance sideways at the pony-tailed brunette. "This is Sophia, Gus, ma boy!" he said triumphantly.

Smiling, Thoroughgood produced a mock bow and offered a light handshake to the full-lipped girl, whose shoulder-length tresses were so dark they were almost jet. "Nice to meet you, Sophia. Don't let him bore you by talking about Celtic all night!" he said, aware that his words were delivered with a slight slur.

"He'll be talking to himself if he starts that nonsense," she replied with a delicious smile and a slightly throaty laugh.

But McNab was keen to lead the conversation to a more serious theme. "Look, mate, we just passed that reptile Declan Meechan round by the bookies. I hear Jimmy Gray is giving him free rein to run the West End." He paused. "Your distracted state wouldn't have anything to do with a chance encounter with him?" asked McNab, his concern for once clear.

Thoroughgood shrugged his shoulders. "Aye, there's no doubt you're a DC in the making! So how did you manage to join these dots together?"

"'Cause after what you told me on the phone last night, mate, I'd say you've got yourself involved in the Bermuda of all love triangles. So I'd hazard a guess that right now you're takin' the fast track straight towards the home address of a young damsel who resides in Belmont Street and it just seems funny that your love rival is sporting a grin as smug as the Cheshire cat after getting the cream, while you are so distracted, half-pissed into the bargain, that you cannae negotiate a few dodgy cobbles!"

A grimace was the best Thoroughgood could offer by way of reply.

Chapter Thirty-Five

THOROUGHGOOD STOOD across the street and looked up at the third floor of 23 Belmont Street, an overriding feeling of déjà vu enveloping him as he recalled the first time he had come calling for Celine, determined to put his cards on the table and let her know just how he felt about her.

That was over a year ago and now here he was once again, same old Harrington jacket zipped up, hands shoved deep into his pockets, uncertain about the welcome that would await him, unsure that another impromptu late-night visit was the right course of action and all the time wondering if Meechan's taunting words would prove that he was wasting his time.

As always, the chipped black storm door lay carelessly ajar and he felt a surge of irritation at the fact that Celine's landlord had still failed to upgrade the doorway with a security entrance.

Reaching the bottom step of the stairwell, Thoroughgood took a deep breath and then bounded up the steps two at a time as per usual, and before he knew it he was on the top floor facing the name panel on her front door.

So the moment of truth had arrived … again … and for the first time it occurred to Thoroughgood that perhaps, given the five pints of Fürstenberg he'd quaffed, his uninvited visit wasn't the best idea.

But then the voice in his head took centre stage: 'Fuck it, Gussy boy, you need to know, one way or another.' He rapped on the door with his right hand, took a pace back and said a silent prayer for divine intervention from the man above.

As the moments passed, he could hear her light footsteps coming across the panels of the flat hall's wooden floor and then the door opened just as the opening line of David Bowie's 'Modern Love' advised 'I know when to go out, I know when to stay in.' Celine stood in front of him, all Caribbean sun, in a light, almost chiffon-type floral-print three-quarter robe, her hair bound in a towel, the traces of moisture that escaped from it confirming that she'd just come from the shower as his heartbeat started to race.

With Bowie blasting in the background, Thoroughgood, his slightly intoxicated state anything but a help, played a disastrous opening gambit: "So tell me, Celine, do you believe in modern love?"

Her eyebrows arched in reply and she narrowed her eyes suspiciously. "Have you been drinking, Gus?"

He smiled awkwardly and shrugged his shoulders. "A couple of pints at The UB Chip, nothing major. Can we talk … please?" he asked, making a conscious effort not to let his newly acquired speech impediment resurface.

She leant against the front door and as she did the sway of her hips started to do strange things to Thoroughgood's head, but folding her arms Celine replied coldly: "Talk about what, Gus? You haven't shown much desire to speak to me over the last few days, so what's changed now?"

Thoroughgood looked up and collected his thoughts. "A conversation I had with Declan Meechan about an hour ago."

It was a line that seemed to take Celine completely by surprise and one that melted her previously icy self-composure. Pushing the door back, she said: "I s'pose you better come in, then."

Ten minutes later, Thoroughgood found himself once more parked on the outsize white leather settee, shifting uncomfortably while he waited for Celine to finish fixing herself a Bacardi & Coke. He resolved that this was not going to turn into a one-way grovelling session because, as the voice in his head confirmed, 'You ain't the one in the wrong here, mate.'

The fact she kept those delicious chocolate-brown eyes fixed down on her drink preparations and would not look his way once, never mind say a word, was hardly filling him with hope and indeed the only words that could be heard were Bowie's lounge-lizard smooth lyrics to 'China Girl'.

Eventually she slinked around the open-plan kitchen maisonette and as she walked towards him he noticed that in her left hand was a can of Oranjeboom, which she handed to him in silence.

Celine sat down just a foot away from him, the rich and spicy notes of her favourite 'Poison' perfume started to intoxicate him for the second time that night.

She sipped slowly on her B&C but Celine's reluctance to look his way was starting to fill Thoroughgood with a mounting dread that something had indeed happened between Meechan and her: that now Celine's awkward sullen silence was nothing less than a confession of her guilt.

As dread gave way to a burning anger, Thoroughgood snapped the Oranjeboom's ring pull open and took a long swig, then set the can down a little too heavily onto the dark glass coffee table in front of him.

His ire starting to unhinge him, Thoroughgood leant forward and said: "So why don't you tell me about you and your friend Declan?"

Celine placed her drink down next to a copy of Hello! magazine, her eyes taking in the agitated tremor of movement through Thoroughgood's legs in time to the guitar solo at the heart of China Girl and as Bowie told them to "Sssh," she spoke.

"What exactly did Declan say, Gus?"

Thoroughgood took another mouthful of Oranjeboom. "Well, Celine, as it happens he told me that he wants you. But let me ask you a question, the only one that really matters: has he had you already?"

So rapid was the almost feline speed with which her left hand shot out and administered a stinging slap, Thoroughgood, in his half-inebriated state, didn't see it coming.

"For Chrissakes, Celine," he hissed rubbing his jaw. "Just what do you expect me to ask when he follows me to The Chip, tells me he wants you and claims you've already made a 'decision'?"

Bowie hit the almost insouciant notes of 'Let's Dance' with casual arrogance and Thoroughgood swore. He jumped up and headed over for her Amstrad stereo tower. "I'm sorry ... I can't take any more fuckin' Bowie," he snarled, before whipping the needle from the LP, then turning back to glower Celine's way over his can of Oranjeboom.

She pulled her knees up to her chest and wrapped her arms around them and although Celine's vulnerability pulled at Thoroughgood's heartstrings, his anger would not be assuaged.

Rifling a hand through his black strands, a dread realisation seeped through him and nausea started to pervade through his body. "Jesus, Celine, what have you done?" Thoroughgood asked, his words trailing off.

Her eyes welled with tears. "I'm sorry, Gus," she said and in three words he felt his world collapse.

Rubbing his fingers over his mouth, Thoroughgood couldn't help himself demanding the gory details. "So it was the other night after Bonham's? Must've been. What happened, did the Dom-bloody-Pérignon go to your head? For crying out loud, Celine, what happened, did he promise you the earth, tell you the sky's the limit and the next minute you've dropped your knickers and wham, bam, he's seeing the stars?"

Pacing back and forward, the dam of his self-restrain burst, Thoroughgood couldn't help his rage pouring out. "Didn't that whole business with Dawson mean anything to you? Chrissakes, Celine, do you think you would have got out of that one alive if me and Hardie hadn't come calling and this ... this is how you repay me?" he seethed, shaking his head in disbelief and placing the can down shakily on the Amstrad.

But as he did so, Thoroughgood almost failed to hear, perhaps refused to comprehend, the words that were now coming out of Celine's mouth, words that drove the ultimate dagger through his heart. "I'm sorry, but I … I don't think I love you, Gus," she said from behind her knees.

So Meechan had been right, she had made a decision and now it hit him like one of Iron Mike's right hooks and despite himself, Thoroughgood's hands reached for his head and clamped onto his face with increasing pressure as he closed his eyes and tried to shut out the awful truth.

Then gritting his teeth, he ripped his fingers away and stared her way. "And that, my darling, is all I need to know," he said. Taking a deep breath, he stalked past her, desperate to lose himself in the night.

As she watched him go, Celine buried her head in her arms and sobbed.

Chapter Thirty-Six

THE GREEN TRANSIT pulled up at the side of the kerb and McGrain, his face taut at the knowledge they had reached a crucial juncture on the job, turned to Spider. "OK, big man, so get the motor parked up somewhere discreet and then make your way back to us as soon as you can. Gregsy will be keeping a look out for you at the rear of the bank. Keep your eyes open and yer wits about you, just in case there is anyone dodgy about and if there is, then we need to know on the walkie-talkie tout de suite!" he concluded, flicking a quick wink his mate's way.

Spider stretched his uninjured hand towards his old brother-in-arms and the two closed palms and locked shoulders in a gesture of comradeship that dated back from their days in the Legion. "Aye, when this is aw done, Tony, we can lay back somewhere hot and raise a glass to Ferg."

"Agreed," replied McGrain, a slight hint of emotion clouding his eyes despite his grimace. He clicked his door handle down and swung his denim-clad legs out of the vehicle, making his way towards the rear of the van and opening its doors.

When they sprang open, they revealed Gregsy and Parlane on opposite sides of the van, their faces etched with tension. McGrain smiled at them reassuringly. "Okay, boys, all we need to do is get in there without being spotted by any clever dick who thinks we look a bit dodgy, 'cause once we are in then nothing is gonna stop us pulling off this turn. Now bring your kitbags and let's get movin'," he rapped.

They jumped out of the van and McGrain slammed the doors shut. He administered a firm slap on the metal to let Spider know he was good to go and was rewarded with the Transit drawing away almost instantaneously, a bandaged hand waving out of the driver's window.

They made their way up Sugham Lane past a large whitewashed house and over semi-broken, weed-strewn tarmac, lined sporadically and incongruously with an oak tree and then some smaller beech trees that swayed in the dying of the evening light.

As he led the other two, McGrain constantly scanned for anything that might pose a threat to his best-laid plans.

The sound of a window snapping shut from a first-floor bedroom caused him to twitch and raise his right palm in a gesture to stay his confederates, but seeing there was no threat, the trio quickly moved on.

"300 yards to go, it's shootie-in!" volunteered Parlane helpfully, his hands dug deep in the green army jacket he had been given.

As they continued to make their way up the lane at a brisk walk, Gregsy's gaze took in the rear of the bank. "Nice one, the alarm's been deactivated: no lights on and the security camera's pointin' tae the stars. That's gid work, yer inside man knows his stuff, Tony!" He paused. "But that white van at the top of the lane could be a wee problem."

McGrain had spotted it and he gave a curt nod of his head. "Aye, there's a fuckin' Chinese takeaway, The Golden Sunset, just across the lane and I'd wager good money that's their delivery van. Just keep yer eyes peeled, 'cause if Charlie Chan comes blunderin' out, we've got a fuckin' problem," he said, before continuing at double time, his heavy Legion kitbag slung over his right shoulder.

Walking past a graffiti-daubed, flat-roofed garage, the grimy rough-cast of the bank's rear extension, which had been built to provide a staffroom, loomed large and Parlane, his shoulders starting to drop as he began to relax, said: "Nearly there, it's a piece o' piss, McGrain."

But he had spoken to soon.

Just as they passed a small wall 10 yards away from the rear of the bank, the sound of an accented male voice singing could clearly be heard coming around the corner from the main street at the side opposite to the NatWest.

And to their disbelief a small Chinese man ambled out in front of them, his arms filled with a cardboard box from which a series of white plastic bags could be seen billowing in the night breeze, as he walked along the side of the van.

McGrain appraised the potential threat and instantly barked his orders: "Okay, if he gets in the van without looking' our way we let him go; if his eyes wander, I'll deal with him and you two get yourselves in the back of the bank pronto, got it?"

"Nae bother, Tony," replied Gregsy while Parlane nodded.

The delivery driver – a slight, balding middle-aged man – made his way to the rear of the van. Balancing his box on his left knee, he jammed it against one of the vehicle's rear doors while he shot his right hand round and tried to click open the door handle without dropping his precious cargo.

Behind him, around 10 yards away and closing, three sets of eyes bored into his back and prayed he didn't turn around.

Eventually the van's right side door sprang open and the deliveryman clamped his now spare right hand back on the box and shoved it into the rear of the vehicle, all the time singing away to himself.

But as the box slid through the door, one of the plastic bag's handles caught the door lever: the bag was drawn up and a square silver foil carton tipped out and dropped onto the ground with a splat, spilling what looked like a portion of fried rice onto the weed-punctured tarmacadam.

The deliveryman swore and proceeded to scoop up the rice with his hands, attempting to re-fill the container with its former contents; but as he did so, guilt got the better of him and he looked up furtively to see if there was anyone observing his devious actions.

It was then that he saw the three grim-faced Glaswegians watching him from half-a-dozen yards away, just to the left of the bank's rear entrance and as the deliveryman's nervous glance flicked towards the building's back gate, suspicion etched itself across his face.

From the middle of the three-man line-up, McGrain stepped forward and quickly covered the ground between him and the startled deliveryman. As he did so, he reached inside his army jacket and pulled out a sawn-off shotgun, ramming it against the driver's head.

"Awright, Fu Man-fuckin'-chu, make one dumb move and I'll blow the head off yer shoulders. Now get the box back out and do as I bleedin' well say and maybees you might live to enjoy some prawn crackers for breakfast tomorrow," he spat.

Chapter Thirty-Seven

THE DELIVERYMAN'S EYES saucered in fear and his instant reaction was to raise his hands high and start to babble shrilly in his native tongue. McGrain could neither understand nor had time to decipher his panic-laced words and he rammed the sawn-off under the driver's jaw and forced him up against the van's doors.

"Shut the fuck up," he spat, the violence and tone persuading the driver that silence was the best policy. As his tongue stilled, McGrain spoke, calmly yet with an edge of menace: "Do you understand me?"

"I, I do, sir, yes, yes, I do, sir," trembled the deliveryman.

"Excellent, then do as you're told and you might just make it out of this alive. Now get the fuckin' delivery out of the van and start walking that way," ordered McGrain, pointing with the sawn-off to the rear of the bank, his gaze steady but simmering with violence.

"Very good, sir, very good, sir," stammered the deliveryman, shakily doing as he was bid. When he turned back, his arms were laden with the box full of takeaways. McGrain forced the door shut with the sole of his Doc Marten and flicked the barrel of his gun in the direction he wanted his new friend to travel.

A few yards down the lane, the sawn-off still levelled against the back of the deliveryman's head, McGrain took a last sweep of the immediate area and, confident that no prying eyes had seen the drama that had just unfolded, shoved his captive in through the bank's rear entrance gate, which Parlane was helpfully holding open.

"A chinky for supper, ah, you should'ne have bothered, McGrain, man!" he quipped.

McGrain was in no mood for joviality. "I assume you've got the keys for the gate from the security cupboard? So just shut it behind us and get the fuckin' thing locked, then as soon as you're satisfied no one has seen anything, get yourself indoors."

For once, Parlane refrained from a wisecrack and replied with a curt nod of understanding as McGrain frogmarched the deliveryman at gunpoint in through the rear door of the staff entrance and into the kitchen, where Gregsy had helpfully placed their three large kitbags on top of the worktops.

The panic-stricken takeaway driver began to stammer again and beg to be freed: "You let me go, mister, and I bring you something nice," he pleaded.

"Now listen good, Charlie Chan. Put the box on top of the pool table, and then sit down on that fucking chair and get your hands out in front of you, keeping them together," ordered McGrain, while nodding to Gregsy to go to one of the kitbags. "Get the tape out and bind his wrists, but leave his mouth free, for the time being …"

Within moments, Gregsy had done as he was bid. The sound of the backdoor being locked echoed through into the kitchen and Parlane joined them. "Aye, dinner aside, you've gotta real problem, Houston!" he said.

"Never mind the one-liners … what's happenin' outside, Parlane, is the lane clear?" snapped McGrain.

"Quiet as the grave, though that's only gonna last until the punters at the chinky start phonin' in and greetin' about their dinner no turnin' up. The van's a fuckin' problem and it needs tae be dumped sometime fuckin' soon, McGrain," concluded Parlane, before adding: "Ya dirty slant-eyed bastard, scoopin' up that rice aff the deck and stuffin' it back in tae the carton … ah, ya mingin' wee …"

As Parlane advanced, the delivery driver brought his knees up to his chest and pulled his forearms down, shutting his eyes and beginning to blub incoherently.

But McGrain blocked Parlane's route to goal with a single step. "That isn't going to help, now back off, Parlane," he said, then turned to Gregsy. "Get on the walkie-talkie and see what's happening with Spider. We need him back here pronto tae move the delivery van." McGrain turned his leaden stare the deliveryman's way. "Okay, Charlie, so tell me how many people you got working in The Golden Sunset and how long before they're gonna be trying to contact you?"

But before he could answer, Gregsy had bound his wrists and rifling through his pockets found both the vehicle keys and an outsize mobile phone, which he placed on the pool table with a knowing smile.

McGrain flicked a tepid smile at him. "Okay, Gregsy, you're gonna have to babysit Charlie here so that when the mobile goes he gives the right answer, while you keep lookout from the back of the shop, Parlane." Then he leaned forward until his face was just inches away from the trembling driver. "I asked you a fuckin' question, Charlie …?" the threat in his voice, even though his words had been spoken in an even tone, was unmistakable.

"Sorry, mister, they bell me on mobile if take more 15 minutes make first delivery," he stammered at 100 miles an hour.

McGrain looked at the kitchen clock on the wall above the sink. "Fuck, so we have less than 5 minutes before they start askin' questions. We need that fuckin' van moved pronto. Gregsy, try Spider again. If you don't get him this time then one of you will have to get it moved."

Gregsy shook his head in concern. "This ain't good, Tony. All this traffic comin' and goin' from the back of the bank, sooner or later someone's gonna see something we don't want them tae and put two and two together. After all, it's a bleedin' bank."

McGrain nodded grimly but said nothing, his mind assessing the whys and wherefores of their predicament and the danger it was now placing the entire job under, but before he could speak, Gregsy's walkie-talkie crackled into life. "Le Boudin to L'Étranger. Van parked up nice and discreet, I'm coming up the lane, get the back door open,"

Spider said, using the codename he'd picked up in the Legion: 'le boudin', or blood sausage, a nickname for the gear rolled up and carried atop the legionnaires' packs.

* * *

The surprise on Spider's face when he clapped eyes on the Chinese deliveryman was replaced with immediate realisation. Turning to McGrain, he said: "So our chinky friend has blundered into the plot and fucked things right up. We need to get him off the premises, Tony, and tout de suite. I take it that the van at the top of the lane is his delivery vehicle?"

McGrain nodded in the affirmative and then looking over at Parlane, snapped: "Tape his mouth over." His grey gaze returned to his number two. "Okay, I don't see that we've got any choice, Charlie here needs to be taken out of the bank and driven somewhere nice and quiet in his delivery van. Because when the punters start complaining about their takeaways failing to show, the first thing our friends in the Chinese are gonna do is come out looking for the van and when they see it's parked up outside … how long do you think before they get the fuckin' polis involved? We can't have any unwanted attention on our doorstep, Spider, and I need Gregsy for the safe just in case we get any funny business, while Mr Parlane here is better off where I can see him …" concluded McGrain knowingly.

Spider nodded curtly in recognition that he was the obvious choice to ensure the deliveryman's exit from the premises. "Keys?" he asked and was answered by Gregsy throwing the vehicle's jangling key ring his way.

Reaching out without thinking, he caught them in his bandaged right mitt and winced from the pain of his wound. Gritting his teeth, Spider grabbed the deliveryman with his left hand and ripped him from the leather kitchen seat. "Come on, wee man, rice and easy," he said before chortling at his own joke and propelling the heavily sweating man towards the rear exit.

But before he reached the door, Parlane's harsh Glaswegian voice barked out a warning: "For fuck's sake, it's the bleedin' filth!"

McGrain immediately surged past Spider and the delivery driver to hover at Parlane's shoulder. "What do you mean? Where, man?"

Squinting out from behind a net curtain, Parlane pointed down the lane to their right as a marked police car could be seen crawling slowly up the lane before drawing to a stop just behind the delivery van.

"Fuck me gently," spat McGrain.

CHAPTER THIRTY-EIGHT

TEN YARDS BEFORE the delivery van, the marked police Escort drew to a stop and a moment later two white-shirted male officers got out, slamming their vehicle doors shut. Without bothering to lock the Escort, they swaggered up Sugham Lane.

Parlane immediately pushed the curtain back across the glass-panelled door and took a step back. "Here we go, someone's either called the filth to grass up something dodgy or the Lancashire Polis are every bit as greedy and fuckin' lazy as their cousins up the road in Glasgae."

Behind Parlane, McGrain cradled his sawn-off in silent anticipation of the possibilities that were about to play out. To his left, Spider had unsheathed the rhinoceros-horn, ivory-hilted janbiya dagger that was the twin of McGrain's and grazed the deliveryman's throat with its edge. "I'd stay nice and quiet if I was you, Charlie," he whispered viciously.

Although his whole being was shaking, the terrified driver did as he was bid.

Outside, the two cops had drawn level with the bank's wrought-iron rear entrance gate … just as a doubt exploded in McGrain's head. "Fuck it, who was last in through the gate? Is the padlock locked?"

"Shit," replied Spider.

Yards away, in the lane, the smaller of the two cops, a ruddy individual, who seemed to be attempting to make up for his lack of inches by wearing his domed custodian helmet, glanced towards the gate. His blunt Lancastrian voice thrummed into life: "Hey up, Les, what we got hear? Padlock's loose, innit."

His slightly stooped colleague, the three stripes on his shoulder indicating that he was a sergeant, immediately snapped his glance at the bank's gate. "Thursday night: that Glaswegian tart, the cleaner, closes up. Little bitch is training to be an auxiliary nurse, so's I heard, Sid."

"Aye, and you know what they say about a nurse, gaffer?" asked the stocky cop now identified as Sid, before they both answered at the same time in a routine jest that clearly had been repeated since the dawn of time: "There's only two certainties in life and one's a nurse!" Then the duo's chorus of choreographed mirth boomed out.

Inside the bank a sense of mystified amazement swept over McGrain and his men as they listened to the laughing policemen and eyed each other nervously.

Their hilarity over, both officers stood at the gate and to the horror of those inside, its wrought-iron frame sprang open when Sid gave it a push.

"Aye aye, maybe we better take us a closer look," said Les as it squeaked open.

Inside, McGrain nodded towards Gregsy and watched as the peterman flicked the safety off his pistol. "We've got a problem, Spider. Take Charlie Chan back into the corridor. Gregsy, Parlane, get down behind either end of the pool table," he whispered in a barely audible voice, and as his minions did as they were bid he slammed himself against the wall to the side of the kitchen door and waited for the strong arm of the law to make its presence felt.

Outside in the small rear yard, Sergeant Les was running his eyes around the perimeter of the bank checking for anything that was out of place.

As he did so, PC Sid tried the back door and gave a sigh of relief when it remained locked fast despite his forceful attempt to open it. "Door's locked, gaffer," said Sid as he tried to peer through the net curtain into the building, and added: "It's hard to say ... but I reckons all's well."

"That's as maybe, Sid my son, but the alarm ain't on. Might just be an oversight 'cause I heard at the golf club bar the other night that old Revie the manager likes to give our little Scottish tart a quick poke before he leaves, so maybees she had somethin' else on her mind. Hey up, I think you'd be as well to radio in and check all is good."

McGrain had heard every word of the two cops' conversation. He knew that he had to act quickly: once the cops spotted the CCTV camera facing towards the stars then it would be game over and the only way to escape would be to come out shooting.

"I just don't fuckin' believe it," McGrain muttered to himself under his breath. His mounting rage at the cruel hand Lady Luck seemed about to deal him and his boys throbbed through his head as he strained his ears, desperately trying to pick up every word being spoken 2 yards away, from the other side of the door.

Outside, Constable Sid was already talking to his control room: "Panda Charlie, Constable U426 Dawson, reporting alarm inactivation at the NatWest Bank, 380 Heysham Road, please confirm all well, over."

Inside, McGrain signalled to his boys to get ready for the moment of truth. He drew back from the wall, levelled his sawn-off and waited for the inevitable. McGrain had decided that their only chance was to take the two cops by surprise as quickly as possible and hope that they managed to subdue them before a cry for help was put out.

In the small yard, his hands on his hips, Sergeant Les James scanned the rear of the bank, waiting expectantly for his control room to answer.

"'U' Uniform control to U426 Constable Dawson, all well, Bank Manager Revie has called in earlier to backshift to inform them there is a light bulb out on the alarm system and Pointer will be attending first thing in the morning to rectify. Stand down, all well. Repeat, all well."

Dawson couldn't help the sense of relief that swept over him translating into an irreverent pat on Sergeant James' right arm. "We're bleedin' sorted, Les. Now let's go to The Golden Sunset and get the duck 'n' plum sauce in, 'cause I'm soddin' starving, me I am!"

The sergeant's spare features crumpled into a warm smile as he contemplated feeding time. "Aye, Sid, and your hands're on the buzzer, lad," and at that the small yard reverberated with another round of throaty laughter. The two cops made their way out through the gate, ramming it shut so that the catch clanked with the impact, and made their way to the front of the lane, somehow having failed to spot the skied CCTV camera on top of the extension's flat roof.

Inside, McGrain rested the barrel of his sawn-off on his shoulder and sighed. "Sweet Christ," he said and dabbed away the beads of sweat that had broken out on his brow.

Across at the pool table, Parlane said: "Aye, you could'nae make it up, McGrain, how spawny can yous get to hae a couple of comedians like that on yer case!"

CHAPTER THIRTY-NINE

BUT THE SENSE of relief inside the bank was fleeting, for McGrain now found himself starting to worry about what would happen when the two cops made their way off into The Golden Sunset. He took a deep breath and then told it like it was: "Okay, here we go, these cops are a real fuckin' problem for us. Ten to one they'll blurt out something about the delivery van being left outside, or start asking if they can speak to the delivery driver to check if he has seen anything dodgy. All of which means we need to make sure the van is gone before they come back out with their fuckin' chop sueys." Stopping for air, he glanced Spider's way and then barked out an order as if he was still on the parade ground of the Légion Étrangère.

"Okay, Spider, you need to get Charlie here back into the van, get it tae fuck, then do the needful, and I need it done yesterday. Gregsy, you'll follow them out and get Charlie into the rear of the van, allowing Spider into the driver's seat asap, then get your arse back here as quick as you can. Parlane, you'll keep your head down inside the back door holding the fort, while I cover Spider, his little Chinese friend and Gregsy out into the lane and make sure they are gone without any hitches. Understood?" McGrain snapped. He swept everybody in the staffroom with his hawklike stare and was met with an immediate nod of heads.

Parlane unlocked the back door and received a curt grunt of thanks from Spider as he frogmarched the bound, gagged and quaking driver out into the small yard, the curved blade of his

183

janbiya wedged against the side of the man's bare neck, with Gregsy following in their slipstream.

McGrain immediately assumed a position at the gate, peering through its bars to the right, then the left, to make sure there was no unwanted pedestrian traffic from either side of Sugham Lane. Fortunately, it was dead.

The silence was deafening, as split seconds seemed to draw on interminably forever, such was the tension that filled their minds and bodies as they tried to circumvent another mini-crisis that could blow everything to kingdom come.

"Okay, you're good to go, big man," said McGrain and patted Spider on his back. The burly henchman went out into the lane, dropping the janbiya down until it assumed a more discreet position in the small of the deliveryman's back.

The big man closed the dozen yards between the gate and the vehicle in a measured stride with Gregsy riding shotgun at his shoulder, his brooding gaze firmly on the end of the lane, towards the area just outside the front of The Golden Sunset.

From the bank gate, McGrain trained his sawn-off on the front of the lane and said his prayers of deliverance in silence.

Behind him, Parlane's darting eyes took in the unfolding drama and wondered how he might yet turn the crisis to his best advantage … but failed to find any good answer.

As soon as they reached the van, Spider rammed Charlie against the vehicle's rear doors and turned to Gregsy. "Get the baw in the onion bag, Gregsy, and make sure he's lassoed in good and tight. Then get the fuck back intae the NatWest, son."

Clamping his hands on the deliveryman's trembling shoulders, Gregsy answered with a nod of the head, but before he disappeared around the front of the van, Spider called out: "Bonne chance, peterman!"

All the while, Spider's eyes remained fixed on the front of the lane. He opened the vehicle door and jumped into the seat, then rammed the keys in the ignition. Hearing the rear doors open and the clunk of a dead weight on the van floor, he turned 45 degrees behind him to see if Gregsy had secured their captive.

The peterman was in no mood to hang about and no sooner had his prisoner hit the deck than he manhandled him onto a bench seat. Gregsy whipped out a length of rope and started to lash him to the metal spars inside the van wall, the deliveryman gagging with nausea on the cleaner's chamois that was stuffed in his mouth.

His victim secured, Gregsy flashed a thumbs up to Spider and said: "Take care, big man, and keep us posted on the walkie-talkie." Receiving a reciprocal yellowed grin, he turned and bailed out.

Spider turned the ignition on and to his relief the heavy thrumming of the diesel engine burned into life. He relaxed a little into the driver's seat, before easing the handbrake off, and clicking the gear shaft into first. He eased the van 10 yards forward to the junction of the lane and the main Heysham Road, a smile of relief breaking out over his face.

But just as he checked the traffic flow left and right and started to inch the delivery van onto the main road, Dawson and James, their arms laden with their evening snack, walked out the front door of The Golden Sunset.

As they did so, their eyes met and held Spider's dark gaze.

Realisation at the calamity that was overtaking him swept over the big man and through gritted teeth he groaned "Shite!"

Yards away on the pavement, PC Dawson was first to respond: "Hey up, Les, who the fook is that drivin' the delivery van? It sure as hell ain't wee man Mao?"

"Yer damn tootin, Sid me son, why don't you check with Michael the manager—" but before Sergeant James could complete his instructions, Spider put his foot to the floor and the van shot out onto the main road leaving just the stench of burning rubber.

"Never mind that, Les, the van's been fookin' nicked, get on the radio and post a lookout! Let's go, matey, we've got ourselves a bastardin' hot vehicle pursuit!" crowed Dawson, already breaking into a trot back down Sugham Lane, his gaffer following in his wake, all the while breathlessly barking out vehicle description, direction of travel and occupant description to the increasingly excited female controller in 'U' Uniform HQ Divisional control room.

As the two cops charged past the bank's rear gate, Sergeant James let the adrenaline rush he was now surfing get the better of him. "Come on, Sid, by the looks of the big bastard behind the wheel I'd say it's a cert the van's being stolen for use on a much bigger job elsewhere, you never know what we might turn up, matey!"

Crouched down just inside the gate, partially concealed by a wheelie bin, McGrain cradled his head in his hands.

Behind him, Parlane shot Gregsy a worried glance.

CHAPTER FORTY

SPIDER SLAMMED his foot to the floor of the Sherpa 200 but the agricultural 1.8 litre diesel engine wasn't built for speed and barely responded. He ground his teeth in anger at the knowledge there was absolutely no chance he would be able to outrun the police vehicle that any second now would be shooting out of Sugham Lane.

In short, the game was up if he couldn't come up with some ad hoc plan to avert impending disaster.

Checking the driver-side mirror, he saw that the police car had failed to find the main road and Spider's brooding gaze quickly shifted to the immediate horizon, where a hard right that would take him down towards the coast was coming up. Slowly the fragments of a desperate plan began to piece themselves together in his mind.

Taking the right turn almost on two wheels, Spider struggled to control the Sherpa's steering as the vehicle's woeful suspension let loose a shockwave of motion through its metallic shell; from the back, he heard the deliveryman, despite his gag, howling like a demented dog.

Spider smiled viciously.

Yet while the hysterics of his prisoner reverberated around the vehicle, the familiar strident tones of a police siren confirmed that his pursuers were now firmly in his slipstream.

On the passenger's seat his walkie-talkie crackled into life and a harsh Glaswegian voice added to the cacophony. "L'Étranger to Le Boudin, come in, over," demanded McGrain.

Spider reached over and scooped up the walkie-talkie with his left hand. "Go ahead, L'Étranger," he replied.

"Update please?" asked McGrain almost politely; but his voice betrayed the tension Spider had heard on countless operations and jobs during their 20-year association.

As the Sherpa started to descend a hill, the darkness in his mirror was illuminated by the flashing lights of a marked police Escort.

"Merde!" spat Spider and once again levelled his right foot onto the accelerator.

McGrain's voice ground out from the walkie-talkie: "Repeat, as tu un plan stratégique?"

"Oui, mon ami, un plan d'action magnifique, but for now, au revoir, mon frère de sang," and Spider ended the conversation with a blood-curdling laugh that did little to reassure McGrain all was likely to be well.

The road was now leaving the edges of suburbia and where houses had lined either side of the route, there were now steep banks of green grass. As Spider wrestled with the Sherpa's steering wheel on another sharp bend, he was met with the sight of a tractor starting to reverse out of a field.

Ramming the accelerator to the floor once again, Spider managed to thread the needle and get the Sherpa through the rapidly narrowing gap between agricultural vehicle and hedge, the cloth-capped, pipe smoking idiot driving it grinning inanely at him and waving wildly all the while.

As he passed Farmer Barleymow, the middle digit of Spider's left hand shot up and the chuckling smile that had previously beamed from the farmer's ruddy face was replaced by a furrowed brow and a volley of abuse: "Cheeky prat, come back here an' I'll have yer guts for garters!" raged the farmer as the Sherpa sped past.

As he checked his mirror, Spider could see that in his rage the farmer had managed to overdo his reverse manoeuvre and had now rammed the tractor into the grass verge at the opposite side of the road. From the other side of the vehicle, the police car sat stationary and helpless, its lights blazing and siren blasting: all to no avail, as the farmer shook a fist at the irate members of the local constabulary whose progress he had now brought to a juddering halt.

Checking the roadway ahead, Spider saw that about 100 yards to his right what looked like some kind of old, deserted coastal track forked down to the main route, which a sign had just confirmed was the Shore Road.

This was the opportunity that he had been looking for and as he turned the Sherpa onto the sand-washed, barely visible tarmac, Spider once again replayed the likely outcomes that awaited him if, as he had been taught in the Legion, he seized the initiative.

Firstly, as he knew, there was no way he could outrun the cops, and in any case, even if they hadn't already made it, a call for backup would soon see him surrounded.

If he abandoned the Transit and tried to make his escape over foreign terrain he had no prior knowledge of then it would not be too long before he made a mistake that would lead to his capture.

Ruefully, he shook his head in realisation that the course he was now mentally setting was one that would escalate his current situation, yet was the best way out of the increasingly deep hole he was in: and all because of one idiot little Chinese takeaway driver and his grubby little fingers.

Spider brought the van to a halt and clicked the internal catch for the bonnet. He jumped out of the cabin, leaving the driver's door deliberately open to swing in the night wind, and made his way around to the front of the vehicle, then snapped the bonnet open, mounting it on to the supporting catch. Pulling the janbiya free from his green army jacket, he walked round to the rear of the van, opened the doors and jumped in.

Towering over the terrorised deliveryman Spider gave a rueful shake of his head. "Je suis désolé, Charlie," he whispered, then bent down and pulled the driver's head back against the van wall before ripping the janbiya's glinting steel across his throat.

As the blood spattered over his victim and shot across his hands, Spider vaulted out of the van and secreted himself in a grass gulley just to the right of the vehicle, wiping his stained paws on the foliage as he waited for the cops to blunder into his trap.

CHAPTER FORTY-ONE

DESOLATE AND DESPAIRING, Thoroughgood had made his way back to Crown Gardens and opened the front door to number three unseeing.

For the entire walk home he couldn't stop himself replaying the conversations he'd had that evening.

What really got to him was Meechan's confidence that Celine had indeed made her decision but also his own singular ineptitude and failure to find out just why she had really reached that decision when he had had the opportunity.

'I'm sorry, but I ... I don't think I love you, Gus,' might have been a clue, but surely there was more to it than a one-night fling with Meechan? Yet as he now readily admitted to himself, if there had been, he had failed to find out what that was and instead let his pride get in the way.

If there was any point in fighting for what they had ... whatever that was ... it was too late now.

He unconsciously plucked a record from the Ballantine's whisky box and Bon Jovi's 'New Jersey' magically found its way from his hands onto the Sony turntable. Before he knew it, he was being treated to 'Bad Medicine'. The irony of the song's opening line, 'Your love is like bad medicine', penetrated the fug of his inner turmoil, and as his right hand closed round a glass of Lagavulin and his left lit up the Café Crème now dangling from his mouth, Thoroughgood sought some solace by wallowing in visions of the beauty of Celine's golden skin; the smooth contours of her so-perfect face flashed before him so vividly that he could almost taste her.

Yet the realisation that she may now be cradled in Meechan's arms proved too hurtful for him, the ultimate conclusion that perhaps they were, as his grandfather would say, 'just not right for each other', at last all too glaringly obvious.

Yet that was something Thoroughgood was unwilling to accept right here, right now, in this whisky-stained, cigar-wreathed moment of misery, entombed in a crummy living room that was like a monument to late-seventies bad taste and which never ceased to depress him.

As his eyes swept his pathetic accommodation and stopped on the bamboo-blind-covered hatchway that punctuated the three-quarter 'wall' that was supposed to separate the bedroom from the living-room-cum-lounge, Thoroughgood had to admit that there was no wonder Celine had opted for Meechan.

Super-smooth Meechan and his handmade double-breasted suits, Rolex watches and the rest of his gangster bling.

The tortured vortex of his own ineptitude, his pathetic living premises and, when all else failed, the fact that a Partick Thistle supporter was never likely to get a girl like Celine, engulfed Thoroughgood.

'Aye, and when was the last time you were up at Firhill, part-timer?' snapped the voice in his head in disgust.

At last Thoroughgood exploded in rage and launched the whisky glass at the partition wall … admittedly after he had drained the Lagavulin.

As the glass clattered off the wall and dropped to the petrol-green carpeted floor with a dull clunk, the fact that the bedroom 'wall' had been left with a dent rather than the glass smashing left Thoroughgood shaking his head at another piece of confirmation of just what a pitiful existence he was immersed in.

Had it really been worth fighting Dawson and The Shift for this? What had he won? The right to see through his probation, but what did that really amount too?

'Should have gone to Jordanhill and got on the teacher training course, mate,' advised the voice in his head and as it did so he heard a rap on the flat's outside wall … Old Miss Lynch, the anything but merry spinster next door, was letting him know her displeasure in the time-honoured manner of belting her walking stick on the adjoining wall between their two 'residences'.

Turning down the Sony, Thoroughgood's mindset was hardly helped by the next track on the playlist: 'Born To Be My Baby'. But as Jon Bon Jovi's husky voice boomed out of his speakers, Thoroughgood found another face forcing its way into his consciousness … that of Emma McCabe.

He retrieved the whisky glass from the carpet, poured himself another Lagavulin and took a drag on the next Café Crème; Friday morning was fast approaching and it was his weekend off, so what did it matter how he greeted it?

Slowly, though, his green eyes moist but refusing to shed tears, he forced himself to focus on Meechan and the information he had furnished him with.

Swirling the delicious peaty harshness of the malt around the inside of his mouth, Thoroughgood tried to map out a plan of what to do with the information … info that was way too hot for him to handle alone.

There was only one place for it and that was with Numan and Malcolm. It may also be time that he made contact with Collins, for the Cat would be ideal to start carrying out some sort of surveillance on Meechan and prove that two could play at that game.

Sitting nodding to himself in his hideous checked armchair, gazing vacuously at the ridiculous orange wallpaper, Thoroughgood stared into his whisky and winced as Bon Jovi's anthem to unfailing love 'I'll Be There For You' filled the air in an enforced whisper.

As he did so, the voice in his head started to impart some home-grown truth to him: 'Come on, mate, did you ever think it was gonna be any different?'

Despite himself, Thoroughgood gave an involuntarily nod to the negative and took another mouthful of malt. He gritted his teeth and let the voice in his head make a vow for him, a vow that he would use Meechan to blow O'Toole and the Widowmaker out of the water and then turn it all on Meechan, when the time was right.

Because if it meant sucking up the pain of seeing 'her' with him in order to use Meechan to get him out of this shithole, make something of himself and prove them all wrong, then that was exactly what he would do.

Raising the glass of Lagavulin in the air, Thoroughgood made his pledge: "Here's to you, Meechan, may you be the architect of your own downfall and may you only find that out when I bring you to your knees. Sláinte!"

Grabbing the now half-empty bottle of malt, Thoroughgood resolved to meet up with the Unit in the morning … whenever that came.

Chapter Forty-Two

HIS HEAD POUNDED.

The stale taste of the whisky mixed with the residual tobacco of last night's cigars, coating the inside of his mouth in a fur that seemed to stick his tongue to its roof and forcing him to take constant swigs from the bottle of water he had purchased on the way into the tube station.

But now the jolt of the Glasgow Subway's toing and froing was causing waves of nausea to sweep over him as he swayed this way and that, clamping his right hand ever tighter around the steel standing pole to try and stop himself from being thrown from one side of the carriage to the other.

Yet while he battled to keep upright, he began to worry that the slurred voicemail message he had delivered on the Unit's office answerphone ... sometime last night ... wasn't the smartest way to announce he had some info for them, so waves of guilt competed with those of his nausea for prominence within his body.

His eyes shut, his normally dark features now sporting a distinctly green hue, he swallowed a mouth of rising bile back down where it came from and took a deep breath of diesel-tinted air.

"You all right, son?" asked a grating female voice immediately to his right. Startled, Thoroughgood opened his eyes to check if the words had indeed been addressed to him and was met with the enquiring gaze of a woman perhaps in her mid 50s, smart navy raincoat unbuttoned and a bright-yellow turtleneck peeking out, with a red silk headscarf tied around her neck and a pair of thick, dark-rimmed glasses framing lively blue eyes that gave her artfully made-up features a striking quality.

"I've been better," admitted Thoroughgood, offering a tepid smile and then leaning onto the pole, shutting his eyes once again and praying for the end of his journey to come.

"Out on the randan were you, son?" asked the female, her persistence starting to unsettle Thoroughgood, who again opened his eyes and produced a wan smile but found to his amazement that the female, whose dark, once jet-black hair was teased up in a ruffle that sported a white streak through its centre, had started to sidle along the carriage seat and then alluringly pat the newly vacant seat, which she had just so obligingly created.

"Why don't you join me down here and let me take care of your motion sickness, young man," she said, a wolfish smile playing across her heavily made-up face, and before he could open his mouth she opened a cream handbag and pulled out a plastic bottle of Irn-Bru. "Take a sip of this, it'll soon put some lead in your pencil."

Thoroughgood couldn't help a smirk slipping across his face and for a moment his green eyes held her sparkling azure gaze, until another wave of nausea forced him to take a deep breath just as the Tube drew to a jarring halt with such intensity that his legs buckled and he dipped down until his face was level with her predatory gaze.

As their eyes locked again, this time just inches apart, her tongue slipped out of her mouth and ran along the top of her ruby-red, painted lips. "Er ... sorry," stumbled Thoroughgood, desperately trying to regain his balance and escape from a brief encounter that was, perhaps, a case of being in the right place at the wrong time.

As he straightened up, Thoroughgood took another deep breath and smiled again. "Thanks for your offer but this is my stop." Yet despite himself, he flashed a quick wink her way and was rewarded with another feline smile as he turned and set off through the thronging masses of Buchanan Street Underground Station.

Pounding along the pavement, he was soon making his way up St Vincent Street, mixing deep breaths of air with long swallows of water as he attempted to put together the information he was about to furnish the Unit with in a concise fashion.

Ten minutes later, he reached Pitt Street Force HQ, but before entering he quickly popped a Sharp's extra strong mint into his mouth, hoping its super strength would kill any residual stale alcohol still seeping from him.

Passing the silver-haired, immaculately uniformed commissionaire with a smile and a quick mumbled explanation that he was on his way to the fifth floor to see DS Malcolm and DC Numan, Thoroughgood was soon in the familiar brown-tiled corridor occasionally punctured by a window offering an impressive view of the Glasgow skyline that led along to the Unit's office.

Arriving at the grey door, as it always did, brought memories flooding back of the first time he had visited the Unit, his nerves jangling, mouth dry. Although the latter was once more the case, Thoroughgood smiled ruefully at the fact that this time it had not been caused by a case of the jitters.

Before rapping on the door, he noticed that the words 'Proactive Unit' had now been placed at head height and he shook his head ruefully at this development before knocking and being met with the unmistakeable sing-song of Malcolm's slightly lilting accent: "Come!"

As he entered the room, he found that the paint pots, cardboard boxes and ladders that had been present on his previous visit almost a year ago had been replaced with large Amstrad computers on each desk and Thoroughgood was struck by just how neat and concise everything was. It was all clean lines and cold precision, the only exception being a transistor radio placed on one of the windowsills, playing The Terry Wogan Radio 2 Breakfast Show.

From the corner of the room, a slightly gruff voice sprang into life: "Few sherbets last night was it, young Thoroughgood?" asked

DC Dennis Numan, springing out from behind his Amstrad and covering the distance between them in one bounding stride before almost snapping his hand in two with a vicelike handshake.

Thoroughgood winced awkwardly and mumbled: "Gotta lot going on, Dennis, and I have some info you need to hear."

"So, it wasn't just drink talking then, Angus!" laughed Malcolm.

"By Christ, is old Harry Currie that bad he's been driving you to the drink? Surely life in the CP ain't that grim?" asked Numan from behind his trademark wolfish grin.

"Nope, old Harry is ... not what I thought he was gonna be. It's the rest of the shit that seems to keep flowing in my direction that ..." and at that Thoroughgood shrugged his shoulders and retreated into silence.

"The Creepers giving you nightmares?" asked Malcolm and his words drew a startled look from the young cop at the realisation the newly christened Proactive Unit had clearly still been taking more than a passing interest in his progress – or lack of it.

"But that ain't why you're here, Gus, ma boy, is it?" asked Numan getting to the bottom line.

Thoroughgood shook his head and then, as Malcolm gestured at an empty chair to his left, he sat down and got to the point: "There's a lot to tell, and to be fair The Creepers are maybe a wee part of that, but have you ever heard of Declan Meechan?" he asked, his eyes flitting from Numan to Malcolm as he waited tensely for a reply.

The arching of Numan's greying eyebrows was all the confirmation he needed that the answer to that one was very much in the affirmative.

But it was Malcolm who replied: "You mean the coming man? Oh yes, we've heard of Declan Meechan, a young fella with more fingers in the pie than you've had hot dinners. Also someone who sees himself very much as the heir apparent to Jimmy Gray's West End Empire and from what Dennis has just uncovered, the crown prince is increasingly impatient to ascend to Gray's throne!"

"So why do you ask, Gus? Meechan is a bit of a stretch from your territory, isn't he?" queried Numan.

Thoroughgood rubbed his chin awkwardly. Aware that his explanation was messy and keen to avoid having to admit that his personal life had once again spilled into his professional, he took the circuitous route. "It's not just Meechan I'm here to speak about. Did you know that DI Ronan O'Toole is touting to Tony McGrain and vice versa?" he asked by way of an answer.

"O'Toole, that tosser? Aye, there have been rumours about that for long and weary. Funnily enough, there have also been rumours that O'Toole's been giving one to McGrain's missus, Pauline … aye, but that's gold-plated info for a CP cop to be coming by … no disrespect, Gus!" laughed Numan, clearly impressed by the quality of the data he was now being furnished with.

"Last year it was Davison and Rentoul and now it's O'Toole: how do you manage it? Rubbing up nasty pieces of work seems to be your specialist subject, Gus! Ever thought about a gig on Mastermind? I'm sure you could give old Magnus a run for his money!" jested Numan.

"I think I'll pass on that one," replied Thoroughgood with the obvious pun.

"Okay, joking aside, tell me how you've got under DI O'Toole's skin? More importantly, how the hell did you come by these particulars—"

But before Malcolm could finish his sentence, Numan did it for him: "Meechan?" he asked, his grey eyes boring into Thoroughgood's grey-green features like a wolf scenting its prey, and was met with a nodded affirmative.

"But what you've got to ask, son, is if Meechan has come by that type of info, then who has he got on the inside feeding it to him?" asked Numan.

"We know that McGrain's two main henchmen are big Fergus and Spider; what we need to be doing is some detailed intelligence work on them and seeing if we can come across anyone else who might be on the road with McGrain and his team and whose loyalty dear Tony may not command. Looks like you've gotta busy afternoon ahead, Dennis, as I've got to get this bloody review for ACC White finito by close of play or we may no longer be in existence!" said DS Malcolm, shrugging in frustration.

"No bother, gaffer. I'll make a few phone calls and put the feelers out. As we both know, in Glasgow someone's always willing to talk if they have their palms crossed with enough silver or are convinced it's wise to loosen their tongues by other means of persuasion," said Numan, sending an evil wink Thoroughgood's way that made it clear he would be spending the next few hours doing what he loved best.

CHAPTER FORTY-THREE

THE VETERAN DC's intuition had startled Thoroughgood and after a pause, he jerked his eyes in Numan's direction, holding his inquisitive gaze and shrugging his shoulders in resignation. "How did you know it was Meechan?"

"You could say it was an educated guess; although I'm not sure how you would come in contact with Meechan, other than perhaps a chance encounter in one of Gray's bars. But when a guy is on the make, on the way up like Meechan is, and is as ruthless as it would seem that he is, then I would think he would be delighted to fire-in anyone who he sees as a potential threat to his ambitions and by so doing cultivate a friend who may have similar ambition, albeit on the right side of the law."

Under the twin stares of two sets of avaricious eyes Thoroughgood grimaced but stayed silent and Numan continued with his monologue: "It's in the time-honoured tradition of these things that, the 'coming man', as Cormac called him, will want to cultivate a friend who is of a similar age and mind to him in the service in order to mutually benefit and also acquire a layer of protection … Christ, how'd ya think O'Toole and McGrain got into bed?" concluded Numan.

"All of which begs the question, if Dennis' hunch is correct, how did you – pardon the expression – come to share some pillow talk with dear Declan?" asked Malcolm, a twinkle of amusement fleetingly creasing his face.

But before Thoroughgood could answer, the office door burst open and in walked the familiar denim-clad figure of Kenny Hardie, holding a tray of four chipped mugs from which the pleasing aroma of coffee assailed Thoroughgood's fragile senses.

"All right, lad, the gaffer said you might be in need of this," he said, proffering a careworn Glasgow Rangers mug Thoroughgood's way. "You're a Thistle man aren't you?" smirked Hardie.

The young cop smiled knowingly at Hardie's mischief and a round of laughter broke out around the office as Thoroughgood sipped from the mug and produced a mock choking noise.

But Malcolm was in no mood to let Thoroughgood's temporary reprieve stretch out. "Gus here was about to tell us about how he has become Declan Meechan's new bestest chum …" he said, winking at Hardie.

Hardie's eyes snapped Thoroughgood's way and his forever unruly moustache seemed to twitch in appreciation at the impending conversation.

Clearing his throat, Thoroughgood finally cut to the chase: "Celine has started to work for him," he admitted with a grimace.

"Your girl does'nae half have a nose for trouble, Gus. I'd have thought after that business with Dawson last year she'd have been looking for a new career, one that doesn't involve working for some crim on the make or underworld kingpin," said Hardie with feeling.

"Well she's no longer my girl, Kenny, and you're right, her choice of work colleagues leaves a lot to be desired; but it is also one that could prove very useful to us … er, you," concluded Thoroughgood awkwardly.

"Go on," said Malcolm from behind his coffee mug.

"Meechan has basically made me an offer I couldn't refuse and he did so knowing I would be taking the information he pushed my way straight to your door. He was also well-versed in the Dawson business," concluded Thoroughgood.

Again Numan proved just what a shrewd judge of character and a sharp reader of situations he was. "So Declan gets the girl and you get the info and as time goes by, Meechan will make himself every bit as invaluable to you as McGrain has to O'Toole until he is so bulletproof he is even being fed tip-offs about polis raids!"

This time it was Thoroughgood who was taken by surprise and he almost choked on his coffee at Numan's revelation. "Bloody hell, Dennis, you're kept well informed, even on floor five of the ivory tower!"

"The clue is in the name, Angus, or didn't you spot our new title on your way in? We are now the newly christened 'Proactive Unit', thanks to the patrician interest now being taken in us by ACC White. Sadly, although we don't have much doubt that was indeed the case, proving it will be another matter, especially with O'Toole's pitbull Jimmy Lynch taking one for the team on the way in," concluded Malcolm ruefully.

"It's so bleeding' obvious that the raid on Rossi's was stage-managed, it's unbelievable, and the sad thing is I'll bet that muppet Lynch doesn't know he was made a patsy to try and make it look botched rather than a set-up. Anyway, it all amounts to the same thing, which is that McGrain and his team have scarpered to God-knows-where and O'Toole is strutting about Bayne Street like the North's version of a bulletproof Wyatt Earp. Anyway, what else has your new bestest chum Declan been whispering in your shell-like?" asked Numan.

Thoroughgood took a deep breath. "First, I think I can help you with where McGrain has gone. According to Meechan, he and his team are off down south on a job and it must be a major one, because the proceeds are to be used to fund an IRA bombing campaign in the major cities of England."

The only sound in the office was that of Malcolm pencilling notes and circling what he had just scrawled out. Then the DS' erudite gaze flashed Thoroughgood's way. "You said firstly, so what's for afters?"

"Have you heard of The Blood Acre?" asked Thoroughgood from behind a poker face and was once again met with the sound of silence.

Eventually Hardie's rumbling tones burst into life: "Sounds a bit melodramatic, whatever it is."

"Yeah that's exactly what I said when Meechan told me! It comes from the Bible, Acts Chapter 1, verse 19. The Blood Acre – in Aramaic it's called Akeldama – and that's what he calls the place where we'll find McGrain's victims, and according to Meechan where we may well find the evidence to tie him to O'Toole and take both of them down," finished Thoroughgood, unable to control the adrenaline coursing through his veins and finishing in a bit of a rush.

"Interesting … very interesting," said Malcolm, rubbing his chin thoughtfully before taking a deep breath. "But I think we need to deal with the first revelation according to the Book of Angus! The priority has to be to stop McGrain before he pulls off this job and gets his hands on the money to fund his Provo pals creating more murder and mayhem down south. Kenny, mate, can you get down the corridor and furnish Special Branch with this information, then get his description and that of his sidekicks Spider and Fergus McAteer circulated? We need to start spreading the net like … like it was yesterday," Malcolm finished lamely, and was met with an arching of Hardie's eyebrows and a curt nod.

As the DC exited stage left, Malcolm turned his attention back to Thoroughgood. But before he could speak, Numan beat him to the verbal punch: "Okay, Gus, so what about this Blood Acre … has Meechan got a clue where it may be?" he asked.

"Not yet, but you can bet the info will come his way eventually," replied Thoroughgood.

"Aye, well, we're running against the clock on whatever McGrain is up to in England and we've got a lot of calls to make on it, but ultimately if McGrain is gonna get picked up it will be by our friends down south. But when it comes to DI O'Toole, I wonder if we might force his hand …" said Malcolm, letting his words taper off.

"What do you mean, DS Malcolm?" asked Thoroughgood, unable to stop himself giving his superior his full title.

"I think it's time you and your CP mates got a bit of help hooking The Creepers."

CHAPTER FORTY-FOUR

WHILE THE UNIT'S priority was clearly to get as much info as possible on McGrain and his team circulated down south, they were under pressure to complete a six-month review of the newly christened Proactive Unit's progress for ACC White, and so, coupled with the fact that Thoroughgood was on his weekend off, The Creepers were granted a temporary stay of execution.

He slipped through the gears of his MG Metro, three strong black coffees after his meeting with the Unit, and brought the vehicle to a stop just opposite Davidsons Chemists in Saracen. Then he sat back to wait for a familiar figure to appear outside its doors.

For at noon the local pharmacy dispensed methadone to those junkies who were desperate to beat their addiction and Thoroughgood had heard a whisper through a contact at the local Housing Office that their number now included a lovestruck Collins, who had apparently fallen for a social worker who had been attached to Lennox Hill Health Centre.

Shaking his head in disbelief at this development for the umpteenth time, Thoroughgood drummed his fingers on the dashboard and finally his patience was rewarded by the sight of a dark Berghaus-enveloped figure loping up to the Pharmacy's front door … Collins had come for his script.

Thoroughgood slipped the Metro into first and brought it kerbside just short of the grim, tenement-lined junction and moments later the Cat reappeared, still as furtive and surveillance-conscious as ever.

Although Thoroughgood had taken time to check Collins out on the Police National Computer and had it confirmed that there were – surprisingly – no outstanding warrants for him, the now 'former' cat burglar couldn't help himself making a panoramic scan of the surrounding area for anything that might pose a threat.

Watching Collins, Thoroughgood could see that certain old habits obviously died harder than others and cynically, despite a moment's happiness that his ex-informant was at least taking the first steps to cleaning himself up, the voice in Thoroughgood's head burst into life: 'A tenner says the Cat'll be back on the smack before the week's out!'

Thoroughgood flashed the Metro's lights but he needn't have bothered, because Collins had already made him and administered a wagging finger by way of letting the cop know he was less than pleased to be the subject of his unwarranted scrutiny.

Nevertheless, Collins crossed the road and hunkering down at the MG's passenger window he waited for Thoroughgood to roll down the glass. "Long time no see, boss. Yous hurt me bad when you left me aff yer Christmas card list!" he said, breaking into a gravelly chortle, before adding: "Am figurin' this ain't a courtesy call to see how my rehab is coming along. Soes how can the Cat be o' service?"

For a moment Thoroughgood remained silent, stunned by the spectacular improvement in Collins' previously rotten dental work: for where rotten molars and black holes had once been, now brilliant white ranks of sparkling teeth almost blinded him with their radiance.

Collins' had not missed the impact of his new dentures. "Made ma sel' useful to the local dentist up on the hill when he had his motor tanned and lost a folder wi' his patients records in it, that, by chance, obviously like, came my way. Most beautiful choppers ave ever had, ain't they jist, boss?" smiled Collins, reinforcing his pride in his gleaming new choppers.

Stifling a laugh as best he could, Thoroughgood just about kept his mirth from showing. "Why don't you jump in and let your Uncle Gus take you for a drive and a coffee down the Ally Parade?"

Collin's still sallow, sunken features, creased in diehard suspicion. "Noo just why wid ye be wantin' tae dae that, boss man, after you bein' a stranger for so long, like?" asked Collins.

Thoroughgood shrugged his shoulders. "Because you're the best in the North at what you do and I need your help to lock up a nasty bunch o' bastards who are terrorising my community beat … and because the Cat'll be paid well for his work!"

Collins gave a gurgle of delight. "Ah, why didn't ye say so, boss …" he said, and without delay he opened the Metro's door, jumped in and buckled up.

Fifteen minutes later they were nursing white polystyrene cups, seated in the MG in the car park just 30 yards away from the Snack Wagon that lay in the almost sinister shadow of the former Wills Tobacco Factory, straddling the boundary between 'E' and 'D' divisions, or the North and the East, as anyone who wore a monkey suit referred to them.

Thoroughgood was first to cut to the chase: "So tell me, what's finally helped you see the light, Collins? I mean the new dental work, off the smack and, to be fair, you look like you've actually made the acquaintance of a bar of soap!" he concluded, unable to stop a smile from slipping across his face.

Collins was far from amused and his left hand shot up. "Noo hold on a minute, boss man, we're here to talk about business, naw ma health, touched tho' the Cat is that yer showin' such concern over him." Taking another mouthful of coffee, he let the three sachets of sugar work their magic on the inside of his mouth before swallowing. Then he bit off half of the Mars Bar he had insisted on having along with his refreshment, all in one mouthful.

Thoroughgood, sitting just a foot away, regarded this study in not-so-still-life with undisguised fascination. "Jesus, Collins, I've missed you too," he said and burst into laughter that for some strange reason seemed to infect Collins and before they knew it, the Metro was almost rocking with their unlikely mirth.

Finally Thoroughgood managed to take a sip of his own coffee and 'got down to business' as he'd been bid: "Ever heard of The Creepers?"

For a moment Collins seemed to be ignoring him, such was his fascination with the last part of his Mars Bar, which he had dipped into his coffee and was watching melt into the brown liquid.

Eventually he met Thoroughgood's inquisitorial gaze. "You kiddin' me, boss? Ain't nothin' the Cat does'nae know aboot what's goin' on in the North, as yous coppers caw it!"

Then swallowing the remnants of the coffee-soaked Mars Bar in one fell swoop, he wiped his mouth with the back of his hand and grinned his newly brilliant gloss smile. "Me an' Alby Stringer used to be best buddies back in P7 o' The Hill Primary, aye, a remember when the heedy old Ma Gibson belted the livin' daylights oot o' us for nickin' milk bottles!"

Thoroughgood's initial shock at the Cat's admission was soon replaced with impatience to cash in on his connections. "So if you and friend Alby are so tight, does that mean you're not gonna help me give him and his two little brothers Frankie and ..." Thoroughgood came to a stop as the name of the third of the brothers Grim eluded him, but help wasn't far away.

"You mean wee Johnnie? Aye, the runt was the worst o' the litter there, no doubts aboot it!" chipped in Collins helpfully.

"Aye, but will you help me bring The Creepers' reign of terror to an end and give them the pokey, Collins, for Chrissakes?" snapped Thoroughgood, his patience giving way.

"Aye, it wiz nice to hook back up wi' ye tae, boss!" smirked the Cat, pretending to be offended.

"All right, Collins, but since you know them so well, you'll be well aware of the carnage these horrible little shits are causing: they need to be stopped. We know they have a safe house in—"

But before he could get the words out, Collins interrupted him: "13 Torrybrook, tap dancer left!" he smirked.

"For fuck's sake, Collins! You clearly know it all, so why the fuck has the newly cleaned-up Cat been sitting on his paws while The Creepers have been wreaking havoc on my beat when you knew full well that I needed your help?" raged Thoroughgood.

"Simples, boss man. First, 'cause the Cat knew you'd come callin' for his help … eventually. Seconds, cause I wanted tae make sure you wiz'ne workin' wi' these fuckin' madmen in the Unit … that bawbag Numan … well he's a 24-carat nutter, hingin' me oot the back o' a van at 70 miles per hour on the M8 like that … a feckin' nutter!" concluded the Cat, the terror revisiting him at the replay of one of his last meetings with the Unit writ large in his eyes.

This time it was Thoroughgood who smirked, but holding his left hand up in an admission that the Cat had a point, he sought to ease his informant's fears: "Okay, okay, that business was a bit OTT but, well, you were a naughty boy, Collins, you have to admit …" As the informant's eyebrows shot up and his lips began to move in protest, Thoroughgood continued to horse-trade: "You help me lock The Creepers up for a long stretch and you can have everything – within reason – that you want. Which, out of interest, would be?" asked Thoroughgood.

"All right, boss man, you asked for it … The Cat wants a hoose, wi' a front door and a back garden up at Wallacebrook and—"

Thoroughgood couldn't help himself butting in: "There's more?"

"Aye! I want yous tae put me on an HGV driver's course …" and after a short stunned silence drew out, Collins added: "Who's laughin' now, boss man?"

But returning fire with a mischievous wink and a slight inclination of the head for feeling, Thoroughgood said: "So it's true, the Cat's in love … bloody hell, she must be some bird!"

Across the Metro, Collins' eyes narrowed and then the corners of his mouth hitched up as a smile broke cover. "Damn tootin' she is, boss man!" and at that he stretched out his hand. "Deal?"

"Deal!" replied Thoroughgood and they both burst into laughter once again.

CHAPTER FORTY-FIVE

THE REST OF THE DAY had been spent doing his best to get rid of the rotten taste of whisky and cigar that wouldn't leave his mouth and finally after a five-set squash marathon with his old friend Ballistic, Thoroughgood found himself seated at the bar of the Scottish Squash and Rackets Club, as he was apt to be on any other Friday off at 6 p.m.

"Aye, laddie, so you just don't learn do you, Angus!" said Ballistic, the chemist-cum-captain in the Territorial version of the Parachute Regiment, who over the time they had spent downing post-combat pints following their weekly encounters on the wooden boards had almost assumed the role of a big brother to his junior opponent.

"Well what else is there to say when a girl tells you she doesn't think she loves you?" asked Thoroughgood, staring into the bottom of his pint pot morosely.

"You could always try and make her change her mind …" retorted Ballistic with an implied question.

Two feet away, balanced on his tilting barstool, Thoroughgood rolled his sea-green eyes at his mate. "There's as much chance of me doing that as you beating me … old man!" and a trace of a smile flickered across his almost mournful features.

"Cheeky pup! Thought I was gonna take you tonight, boy: by Christ, I could almost smell the whisky sweating out yer pours! So, tell me why the turnaround? A month back Celine was the woman of your dreams but, to be fair, over the last few weeks, it's been obvious to a one-eyed blind man that there was … er … trouble in paradise," concluded Ballistic with a shrug of his powerful shoulders, which were sheathed in the sleeveless, garish yellow Parachute Regiment T-shirt he always wore after a Friday squash match and before he hit the West End on the pull.

Thoroughgood signalled to Agnes the barmaid that a second serving of Tennent's was required and then turned back to Ballistic. "Your answer in two words is Declan Meechan and he's a ... a fucker, there's no other word for it."

The Anglo-Saxon had barely slipped from his mouth than Agnes had reached across the bar and slapped a copy of the club's Glasgow Herald off Thoroughgood's head. "Angus Thoroughgood, I will not tolerate language of that ... well ... sort in this club, or anywhere else for that matter. What would your mother say if she heard you, a man of the law ¬¬– and an educated one at that – indulging in such disgraceful profanity?"

Agnes' rage scorched him and the bright shade of red that now lit up his previously ashen features reflected Thoroughgood's embarrassment.

"Aye, laddie, I think you best apologise to Agnes and don't let it happen again or Uncle Ballistic will be forced to punish you with his cat-o'-nine-tails!" chortled Ballistic, his moustache twitching with mirth uncontrollably.

Raising the palms of both hands, Thoroughgood admitted his transgression with suitable contrition. "Agnes, I'm really sorry. That was ... unacceptable. You're absolutely right, my mother would be completely disgusted. I promise you I'll never make that mistake again. Can I put a sweet sherry behind the bar by way of an apology for my lack of vocabulary?" he pleaded contritely.

Beside him, Ballistic's mischievous dark eyes ricocheted from one side of the bar to the other in glee at the mini-drama playing out before him that was sure, somehow, to find its way back into the club dressing room to ensure the mutual delight of the rest of their teammates and playing partners.

"A lack of vocabulary is it, laddie? I'd say that's the last thing you suffer from, Angus Thoroughgood!" laughed the TA captain.

But Ballistic's undisguised enjoyment was soon met with Agnes' ire and wagging her finger in his direction, her anger sparking through her thick black-rimmed glasses, she rapped: "And you, Captain RB Falcon, can just hawd yer wheesh as well and stop leading Angus astray: he was a nice, polite young lad when he joined the Scottish Squash and Rackets Club and look what you've done to him," she barked.

This time it was Thoroughgood who smirked at his mate's discomfort.

Pointing at himself in over-egged shock, Ballistic pled his innocence: "Me … lead Constable Thoroughgood astray? You've got it all wrong, Agnes, I am his confessor, not his devil, I assure you," and for good measure Ballistic melodramatically shook his head furiously to underline his disbelief at Agnes' scurrilous accusation.

Sending a warning glare Ballistic's way not to wind Agnes up anymore, Thoroughgood soothed her: "Please, Agnes, here's a tenner for these two pints and fix yourself a nice large sherry for closing up. We'll neck these beers and be out of your hair and please accept my sincere apologies for my slip of the tongue," he said, nodding his head in contrition.

"Well that would be very generous of you, Angus, and that was a nice apology too!" smiled Agnes.

As he looked over to Ballistic, he saw that his confederate was in the process of completing his party piece of downing a pint in a oner and as the last of the amber nectar disappeared down his throat, Ballistic let out a satisfied sigh. "Aah that's better, helps dull the pain of Agnes' cruel accusations," he said, winking across the bar and then flicking his eyes towards Thoroughgood's pint to tell him to get a move on. "Bonham's?" he added, and was met with a relieved smile.

Twenty minutes later, Ballistic pulled back the brass-handled door of their favourite hostelry. "Aye, you'll no' be making that particular slip of the tongue again with old Agnes, though I'd wager she might no mind another type of—"

But before he could finish his sentence, Thoroughgood interjected: "For crying out loud, Ballistic, she's pushin' 65!"

"True, laddie, but you know what they say, the older the Stradivarius …"

" … the better the tune," replied Thoroughgood, rolling his eyes to the darkened heavens and laughing as they entered under the mosaicked Bonham's sign and jostled their way towards the bar as the big beat of New Kids on the Block's 'Hanging Tough' banged out.

"Dear Gawd, I need to be having a word with Anna about that!" quipped Ballistic, who when he turned Thoroughgood's way found his young friend had covered his ears with both hands.

The former was first to arrive at their favoured far end of the 15 foot long marble-topped counter, located just next to the doors that led to the staff stairway linking the ground floor with the first level of the former picture house. Finding a couple of twenty-something, mop-headed geeks in his chosen spot, Ballistic utilised some gentle persuasion to help them move along nicely.

"Aah, boys, I've just met yer mammy on the way in and she says it's bath night! Time you two weans were heading home!" bawled the TA captain. Despite the noise making it hard to make out what he was saying, his piratical smile and a broadening of his straining Parachute Regiment T-shirt quickly focussed their attention and made it clear that argument was futile.

As the two 'weans' skulked off to the other end of the bar, an enticing female voice from the other side of the bar piped up: "A little intimidation works every time for you, Ballistic!"

"Ha, Anna, the blonde goddess of Bonham's! Let me buy you a drink after closing and I'll show you Uncle Ballistic's more tender side!" replied the TA captain wolfishly, before adding a cartoonish "Grrrrr," as Thoroughgood stifled a laugh in the background.

"I don't think so, I prefer my men with their brains elsewhere than between their legs!" Anna quipped and was met with a startled mock look of hurt innocence from Ballistic just as the bar manageress set down the second of the two pints of Stella she had started pouring the minute she had seen her two customers enter Bonham's.

"Please can you do something about that ... that noise? What about some Hipsway?" asked Thoroughgood and was met with a coquettish rise of Anna's artful eyebrows.

But while Ballistic continued to eye the black jumpsuit-clad bar manageress ravenously over his pint, Thoroughgood's attention was soon drawn elsewhere, because located in the wall seats situated inside a slight enclave behind the stairs amid a clutch of females was Emma McCabe.

His eyes fixed on her, he forgot his barroom obligations and had his wandering attentions snapped back to the here and now by Anna pointedly clearing her throat. "That'll be £2.50!" she said and after a moment of delay, an embarrassed Thoroughgood fished into his Harrington for his wallet and some cash.

His lingering stare had not been missed by either Anna or Ballistic. "Correct me if I'm wrong, Angus, but ain't that the poor gorgeous lassie whose mother ...?"

Laying 3 one-pound coins on the marble, Thoroughgood sent an awkward smile across the bar towards Emma, who softened her refined but wistful features. Unsure how to react, he turned back to the bar, where the eyes of both Anna and Ballistic awaited him.

"So tell me, Gus, I'm a bit confused at the chemistry that still seems to linger between you and WPC ...?" enquired Anna before continuing when Thoroughgood didn't reply: "Interesting ... so has the little altercation you recently had in here with Celine and her new friend, who has now poached my chargehand, ended your romance with her?" concluded Anna, cattily emphasising the word 'her' to underline the dislike she had always nursed for Celine.

As Thoroughgood shrugged stiffly, to his surprise Ballistic rode shotgun to his rescue. "Miaow, the kitten's got claws! Come on, give the laddie here a break, I think his heartstrings are getting tugged in so many directions he does'nae know whether he's coming or going."

"Uncle Ballistic turns agony aunt!" said Anna, her silvery eyes sparkling her appreciation at the now evident, but previously hidden, sensitive side of the TA captain.

Clamping a hand on Thoroughgood's shoulder, Ballistic offered some worldly advice: "Look, Angus, you told me Celine has made her choice, so if you have any sense of regret regarding what might have been with the gorgeous creature sat 15 feet away, then may I make a suggestion?"

Thoroughgood's eyes narrowed in suspicion. "Which is?"

"Get your arse in gear and get over there!" and although an initially wary smile started to flirt with the edges of Anna's mouth, in moments all three of them broke into laughter.

Thoroughgood smiled nervously but he needed no second bidding and before he knew it he was hovering awkwardly behind the group of females and clearing his throat. "Evening, ladies, er ... well, sorry to interrupt but just wondering if I could, em, well, have a word, Emma?"

Thoroughgood realised that Emma's friends were off-duty cops, and before she could answer, the girl to her right, a bottle-blonde whom he thought he'd once come across during a spell on mutual aid in Paisley replied for her: "Well, if it isn't Bayne Street's very own knight in shining armour! We thought you were all loved up with a gangster's moll, didn't we, girls ...?"

Despite himself, Thoroughgood couldn't stop his jaw tightening as the realisation this had been anything but a good idea hit him and ignoring his tormentor, he locked eyes on Emma. "Look, I'm sorry to interrupt your night out, Em—" only to find himself interrupted for a second time.

THE BLOOD ACRE

Raising her hand, Emma said: "It's okay, Gus, let's have a quick word …" – and turning to her group of friends she added – "outside!" and was met with a chorus of catcalls that she studiously ignored. Sending a cute smile his way, she rose and walked to the door as her friends broke into a spontaneous round of applause.

A moment later, Thoroughgood found himself outside the bar staring into her eyes. "How are you, Em?" he asked nervously, playing with his Harrington's zipper.

"I'm great, Gus … but is that why you interrupted my night out, to enquire about my health?" she quipped impishly, her eyes sparkling.

"I guess not …" he replied, and holding her gaze for a minute leant forward and kissed her.

CHAPTER FORTY-SIX

IN THE AFTERMATH of Spider's rubber burning exit, with no replies to McGrain's repeated calls on the walkie-talkie, the fevered conjecture inside the NatWest had now turned into sullen silence.

Despite himself, McGrain could not help pacing the carpet in front of the pool table as he tried to mentally cover every scenario that might be playing out around his old comrade.

"If they've got him, it ain't gonna take the cops that long to work out that yer pal is here for something a bit more important than nickin' a feckin chinky's delivery van. Maybe the two plods we had outside the door are'nae capable of puttin' two and two the gether but local CID are bound tae work out there's a bleedin' bank conveniently located next to where the motor got blagged and then there's whatever has happened to Charlie Chan ..." said Parlane, the tremor of a smile, almost subdued, just flickering on his angular face.

"He's right, Tony. Even if Spider gets off his mark okay there's plenty that'll be left in his wake. Christ, even the Keystone Cops would come back for a look at the bank. Dime to a dollar they're gonna want tae speak to the staff at the chinky," said Gregsy, adding his concerns to those of Parlane.

"The peterman's right, McGrain: I say we sack it and get tae fuck pronto, while we still have the chance tae do so," concluded Parlane from behind flexing fingers.

Abruptly McGrain stopped his pacing and stood, looking down menacingly at them, his hawklike features sheathed in shadow. He took a step forward and levelled the sawn-off shotgun he hadn't put down since the cops had first appeared in the lane outside against Parlane's head. "You'd fuckin' love that, my friend. Love to see this job go tits up and me skulking back over the border with ma tail between my legs. Well, it ain't gonna be happening, Parlane, because there is far more riding on this than just getting our hands on admittedly serious wedge."

It was a schoolboy error, his tongue loosened by anger, and McGrain knew it immediately. Parlane's furtive eyes snapped up from under the barrel of the gun and homed in on McGrain's face.

Staying cool under the severest pressure, he asked: "Awright then, McGrain, so whit could be more important than three million in used notes?"

While Gregsy remained silent, the twitching of his head a foot to McGrain's right underlined the level of his folly, and eventually the peterman's curiosity manifested itself in words: "He's gotta point, what could be more important than a place in the sun and no' having to look over your shoulder for the rest of your life?"

But McGrain had recovered himself and slanting the sawn-off up on to his shoulder, he laughed harshly. "Smart boy, Gregsy, aren't you … you've just answered your own question, young man. This isn't about just the money – it's about getting out. It's my last job … and by definition the biggest one I've ever pulled. There's no way I'm gonna be pulling out now we are here and in position, on the brink …" Then he stopped and looked down at his Cartier, checking it against the kitchen wall clock, its ticking irritatingly continuing to tattoo the silence with its metronomic beating.

"Look, that's 0115 hours, and we've had no cops back checking out the lane or the chinky, so whatever Spider has been up to, he's been leading them a merry dance. We have just under 7 hours until Revie the bank manager opens up, so here's what I'm proposing: we divide the night into 3 two-hour watches and then we are all ready to form a welcoming committee for the manager at 0730 hours."

Gregsy shrugged his reluctant agreement but couldn't help himself voicing his concern: "So what you're saying is … that we ride our luck, stay tucked up and wait and see?"

McGrain's smile was partially hidden in the dark but his agreement was still evident enough and turning his gaze Parlane's way, he said: "You're 7 or 8 hours away from a quarter of a million in used notes finding its way into your back pocket, my friend, and what's even better for you is that the man you've hated, loathed and wanted to have rubbed out for the last 10 years has just told you he is vacating his manor and leaving the field open for you to do what you want. For Chrissakes, Parlane, if that isn't enough reason to stay put and see how this one rides out then what is?"

It was a shrewd gambit and McGrain could almost see the workings of his nemesis' mind playing across features that no longer broiled with hatred but instead were now starting to see a major, perhaps defining, opportunity coming his way.

Parlane was hooked. "Ah come on, McGrain, there's no way you're telling me that you and Pauline would fuck aff tae the Costa Bravo or wherever else in the sun that yous fancy and leave me to take over your manor. Nah, I dinnae buy it."

But McGrain knew that the implication of his rival's protestation was that he did exactly 'buy it' and smiling soothingly he replied: "Look, Parlane, I've had enough of this life and when I left the Legion I invested in a property on the island of Martinique. I've been feathering it ever since and that's exactly where we're heading once this is done. You can have the whole of the North Glasgow to yourself … if you want it … and what's more, you'll have the type of serious dough that will allow you to reinforce."

Despite himself, Parlane couldn't help his eyebrows from arching, aware that his every twitch was also being monitored by Gregsy. For the first time he seemed almost ready to admit that McGrain's offer was a tempting one, but then his eyes narrowed and the anger that was never far below the surface with him sparked again. "You ice ma wingman and think you can buy me out wi' cheap words and blood money, McGrain, dae ye? Well—" but before he could complete his rant, McGrain stayed him with a raised palm.

"I think you're forgetting I've also lost a comrade hors de combat at your hands. What I'm saying is this is the perfect chance – the only chance – to put that all behind us, come out of it sorted and go our separate ways knowing that what was causing us to tear each other apart has now given us the chance to … to make a better fucking life … do you understand that? What do you say, Colin?" concluded McGrain, his patience suddenly starting to fray at the edges.

Before he could answer, Gregsy did so for him: reaching to his left he patted his confederate on the back. "Tony's right, Parlane, this is it for all of us and all we have to do is stay cool and get the job done. The polis are'nae coming back tonight. Come on, why don't you shake on it and then I'll take the first watch," and then cheekily he added with a grin: "Colin!"

Even for someone who's very being had been fired by loathing and hatred and a love of violence for the sake of it rather than just its means, Parlane could see that only a fool would continue to bridle and eyeing Gregsy's impish freckled features he smiled. "How'd you bastards know whit my first name wis?"

Seeing his opportunity had arrived, McGrain removed his right hand from the butt of the sawn-off and offered it Parlane's way. "Let's shake on a fresh start, what d'ya say … Colin?"

The smile on his face and extension of Parlane's right hand was all the answer he needed and as the kitchen clock continued to beat, the two of them joined in a firm shake that underlined their mutual determination to get the job done.

Taking first watch, Gregsy wandered down the corridor and into the front of the NatWest using the time to familiarise himself with the layout of the bank; for in a few hours' time, when the manager and the staff started to arrive, he would need to be aware of every nook and cranny. Although they had spent hours on the blueprint during their short sojourn at The Royal Oak, no building was ever exactly the same as its plan, as the peterman had already discovered on more than one occasion.

Necking a can of coke he had taken from the kitchen fridge, he walked along the rear of the counter, checking for any boltholes where an experienced teller may have placed some extra insurance for the type of eventuality that would shortly be playing itself out.

Three sections down, he discovered exactly what he was looking for: an old cricket bat leaning discreetly against a large wastepaper bin just under the counter. "Sweet," exclaimed Gregsy, chortling to himself in smug satisfaction at his discovery.

Content that he had covered the front of the premises with suitably intense scrutiny, he returned back down the corridor and took a left into the room that held the walk-in safe.

He observed the stainless steel of the vault door and started to put into place an emergency plan, just in case Mr Revie was unhelpful.

The technology was old and Gregsy was confident that he had the type of accoutrements in his bag of magic tricks that would provide both an impressive pyrotechnics show and a sprung door, should it be required.

As he wandered back through the staffroom he found himself replaying McGrain's statement: 'You're 7 or 8 hours away from a quarter of a million in used notes finding its way into your back pocket, my friend, and what's even better for you is that the man you've hated, loathed and wanted to have rubbed out for the last 10 years has just told you he is vacating his manor and leaving the field open for you to do what you want.'

For the import of McGrain's words could just as easily have been directed towards him and they left the peterman wondering just what he would do with his share of the dough.

But that was not the only worry nagging away inside Gregsy's head, for Parlane's whispering campaign had also left him wondering just what McGrain's true intentions were if they did manage to pull the NatWest job off.

Could he really be trusted?

And what had become of Spider? The fact the cops knew the Chinese delivery van had been stolen was sure to mean they would come back to The Golden Sunset. Gritting his teeth, Gregsy tried to still the nagging doubts that were starting to give him a migraine.

As he returned to the staffroom and saw McGrain and Parlane doing their best to catch some shut-eye on assorted chairs, Gregsy shook his head in irritation at his own folly in looking further ahead than the next few hours.

Hopefully by then they would be long gone and, despite himself, he slowly whispered a prayer to the man above that all would be well.

Checking the kitchen clock he saw that it was almost 0330 hours, just over 4 hours to show time. He made his way over to Parlane and gave him a shake. "You're on, mate," he said.

Chapter Forty-Seven

GERALD REVIE drained the remnants of his coffee cup and wedged the half-slice of toast in his mouth as he tightened his navy-and-red club tie around the neck of his pristine white shirt, its starched collar so rigid it could have seen Sunday service with the local vicar.

Swinging his single-breasted navy-blue suit jacket over his shoulders he smiled with satisfaction as his wife Julie packed his Tupperware sandwich box into his brown leather double-gusset Chelsea briefcase and then inserted the day's edition of The Times.

"Thank you, darling! What's on the menu today?" he joked, knowing full well what the answer would be.

"It's Friday, Gerald, isn't it ... which means?" answered Julie, smoothing down the sleeves of her black polo neck, then adding impatiently: "Now if you don't mind my tee time with the girls this morning is 8.15. I'm quite sure you can get yourself out to work without any further help from me."

"Tuna and mayonnaise, my darling, will do just nicely ... as always," answered Revie as his wife swept abruptly out of their spacious farmhouse-style kitchen.

Fixing her heavily lacquered hair until she was satisfied that even a freak tornado winging its way across the immaculately manicured fairways of Heysham Golf Club would struggle to whip a golden strand out of place, Julie looked back at Revie as he devoured the final piece of his toast and peanut butter. "Now, Gerald, I don't want you sloping off for a fly pint tonight after work. If you remember, we are due at the Fitzpatricks' for dinner at 7.30. If it isn't too much trouble for you …" she left her sentence open and scorched him with those almost crystalline grey eyes that had captivated him all these years ago when they had met as students at Lancaster University and now filled him with dread every time they shone his way.

Smiling wanly he nodded that her wish was indeed his command and would be obeyed without question and was met with a curt "Good." With that, Julie Revie was gone out the hall and through the front door.

Moments later, Revie followed her down the driveway of the large four-bedroom detached house they had called their own for the best part of a quarter of a century and which had proven perfect for raising their two children, Kenneth and Camilla, who had now flown the nest and were studying politics, and film and media in old London town.

The smile restored back on his face by fond memories from years gone by and a job well done when it came to the raising of their children was, however, soon enhanced by the replay of the previous evening's fumble with Senga, the young Scots cleaner, which had come flooding back … graphically.

Whistling the tune from The Dam Busters, Revie's eyes lit up as he walked along the pavement, the misery of his now loveless life with Julie momentarily forgotten and replaced with the images of his lovemaking with the earthy young Glaswegian cleaner who, worryingly, Revie now admitted to himself, was starting to become more than just a Thursday night fumble to him.

As Gerald Revie arrived at the pedestrian crossing on Heysham Road he looked across at number 380, his pride and joy, his branch of the NatWest, run by him like clockwork for the last 10 years.

Revie pressed the pelican crossing button, checked his watch and noted with smug satisfaction that he had shaved over 40 seconds off the morning walk to work. "6 minutes 18 seconds, comfortably under the 7-minute mark," he said to himself, patting the paunch below his open jacket, convincing himself that there was increasing room within his trouser waistband, puffing out his chest and standing a little straighter.

As the audible warning advising it was time to cross rang out, Revie made his way briskly across the two carriageways of the town's main road, already salivating at the prospect of the buttered roll and sausage he would ensure the office junior brought his way for 8.45 a.m. sharp and was ample reward for his new PB.

It was a little game Revie played with himself every Friday at this time if he managed to match or improve his best and smiling like a naughty schoolboy, Revie had to admit that for him routine was the key to a happy life, or at least a bearable one ... until Senga's arrival.

"My little Scotch minx," he whispered to himself and was lost once again in the passion of last night's treasured moments of secret lust.

Taking hold of the black metallic railings of the slanted, slightly raised access ramp he had insisted be installed to aid wheelchair-bound customers, Revie dipped into his jacket pocket for the office keys and proceeded to unlock the black storm doors, making a mental note that he must make sure he contacted Pointer Alarms the minute he reached his desk.

Revie pinned the storm doors to their wall brackets, opened the glazed, semi-frosted interior door and strode into his branch, turning his gaze to the grey carpet tiles that covered the public side of the branch.

"Good girl," he smiled as his examination of the floor failed to provide a single crumb, piece of litter or other debris that would have allowed him to playfully scold Senga later.

Next, as usual, Revie placed his treasured Ashwood Chelsea brief-case on the counter at the first serving point and then began to make his way along the front counter, making sure that the leather that covered the public side of it had been polished adequately, and inhaling deeply the honey-rich scent of the beeswax he made Senga apply lovingly to the leather blotting.

Arriving at the third cashier point, Revie ran his hand tenderly across the leather and lifted his fingers to his almost Romanesque nose. "Aaah," he said out loud, as the delicious scent aroused his senses and once again he shut his eyes and pressed the mental replay button of his last night with Senga.

But as he did so, he felt something cold and wooden ram up against the underside of his jaw and the light scent of the beeswax was replaced by a long-forgotten whiff from his childhood. Blinking his eyes open, he discovered his jaw was now resting on a willow cricket bat. "Early this morning, Mr Revie," said a gravelly, unfamiliar voice in an earthy, unmistakeably Glaswegian accent.

"What the hell …?" stammered Revie but he got no further before the pressure of the cricket bat on his throat became so great that talking was the least of his worries. Staring into a stocking mask, Revie could make out the intimidating hawkish features of a dark-haired male.

The sudden grip of a powerful hand on his right shoulder spun the bank manager around and then he was confronted with a new menace as the twin barrels of a sawn-off shotgun greeted him at chest height.

"You got some kind o' problem there, mate?" asked Gregsy from inside his stocking mask, but before Revie could answer, his sheathed tormentor jerked the sawn-off towards the near end of the counter, which had been slung open and where McGrain now stood with the cricket bat casually slung over his right shoulder.

"Anyone for cricket?" he quipped and began to pat that bat's end menacingly off his left palm.

As he arrived opposite McGrain, the terrified banker found himself forced against the corridor wall by a third stockinged-up male. Again, a harsh Glaswegian voice made it clear that if Revie wanted to escape from his current predicament with his life he would do as he was bid. "Where are your fuckin' keys, Mr Bank Manager?" it asked flatly, but having already started the process of patting down Revie, his interrogator soon came to the jangling jacket pocket that provided the answer he'd been looking for. Taking the keys out, Parlane tossed them to McGrain, who caught them with his free hand.

"Okay, I'll re-secure the entrance. Get him down into the strong-room and make sure he is ready to spill everything we need the minute I get there," ordered McGrain.

But the banker at last discovered his voice: "Wait a minute, you can't think you'll get away with this? I, I, I don't know the code to the safe, so you're wasting your time," stammered Revie in a show of futile defiance.

His words had been spat in McGrain's direction but were met with his back, as the crime lord was already making his way through the opening in the counter. He slowly turned back towards the bank manager.

A yard away from Revie, McGrain smiled through his mask, show-ing off twin rows of perfect teeth punctuated by two clear gold crowns and for a moment the two men faced each other, one breathing heav-ily and sweating furiously as a mixture of fear and anger enveloped him, the other cold and calculating, assessing his prey.

Then McGrain took a step back, hefted the cricket bat and shouted: "Six!" He smashed the bat off Revie's right knee and was met with an agonised screech as the banker fell to the ground clutching his battered joint.

McGrain hovered above his fallen captive, the cricket bat held like a club over his head. "Now listen to me, Mr Bank Manager, we know every little thing about you ... the route you take to work each morning, how long it takes you, how you like your sausage slightly overdone on a buttered roll just before opening on a Friday morning and the fact yer missus is a torn-faced bitch who'd rather be playing golf than sharing the breakfast table with you. So do you think if we knew all that then we wouldn't know that you personally open your safe to check all the funds are correct and present every morning?"

As the cricket bat remained poised above Revie's head like the sword of Damocles, the banker could see every last dent and crack in the willow and he started to forget the pain in his throbbing right knee and curl into a protective ball; but from behind his raised hands Revie couldn't help curiosity from getting the better of him: "And how, for God's sake, do you know that?"

McGrain hunkered down, cradling the cricket bat across his knees, and said amicably: "Let's just say a little Scotch minx told me!"

Then he turned to Gregsy and Parlane. "Gag and bind him and take him to the strongroom. Then get everything ready. No cock-ups, boys: time is getting tight."

CHAPTER FORTY-EIGHT

MAKING HIS WAY over to the NatWest's front door, McGrain quickly slipped off the stocking mask, for the last thing he needed when he re-secured the storm doors was for some punter in the street to see a masked man in the bank's doorway.

It was now that the paint-blotched boiler suits they were all wearing would hopefully come into their own, but nevertheless McGrain cautiously peered through the semi-frosted glass door, and the branch's details printed on it, just in case anything on the other side might be able to compromise him.

In the background, Revie's mixture of pain-wracked protestation and angry resistance started to fade as Gregsy and Parlane dragged him off towards the strongroom. McGrain allowed himself a comforting pat of the ring of keys that he now had in his boiler suit pocket.

By the time he reached the strongroom, the boys would have their kitbags prepared and ready for him to supervise the opening of the safe door and the removal of the used notes ... a moment that McGrain, despite himself, found he couldn't stop visualising.

With a shake of his head he banished the vision, but was forced to admit things were looking increasingly good: although they had monitored local radio stations throughout the night, there had been no mention of what had happened with the pursuit of Spider, despite the episode with the laughing policemen.

But that in itself was now a major headache. "If Spider doesn'ae show, then just how the hell are we gonna get out of here, Tony?" McGrain muttered to himself.

But that was a problem that he didn't have time to answer right now, although his inventive mind had already explored two possible avenues of departure that caused McGrain to smile, inadvertently, to himself.

Slipping the Yale key into the glazed door he opened it and looked out at the busy main road, then checked his watch, as timing was absolutely crucial. It was 0743 hours and the office staff didn't start arriving for almost 17 minutes … 'Plenty enough time,' said McGrain's inner voice reassuringly.

But as he reached down to slip the hooked metal rod that secured the left storm door to the entrance foyer wall, a female voice startled McGrain: "I didn't know we were expecting decorators this morning?"

The fleeting shock that waved across McGrain's unshaven angular features was suppressed with a barely audible inhalation of air and recovering himself almost immediately, he bowed deferentially before courteously beckoning the middle-aged brunette in through the front door.

"Good morning!" said McGrain, smiling with all the charm he could muster, before adding: "I'm sorry, miss, it looks like Mr Revie may have forgotten to mention to you we would be working on the front of the bank today and over the weekend."

The female, he noticed, had a surprising vibrancy in her eyes that belied the rest of her non-descript appearance, wrapped as she was in a bottle-green raincoat. Scanning his boiler suit for reassurance, she was anything but convinced. "But Mr Revie always ensures that all internal painting and maintenance is done on bank holidays."

As the woman passed McGrain's beckoning hand he adroitly pulled the second storm door closed, taking care not to slam it shut, all too well aware that if he startled the female, any subsequent screams could bring everything crashing down around him.

Then, the bank employee now safely inside the branch, he locked the Yale and turned to face the woman. "Can I get you a cup of tea while you wait for Mr Revie to finish going over his instructions with us?"

Although she was clearly still disconcerted by the out-of-the-ordinary situation she had come across, the woman seemed to be reassured with this offer and the new knowledge that her boss was on the premises.

Spotting a name badge pinned on the breast of the dark uniform bank jacket that peaked out from under her rain coat, McGrain continued: "That would be my pleasure, Miss Partridge. When we are working south of the border I'm always aware that the reputation of my countrymen is at stake and I always try to show that not all Scotsmen are lager swilling, tartan-clad louts!" smiled McGrain, reassuringly ushering Miss Partridge down the corridor towards the staffroom.

As they proceeded, the noise of raised voices reached them. Easing past Miss Partridge, McGrain said: "Mr Revie is just in here, if you would like a quick word with him?"

Again a look of bewilderment crossed Miss Partridge's dowdy, make-up-less features and she started to voice her concerns: "But why would your painters be in the strongroom when you said—" but before she could finish her sentence, the bank employee found herself being propelled by a forceful right hand into the strongroom.

The door slammed shut immediately behind her. Startled, she began to turn around, only to be met with McGrain's Glock. "I'm sorry, Miss Partridge, but your punctuality has meant that you've walked into something you shouldn't have. Now whether you get out of it will depend on you doing everything I tell you too. Do you understand me?"

"What … what is going on?" she spluttered, her body wracked with an involuntary shudder, as McGrain firmly pushed her against the room's right-hand wall.

Looking over, he checked to see that Revie had indeed been bound and gagged as instructed, sitting with his back against the opposite wall, knees to his chest, eyes spitting belligerent defiance.

Immediately he barked instructions to Gregsy and Parlane: "I'm afraid Miss Partridge here has caused us another headache we could have done without. I need her secured like Revie and then taken through and locked in the kitchen."

The words were barely spoken before Gregsy had slapped a large strip of silver electrical gaffer tape over Miss Partridge's mouth, smothering the scream that had started to escape. With McGrain clamping her wrists tight, he tied them expertly before pushing her towards Parlane, who, for once lost for words, did what he was bid without comment.

As Parlane shoved the quaking female out of the strongroom, Gregsy couldn't help articulating his disbelief at this latest potentially disastrous development: "For fuck's sake, you could'nae make this up. Am starting tae think this job is fuckin' doomed, Tony?" he groaned and then immediately regretted he'd used McGrain's Christian name in front of the bank manager.

The anger that mistake had sparked in McGrain was immediately suppressed, with some effort, and his eyes pulsing, he snapped: "It's nothing we can't handle. Now what's the score with the safe?"

"It's as we were told, combination activated ... but it's gonna be a toughie without the right numbers. Although I've got the tools, we'd be struggling against the clock. But all we need is Mr Revie to ... cooperate ... and we will be home and hosed," replied Gregsy, smiling.

"Get him on his feet," ordered McGrain. Gregsy duly grabbed the bank manager by the crook of his arm and hauled him upright, then after a flick of the head from McGrain he ripped the silver gaffer tape sealing Revie's lips free and gave the bank manager a playful pat on the cheek. "It's time you sung for your supper ... or rather breakfast, Mr Bank Manager!"

But Revie had other ideas and pulling his shoulders straight he stared straight back at Gregsy and McGrain. "So your little Scotch bitch has betrayed me?"

McGrain took a step forward and eyeballed Revie from inches away. "The only person who has betrayed you, Mr Revie, is yourself. Now, if you don't mind, tell my young friend here what the activation code is and let's get this done as quickly and painlessly as we can and then we can leave you to get on with your … life."

Revie met McGrain's words with a stony silence and held his dark eyes defiantly for a moment. "But we both know that this story isn't going to have a happy ending … for me," he said flatly.

"And why would that be?" asked McGrain, knowing full well the answer.

"Because, Tony, I know your name and thanks to your little act of … subterfuge with my colleague I now know what you look like. I'm sorry, but you'll be getting nothing from me because the minute I supply you with the combination I will have signed my own death warrant," spat Revie hotly.

Before his words had gone cold McGrain, backhanded him viciously, causing the bank manager's knees to dip and sending him staggering back against the concrete wall. "How very noble of you, Mr Revie; but then, from what your little Scotch bitch tells me, you live such an unhappy life you place no real value on it. Yet sacrificing yourself would be an act of futility because my young friend here has a bag of tricks in which there is the means to overcome your security if you are stupid enough to refuse to help us … but I have a feeling it won't come to that," smiled McGrain, doing his best to subdue his mounting anger and impatience.

Revie looked over towards Gregsy's kit bag with disdain. "So what's your preferred modus operandi? Thermal lance or plasma cutter, or do you have some kind of space-age drill? It matters not, you will not succeed."

Revie's defiance had now irked Gregsy's professional pride and the peterman took a step forward and grabbed him by his navy-blue suit lapels. "How come, baw-jaws?" he demanded.

Revie smiled knowingly. "Surely you are familiar with the term 'thermal relocker'?"

"A right bleedin' smart arse aren't you, Mr Bank Manager," spat Gregsy, a tremor of concern flickering through his eyes as they met McGrain's.

Seeing the surfacing of doubt a knowing smile creased Revie's square features and he said smugly: "When you have 3 million pounds in payroll within your security it pays, pardon the pun, to take suitable precautions. I'm delighted to say that our safe incorporates a thermal relocker in conjunction with a glass-based relocker, operated by a fusible link as part of the relocker cabling which will activate when the temperature of the safe exceeds a certain level and specifically designed to combat the efforts of those ill-advised miscreants armed with thermal lances or crude torches," concluded the bank manager triumphantly.

But McGrain met his smile with a poker face. "Sounds like one of them soddin' Public Information Films. Christ, before we know it Rolf Harris'll be turning up to tell us how to put our flippers on!" and he barked a short laugh Gregsy's way.

McGrain's verbal dog-leg, delivered in his guttural Glaswegian accent, clearly disconcerted Revie, who plainly didn't have a clue what the criminal was on about.

Then McGrain's passive expression was replaced with a sinister half-smile. "You might not place any real value on your sad, pathetic existence, my friend, but I know someone who certainly wants to hold onto life ..." McGrain let his words taper off into silence and then before Revie could react he turned to Gregsy and said: "Get Miss Partridge."

Leaning into Revie's face he said: "Capiche?"

CHAPTER FORTY-NINE

MOMENTS LATER, Gregsy and Parlane returned with the female bank teller, her features florid with fear and the gaffer tape stifling the sobs that continually racked her tortured being.

McGrain met her terrified gaze with a reassuring smile. "I'm sorry about this, Miss Partridge, but I'm afraid your life is now in the hands of your bank manager ... and I have to be honest and say I'm happy it's you that's in that predicament and not me!" Then snorting harshly he rapped: "Get her on her knees."

Parlane quickly forced Miss Partridge down and as her skin hit the cold concrete of the strongroom's floor McGrain noted that her tights laddered, and for a moment he felt some pity at her increasingly desperate appearance ... but it was fleeting.

Pulling the Glock back out of the shoulder holster fitted under his boiler suit he slotted a silencer on its barrel and rammed it against her forehead. Turning to Revie he said: "Maybe you don't care about your own life, but are you prepared to gamble with someone else's? Give my man the fuckin' combination ... now," he demanded, his words resonating with deadly intent.

But Revie was made of sterner stuff than McGrain had anticipated. "You're calling my bluff ... Tony," he replied through gritted teeth, taunting McGrain with the use of his Christian name, although his gaze never left Miss Partridge's imploring eyes as tears cascaded down her blotchy cheeks.

"You think so?" asked McGrain.

Revie said nothing but his jaw was set and he showed no sign of caving in as his teller sobbed profusely, pleading incoherently from behind the gaffer tape.

"Okay, Revie, so you would have the blood of an innocent on your hands just to keep some company's payroll snug in your safe? It's your call …" McGrain pulled the Glock's slide back and released, allowing the mechanism to spring forward. "There we are, all cocked and ready to fire," he said and gently placed his left hand on top of Miss Partridge's short brown, bobbed hair.

"I'm sorry, Miss Partridge, we have only just met and already I must bid you au revoir," he said, then clamped the fingers that had been so softly slipping through her tresses into a vicious grip. Sending one last look in Revie's direction, McGrain said: "May the lord have mercy upon your soul," and began to draw back the Glock's trigger just as Revie finally broke: "No, no … stop it, stop it I'll give you the combination, you Scotch maniac …"

McGrain's smile was tinged with relief. He holstered his Glock and raised Miss Partridge to her feet, but checking his watch saw that it was now 11 minutes to 8: time was starting to beat them. If things didn't start happening, the likelihood of more members of staff blundering in would make the job virtually impossible to pull off.

Quickly he nodded towards Gregsy to take charge of the operation and the peterman smiled through his stocking mask and took a step forward towards the 6-foot walk-in steel safe.

As Gregsy did so, he grabbed Revie and dragged him with him, then turned the bank manager until they were face to face. "So whit we've got here is a standard Group 2 combination lock, the usual for most quality safes used by banks and the like and now you're gonna gie me the combo, smart arse … cause if you don't I'm gonna flick this bad boy on and barbecue me some bank manager!" spat Gregsy, producing his blowtorch and ramming its head up against Revie's cheek.

Revie, his face chalk-white with terror, nodded that he was prepared to play ball and as he did so a strand of greying hair flopped down from his comb over and slid across his face. "Okay, okay, I get the message," said the bank manager and held his hands out to have their binding removed.

A couple of yards away McGrain and Parlane's eyes bored into Revie, while the only sound in the strongroom was Miss Partridge's continual sobbing and the metronomic ticking of a wall clock that was a constant reminder time was no longer on their side.

Gregsy grabbed Revie's wrists and pulled him close to him: "Now this is your final warning, Mr Bank Manager, 'cause I dinnae trust you one wee bit and I just want you tae know exactly how a Group 2 safe works … in other words, whit's called the opening index. So let me spell it out for you soes there are no slip-ups, like. A Group 2 safe follows the standard pattern, which is turn the feckin' numbers tae the left and they increase and turn them to the bleedin' right and it's the opposite … got it?"

Then Gregsy removed the binding from Revie's hands and watched as they slid up towards the dial.

Leaning forward, the peterman spoke menacingly in his ear: "I'm watchin, and watchin real close, and for the last time, I knows how it works, auld man: four clicks tae the left, stop at the first number, three times to the right, stop at the second number, two clicks to the left, stop at the third digit and then once to the right, real slowly, and as you do so I'll be listening for the lock engaging with a little titchy bit o' resistance and then its fuckin' eureka!"

Revie glanced Gregsy's way, so that their eyes locked less than an inch apart. The bank manager offered a tepid smile of acceptance that he had no other option but to play ball.

Revie slid his newly freed hands up to the dial and proceeded to follow Gregsy's instructions, but as the face of the dial slid onwards up through the numbers, a new sound filled the strongroom: Miss Partridge was desperately trying to talk through her taped mouth.

Gregsy clamped a hand on Revie's shoulder and snapped: "Hawd it there, baw-jaws." He turned Parlane's way. "Look, will yous shut Sue Ellen there the fuck up! I cannae hear masel thinkin' with her whimpering. If the dial is alarmed and Mr Bojangles here loses concentration one mistake and we could be fucked."

"Awright, peterman, keep yer hair on," retorted Parlane and turning to Miss Partridge, who was already starting to cower in fear, he raised his hand to cuff her; yet before his paw could make contact with her jaw, it was held in a vicelike grip by McGrain.

"Hold it there, I think Miss Partridge wants to tell us something," he said and manoeuvring himself between Parlane and the bank teller he gently removed the gaffer tape from her mouth. "What's on your mind, lady?"

Miss Partridge took a deep breath and then wiping the mixture of tears and nasal detritus that smeared her face with the back of a dainty but quivering hand, she said: "The code is 1910, the year that Heysham Golf Club was established. Gerald is a former captain … it … it's a standing joke that everyone in the branch knows the code and …" But before she could finish, McGrain held up his right index finger for silence and turned Revie's way.

Next to the bank manager, the realisation at what had just happened was met with an explosion from Gregsy: "Ya dirty treacherous auld bawbag!" he screamed in the bank manager's face.

Feet away McGrain was more eloquent: "You have just slipped the dial right past number one, Mr Revie … haven't you?" he asked almost in passing.

Gregsy rammed forward and pinned Revie against the safe door, brandishing his blowtorch in the bank manager's face. "I'll fuckin' turn yer face to bacon, auld man," raged the peterman.

McGrain remained composed and stepping forward he said: "Oh dear, Mr Revie, you've made two fatal mistakes, I'm afraid. Firstly, I would have thought when it comes to something like a safe code, loose lips sink ships. Second, in trying to set the safe alarm off by clicking the wrong code you've compounded your earlier mistake and now …" – McGrain levelled the Glock at the bank manager – "and now, Gerald, we have no further use for you," and with that he stepped forward and shot Revie through the head.

As the bank manager crumpled onto the concrete floor, Miss Partridge broke into a horrified scream, which was immediately stifled by Parlane's hand.

"Over to you, Gregsy: we need it sprung and we have no time to spare," said McGrain.

"Consider it done, boss," replied Gregsy while McGrain bent down and dragged Revie's lifeless body over to the corner of the room, where he propped up the fresh corpse.

Then he turned and made his way over to Miss Partridge. Caressing her left cheek tenderly, he said: "I thank you from the bottom of my heart, dear lady, and for it you will keep your life …" but before he could finish his sentence, Gregsy's triumphal cry of "Get in there!" drowned him out.

McGrain turned to see that the giant steel safe door had sprung open and standing in the opening was Gregsy, his arms already laden with used notes.

From behind his left shoulder, Parlane's voice grated into life: "God save the Queen!"

Chapter Fifty

AS PARLANE AND GREGSY worked manically to fill the kitbags with the seemingly never-ending wads of notes, McGrain stood deep in thought.

The whole thing was a mess and confronting him now was the problem that had left him sleepless all night ... just how the hell were they going to make their exit.

Miss Partridge's presence was also a major headache, for how could he leave her alive when she had been witness to the killing of Revie?

The reality that she would have to be iced was deeply troubling to a criminal who lived his life by the credo that the business of the underworld, where at all possible, should not be inflicted upon the innocent ... yet now it would be impossible to stay loyal to that diktat.

As the final bag was filled with the used bank notes and Parlane tied it off, McGrain shook his head at the twin dilemmas that were driving him to distraction ... and where the fuck was Spider, what had happened to his vieil ami? The folly of allowing him to leave with the keys to the green van had hammered away at McGrain constantly ... a schoolboy mistake that had now rendered all their meticulous planning redundant.

But he was snapped from his angst by Parlane's irritating voice, and words that confirmed that McGrain had in fact three major problems that needed dealing with.

"Awright, McGrain, so whit now, Mr Big?" he spat, his grey eyes flickering with contempt at the elephant in the room: they had just pulled off a 3-million-pound robbery but had no means of escape.

"Let me worry about that, Parlane. Now let's get the four bags through the back to the staffroom and get ready to get the hell out of here," snapped McGrain. But as the words left his mouth he saw the doubt written large over Gregsy's freckled features, sweat tracers running down either side of his face while a tousle of ginger hair had escaped from the stocking that now perched at a ridiculous angle on his bonce.

"For fuck's sake, McGrain, will you just tell us how're we gettin' the hell oot o' here? In case you hav'nae noticed, we've got a dead bank manager on our hands," demanded Parlane, articulating the silent question etched on Gregsy's flushed face.

Keeping his temper in check with a considerable effort, McGrain spoke with icy precision: "You'll have the answer to that question in a minute, Parlane. Now let's just get the sacks through the back." He paused momentarily to check the wall clock. "That's 0756 hours, we may have less than 4 minutes to get out before the rest of the staff start arriving … you need to trust me and stop wasting time doubting me … okay?"

"Now you take the bags into the staffroom while I take a look out the front of the building and make sure there is nothing happening out there that shouldn't be and that we have no unwanted visitors coming our way. Just stick with me, boys, we're gonna make it out of this with or without Spider," concluded McGrain with feeling; but the uneasy looks on his two henchmen's faces showed they were anything but convinced.

* * *

In the bank's kitchen, Cynthia Partridge sat knees drawn tightly up to her chin, trying desperately to force herself to calm down and stop the huge sobs that had been wracking her body for the last 15 minutes.

Fifteen minutes in which her safe, cosy little world had been thrown into complete chaos. For things like this, reasoned Cynthia, just didn't happen to a girl like her.

243

She knew that the rest of the staff thought of her as nothing more than a dowdy, middle-aged spinster whose life revolved around the church, a wallflower for whom life had passed by, but Cynthia was no fool and she knew where every skeleton was buried in Heysham's NatWest branch.

She had known about Revie's affair with the young cleaner Senga, just as she had known that his deputy Jackie was 'involved' with Ben, the young summer student, who started each day faithfully taking their office messages and, so the rumour went, was apt to finish it on a tartan travel rug with the deputy bank manager astride him on one of Half Moon Bay's beach dunes.

Now Revie was dead and her mind kept replaying the moment he had been shot: yet Cynthia had felt anything but sadness at his execution. After all, what appreciation or consideration had he shown her during the 10 years she had been his chief teller? He had never failed to overlook her for any promotion that was going, and ultimately what he had thought of her had been shown by his initial reaction when 'Tony' had threatened to kill her. His decision to try to trick the robbers would have got them both killed if she hadn't intervened.

But perhaps most disconcerting of all was the fact that, despite everything, Cynthia had felt a surge of arousal when spoken to by their leader: his understated menace mixed with unexpected kindness had … proven strangely, disgustingly attractive to her.

Chiding herself with a sharp shake of her head, she forced these ridiculous thoughts from her mind and turned to the awful truth that was gnawing her with fear.

For the fact she would be able to identify the faces of the robbers, knew that their leader was known as Tony, could hardly fail to tell through their accents where they were from, all meant that despite everything Cynthia could only come to one appalling conclusion … her death was moments away.

And that realisation now started to spark a cycle of memories replaying on the silver screen in front of her mind's eye: the high hopes of her university life when she had wanted to build on her media and drama course to create a career in TV production only to have her aspirations thwarted by a tyrannical father who had forced her to go into the bank.

Then there had been the love of her teenage life, Hugh, the floppy-haired, sweater-wearing rugby player who had been a dead ringer for T. Rex's Marc Bollan. She had met him at a gig in the student's union at Leeds Polytechnic and had fallen head over heels, only for her father to once again kill off love's blossoming young dream.

Now here she was 43 years old with nothing of any substance, no joy in her life: in fact, Cynthia was forced to admit it was more of an existence than a life and one that was interminably dreary and grey and now about to come to its end in this so-called bank, which was no more than a horrible converted house.

It was too much for Cynthia and once more she dissolved in a torrent of tears until she could barely make out the kitchen door such was her grief at the futility and pointlessness of her life: a life that could hardly have been any less ordinary ... until this day ... the day that would be her last.

But Cynthia's self-torture was brought to an abrupt end as the kitchen door flew open and McGrain stood above her, his unreadable dark stare filling her with doom.

As he walked over to Cynthia, she cowered, drawing into herself, but McGrain hunkered down beside her and with that disconcertingly soft touch of his slipped the gaffer tape from off her mouth. "Look, Miss Partridge, I'm sorry you've become embroiled in all of this, had to see what you just saw, but despite that there is a way out of this for you and us. Can I ask how you got into work this morning?"

But before she could answer, a knock on the rear door tattooed out and Cynthia saw the tremor of panic that flickered through his dark eyes instantly suppressed.

Slipping the gaffer tape back over her lips, he said with a wicked smile: "Now don't go anywhere!" Then sliding his Glock from its shoulder holster, he was gone, the kitchen door slamming shut behind him.

In the staffroom, Gregsy had already drawn his weapon while Parlane had picked up the cricket bat that McGrain had discarded earlier and was advancing menacingly towards the bank's rear door.

"It's gotta be the fuckin' cops, I knew they'd come callin' back in the morning, bastardin' rozzers always show up when you least want it," spat Parlane.

But from outside in the lane a familiar deep rumbling baritone spoke: "Es-tu à la maison, monsieur le Président?"

Despite himself, McGrain broke into a relieved laugh. "Thank Christ for that: Spider's back!"

Chapter Fifty-One

AS SPIDER TOOK up a position in the middle of the staffroom, he received a warm slap on the back from Gregsy, which underlined the relief coursing through the room.

But with every minute that passed taking them a step closer to discovery and disaster, McGrain was only interested in one thing. "Please tell me you have the motor nearby?" he asked, his agitation undisguised.

"It's reversed up outside in the lane, Tony, ready to be loaded and good tae go," rapped Spider, wincing at a sharp jet of pain from his injured hand. As McGrain's eyes slipped down towards the wound, he saw that the bandage that enveloped it was drenched in crimson.

"Look, I'm okay, mon ami, just been a busy boy, like, but aw that can wait. C'mon, lads, let's get the wedge out o' here and head for the fuckin' hills!" said Spider in a rat-a-tat-tat delivery.

Reassured by his old comrade's braggadocio, McGrain smiled in agreement, before adding: "Okay, boys, get to it while I have a chat with Miss Partridge."

His words caused a look of confusion to cross Spider's grim features, but before he could say anything it was Parlane who bridled. "Look, McGrain, what is there tae say to her, we cannae be walking away from here leaving a loose end that could all see us in Peterhead for the rest of our naturals. For fuck's sake, man, if it's a problem gie me yer shooter and I'll take care of the bitch masel," he spat.

At the side of the room Gregsy watched with undisguised fascination, but a blood-soaked hand reached out and grabbed Parlane's right shoulder and as an unspoken glance of understanding passed between McGrain and Spider, the latter, in a tone that brooked no argument, spat: "Why don't you leave that to Tony and get the fuckin' money in the van before something nasty happens to you, Parlane?"

Despite the anger that blazed through his eyes, Parlane eventually shrugged his shoulders and grabbed the nearest kitbag as McGrain turned and made his way back to the kitchenette.

Opening the door, he saw Miss Partridge look up, her desperation having suffocated the earlier liveliness of her eyes and McGrain was immediately assailed by a disconcerting sense of regret.

Reaching down, he helped Cynthia Partridge to her feet and for a second time lightly removed the gaffer tape from her smudged lips. Looking into her eyes, McGrain could see that the hint of attraction that he had thought sparkled from her at their first encounter flickered towards him again.

"Don't worry, Miss Partridge, it's gonna be all right; but it's time for me to go," he said, almost in a whisper, in a voice that was tender and tinged with melancholy.

As he wiped the trails of moisture from under her eyes, McGrain was met with a sob and Cynthia blurted out: "But what's going to happen to me?"

"You're gonna be fine, Miss Partridge," he said. Then he leant down in one motion and kissed her ravenously on the lips, which he had been dying to sample since he had first clapped eyes on her at the bank entrance. As he did so, a tress of her chestnut hair fell across her eyes and Cynthia let out a slight sigh of arousal at the rekindling of a passion she had not known in years and had thought she would never experience again.

McGrain dexterously manoeuvred her around, feeling her back excitedly arching under his touch. He leant down further, kissing her on the neck and trying to suppress the arousal that was starting to burst through his body as the warmth of hers permeated his being and she moaned once again under his lips.

In one motion he slipped the janbiya out from inside his boiler suit, whispered "I'm sorry, Miss Partridge," and ran its vicious edge across her throat, to be met with a startled scream that almost instantly was replaced with a gurgling as Cynthia's lifeblood spurted out and cascaded down the arms of his white boiler suit.

Gritting his teeth and shutting his eyes, McGrain held her tight in his killing embrace and waited for the life to drain from Cynthia Partridge. When her writhing eventually subsided to a deathly stillness, he lay her down on the kitchen floor.

Shaking his head in disgust at his own actions, McGrain said: "May the Lord forgive me," and then, waves of nausea surfing through him, he grabbed a dish towel and wiped his hands clean as he walked out of the kitchen, before stuffing the towel into the boiler suit's breast pocket.

Forcing his emotions into check and taking a deep breath, McGrain regained his self-control and cast his gaze around the premises, making sure that his men had left no telltale debris behind them that could eventually help point a finger their way.

Satisfied that nothing had been left that might signpost the road to Glasgow, he turned to leave the staffroom but before he left, McGrain cast one final glance back through the kitchen door and as his eyes locked on Cynthia Partridge's inert body, they moistened. Then he walked out the back door of Heysham NatWest as quickly as possible.

Outside sat the green van, diesel engine running, with Spider behind the wheel offering him a thumbs up. McGrain skirted round the bonnet and jumped into the front passenger seat.

"We have 30 minutes to make the rendezvous or our friend will no longer be waiting … don't spare the horses, my friend!"

Looking at his brother-in-arms, Spider knew that right now silence was indeed golden, and his face masked in a grim smile he gave a curt nod then levelled his foot to the floor. The green Transit surged down Sugham Lane, leaving behind their bloody deeds.

But while the front of the Transit was drowning in brooding silence, the back of the vehicle reverberated with triumph. Parlane ripped off the wire binding one of the kitbags and delved inside, pulling three wedges of used notes out and starting to finger them as a manic smile developed across his taut features. "I cannae quite believe it, we've fuckin' done it and now am sittin' in the back of a motor with three mill' for fuckin' company!"

He threw one of the packets of notes across the back of the van at Gregsy, who caught the money and, his eyes dancing with jubilation, sniffed the notes. "You're right, Parlane man, after all that shit with the cops and the delivery man, big Spider goin' AWOL and then that shite Revie the bank manager and the teller bitch walkin' in on us, it's nothin' short of a bleedin' miracle we've pulled it aff!" Then he laughed out loud and shouted at the top of his voice: "Yahoo, ya bass!"

In the van's cabin, McGrain turned their way and managed a wan smile. "Aye, we may have pulled off the robbery but we still need to make good our escape, so enjoy the moment but don't get carried away, boys, as there's plenty still to be done," he counselled.

"Fuck's sake, Tony, the rest'll be pure toffee compared to the shit we've had to come through to pull the joab aff," Gregsy laughed, then ripped his boiler suit downwards, tied the sleeves back around his waist and swivelled round in his seat so that he could get eyes on Spider. "Hey, big Spider, ain't it about time you told us why you went missin and whit ever became o' Charlie Chan and the boys in blue that were on yer tail?"

Parlane chorused his agreement: "Aye, c'mon, big guy, that paw o' yours looks in a right old mess, plus judging by that moose under yer right eye someone managed to land a glove on you, pal …?"

Spider's dark eyes flitted in his driver's rear-view mirror as he adjusted his gaze to meet his two comrades in the back of the Transit.

"Afraid wee Charlie bought it pretty sharpish and I used him as the bait for Bill and Ben the fuckin' Flower Pot Men to blunder into the trap … put it this way, Lancashire Cops are now a sergeant and copper down!" and a slow rumbling chuckle started to bubble up through his chest.

In the rear, Parlane smiled viciously. "Couple o' feckin' muppets awright, whit was aw that heein' and hawin' they were doin' at the back o' the bank, like? Aye, it musta been a pleasure to bleach the two o' them! Filthy rozzer scum," he ended with feeling.

In the front of the vehicle, McGrain couldn't stop himself checking his passenger mirror to make sure they were not being followed but the rear view was clear and as he looked forward he smiled with satisfaction as the coastal road started to wind out in front of him.

But McGrain was not the only one who was taking an interest in their route. "So whit noo, McGrain, am presuming we're headin' for a safe house tae divide the dough up? I'm takin' it you'll be torchin the tranny and have another motor good tae go …" asked Parlane.

"Of course. We're taking a slight detour off the beaten track and making for a location called Throbshire Point on the headland, where all will be revealed, but you can rest assured that every eventuality will be taken care of there," said McGrain, his face stony.

Chapter Fifty-Two

THE TRANSIT TOOK a right turn and Spider nudged the vehicle along a narrow tarmacadam roadway that was dusted with sand and ran parallel to a stony beach on which the tide lapped with a soothing repetition. For a moment, McGrain lost himself in the Irish Sea's grey depths.

But he was snapped from his thought by Spider's gruff voice: "L'Irlandais est dans l'église!"

In the back of the van, Parlane surprised them with a revelation of intelligence: "The Irishman is in the church? What the fuck is going on, McGrain?" he demanded.

But the Transit was now drawing to a stop as the roadway, such as it was, ran out in a cul-de-sac where a yellow Bedford HA Van with the word 'Telecom' printed on it in royal blue and a couple of ladders running along the rack attached to its roof was parked.

The vehicle was empty but as McGrain and Spider looked up to the right at the ancient ruined church that haunted the clifftop, they saw a stocky individual scanning them from his vantage point, leaning against the broken stone walls that arched around the building's empty doorway.

Turning around, McGrain met Gregsy and Parlane's puzzled stares. "Right, lads, our new transport awaits; admittedly it's a little cramped but it will do the job nicely. Now I want all the old boiler suits put into the black bin liners you'll find in the Bedford and then transferred to the Transit for torching along with any other shit that might come back to haunt us ..." and at that he ground to a halt before fishing out the blood-stained dish towel he had used to wipe Cynthia Partridge's vitals from his hands. Bundling it up with the boiler suit he had already peeled off during their journey, he threw them at Parlane, then grimacing added: "Same goes for that. Then get the money sacks into the back of the Telecom van while I have a quick word with our Irish friend ..."

But before he could finish his orders, Parlane interjected: "Ain't you forgettin' something, McGrain: when do we start divvying it up?"

"Fair enough ... Colin, you've done everything asked of you and it's a legitimate question. Your 250k will be yours in about 10 minutes," replied McGrain flatly.

Parlane's eyes lit up and despite himself he couldn't stop his tongue breaking free and tickling the left side of his mouth.

McGrain arched an eyebrow and then he turned to Spider. "Okay, mon ami, you know what to do."

Spider winked that he did. McGrain jumped out of the Transit and made his way up a beaten earthy track, taking care to avoid treading in the dog shit that sporadically blighted it, as he climbed to the ruined church.

Five feet away from the ancient edifice's doorway, a voice sheathed in a bitingly harsh Belfast accent spoke: "Tá sé go deas tú a fheiceáil arí [Good to see you, my friend]."

"Tusa freisin, Conall [You too]," replied McGrain.

The Irishman had a thick mop of centre-parted red hair, complimented by a piratical beard that was almost as dense and from behind aviator-shaped glasses intense dark brown eyes read McGrain's features for signs of the impact of the last few days: but saw none.

"Your little pick-me-up from the Legion – what was it called again ... ah yes, Pervitin, wasn't it – has worked well for you, I take it?" asked the Irishman, his checked scarf billowing about above a tweed jacket.

McGrain smiled. "Of course, Conall, my little white pills have indeed done the trick. Did you know that the First Panzer Division were supplied with 20,000 of them on the eve of the Ardennes Offensive back in 1944? Of course you know how many stormtroopers found their way into the Legion after the war. The chemical technology behind Pervitin, in essence methamphetamine, is the ingredient that kept the Panzers marching all night and fighting all of the next day, so why wouldn't we make the most of the Nazi's secret weapon when their fugitives joined us in the Legion in their droves?"

"To be sure, to be sure. Was there any collateral?" asked Conall, gripping his scarf tight.

McGrain nodded curtly. "I'm afraid it turned into a mess and the bank manager and his chief teller both had to be silenced, while two members of the local constabulary are also no longer on duty; and a Chinese takeaway has a vacancy for a new delivery driver. So we need to get this sorted and be on our way, mo chara."

The Irishman smiled viciously. "What do I care a fig about how many Brit fockers buy it? But now all that matters is that you are here and so is the money."

"All three million is bagged up and being transferred into the Bedford. As agreed, one million will be kept for myself and my men to be split three ways. So you have two million for the cause, which will help you buy an awful lot of semtex and Armalite AR-18s," replied McGrain curtly.

"Yes, the two mill' will prove good value with our Libyan friends, Tony. But the ferry is leaving for Belfast in …" Conall stopped and pulled his jacket sleeve up to reveal a watch with a black leather strap, before adding: "Just over half an hour …"

"That's no big deal, Conall: by then the Bedford and its three newly uniformed BT Engineers will be on the car deck," replied McGrain.

His answer induced a look of confusion drawing across the Irishman's benign features. "But there are four of you, Tony?" he asked.

"Not for much longer," replied McGrain and he extended a hand filled with a Manilla envelope to the Irishman. "I took a wee extra look at a couple of personal safety deposit boxes and came across some nice little jewels you'll be able to fence with your contacts for some extra expenses. That'll keep you comfortable while you plan for the fruits of our labours to take their spectacular effect all across the Englisher's so-called green and pleasant land," smiled McGrain.

Taking the envelope, Conall opened it and the contents lit up his face with joy. "Sweet Mother Mary, I did'nae know Queen Elizabeth banked with the Heysham branch o' the NatWest?" he laughed out loud and at that the Irishman took McGrain's right hand and, shaking it firmly, said: "Tiocfaidh ár lá [Our day will come]."

Turning through the ruin's empty doorway, he picked his way among the broken stone and disappeared over the headland.

CHAPTER FIFTY-THREE

DRAWING AN index finger down a stubbled cheek, McGrain turned back towards the becalmed sea and saw that Spider, luminous in a yellowy-orange Telecom boiler suit, had begun to douse the Transit in petrol.

Making his way back down the path, McGrain allowed the slight twist of a smile to form on his face ... he was going to enjoy the coming moments yet he could feel the extreme effects of fatigue starting to send slight tremors through his body and pulling out the red and blue container of Pervitin he had carried with him since his days in the Legion, he popped the top, removed a white tablet and swallowed it dry.

By the time he reached the tarmacadam and took up a position just in front of the two vans, he could already feel its effects: the rush of energy, the extreme sharpness of focus and the falling away of all the worries that had begun to plague him with the creeping of nervous exhaustion.

Now they were replaced with a cold fury and hunger to extract final revenge for the death of Fergus and as he checked the rear of the Transit had been emptied, he saw to his delight that Revie's cricket bat was still stowed against the left-side bench just inside the door.

Reaching in, he pulled it out and hefted it against his right shoulder and then walked over to the Bedford, silently observing for a moment as Gregsy started to pull on his new Telecom overalls while Parlane, who had just handed the garment to the peterman, seemed mystified by the fact he couldn't find a suit for himself.

"Whit's happenin', McGrain, seems to be we are a suit short?" asked Parlane, his gaunt face puzzled.

"No, Colin, there's no mistake: it's time for you to say au revoir. But before you do, I'm afraid you'll need to make some restitution for the death of my comrade Fergus ..." McGrain let his words taper off as he waited for Parlane to erupt.

He didn't disappoint and taking a step towards McGrain in a finger jabbing, spittle-flecked rage, he let rip: "You fuckin' baw-bag, I've done everything you asked, McGrain! We had a bloody agreement and we both lost men over this, or have you forgotten I'm a man down tae?"

But Parlane's anger started to subside as he felt the cruel, needle-sharp steel of Spider's janbiya held against his back and the big man's powerful right forearm wrapping around his neck. "I'd shut the fuck up if I was you, Parlane," sneered Spider.

McGrain turned nonchalantly to Gregsy, pointing the cricket bat threateningly in the peterman's direction. "It's my hope, James, that I don't have to use this on you, but quite frankly I know this piece of vermin has been whispering poison in your ear and I don't know if I can trust you. So you will help me lash him down in the back of the Transit, no questions. Just do as you're told and you will get your reward," concluded McGrain.

At that, Spider started to force the furiously struggling Parlane towards the back of the green Transit and as they reached its doors McGrain lowered the cricket bat he had taken from the NatWest and lovingly ran his left hand over the crevasses and scars caused by ancient actions.

"Time to face the music and smile sweetly, Parlane," he said and Spider forcibly span him round. As the two came face to face, McGrain shouted "Six!" and swung the bat in a sweep that would have graced the hallowed turf of Lords, watching in cruel delight as the willow connected with Parlane's cranium and his nemesis crumpled beneath the blow.

As he came around moments later, the first thing Parlane felt was the biting tightness of the ropes that lashed his ankles and his wrists to the floor of the Transit.

His head throbbing, he nonetheless shook it to try and get the fog that shrouded his vision to clear and as his sight returned fuzzily, Parlane found himself facing a scene that filled him with sheer terror.

McGrain, his pupils dilated and a feverish energy working his features, now held the exotic, cruel blade he'd inherited from his legionary service. McGrain saw Parlane's gaze and began to lecture him: "I thought James may have made you aware of the delights of a janbiya, another old Legion companion of mine. Now I'm going to demonstrate what a lethal weapon it is … on you, Parlane," smiled McGrain tauntingly.

Parlane tugged furiously at the ropes that were binding him tight to four fixings on the van floor.

"There will be no escape for you this time, Parlane. I had hoped to use your death to cover our tracks, but our situation changed …" mused McGrain, hunkering down next to Parlane's head and slipping the janbiya's curved blade under his chin. "Rest assured, though, I'm going to give you a send-off fit for a king … you, my dear Parlane, are going to have your very own funeral pyre, here in the Transit …"

Before he could continue his cruel taunting monologue, Parlane interrupted him desperately: "Come on, McGrain, this is fuckin' nuts … after all we've been through, the agreement we had reached, for Chrissakes, man, you said you were chucking it and heading for the sun …" fired the prostrate Parlane, his eyes straining at their sockets, in a machine-gun delivery as the hopelessness of his situation started to engulf him.

"But before I apply flame and Spider sends you over the cliff and into the sea, it's fitting that this magnificent 19th-century, hand-crafted Ottoman antiquity enacts vengeance on you in a manner entirely appropriate for your assorted misdemeanours to me and mine over the years. Do you know what it means to be hung, drawn and quartered?" asked McGrain pleasantly.

It was clear from the startled expression that whiplashed across Parlane's angular features that he was all too well aware of the meaning but his natural default position of sneering, vicious anger resurfaced in a show of desperate defiance: "What madness is this yer spouting now, McGrain, you maniac … how many of them little white pills have you popped, you fuckin' lunatic?" he spluttered.

"Just the one," laughed McGrain, "but let's not stop that getting in the way of your history lesson. Being hung, drawn and quartered was a particularly barbaric medieval form of punishment imposed upon traitors pursuant to ancient common law: namely, partial hanging, disembowelling and cutting of the body into quarters … but the good news for you, Parlane, is that before your funeral pyre plunges into the Irish Sea you will only have one of this gruesome triumvirate inflicted upon you!" said McGrain, almost sheened by his drug-induced ferocity.

At the rear of the van, Spider swung himself into the Transit and kneeled down at Parlane's midriff, ripped his shirt open, then produced his own ivory-handled instrument of death. "Just say the word, Tony," he spat, but McGrain's keen eyes strayed across his shoulder to locate Gregsy's disbelieving, ruddy face.

"Non, mon frère, that honour shall be bestowed on young James," and his dark gaze locked on Gregsy's startled features, challenging him to refuse.

The peterman knew he was between a rock and a hard place, yet his revulsion meant he had to protest: "In the name of the wee man, McGrain, is this naw the type o' thing the bastardin' English did tae the Wallace? I'm sure we did it in O Level history … for fuck's sake, McGrain, tell me yer jokin'!" he pleaded.

"This is no joke, but the ultimate test of your loyalty, James." McGrain's pointed his Glock Gregsy's way. "Now get in the van, Mr Fuckin' Peterman and do as you're told."

Seeing he had no choice, Gregsy got in and at a nod from McGrain Spider handed him his curved blade. "The good news is that we're naw gonna bother cutting his baws aff, wee man. Now just rip him across the gut and I'll do the rest ..."

"For Chrissakes, McGrain, stop this, stop it ... I'll do anything you want, any fuckin' thing ..." begged Parlane, looking up at his sneering tormentor.

McGrain stroked his captive's cheek tenderly and sidled past his lashed body before jumping out of the van and taking up a position at its rear doors.

For a moment he stood there in silence and this time it was the increasingly queasy Gregsy who pleaded on behalf of the accused: "Come on, Tony, this, this ain't right ... it's way too much ..."

But Spider had already clamped his powerful right hand around his wrist and was drawing Gregsy's paw and the janbiya it held now ever closer to the exposed skin of Parlane's midriff.

"Sweet Jesus, please, McGrain, stop him ..." begged Parlane.

At the back of the van, for a moment, McGrain rubbed his unshaven chin and appeared to be considering a stay of execution, but his show of doubt was just pantomime. "Slice him James ... it's him or you ..."

As Gregsy hesitated, McGrain took a step forward and jammed the Glock against the back of his head. "You have until three, peterman ..."

"Jesus, naw dinnae dae it, Gregsy ... for fuck's sake, McGrain ..." pleaded Parlane, but the sound of the safety catch being released on the Glock was the last straw for the peterman and closing his eyes he ripped the Damascus steel across Parlane's midriff, immediately feeling the hot jets of blood slosh over his hands as his victim screamed like a banshee in the night.

Next to him, Spider grabbed the janbiya and shoved Gregsy away. Reaching into Parlane's innards, he yanked out his bloody intestines and held them high above the agony-wracked, almost unconscious criminal. "Fuck you, you piece of sewage," he snarled and cut through their bloody rope like knots, slamming a ruby slime-enveloped chunk into a bin liner next to him before ramming the rest of the intestines down on top of the semi-conscious hitman.

As Parlane's eyes rolled, Spider taunted him: "Ain't it nice to know, dear Colin, that a piece of you'll be forevermore buried back home in Glasgae where ye belong. Buried in The Blood Acre!" and then he grabbed the bin liner and vaulted back out of the Transit as his mortally wounded victim continued to fill the air with a mixture of howls and screams that would not have been out of place in the deepest depths of hell.

At the side of the van, Gregsy was being violently sick, but next to him McGrain was a picture of calm as he struck a Swan Vesta off the side of its box and tossed into the back of the vehicle.

As Parlane's howls dipped in pitch to a barely audible series of moans, the flames started to take hold and after one last satisfied look at the effects of his handiwork, Spider ran round the side of the motor, turned the engine on, released the handbrake and clicked the van into first. With a final gun of the accelerator, he set the vehicle in motion and, just 10 feet before the cliff face, jumped out and regained his feet just in time to see the vehicle plunge into the inky depths below.

Yards away, McGrain hauled Gregsy to his feet. "You have a choice, James ..."

"Which is?" croaked the peterman, as he swallowed down more vomit.

"Come with us to Belfast ... or follow in Mr Parlane's slipstream."

Chapter Fifty-Four

THE WHITE TRANSIT van with the twin rag-tied ladders running over its roof rack sat at the corner of Balornock Road, 300 yards away from the bar, lights out and no evidence of anyone home; but through the blackened rear windows a Nikon camera with a zoom lens ensured that no detail of the life that came and went at The Cairns Bar was missed.

For Collins had been as good as his word and the safe house where The Creepers were trading their ill-gotten gains had been identified as the Balornock Pub that straddled an area of wasteland and golf course that made it easy for various species of local wildlife to come and go as they went about their nefarious activities.

Numan and Malcolm, resplendent in their white painters' and decorators' boiler suits, manned the van emblazoned with 'The Brush Off: Painters and Decorators, No Job Too Small' from the Balornock side of the pub at the top of Lamont Road. Meanwhile, Thoroughgood and Harry Currie had parked their red Bedford Van at the Bishopbriggs side of the lane that wound its way between the marshland and Little Hill Golf Course and were now picking their way carefully on foot, rain stinging their faces, to the rendezvous point scouted by Thoroughgood.

It was also where Collins had agreed to meet them.

The bar itself was nothing much to look at: a single-story building that was a mixture of cream-painted brickwork and maroon-coated woodwork. Inside at the bar, his nose deep in the pages of his Sun, sat a denim-clad male with a monstrous black moustache with a mind of its own and a head of hair that was almost as unruly.

Draining the remnants of a pint of Tennent's, Kenny Hardie cleared his throat roughly and gaining the attention of the bar manager, Frankie Docherty, he said gruffly: "Put another one in there would you, pal?"

Docherty, a bald, pot-bellied man with jowelly features eyed the newcomer with suspicion as he had done since he had turned up just after 10 p.m. For Monday night was slow even by The Cairns' usual standards, which had meant that aside from Hardie only three other gents of an OAP variety were nursing their 'hawf and a hawfs' over a game of dominos in one of the bar's dingy linoleum-lined corners.

Pouring the Tennent's, he watched the male with narrow eyes. "Sure thing. Sorry, whit did you say yer name was?"

"I did'nae," answered Hardie in a voice that was so low it could have been coming from the soles of his Adidas Samba trainers.

But Docherty wasn't to be put off by his brusque reply. "So what brings you to our cosy wee corner of Balornock, mate?"

"Not that it's any of yer business … mate … but my old Auntie Fanny pegged it and has left me her hoose down the bottom o' Lamont Road. So I was gaspin' for a pint after gieing the auld place a fresh lick o' paint and thought it wiz time to gie my new local a look!" replied Hardie with an insincere smile, as he pushed two pound coins across the bar.

While his job was to cover the front of the bar and occupy its owner, known as Frankie-Fingers for his ability to get his dibs on virtually any item of contraband ever requested of him, Hardie had been less than impressed by having to spend his night on a detail, that although, of course, in the interests of authenticity was blessed with some liquid consolation, was, he thought, hardly likely to provide much to write home about.

Yet although the tip-off from Collins had suggested the fun and games would all take place at the rear of the boozer, Hardie had to admit to himself that Frankie-Fingers was indeed looking a little bit twitchy. As the bar manager checked the clock above the gantry behind him for the third time in the last 15 minutes, Hardie lowered his Sun and said: "Aye, no wonder your clock-watchin', pal, is it always as slow as a wet weekend in Butlins?"

Docherty curled his top lip and snapped: "Whit do you expect from a boozer in the arse-end o' Glasgow on a shitty Monday night … mate? But you know what the good news is, that's last orders and you'll be able to go back to Auntie Fanny's in a quarter of an hour—" but before Frankie-Fingers could finish his reply, the sound of a phone ringing through the back of the bar grabbed his attention and judging by the speed with which he went to answer it there seemed little doubt that Docherty had been waiting for the call.

Hardie did his best to lean over the chipped dark wooden counter and strain his ears for all they were worth in order to gain a snatch of the conversation, but the assorted noises of the fruit machine now helpfully being played by one of the bored pensioners, and his cronies accusing him of rudeness for deserting their domino table, made it all but impossible.

Yet as he glanced at the gantry clock and saw the hands pointing to 10.50, Hardie knew that if Collins' information was accurate the call was almost certainly to alert Docherty to the fact his visitors would be arriving sometime soon.

Finishing his pint, Hardie stood up and arched his body over the counter like an arthritic limbo dancer warming up and was rewarded by a temporary stilling of the fruit machine behind him, which in turn allowed a snatch of Docherty's conversation to drift his way.

"The deal was 11.30 tae allow me to close up and get the punters oot. Whit dae ya mean there's been a change o' plan? Tell me how the fuck am a supposed to shut up shop and deal wi' yous at the same time, Alby … you knows it's just me on a Monday night," rat-a-tat-tatted Frankie-Fingers in his strangely high-pitched, staccato delivery.

For a moment only the sound of silence seeped through from the rear of the bar. Then Docherty's whine perforated the airwaves once again: "Awright, I get it, it's just a few old gits and some jakey readin' a Sun, so I can throw them oot nae bother," and with Hardie bristling at the bar counter after being referred to as a jakey, Docherty slammed the phone down and made his way back to the counter, where he was met with a particularly titillating image of Linda Lusardi smiling at him from page three.

Grabbing the top of the paper he smiled at Hardie. "I'm sorry, mate, but due to illness in the family I'm shuttin' up shop a wee bitty early tonight. Okay, gents, it's time to drink up and get tae: Monday night at The Cairns is officially over."

* * *

As Currie and Thoroughgood trudged down the leaf-strewn lane that would take them from Auchinroan Road through to the waste ground at the rear of The Cairns, they heard a three-note whistle penetrate the dark and rain from their left flank. There, peering over the dyke that marked the boundary of Littlehill Golf Club, was Collins, his Berghaus-sheathed arms leaning along the top of the wall and his pristine white smile lighting up the gloom.

"Well, if it ain't Bayne Street's answer tae Starsky & Hutch!" he quipped.

Collins' smart-mouthed remark went down like the Titanic with the senior cop. Currie, decked out in a three-quarter length purple Jack Wolfskin anorak and matching Calgary waterproof hat that made him look like he was ready for an expedition to the Cairngorms rather than a night out in Balornock, snapped his right hand across the dyke to grab the informant, who just about managed to elude Currie's clawing fingers. "That's a smart mouth you've got on you, son. I just hope for your sake that your info is spot on and naw gonna be leading us on some wild goose chase."

Collins flashed his pristine grin. "Why don't I gie you a hand over the dyke, old-timer ... or d'ya think yous can make it yersel'?" laughed the tout.

"All right, gents, let's just keep the noise down and get behind the wall," soothed Thoroughgood, cupping his hands and nodding to Currie that he would be best going first up and over the wall.

Moments later, after a bout of mumping and moaning, the senior cop landed on the golf course side of the dyke with Thoroughgood dropping down adroitly a yard away.

"Look, a dinnae want tae be out in the pissin' rain on a shitty Monday night any more than yous, but this is it. The Creepers, like a said when a belled ye earlier, are on their way in for the back o' 11 and from whit am hearin' they've got somethin' very tasty for Frankie-Fingers to get his dabs oan!"

Currie remained sceptical. "Okay, Billy Big-Time, and what's that?"

But Collins was keen to prefix the info with his own set of terms and conditions. "Aw naw, not until the Cat gets his deposit …" and at that he eyed Thoroughgood before adding: "Well, guv'nor?"

Before Thoroughgood could reply, Currie, his eyes popping, shot out a retort: "Now hold on a minute, what's goin' on here, Gus …"

But before he could finish his protest, Thoroughgood fished out a small black plastic wallet with 'Strathclyde Police' embossed on it in faded gold leaf writing and slapped it against the tout's chest. "There you go, Collins, a ton up front as agreed." As he did so, he studiously avoided Currie's disgusted gaze.

"Aye, and a fuckin' bargain at the price tae, if I dinnae say so masel!" rapped Collins.

But Currie was far from convinced. "Christ, Gus, I thought you would have learned a lesson after that business with Nicholas! So never mind givin' us your chat, whatever your name is. I want to know exactly what it is The Creepers are supposed to be bringing in or I will personally take that ton back off you and boot your arse up the 18th fairway," raged Currie, his eyes bulging from their sockets.

"All right, grandad, keep yer hat on," replied Collins, before checking his watch and adding: "Sometime in the next 15 minutes am expecting Alby and his brothers to be rocking up in their shitty wee Nissan Homy and in the back I expect tae be some very tasteful silverware and artwork from a joab they pulled in a big hoose out in Lenzie last night! And dinnae be thinkin' that'll be aw they'll have in the motor for old Frankie-Fingers ..."

But before Collins' could continue, Thoroughgood interrupted: "Wait a minute, that'll be Kelvinmore House, it was done last night: I caught it in the Daily Briefing Register earlier on. Lord and Lady Kelvinmore were left gagged and bound after they were dragged out their four-poster at knifepoint. The old boy got thrown down the steps of his grand staircase and was left with a fractured skull for his protestations. The DBR said there was some priceless artwork stolen but didn't specify just what ..." concluded Thoroughgood as his eyes narrowed in on Collins.

"Aye, well, from whit am hearing there is an auld – whit-dae-you-call-it ... mister ... is it? – been whipped aff the wall in Lord Kelvinmore's study up in wan o' his turrets and the silverware is gonna make Alby a tasty sum once it's melted down ... but to make that all happen they need a fence who can get gear as hot as the Ashoka's vindaloo movin' and Frankie-Fingers is the man for that," smiled Collins, adding a wink for good measure.

This time it was Currie who spoke up: "Master: Old Master is the term, you bloody eediot. Well, Kelvinmore has always been secretive about his art collection but how the hell would The Creepers know where to look for an Old Master and know exactly where it was hung like that?" he asked puzzled.

"Simples, auld yin the gardener has been knockin' aff Lord Hawhaw's daughter when she's home from her fancy fee payin' school and he's one o' Alby's first cousins ... so dae a need to put two-and-two together for yous?" asked Collins, his eyes twinkling with mischief.

"Bloody hell," said Thoroughgood, but before he could say anything else the night was filled with the noise of a diesel engine thrumming its way ever closer and drawing parallel with the front of The Cairns, a black Nissan Homy drew to a temporary halt as its three occupants nervously scanned the area for anything out of the ordinary.

Satisfied that the coast was clear, the Homy drove down the road's sharp incline, turned left into the large rundown car park and then reversed towards the rear of The Cairns, where the two rusting metal burgundy doors located in the bottom-left corner of the rear wall had opened and Frankie-Fingers stood illuminated by the light of his cellar.

Seconds later, the driver's door opened and out jumped a slight male with a navy-blue jerkin zipped up to his neck and a New York Yankees baseball cap pulled down tight over his head, which meant the black-framed glasses he wore were only just visible.

"Game on, it's Albert Stringer all right!" exclaimed Thoroughgood, barely able to suppress the raw excitement coursing through his voice.

To his right Collins chimed in: "Just like I said it wid be, chief." But Thoroughgood was already on his walkie-talkie relaying the news to Malcolm and Numan.

Chapter Fifty-Five

STANDING FREEZE-FRAMED in the cellar doorway, his fingers fluttering excitedly from clasped hands that perched on his chest, Docherty twitched his digits in the trademark manner which had helped, alongside his illicit sideline, contribute to his nickname.

Drawing to a halt 2 feet away, Alby Stringer took a final look around the car park, scanning the house at the end of Balornock Road, which had a partial view of the rear and side of the pub.

But contented that the dwelling was in darkness and that there were no other signs of life that might provide a threat to his business, he smiled at Frankie-Fingers and offered a tepid handshake.

"Awright, Frankie, you were'nae jokin', it's pan breed sure enough and jist as well, man. 'Cause the shit we've got in the Homy is the haul o' a lifetime … nae feckin' doubts aboot it, man," said Stringer, holding his hand out as, right on cue, his siblings sprang the boot door of the van open.

Some 200 yards away, from their concealed view behind the dyke, three sets of watching eyes widened at the delight that lit up Docherty's ruddy features, while from the blackened back window of a white painters' and decorators' van a Nikon started to click.

"Sweet Christ!" exclaimed Frankie-Fingers, his eyes zeroing in on the gilt-framed painting that was being removed by the younger Stringer brothers. "I'd bet ma shirt on it … it's a bleedin' Goya!"

"Maybees aye, maybees naw, that's what your cut's for, but let's get it inside your cellar and the rest o' the shit with it before the rain soaks it and some fuckin' dug-walker does'nae go stumbling across something he should'nae be clappin' his mince pies oan!"

And before he could reply, Docherty found himself forced to flatten his corpulent body against the left-hand wall of his cellar as the imposing painting was carried in by Frankie and Johnnie Stringer. But as they drew level with him, Johnnie lost his grip on the frame and the painting started to slip towards the cellar floor; just in time, Docherty's hands shot out underneath the frame and held it steady.

"In the name of the wee man will you be careful with this … have you any idea how much this painting may be worth?" he raged.

"Naw, big man, but I'd say you're ready to step in for the Celts if big Packie Bonner rips a hamstring, so there's nae need to be worrying! Anyhow, am sure yer gonna tell us, like," retorted Johnnie, his feral features sparking with anger.

Reassured that the Stringers now had control of the painting, the fence removed his fingers from underneath its frame. "At Sotheby's in New York earlier this year the 'Suerte de Varas' was sold for $7.9 million," beamed Docherty triumphantly.

A yard away, Alby Stringer's nasally tones erupted: "Yer fuckin' kiddin me, Frankie?"

"Do I look like I'm jokin', Alby? If I'm correct then this work is called 'Charles IV of Spain and His Family' and was painted by Francisco Goya between 1800 and 1801. Look at the detail here …" said Docherty, as he took a step closer to the canvas and traced a finger lovingly over it. "See the guy painting on the canvas at the left-hand side at the back of the royal family? That's Goya himself … there's long been rumours that old Kelvinmore had something special in his private collection but an Old Master, with such provenance … it beggar's belief …"

Shaking his head in a mixture of surprise and irritation at Docherty's delight, Stringer snapped: "So tell me, Frankie … just how does a bar owner in Balornock come tae know so much aboot aw this shite?"

Fingers smiled knowingly. "I'm from a travelling family, Alby, and back in the seventies for some pocket money I used to head down south and help out my Uncle Chad when him and his boys went out on the rob around various country houses in Oxfordshire and some other English shires. Over the course o' time I got to know quite a lot about art and the like and when I came back up north they needed helpin' out making some particularly hot stuff disappear and it just grew arms and legs from there," said Docherty.

But Alby Stringer was already becoming impatient with his art lesson. "That's aw very well, Frankie ... but provenance ... I could'nae gie a monkeys if it wiz the man from the Prudential who fuckin' painted it ... alls I want's tae know is can ye shift it for us?"

Behind him, the weasel features of Alby's younger brother Johnnie appeared. "Alby's right, Fingers, if this is whit you say it is and yer man stands it up then how the hell are we gonna get it shifted and get a decent bang for oor buck, like?" he demanded.

Docherty scratched his egg-shaped dome and a knowing smile started to slip across his features. "'Cause there's always some punter somewhere who will pay top dollar to add an Old Master to his private collection. This Goya has been missing from the public eye for over 50 years since the Spanish Civil War and it was rumoured that General Franco used some of his country's art treasures to pay off those who had supported him in his hour of need ... but how the hell it came to be in Kelvinmore's collection ... well, your guess is as good as mine ... it's unbelievable ..."

For a moment the only sound in the cellar was that off Frankie Stringer continuing to unload the high value contents of Lord Kelvinmore's household and irritated, he spat in his whining voice: "For fuck's sake, am ah the only wan here who's gonna dae any work ... this stash will'nae unload itself, ye ken."

"Awright, Johnnie, get back tae work, will you, and bring me oot these wee gold boxes we came across next ... before Frankie here has a heart attack …" said Alby, his eyes twinkling with mischief and a crooked smile breaking across his sallow features.

As the seemingly endless flow of golden candelabra, plate and other fine antiquities came to a stop and Frankie Stringer closed the Homy's boot, Johnnie removed a box from the front seat and joined his three confederates in the cellar, presenting a Barkers Brogues shoebox to Docherty and slipping the lid off. "Whit dae ye make o' this, Fingers?" he asked.

Such was the joy and wonder that lit up Docherty's face it was hard to tell if he was going to laugh or cry. "Sweet Mother Mary …" he stammered as he clapped eyes on six intricately designed gold and mother-of-pearl containers.

"Well … so whit the hell have we got here, Arthur bleedin' Negus?" demanded Alby Stringer, before barking out a harsh laugh.

For a moment, lost in wonderment at the sight before him, Docherty remained in stunned silence, before he started to shake his head. "I'll tell you whit we have here, Alby, son … these little beauties are 18th-century German snuffboxes and for specimens as ornate and finely handcrafted as these, we could be talking anything up to £500k a pop … Jesus H Christ, Alby, just what have you gone and done!"

"Never mind that, Arthur … the bottom line is, can ye fence' em and just what can I expect back?" rapped Stringer.

Casting his eyes over the contents of his now half-filled cellar, Docherty's brain started to do the maths and after a couple of moments of chin stroking he smiled. "Okay, so I will be able to get rid of the standard stuff like the gold plate, silverware and other household bric-a-brac via the usual channels and you can expect a good few grand back, but the Goya and the snuffboxes … well, they're gonna take time, Alby … as I'm sure you'll understand. This is all going to have to be catalogued and labelled up and presented to the right people, it's naw just a case o' takin' it doon the Barras and seeing what I can punt it for."

"Awright, Frankie ... dae a look like a gotta zip up me back ..."
but before Alby could finish his sentence, the sharp crack of a piece
of wooden foliage outside alerted the gang to the fact they might
have unwanted company.

CHAPTER FIFTY-SIX

"WHIT THE FUCK wiz that?" snapped Alby Stringer as his three confederates froze with apprehension.

"I'll bet it's the local young team, been havin' problems wi' them and the shite they keep daubin' on ma walls," replied Docherty, before adding: "But I know how tae deal wi' a bunch o' wee scroats," and he walked over to a black bin positioned at the foot of the stairs that led up to the pub itself and after fishing about he removed a machete. Turning to face the Stringers, he said: "I'll teach the wee bastards a lesson once and for all."

"Whit else you got in there?" asked Johnnie, and the younger of the three Stringers jogged over to the bin and gave out a yelp of satisfied delight at the sight meeting his eyes: "Ya beauty!" he said, before presenting a chair leg with nails of various sizes protruding from up and down its length. "C'moan, Alby, lets gi' this young team a wee lesson," he said, throwing a pool cue towards his elder brother and following Frankie-Fingers to the cellar doorway.

"Aye, fair enough," said Alby, his mitts wrapped reassuringly around the cue. "We cannae be havin' the local shite puttin' our big pay day in jeopardy. On ye go, Fingers, open the door and let's gi' them a pastin'!"

But as he rearranged the last of the loot at the left-hand side of the cellar, Frankie Stringer shook his head in trepidation. "Look, bros, I think we needs tae be careful here, this could get real messy. Plus whit if it's just some auld dug-walker like you said?"

But 10 feet in front of him, Docherty was already pulling the up-and-over door to the ceiling of the cellar. "Dinnae be worrying about that, wee man, if it's a case o' mistaken identity, I'll throw in a bag o' Winalot for Snorbitz, like, and everything will be smellin' o' roses!" chortled the fence.

But as the metallic door snapped up and over, the sight meeting the Creepers stilled Docherty's grating laughter instantaneously.

The denim-clad male who had previously been in residence at The Cairns' Bar stood 10 feet away, a glinting grin twitching from underneath his Pancho Villa moustache.

"Seem to have lost ma Dalmatian, Winston; just wonderin' if he's wandered into your cellar, pal?" asked Hardie, and just as he finished his opening gambit, two males clad in white painters' boiler suits walked out from the shadows on either side of him.

As a look of utter bewilderment started to spread across Docherty's face, the denim-clad male's right hand shot out and in it he presented a plastic card. "DC Hardie, Strathclyde Polis. Frankie-Fingers, yer fuckin' nicked and I'd put that machete down sharpish if I was you!"

As realisation started to break over Docherty the Stringers decided to adopt an every-man-for himself-policy. "It's the fuckin' rozzers, boys: bolt!" shouted Alby to his brothers and the three Creepers charged out from the cellar just as Docherty began to raise his machete in an arc towards Hardie's extended hand. "Polis ma arse!" he screamed.

But the DC had been watchin' Fingers with the intensity of a hawk and was ready for his attack. Before the blade had reached head height, Hardie's right hand buried itself in his midriff and he watched with delight as the fence crumpled onto the wet tarmacadam, groaning and clutching his guts. "Jim Watt, eat yer heart oot!" said Hardie.

But while his confrontation with Docherty had come to a premature end, the Stringers were determined that they wouldn't be going anywhere without a fight and Johnnie Stringer charged out of the cellar, lobbing the nail-spiked chair leg into the night and shooting into the treeline that flanked the rear of The Cairns.

Yet as he did so, a grey-haired male with mad eyes loomed in front of him, hooked a Doc Marten boot around his legs and was rewarded with the sight of the youngest Stringer brother hurtling through the air and landing in pile of leaves.

Before he could move, a knee rammed into the small of his back, his wrists were ripped round behind him and twin steel bracelets snapped on them until they bit deep into his skin. "Nae luck, wee man, the game's up!" said Numan.

While Johnnie had taken the right turn out the cellar, Frankie Stringer, who was last to make his appearance, found his hope of a great escape brought to an almost immediate end.

Sprinting out into the dark, he collided with a wooden baton that rammed against his windpipe and in one fell swoop took the air well and truly out of his sails, leaving him clutching at his throbbing throat and gasping for oxygen.

But while his siblings and Docherty had all had their bids for freedom brought to a shuddering end, Alby Stringer's darting eyes had charted a zig-zagging course that took him in-and-out of the series of tag matches that had filled the night air with assorted expletives and groans.

For Alby knew exactly where the best hope of escape lay and that was either down the footpath to the left of The Cairns or across the fairways of the Littlehill Golf Course and as he left behind the free-for-all in the car park, he saw the 5-foot-high stone dyke that marked the boundary of the golf course appear sketchily in the night.

But as he hit the juncture of the footpath with the boundary of the wall, he found the lane blocked by a looming figure clad in state-of-the-art arctic wear.

"Aw naw you dinnae!" smirked Currie and in doing so made Alby's mind up that his only hope of eluding the strong arm of the law was to vault the dyke.

Swinging himself up onto the top of the wall with the grace of a male Nadia Comaneci, he landed cleanly on the sodden turf at the fringes of the 18th green.

"It's always nice to land a wee birdie on the last," quipped a voice from the black and no sooner had Alby's chalk-white features creased with surprise at the anonymous words of welcome than a right hand smashed off his jaw and he pirouetted with supreme grace into a bunker flanking the green.

Standing above his captive, Thoroughgood's relief at a job well done manifested itself in a harsh laugh just as Collins appeared at the other side of the sandpit.

"I'd say that wiz a perfect 10 for artistic impression, boss, whit you think?" said the tout.

CHAPTER FIFTY-SEVEN

ALMOST AN HOUR LATER, the charge bar at Bayne Street 'Z' Division HQ resembled Sauchiehall Street as The Creepers and Frankie-Fingers were lined up ready to be processed.

Surveying the trooping of the dammed, Sergeant Sam Storey beamed with delight at the work of his men and turning to the Duty Officer Dougald McGarry, he said: "A sight for sore eyes, Inspector McGarry, wouldn't you say ... The Creepers bagged and tagged and the most notorious fence in the north of the city, who has repeatedly eluded the charms of the Fine Art Squad and our local CID, all taken down by Community Policing Department ... er, with a little help from our friends at the Proactive Unit, Force HQ," he nodded respectfully in the directions of Malcolm, Numan and Hardie.

McGarry's pince-nez glasses seemed almost to defy gravity as they slipped to the bottom of his aquiline nose but somehow clung to it, while his eyes looked up across the bar at the assorted assembly of cops and neddery. "Aye, Sergeant Storey, your boys have done you proud, there's no doubt about it. From what I'm told it's going to take a month to catalogue the content of Mr Docherty's Aladdin's cave, never mind the locating of a long lost Old Master here in the North ... it's quite unbelievable really!"

While this bout of self-gratification was taking place, Thoroughgood felt a tap on his shoulder and was met with a curt nod of the head from DS Malcolm to join him at the back of the prisoner processing area.

"Look, Angus, it goes without saying this is brilliant work and from what I've heard the Night Shift Super is on his way to Bayne Street to offer his personal congratulations. Your name will be on every gaffer's lips at Force HQ, including the chief. Between the painting and the German snuffboxes, this turn is worth millions ..." Malcolm's word tapered off into an awkward silence.

"But?" asked Thoroughgood, his elation draining from him.

"But, needless to say, while you might be lauded from pillar to post among your friends in uniform, I'm afraid it will only stoke the enmity borne you by DI O'Toole. He will have to be careful that his resentment doesn't manifest itself as outright and obvious jealousy but make no mistake, given him and Lynch gave Alby Stringer a tug and got he-haw, he'll take this as a personal insult to his ... authority and, if it wasn't out before, the knife will be well and truly being sharpened for your back," warned Malcolm.

Thoroughgood shook his head ruefully and opened his hands in a gesture of bewilderment, but before he could say anything Malcolm piped up once again: "The other thing you need to know is there has been an interesting development with O'Toole's friend McGrain. It's possible, although unconfirmed, that friend Tony and chums may have been involved in a bit of a shootout on the M74 ... which now means they are down south and ready to pull whatever job it is they have planned. So McGrain and his team are now in the wind and my hope is that will blow them back towards Glasgow ... to that end we will be watching persons of interest ... like the good DI ... But I need you to hook back up with your new best friend Mr Meechan and shake that tree ... understand?"

The young cop nodded his head in the affirmative but before he could say anything, a whining Glaswegian voice 3 yards away grated into life: "A want ma lawyer, that bastard o'er there has broken ma feckin' jaw," spat Alby Stringer, giving Thoroughgood a death stare.

From the other side of the charge bar, Inspector McGarry cast a sceptical gaze Stringer's way. "Is that so, Mr Stringer? Would you like to step forward and substantiate your claim?" asked the Duty Officer and as Stringer reached the charge bar, McGarry lifted the giant leather-bound charge book with both hands and smashed it down on Stringer's head.

For a second time that night, Stringer dropped like a stone as all hell broke loose at Bayne Street Police Office.

* * *

From behind his desk, Sergeant Sam Storey produced a bottle and three glasses. "If ever there was time to toast a success then this is it, gents. I like to keep a good bottle of Highland Park for such celebrations," he said, pouring the golden liquid and pushing back an unruly strand of his comb over.

To Thoroughgood's right, Harry Currie smiled and said: "To be fair, gaffer, it's all down to young Gus here and one of his touts. After that business with Nicholas, I was'nae sure you could be trusted to run a tout as opposed to be being run by one but you've come up trumps with this …"

Thoroughgood quickly helped his neeber get over the sudden attack of amnesia. "Collins is his name and that reminds me, we need to make sure he gets taken care of … sarge!" he said, eyes searching Storey's supine features for confirmation that Collins would get his just desserts.

Finally, after savouring the contents of his whisky glass, Storey replied: "And what exactly was Mr Collins looking for?"

Thoroughgood cleared his throat nervously. "Er, one large, a council house in Auchinroan with a front and back and well … er … an HGV driving course …"

Storey just about spat out the contents of his next mouthful of whisky. "He wants what? An HGV driving course? God's eyes …"

But the words had hardly escaped his mouth before Harry Currie exploded into a fit of uncontrolled, raucous laughter that was soon echoed by his companions.

Recovering himself eventually, Storey's lips pouted like a trout and he shook his head. "Aye, he does'nae want much does Mr Collins but then we can hardly quibble with the turn he's served us up."

Thoroughgood smiled as much in relief that his tout would get the reward he deserved as anything else, but couldn't help himself voicing another concern that was gnawing away at him: "What about O'Toole and Lynch, gaffer?"

"What about them? You leave them to me. What this turn has done in one fell swoop has ended O'Toole's hopes of taking control of all our extracurricular plain-clothes operations and using our resources for his own end and in effect turning us into a poor man's CID. So you can leave O'Toole to me. I'm sure SDO Newton will be delighted when he sees my report waiting for him in the morning and most keen to put DI O'Toole's vaulted ambitions in their place. Unfortunately, when it comes to your own hopes of a CID Aide, I know that as ridiculous as it may seem, given the turn you have just orchestrated, O'Toole is now even less likely to admit you."

"It's no big deal, sarge, the main thing is that The Creepers will be remanded and soon doing serious time for their assorted misdemeanours—" But before Thoroughgood could complete his sentence, there was a knock on the door and Storey looked up suspiciously.

"Come in," he called out and as the door opened Storey's face was lit up with amazement at the entrance of DI Ronan O'Toole.

"Good evening, gents, I thought I would make the effort to be among the first to congratulate you, young Thoroughgood, and also you, Senior Constable Currie, on your … notable success. To have snaffled The Creepers and Frankie-Fingers in one fell swoop, then netted an Old Master and a set of 18th-century German snuffboxes in the process has to rank among the greatest turns ever pulled off in the history of 'Z' Division. It is certainly one that, it goes without saying, must be rewarded," said O'Toole, beaming a slightly forced smile but nevertheless offering a handshake first to Thoroughgood, then Currie and lastly Storey.

But as always with O'Toole, there was a sting in the tail. With the tightening of his jaw betraying the suppressed rage that he was wrestling with, he said: "Clearly I'm a bit disappointed that you thought to mount this operation without advising 'Z' Div CID of your activities concerning a person of interest for us ... but given your ... well, spectacular results, it would seem churlish and petty to put you, Sergeant Storey, and your men on paper, after all we are all on the same side ... aren't we?"

Storey produced a smile of stunning obsequiousness and dipped his head slightly in respect. "Although, perhaps it doesn't seem that way sometimes, Detective Inspector O'Toole ..." said the CP sergeant, sarcastically drawing out the DI's surname into a temporary silence before continuing: "that is indeed the case, so why don't you join us for a wee goldie ... I'm sure a man of your calibre is partial to the charms of a 12-year-old Highland Park."

His brown eyes pulsing and his teeth gritted, O'Toole, with considerable effort, retained his composure. "I'm afraid I'm only an hour into night shift and as much as I would like to, your little haul is going to require quite a bit of backup work in terms of further interviews, never mind getting the paperwork mountain underway, while the CID clerk will also have to be primed. So if you don't mind, I will politely decline your offer. But what I will say, Constable Thoroughgood, is that I will be recommending that you are rewarded for your efforts with the next available CID Aide. We must make sure that a talent like yours, Thoroughgood, and your network of informants is put to best use for the good of the Criminal Investigation Department, where it belongs," concluded O'Toole, with a smile that seemed to underline his remarks were almost more of a threat than the promise of a highly prized reward.

But with that the DI nodded his head and gave a squeak-heeled about-turn on his loafers before exiting stage left in a precise manoeuvre. Behind him, the stunned silence was deafening.

CHAPTER FIFTY-EIGHT

THOROUGHGOOD SAT perched on the end of The Ubiquitous Chip bar and checked his watch for the umpteenth time. As usual he was early, this time so that he could chew on the events of the last 24 hours, which had seen him lauded but left completely confused as to which direction he was in fact going.

O'Toole's offer of an Aide was the last thing he'd expected and one that he now viewed as a poisoned chalice. In the aftermath of the DI's departure from the CP sergeants' room it was clear that both Storey and Currie agreed with him. Yet the realisation of a CID Aide had been at the front of every hope and ambition he had for his police career and now that it was being offered to him it came doused in danger.

But the reason for his arrival at the UB Chip further complicated his acceptance of any such Aide and the necessity to work under the direct supervision of O'Toole it would bring, for he was here to meet Meechan and in turn learn as much as he could about the whereabouts and activities of O'Toole's alleged star informant … Tony McGrain.

Sipping at his Fürstenberg, Thoroughgood also found the faces of Emma and Celine starting to jockey for position in front of his mind's eye.

Shaking his head, Thoroughgood raised his eyes in exasperation and asked himself 'Can it get any more complicated?'

Yet he knew that there really was no dilemma. As he kept telling himself, Celine had made her choice and that choice was the ambitious, dangerous criminal who would soon be joining him at the bar.

Meechan, the coming man of the Glasgow criminal underworld, who wanted to build a relationship with him that would act as a firewall against his own criminal rivals, while also ensuring that the gold-plated information he provided Thoroughgood helped suppress his feelings for Celine.

But now these feelings, whatever they were, had been further muddied by what had happened with Emma. Poor, tragic Emma, who had seen her brother killed in a car crash when she was an infant and lost her mother to the ravages of cancer before reaching her mid-twenties.

"A man deep in thought I see," said a familiar, slightly lisping Northern Irish accent in an amicable tone that was nonetheless laced with lingering contempt.

Meechan had arrived and after a curt nod of greeting he ordered two pints of Fürstenberg and gestured to a table next to the fire that had just been vacated by two suits.

A few minutes later, Meechan laid their beers down and said: "I hear congratulations are in order: your turn up at The Cairns Bar has sent shockwaves through Glasgow. A turn like that can only come from blue-chip information, so from where I'm sitting you should also be congratulated for your cultivation of the snout who provided it … but then that's something you are proving increasingly adept at!" concluded Meechan from behind that hooded gaze of his, which Thoroughgood found slightly unnerving and made Celine's burgeoning relationship with 'the West End businessman' even more unpalatable.

Aware that Meechan was waiting for a reaction to his charm offensive, Thoroughgood gave none and instead took a deep draught from his pint.

Yet as he lowered the Fürstenberg back onto the table, Thoroughgood knew that the onus was very much on him to make the running … for Meechan had what he wanted … 'in more ways than one,' chimed the voice in his head helpfully.

But as he turned his gaze towards him, he found Meechan's almost sonorous voice already in action: "Let's start with the bad news first, shall we? McGrain is in Ireland, being housed by his friends across the Emerald Sea and I don't expect him back anytime soon ... but ..." and Meechan let a theatrical silence draw out.

Their eyes locked and Thoroughgood knew that the silence was a deliberate attempt by Meechan to underline that the balance of power in their collaboration lay firmly with him. He gave in to the inevitable: "But?"

"But one of his gang is pining for his home town and wants to come back to Glasgow to see his old ma, who is undergoing chemo at The Western!" said Meechan, the slight tremor of a smile twitching across his saturnine features.

Before he could control them, Thoroughgood's dark eyebrows twitched. "You're kiddin' me, Meechan ... what you're telling me is that you have access to a member of McGrain's team?"

"Oh, it's better than that ... Angus ... I put him there to serve this purpose ... a human Trojan Horse, if you will, all-seeing, all-listening and now tarred with the guilt that has covered McGrain and his men's hands in the blood of innocents!" concluded Meechan, studying his pint pot.

His baiting of the young cop was too much and despite himself Thoroughgood's right hand reached out and clamped onto Meechan's wrist as he lowered his Fürstenberg. "The blood of innocents ... what do you mean, Meechan?" he demanded, trying to link Meechan's titbit with the quickly mumbled conversation he'd had with DS Malcolm at Bayne Street's charge bar.

"I mean that a branch of the NatWest was turned in the Lancashire Port of Heysham and in the process the bank manager and a female teller were executed. I mean that in another incident less than a mile away two coppers and a Chinese delivery man were found with their throats slit ... what does that all add up to, Angus ... do you think?" asked Meechan, his grey eyes burning with intensity.

"Jesus," said Thoroughgood, and then the wheels of his mind turning, he added: "Wait a minute, I'm sure I caught that one on the Radio 2 news the other day … the three million job, wasn't it?"

"Precisely. Three million pounds in used bank notes now all in the hands of the IRA's main fixer in England, Connall McGrath, or The Leprechaun as he is known. All taking place just a couple of miles away from a fast ferry to Belfast. So, Gus, just how much Semtex do you think three mill' buys?" asked Meechan, making his point with interest.

Thoroughgood held his hands up. "All right, Meechan, you've got me hook, line and sinker. So you have an infiltrator in the gang and he's coming back to Glasgow … the bottom line is, are you willing to give him to us and how do we huckle him?" he asked, his eyes locked on Meechan.

"I see I have your attention now … Angus. But I'm afraid I am not ready to give you all of that … just yet. Because, naturally, for information of this standard and an ongoing service of similar quality I will need to have our arrangement formalised and the protection that goes with that in writing. So what I need you to do is to go back to your handlers in the newly christened Proactive Unit at Pitt Street and tell them I want to be formally enrolled as your informant and I also want a concrete reassurance that my boss Jimmy Gray and I will have a certain amount of leeway when going about our business here in the West End."

Then buttoning up his navy-blue Prince of Wales check double-breasted suit, Meechan quaffed the remnants of his pint and stood up. "So there you have the rub of it, Angus … we have reached the point of no return, the start of a beautiful friendship or the end of something so promising yet agonisingly, tantalisingly, out of reach. If I was you, I'd be having that conversation with the persons you need to sometime very soon," said Meechan with a glint-eyed flourish, and then he left the bar.

CHAPTER FIFTY-NINE

MEECHAN WOUND his way down the UB's stairs and headed out onto the cobbles of Ashton Lane, flicking up the lapels of his suit jacket to guard against the sting of the early evening cold.

As he did so, a voice as rough as a sack of gravel penetrated his thoughts: "Awright, sir, gonna help oot a poor doon an' oot wi' a quid for a cup o' tea?" asked the beggar in a soiled beanie with a dark Berghaus zipped up to his chin, sitting cross-legged on what looked like a tea towel with a curled-up Jack Russell for company.

Meechan looked down on the beggar, sending a disgusted sigh the unfortunate's way. "Lucky beggar. Bet you're worth more than I am, wee man," and as he fished out a handful of shrapnel, the beggar whipped off his beanie and held it out, allowing Meechan, who couldn't help himself barking out a harsh laugh, to empty his change into the hat.

"Top of the day to you, sir, yer the King o' the Cobbles!" said the beggar, but Meechan was already walking away, his mind working overtime on the next piece of the jigsaw he needed to assemble.

As Meechan walked past the Cul de Sac, the beggar got up and folded his tea towel into precise quarters, gave the Jack Russell a rough pat on his head and was met with a snarl.

"Easy, mutt," he replied, then clamping his beanie back on his head he peered around the corner into the blackness of a winding wrought-iron staircase, where a white-haired ancient sat guzzling on a can of Carlsberg. "Well done, old yin, you were worth every drop o' yer Super Brew," said the erstwhile beggar, before producing the most ridiculously gleaming smile.

"Whit aboot the change?" asked the beggar, looking for Meechan's contribution to find its way to his opened paw.

"Maybe you should use a couple o' quid to feed Patch here some sausages instead o' pourin' it doon yer throat, ya old throbber!" admonished Collins, ignoring his entreaty. Ramming his hands into his Berghaus, he made his way along the cobbles.

As he did so, a dark-haired male in a black Harrington shouted across the street from the doorway of The Ubiquitous Chip: "Ain't you got anything better to do than harass an old jakey?" and was met with a repeat showing of that brilliant smile.

Winking, Collins said: "Just concerned he had enough money to feed his wee dug, guv'nor!" and flicking a wink Thoroughgood's way, he doffed his beanie before sauntering down Ashton Lane, always keeping to the shadows, and just managing to re-sight Meechan as he turned a corner 100 yards away.

As he walked up Hyndland Road, Thoroughgood was warmed by the thought that putting Collins on Meechan's tail might yield some scrap of information that could be useful; yet at the same time he worried that it might provide a return of a more personal nature. Hunching his shoulders, he once again tried to keep his personal concerns from clouding his need to retain a professional clarity.

But reaching the front gate of Cottiers, the converted church that had now been turned into a thriving bar, restaurant and theatre complex, Thoroughgood continued to chew over Meechan's latest serving of titbits.

Who was the homesick gang member? Was McGrain really behind the Heysham job? And if the money was bound for the coffers of the IRA, then how could they be stopped before 1990 became a year known for hundreds of dead civilians south of the border?'

As he slipped through the door, Thoroughgood took a sharp left and headed for the public phone. He punched in Numan's number and waited for his pick up. "DC Numan, Proactive Unit, how can I help you?" the voice at the other end replied, to his relief.

* * *

Thoroughgood looked down at his watch. When he saw that it was 8.17 p.m. a sense of panic engulfed him. His conversation with Numan, covering every angle of his meeting with Meechan and bringing the DC up-to-date with his little idea of using the Cat as Meechan's tail, had left him woefully late.

Scanning the punters that lined the bar, Thoroughgood was met with the faces of the usual Friday night sweethearts and wolfish wannabe Lotharios who did the rounds of the West End bars and probably of each other in a choreographed dating ritual that was likely to conclude at the Western Tennis Club Friday night disco, where the ultimate acts of drunken fumbled foreplay took place.

But there was no sign of Emma and wincing Thoroughgood admitted to himself that it was no more than he deserved. "You're a dobber, Gus Thoroughgood. Could belling Numan not have waited? She probably walked out the door while you were spoutin' your guff!" he admonished himself and nodded as the bartender recognised him and started to pull his favoured pint of Kronenbourg.

Setting his pound coins down on the counter and muttering "Cheers, mate," for service well rendered, Thoroughgood took a draught of the pint.

As he did so, he felt the soothing, honeyed words wash over him: "Hi Gus, sorry I'm late," said Emma, and turning round he met her gaze and didn't even try to stop the relief sweeping over him lighting up his face.

Shocked at the intensity of his emotions, Thoroughgood found himself acting on auto-pilot as he stooped slightly and kissed Emma on the lips. "All that matters is that you're here now, darlin'," he said.

Five minutes later they sat at a table just vacated by a middle-aged couple who seemed to be having a hard time deciding whether the delights of their bottle of Black Knight outweighed their obvious need to get a room, but with the latter evidently winning, Thoroughgood and Emma gratefully took their vacated seats.

"I wasn't sure whether you would have waited for me, Gus, but you know what it's like finding a parking space around here on a Friday night," said Emma, smiling sweetly.

Her words, however innocuous, felt like they had just thrown a bucket of icy water over Thoroughgood, for their implication was obvious, but he tried to recover himself. "Look, Em, I'm just glad you're here," he replied, lapsing into an old familiar term of endearment for her.

"But what about you, Gus? That turn at The Cairns – wow! – how did you manage to pull it off, I mean we're talking millions of pounds worth of stolen art. You're the talk of the steamy at Bayne Street!" purred Emma.

"Good information is everything, Em. Once you have it, all you need to do is make sure that all the basics are covered and I have some very good teachers when it comes to that. But I don't want to waste our time talking about the job … I've had enough of that for one day!" said Thoroughgood, smiling wanly.

"So, what do you want to talk about?" asked Emma, her blue-green eyes holding his in their delicious gaze.

"I want to talk about us. I want to know how you are, Em, want to know if you're strong enough to give us a second chance after everything you've been through with your mum," said Thoroughgood, his words almost trailing off into a whisper.

Emma's eyes pooled with moisture and for a moment Thoroughgood thought that the impatience and directness that had always been his failing had once again undermined his hopes.

Wiping her tears away with her index finger, Emma took care not to smudge her mascara and then took a sip of her glass of house white, wincing at its taste. Surprised by her reaction, Thoroughgood couldn't help breaking into an involuntary laugh and it had the effect of dissipating her sadness.

"Yuch, it's like cat's pee!" she exclaimed and took off her Guess leather jacket with faux fur to reveal a chocolate velvet blouse that left Thoroughgood captivated.

"But you'll drink it nevertheless, or should I get you a Bacardi Breezer?" he quipped and slipped his paw across the top of the marble-topped table and onto her hand. Again their eyes met, but this time there was the warmth of a smile in them.

"Are you ready, well … er … do you want to start again?" asked Thoroughgood, despite himself.

Although she didn't remove her hand, Emma's reply surprised him: "Only you can answer that," she said and deliberately let a silence develop.

Thoroughgood scratched his earlobe and couldn't help looking confused. "I'm sorry, Em, but you have me at a loss … what do you mean?"

"I mean what about Celine Lynott? From what I've heard, you've had a pretty intense thing going on. Maybe that's because you saved her life, but I don't imagine something like that just falls apart at the click of a finger?" she asked and did as she had just said to underline her point.

Thoroughgood shook his head. "I'm afraid the stresses of life bring people together that maybe are not … well … compatible … and maybe that was the case for me and Celine. The intensity of a moment, the drama of a set of events that are now so surreal they just don't seem like they could have happened or belonged to the real world. Then when everyday life, when the mundanity of it all returns and the drama has gone … well, that's when the cracks surface and perspective makes it clear that maybe what was right in the heat of the moment just doesn't work on your average shitty Glasgow Monday morning," concluded Thoroughgood.

"So what you're telling me is that I am the type of girl who fits in just perfectly with your average shitty Glasgow Monday morning?" asked Emma.

This time Thoroughgood laughed … nervously … worried that he had once again put his size 10s in it, but a mischievous smile soon broke out on Emma's face and he breathed again.

"We used to have a laugh, Em. I know you haven't had much cause to smile of late but maybe if we can start to look forward then we might have a chance … this time," he concluded.

"But you still haven't answered my question, Gus: what about you and Celine?" asked Emma for a second time.

Thoroughgood had no need to reply for at the other end of the bar, in full exotic splendour, wearing a black leather trilby and a leopard-print fur coat that had every male head in the vicinity turning her way, walked Celine, her arm linked through that of a sandy-haired, smartly suited male in a Prince of Wales navy-blue checked suit.

His gaze sweeping the room, Meechan's eyes triumphantly met Thoroughgood's and as the latter's attention had now so obviously wandered to the bar, Emma half-turned round in her seat to see what was the source of the diversion.

Looking her way was Celine and her lips pouted slightly as she stared haughtily their way, her eyes smouldering as they dismissively left Emma to lock on Thoroughgood.

For a moment he held her stare and everyone else in the bar seemed to disappear as time stood still.

"And I take it that Miss Lynott has just entered the bar?" asked Emma.

CHAPTER SIXTY

FOR A SECOND her words didn't seem to register; but after a moment Thoroughgood managed to rip his eyes back from Celine to Emma. "She has and as you can see, she also seems to be looking forward pretty quickly. But this isn't about her, this is about you and me, Em, and I'd rather we talked about that somewhere there are no other distractions ... well, I was hoping we could maybe talk about it back at mine ..." suggested Thoroughgood, aware that he may have overplayed his hand.

For a moment Emma studied his face and then she smiled again. "As long as you have a decent bottle of white in your fridge!"

"Sauvignon Blanc okay for you?" he replied, relieved.

"Perfect," said Emma, and standing up she pulled her jacket back on as Thoroughgood finished the remains of his pint.

But as they made their way towards the door, Meechan's sonorous voice called their way: "Leaving so soon, Angus? I was hoping we would be able to join you and your young lady," he taunted.

Before Thoroughgood could say anything, Emma beat him to the verbal punch: "And just why would you want to do that, mister?" Looking at Celine she added: "I'd steer clear of the house white, honey, it's a paint stripper." Then, before anyone could react, Emma grabbed Thoroughgood's arm and led him across the floor.

The voice inside Thoroughgood's head said: 'Thank Christ for that!'

As they moved towards the door, Thoroughgood's eyes moved from Celine's to Meechan's and a faint smile developed across his taut features; but as the sharp night air hit him he was snapped from his torment by a rough Glaswegian accent coming from the shadows of Cottiers' courtyard. "Look, boss, am sorry aboot that, but he made me, bastard's no' as dumb as he looks," said Collins, stepping out into the yard's lighting.

On his arm, Emma squinted at Thoroughgood and said: "Interesting …"

As he looked Collins' way, Thoroughgood didn't know whether to laugh or cry; the shrug he produced seemed to underline that confusion as the informant handed him a piece of paper. "Tae be fair to Meechan, looks like it's turned out okay for yous, boss. He told me to gie yous this … after I'd had a conversation with his shooter … bastard was only packin', like."

Thoroughgood took the piece of paper and unfolded it and there written in immaculate, extravagantly looped handwriting was an address. "Ward B1, the Beatson Oncology Centre, Western Hospital. The Trojan Horse has returned from the Emerald Isle," read out Thoroughgood.

"Whit's that aw about?" croaked Collins.

"Yes, Gus, what exactly is this?" asked Emma, the words Thoroughgood had just spoken bringing back painful memories.

Looking from one to the other, Thoroughgood replied flatly: "It means that Meechan has just given me the location of the man who is at the centre of this whole thing: the problem is I don't have a fuckin' Scooby who he is."

For a moment Thoroughgood replayed Meechan's words in his head: 'I'm afraid I am not ready to give you all of that … just yet. Because, naturally, for information of this standard and an ongoing service of similar quality I will need to have our arrangement formalised and the protection that goes with that in writing.'

So why had Meechan changed his mind and coughed up, or at least provided the location of the man who could be the key to this whole web of intrigue and duplicity?

The next question that assailed Thoroughgood was just how he was going to track down Meechan's Trojan Horse in a cancer ward and despite himself, Thoroughgood's reached up to his head and started massaging his temples.

"So, boss, is it somefin' or nuffin'?" asked Collins.

His hands dropping to his sides, Thoroughgood looked at them both. "You don't know the half of it, Collins. The bottom line is that if I can find out the identity of our mystery visitor to the Beatson then it's the piece that may make the whole jigsaw fit together," said Thoroughgood, his eyes straying towards an enthralled Emma.

* * *

The words on the piece of paper Collins had handed him had sent Thoroughgood's brain into overdrive and the romantic evening he'd had planned with Emma had in turn been dominated by the import of Meechan's luxuriously looped handwriting.

And now Emma had been caught up in the scheme he hoped would ultimately put all the jigsaw pieces together and solve the riddle of what lay in The Blood Acre.

Parking the MG Metro down by Kelvin Hall, Thoroughgood and Emma crossed Dumbarton Road and headed for the rear of the Western Infirmary where the Beatson was situated: for Emma had argued that as she had such recent – although harrowing – memories of the centre, her knowledge of how it worked and where everything lay was without doubt an advantage that he had to make the most of.

Standing outside the entrance he smiled at Emma. "Look, are you sure you want to go through with this, I know we talked it over last night but it's gonna stoke up some real painful memories when you walk back in there?"

Emma's smile was weak and already he could see the torment that was starting to well up inside her. Thoroughgood pulled her close tenderly and spoke gently: "I'm sure we can get the patient info with

296

a warrant. This was a bad idea. Nothing's worse than what this is going to do to you: come on, let's leave it for now and get a coffee."

But Emma pulled away from him and despite the moisture pooling in her eyes she said defiantly: "If Meechan thought it serious enough to give you this information last night don't you think that there is every chance the man you seek will be here in the ward today at visiting time?"

Thoroughgood shrugged, conflicted about enlisting Emma to do something that was obviously going to be a source of angst for her, yet was essential if they were going to lay hands on the key player in this game of shadows.

His features relayed that torment and Emma looked up into his sea-green gaze and ran a hand down the side of his face. "Give me 10 minutes, Gus. I know the duty sister pretty well from my mum's visiting ..." and as her words broke down with a tremor of emotion, Emma turned away and walked through the entrance doors leaving Thoroughgood impaled by guilt.

CHAPTER SIXTY-ONE

As Emma entered Ward B1, the first thing that hit her was the familiar pine-fresh smell of the disinfectant and the thought struck her, as it always did, that Molly Weir had managed to offload a bumper consignment of Flash on the Western.

As she passed the fire doors and approached the reception desk, she saw the familiar bunned hair of Sister Maynard – or 'Hattie' as everyone in the Beatson called her, on account of her uncanny likeness to the nursing matron played by Hattie Jaques in the Carry On films.

But Emma's eyes were soon straying to an empty bed, the only one that lay vacant, in which her mother had wasted away and finally lost her cruel fight with the ravages of cancer, before she had been relocated to Strathcarron Hospice for her deathbed. As Emma replayed these tortured images, the tears that she had known she would inevitably shed upon her return to B1 began to cascade down her cheeks and she fumbled for a tissue inside her jacket.

As she did so, a flinty voice sparked into life just next to her: "Awright, darlin', here you go, I know it's tough, but you gotta hold it taegether for yer loved wan, don't ye?" said a ginger-haired, ruddy-featured male grasping a bunch of Esso petrol station flowers like they were the cure to all known ills. He helpfully fished out a Scotties tissue from his parka.

"Thank you," was the best that Emma could manage in between sobs that she desperately sought to stifle and to her amazement her knight in shining armour gave Emma a reassuring pat on the shoulder: "I knows it's tough, am in tae see ma maw after another blast o' that radiotherapy, like, but as I says you gotta try and suck it aw up for yer loved wan. Is it yer maw or da? Oh by the way, it's Gregsy," added the twenty-something, offering a tepid, awkward handshake.

Emma managed a weak smile as she took his hand, while a part of her computed his appearance, name and the possibility that, just maybe, she had blundered into the man they were after. Taking a deep breath she replied: "It was my mum, she … she was in bed five, over there," she finished in a quivering rush.

"Christ, am really sorry tae hear that, darlin' …" stammered Gregsy, but before he could dig himself a deeper hole a voice croaked from the bed diagonally opposite in the top left-hand corner of the ward.

"Jamesy, son, yer back fae Ireland," said a sallow-skinned woman, her grey-streaked dark hair hanging lankly over a lilac nightgown.

Standing a foot away to Gregsy's right, Emma tried hard to stop this crucial piece of information from betraying it's impact on her face, but she had no time to worry about that as a familiar singsong voice greeted her from the reception desk: "Emma, my dear, you've come back to visit us!" said a delighted sister Hattie in her sibilant Isle of Barra accent and she waddled across the ward to clasp Emma close to her sizeable bosoms.

Then the nursing sister held Emma at arm's length and looked her up and down with a matronly appreciation. "My, you're looking well and how are things? I am glad you've come back to see us, dearie: sometimes it can help you get closure. Come on over to the nursing station, I've just boiled the kettle!" purred the delighted sister.

But as she tried to provide a polite show of gratitude at the warm reception of a nurse whom she had almost come to regard as an honorary aunt during the final weeks of her mother's torment, Emma made sure she kept an eye on Gregsy, for there was now no doubt in her mind that he was their man.

At the top of the ward, Gregsy practised his best bedside manner. "So, Maw, how are you?" he asked, stooping down to envelop his mother in his loving arms, and awkwardly forgetting that he had still to put the bunch of flowers down.

"Jamesy, lad, am so pleased you came but …" and Gregsy's mother dropped her rasping voice to a conspiratorial whisper: "But should you be here? Ah knows you've been up tae yer tricks, ma bold boy, and I'll bet the coppers are hunting high and low for you."

Gregsy grabbed a red moulded chair and slapped the Esso flowers down on the bedside cabinet. He poured them both a glass of water, handed one to his mother and with his free hand plucked a grape from the bunch that was conveniently located in the fruit bowl at her bedside.

Then as he finished chewing the grape he smiled beatifically at his mother, leant down and gave her a quick peck on her jaundiced cheek, whispering: "Look, Maw, these coppers dinnae know their arse fae their elbows, like, we've just pulled wan o' the biggest jobs in England and buggered aff tae Belfast on a ferry with three mill' in oor bags, so if they could'nae get their mitts on us then, whit chance have the rozzers got oh hucklin' Gregsy in Glasgae?"

Propped up on her elbows, the fragile state of his terminally ill mother was underlined by the wheezing that accompanied her attempts to drink the water Gregsy had given her, but as she handed it back to him and rested her head on a pillow, auld ma Greg smiled at her only offspring with the all-forgiving warmth that only a mother can afford her child. "And I hope no one got hurt on this joab, Jamesy?" she asked, her eyes shining with surprising clarity.

Gregsy's hesitation was fatal but as he attempted to splutter a lie, he was rescued by Sister Hattie's soothing Western Isles' voice: "Mr Greg, I assume? You really should have checked in at the reception desk with me but I suppose I was otherwise engaged. I must warn you your mother has just had another round of radiation therapy and although I know she is delighted to see you, please remember what she has been through. Try not to overexcite her, Mr Greg," she admonished.

Gregsy flashed his cheekiest naughty schoolboy grin. "Aye, nae bother, sister, I knows what you mean. I wiz just tellin' maw that the Guinness is so much better across the watter."

Sister Hattie's eyes sparkled with mischievous intent as she replied: "It's the same on the Isle of Barra. I wager they would be struggling to pour a more velvety drop of the black stuff than the pint poured in The Castlebay Bar! Now just remember what I said, young man," concluded Sister Hattie, with a matronly wagging of her finger and a concerned nod at Gregsy's mother who croaked a "Thank you, sister!"

Back at the sister's desk, Emma cradled her mug of tea and attempted to hear Gregsy's conversation over the strains of Hue & Cry's 'Looking for Linda' coming from the transistor on the filing cabinet behind the reception desk. Checking the ward clock, Emma saw that the afternoon visiting time was less than 5 minutes away from its conclusion.

As sister Hattie ambled back to her station she picked up her mug in a fleshy hand and smiled down at Emma. "I'm so glad you came back, my lamb. I know it's been hard to face but we still have some of your mother's belongings that need to be uplifted. Do you mind if I go and get them?"

It was the moment that Emma had dreaded but at the same time knew she must deal with sooner rather than later and she managed a shaky nod of her head in agreement.

Clutching her wrist reassuringly, Sister Hattie smiled and walked over to the locker area, scolding one of her nurses for a poorly made bed with an exaggerated raise of an eyebrow.

Over at bed eight, Gregsy was saying his goodbyes to his mother: "Look, Maw, am gonna fix everything, we're gonna get help with yer care when you get oot oh here. I phoned them Macmillan nurses when I wiz across the watter and it's aw sorted, whit a joab they do …" but seeing his mother had drifted into a fitful sleep he bent down and kissed her tenderly on her forehead and whispered a good-bye:

"Ah'll see you the morra, Ma, sweet dreams!" and with that Gregsy plucked another grape, pushed the chair back and headed over to the reception desk where Sister Hattie had just handed Emma a small polythene bag filled with assorted knick-knacks that had belonged to her late mother.

"It's just some toiletries and a diary your mum kept; I don't know if you knew about it?" asked Sister Hattie almost apologetically.

As she nodded her thanks, Emma could feel herself welling up again and clasping the bag in a trembling hand she saw the black leather pocket diary with her mother's initials 'MM' written on it in her spidery handwriting.

"Thank you," croaked Emma just as a clearly concerned Gregsy smiled his own gratitude towards Sister Hattie.

"Thanks a lot, sister, Maw's sleeping now but can you tell me how she's really daein' like, what's the whit-do-ya-macall-it ... prog ... somethin' anotha?" he said.

"You mean the prognosis, young man. The best person to speak to about that is the consultant, Dr Armitage, and I'm afraid you've missed him for the day, so you will need to come back tomorrow," replied Sister Hattie.

"Aw, come on, sister ... you must be able to gie me somefin?" asked Gregsy, his agitation beginning to show.

"What I will say is that your mum is responding well to her treatment but we know she has a fight on her hands. Now as I said, if you are back here at the same time tomorrow, Dr Armitage will be able to go over the details of your mum's treatment and progress but can I assure you, she is well cared for here and wants for nothing," concluded Sister Hattie, placing a reassuring hand on Gregsy's wrist out of habit.

For a moment he seemed to struggle with a lump in his throat as the emotion of the moment hit Gregsy, before he finally managed a reply: "Aye, well, she's aw I got, sister, so anything Maw needs you let me know," and with that he turned his attention to Emma, who stood opposite him not knowing whether to stick or twist. "Seems like me and you hae a lot in common, sweetheart. I wiz wonderin', could I buy you a wee pot o' tea?"

Emma didn't know what else to do but smile and before she knew it she was being guided out of B1 by a grinning Gregsy who could hardly believe that he'd gone to hospital to visit his terminally ill mother and come out with the woman of his dreams.

But as they walked through the revolving doors and out into the ambulance bays, a dark-haired male approached Gregsy from his right-hand side and rammed the barrel of a handgun into his side from inside a Harrington jacket. "One stupid move and you're toast, pal," said the male, just as Gregsy felt his left wrist being grasped and his palm jerked viciously to face the skies as his body contorted into a horizontal position. "Cuff the bastard, constable," said Thoroughgood.

Emma smiled back. "With pleasure!" she replied and snapped steel bracelets on his wrists with assured dexterity.

"Aiya, ya dirty polis bitch, you've done me up like a feckin' kipper!" screeched the raging Gregsy.

Ramming the peterman against the nearest wall, Thoroughgood patted him down for weapons and was surprised to find Gregsy had come without insurance.

"Travelling light then, Mr Greg?" he enquired.

"What yous expect, copper … that am gonna be taking a Kalashnikov instead o' a bunch of flowers tae visit ma maw in hospital?"

CHAPTER SIXTY-TWO

FROGMARCHED ALONG Dumbarton Road, his handcuffed wrists covered with a copy of The Herald, the silently raging Gregsy soon found himself forced into the rear of the white MG Metro with Thoroughgood sat next to him, the shape of the gun inside his Harrington constantly trained on their captive.

As Emma settled in the driver's seat they both turned their eyes on the glowering peterman, who snapped: "So whit the fuck is this? Ah mean who the hell are yous, Bonnie and bleedin' Clyde? If yer polis I need to be seeing yer ID," he demanded.

From the driver's seat, Emma smiled sweetly and flashed her uniformed warrant card picture his way. "That good enough for you, sweetheart?" she asked sarcastically.

Gregsy curled a lip in a disgusted sneer. "Awright, soes yer the fecking law ... big deal. Why are yous hucklin' me from ma maw's bedside and anyway, whit about aw that fanny you were spinnin me back in the ward ... a crock o' shit wiz it and a river o' crocodile taers tae go with it. You disgust me, bitch!" he raged, the emotions of seeing his mother in such a grave state, and having been apprehended at his most vulnerable, taking him to boiling point.

But the only reward for his outburst was Thoroughgood's right hand clamping around his throat and snapping his head back. "I'd keep it civil if I was you, Mr Greg. Constable McCabe's mother did indeed die earlier this year, so anything she may have said to you about her mother was the truth. But that has got sweet FA to do with why you are going on a magical mystery tour with us ..." he said, letting his words drop off to invite Gregsy to bite, but

304

continuing to grip the peterman by the throat tightly enough to make him rasp.

Eventually the cop released his grip, smoothed down Gregsy's ruffled parka and seared him with the bite of his green stare.

"Ah, fer fuck's sake ... put me oot ma misery will ye, Mr Sweeney!" spat Gregsy.

"First of all, now that we're making introductions it's nice to meet you, peterman. You see, I've done my homework on you, James Greg, and you were the technical expertise behind one of the biggest robberies in English criminal history. You've just walked away with three million in your pockets. We know that three innocents and almost certainly two current serving police officers were killed on this job. That a considerable amount of the funds you helped steal are now being diverted towards an IRA bombing campaign south of the border. We also know who your accomplices were and for all of that you will go down for a long stretch which won't end until you're an old done man. That, quite naturally, will mean you're not there to take care of your dear mother and help see her off when the sad day comes and she pops her clogs," concluded Thoroughgood, the sides of his mouth starting to curl into a cruel smile.

"Dirty bastard," spat Gregsy and, despite his cuffed hands, he lunged across the back seat at Thoroughgood, slamming his forehead at the cop's face, but being met by a sharp elbow that took the brunt of his blow and sent him recoiling with his head spinning. "Aargh, rozzer scum!" raged the peterman.

This time Thoroughgood followed through with his elbow and pinioned it across Gregsy's throat. "Do that again, my friend, and we'll park up somewhere nice and quiet where you will have summary justice meted out. Now I suggest you listen to what I've got to say ... because it's your only hope of seeing your mother again and helping her through the final months of her struggle in the way that any dutiful son with the slightest bit of decency in him would want ..."

For a moment Gregsy shut his eyes and Thoroughgood could see that the peterman was actually trying to blink back tears. Then after taking a deep breath he opened his eyes and stared Thoroughgood straight back. "Then what you got for me, copper?"

For a second time Thoroughgood eased himself back towards his side of the rear seat. "I am told by a mutual friend of ours that in a piece of ground known locally – touchingly – as The Blood Acre, there are a group of corpses that bear testimony to your boss Tony McGrain's ruthless measures. That on one of them there may be something that will help incriminate McGrain and an associate of his who happens to be a current serving and senior police officer, to a string of gangland killings, some of which may also lie buried in The Blood Acre … would that be correct, Mr Greg?"

His reply came in the form of a one-word question: "Meechan?"

Thoroughgood replied from behind a poker face: "It matters not. What does is that you take us to this piece of land and help us uncover the evidence I have mentioned. If you do, and in so doing turn Queen's evidence, both you and your mother will be given the chance to start afresh, somewhere where your old maw can have the peace and quiet to meet her maker with dignity. Where you can be there for her, her ever-loving son, to the end," concluded the cop, scouring Gregsy's features for reaction.

"Fuck me, pal, you should have been a bloody reverend, no' a copper!" replied the peterman, his eyes straying to the front of the MG where Emma held his stare. "Look, miss, I'm sorry about your mum. Whit with you hucklin' me like that I did'nae know whether I was comin' or goin' there," he explained and was met with a smile of understanding from Emma.

Then Gregsy turned his gaze back to his inquisitor. "Well, reverend, your grass is right. On one of the bodies I planted a wee cassette recorder with a tape on which McGrain and his copper mate have a right interesting chat. Maw always told me to make sure I kept somefin' back for a rainy day and that is where it is, inside the anorak of a piece o' shit called Glavin, buried under a willow tree in a deserted churchyard called St Serf's and if the young lady swears on her mother's grave that yous'll be true to yer word and give me and maw what you said you wid then I'll take yous to it right now, Reverend … ."

"Thoroughgood is my name, Mr Greg," replied the cop.

"Jeez, that's a belter!" smirked Gregsy before turning back towards Emma and saying: "Soes are you prepared to do that, miss?"

This time Emma smiled wanly and switching her eyes to Thoroughgood, she sought his permission to give Gregsy what he asked for. Getting the green light, she said: "James, I swear on my mother's grave that you and your mother will get your fresh start if you turn Queen's evidence and … and that I will give you any help I can to make her final days comfortable."

Clearly moved by Emma's pledge to help him through what was to come, Gregsy turned towards Thoroughgood. "Yous better get the motor headed out the M8 … but wan thing, reverend …"

"Which is?" asked Thoroughgood.

"I get carsick if I have to sit in the back seat of a car for any length o' time, so if you dinnae mind I needs to be sitting up front!" he smiled through a crooked grin, and despite themselves Emma and Thoroughgood couldn't stifle their laughter.

CHAPTER SIXTY-THREE

O'TOOLE DRUMMED his fingers on the dashboard of the maroon CID Peugeot 309 and waited for the traffic lights to change. "Come on, come on," he muttered.

McGrain's tip-off that Gregsy had hightailed it back to Glasgow in order to see his dying mother had come too late. What had made matters worse was the information supplied by the overweight Teuchter nursing sister on the ward reception desk that he had left with a girl called Emma McCabe: a girl he knew to be a cop temporarily attached to Bayne Street Group Two shift, whose mother had six months back died of cancer. But more importantly, O'Toole knew she was supposed to have broken Thoroughgood's heart the previous year when she had ended their burgeoning romance to care for her late mother as the old dear entered the final stages of her grim battle with the 'big C'.

That could mean only one thing: that the two of them had hooked back up to set a honey trap for James Greg and he had almost certainly become stuck in it.

Yet that in turn gave O'Toole his main source of hope. Because, he reasoned, if Thoroughgood had pulled off this little stroke with the help of Emma, he was almost certainly operating off-duty, in an unofficial capacity and so without backup.

His mind working furiously as he turned the Peugeot out of the Western's rear access lane, O'Toole tried to work out the pattern of play as it would be if he was in Thoroughgood's shoes ... the end result wasn't difficult to arrive at.

Greg was only any use to Thoroughgood if he could get the peter-man to take him to St Serf's and the only way that would happen was if the cop had persuaded him to turn Queen's evidence, for that was surely the only thing that would make Greg take the bait.

That was blindingly obvious to O'Toole, for if it had been him who had huckled Greg, then he would have been sugar-coating everything with the enticement that both the peterman and his dying mother would be offered a fresh start, safe from the murderous revenge of McGrain and Spider.

So they were on their way to The Blood Acre. For there, O'Toole knew, lay the bodies that could be linked to McGrain but, as the crime lord had suggested to O'Toole in their phone conversation earlier that day, there may be something else lying buried in The Blood Acre that would incriminate him.

Worryingly, if that something was so important that Thorough-good was taking the type of chance he was, off-duty and vulnerable, O'Toole reasoned, it must be gold-plated.

Despite that alarming conclusion, a smile at last slipped across O'Toole's taut features, for half-a-dozen cars up, approaching the split between Argyle Street and Sauchiehall Street, was the pathetic excuse for a boy racer's motor that was Thoroughgood's white MG Metro.

O'Toole eased the Peugeot slightly out of the line of traffic and was rewarded by a view of the MG that confirmed there were three people in it.

Thoroughgood was behind the wheel and in the rear seat was a female with shoulder-length brown hair, while in the passenger seat was the ginger nut that almost certainly belonged to James Greg.

"Gotcha," snapped O'Toole and he fingered the Smith & Wesson nestled in his shoulder holster.

* * *

As the MG shot down the M8, Thoroughgood half-turned towards Gregsy, quickly checking his body language for any implied threat.

He knew he was taking a chance by allowing the peterman to occupy the front passenger seat, where he could threaten his control of the vehicle. Thoroughgood flicked a warning glance in the driver's mirror to Emma to make sure she was keeping a wary eye on their captive.

None of that was lost on Gregsy. "Look, am naw gonna be trying anything, now am I? We have a deal. Bottom line and it's the only one that works for me and my maw. I owe her everything, yous have naw idea whit it wiz like being brought up by a single parent back in Bridgeton in the 70s after yer da ran aff wi' a bus conductress. I owes Maw everything. So, I'll take you to St Serf's just like I said I would."

"St Serf's?" asked Thoroughgood.

"Aye, reverend, you'll love it there … the old ruined church, high on a hill in the middle of nowhere, where you'll find exactly what you need to finger McGrain and his copper mate. Anyway, never mind that, I'm feckin' starvin' … got any nosh?" asked Gregsy, taking the conversation in an unexpected direction.

Slipping his left hand inside the corresponding pocket of his Harrington, Thoroughgood saw Gregsy eyeing him with concern as the peterman waited for a handgun to be produced … instead, the young cop pulled out a banana.

"Here, make yourself useful, James … peel yourself that 'nana: it should help keep you from starving!" he smirked.

"Yer havin' a bleeding larff ain't ya!" snapped the peterman, catching the piece of fruit tossed his way. "So yer tellin' me that you've soddin' captured me with a … with a bleedin' banana …?" And he shook his head in exasperation.

From behind him, Emma's velvety voice piped up: "I think you'll find it was me that apprehended, bagged and tagged you, James. Anyway, I don't think that's an accurate way to describe things. What we're doing is giving you the only chance to turn your life around that you're going to get, never mind be there for your mum when she needs you. But tell me one thing James …"

Emma paused and as she did so she saw Gregsy's eyes flick into the mirror to catch her gaze. "And what would that be, miss?"

"Did you kill any of the people that died down in Heysham or whose bodies lie buried in The Blood Acre?"

His smile was sufficiently delayed to provide the true answer to that question but when his lips moved the reply was a half-truth: "None of the people that died down in Heysham were down to me, miss, you have my word. That was all down to that maniac Spider and McGrain himself."

Then quickly before Emma could resume her interrogation he turned back to Thoroughgood and added: "You need to take the next turn aff in 100 yards … just there, reverend … now we're just 2 miles away from St Serf's down this wee B road. You'll see it looming on yer right-hand side in a couple o' minutes, like."

"So, tell me, James, just what are we looking for in The Blood Acre; or would it be more appropriate to call it St Serf's graveyard?" asked Thoroughgood.

"There you go, right here, reverend," pointed Gregsy. "See it now at the top of the side road lined by the two dykes, there's the old bell tower and the ruined gable end, aye, an' the Garden Cottage just beyond the north wall," he pointed as the ruined church came into view about a quarter of a mile up a single-track road.

"You haven't answered Constable Thoroughgood's question, or mine, so why don't you start talking, James, because sooner or later you'll have to spill, no matter how painful it is," said Emma, trying to get the ball rolling.

"All right, I get it. What happened here was a double-cross and yeah people got killed and I pulled the trigger. But it was them or me and the only escape was to come out shootin'. Nae disrespect, miss, but you were'nae there and I wiz. If I had'nae pulled the trigger I would'ne be giein' you this wee guided tour. But whit I will say is that the maggots who bought it that night deserved everything

311

they had comin' to 'em. They chose their lives and they paid their price. So fuck 'em. Now, reverend, if you pull up just there in front o' the arch we can go get our paws on the prize."

Moments later they stood in front of a rusted, wrought-iron gate partially hanging from a rickety hinge under a stone archway that looked like it might collapse any minute. Ducking under the arch, Thoroughgood dragged Gregsy by the metal chain linking his cuffs, past the rotting wooden door of a gravedigger's hut that, left ajar, swung creaking in the breeze as they walked on into the graveyard.

Despite himself, Thoroughgood found himself surveying its contents. The Kirkyard was home to a collection of some fairly ancient gravestones in varying states of disrepair. The cop stared at the symbols of mortality, angels and hourglasses, skulls and crossbones, the Presbyterian Kirk's replacements for the papist cross. A shiver went down his spine.

As they approached the eastern side of the graveyard the rustle of the trees and the birdsong started to be drowned out by a different noise: running water.

Through the trees that edged a fast flowing burn pouring down off the hillside and running along the eastern border of the graveyard, Thoroughgood observed a delicate wooden bridge that looked like it would be lucky to remain standing for another hour.

Stopping just before a broken pile of stones, Gregsy turned to face his captors. "Okay here we go … soes we go over the bridge and through the trees and there yous'll find The Blood Acre and whit lies in it … ."

But before he could finish his sentence, a crunch of foliage indicated that the rising wind wasn't their only company.

"I think it's coming from the birches on the other side of the burn," said a startled Emma.

Focussing his eyes across the water, for the first time Thoroughgood began to regret the fact he was acting on his own, had dragged

Emma into his scheming and had not been able to make any contact with Malcolm and Numan, other than to leave them a voicemail on the office phone.

Chapter Sixty-Four

TURNING TOWARDS Emma and Gregsy, Thoroughgood smiled reassuringly. "The two of you wait here and I'll take a butcher's across the bridge and make sure we don't have any unwanted company," he said, then headed across the water, feeling the wooden trestles below his feet sag alarmingly as the snap of another piece of twig reported like a backfire.

Unarmed, without even the comfort of his wooden baton, Thoroughgood felt almost naked, as he realised just how vulnerable he was. Setting foot on the far bank he saw a flicker of movement in the knot of birches to his left and taking a deep breath he called out: "Police! If there's anyone there I suggest you come out before I—"

But Thoroughgood stopped in mid-sentence as the source of his alarm became apparent when the reddish-brown hide and startled grey face of a roe deer looked out from the treeline. Laughing with relief, the cop called out for Emma and Gregsy to follow him across the footbridge, greeting them with the good news: "It's okay it, was a deer!"

"Happy days!" laughed Gregsy, but his eyes had already strayed beyond Thoroughgood and their direction of travel was soon taken up by the two cops.

Less than 50 yards away against a partially tumbled down dyke, shaded by a waving willow tree, Thoroughgood could make out a rusted wheelbarrow inside which, conveniently laid at a precarious angle, were two shovels.

Half-turning towards his captors, Gregsy said: "Aye, that's it ... The Blood Acre ... we've got some digging ahead of us but under

314

that ground yous'll find what you need and I'd bet ma maw's life on there being plenty more where they came from not far away."

"Okay, there's no point in hanging about, who's pushin' up the daisies?" asked Thoroughgood, striding out for the dyke as he spoke and leaving Emma to pull the now seemingly reluctant Gregsy along in his slipstream.

"Jimmy Glavin, Boaby Simms and Shug Fowler," said Gregsy in a rush that indicated somewhere deep inside he needed to unburden himself of the events that had haunted him since he last set foot in St Serf's.

As he arrived at the dyke, Thoroughgood noticed that the ground was a pastiche of newly laid turf sods that had barely knitted together. A thought crossed his mind. "Were you present when the three amigos were buried?" he asked, searching Gregsy's features for a tremor of treachery.

"Present? Are you havin' me on, reverend … I fuckin' helped bury 'em with ma own hands. Now toss me a shovel and let's get tae it, 'cause inside Glavin's jaecket is all the evidence you're ever gonna need to put McGrain and his bent cop monkey away for keeps."

Thoroughgood's gaze flickered to Emma and he was met with an unconvincing smile; but after a second's delay he did as he was bid and handed Gregsy one of the shovels before setting to work on the seams of the turf, which resembled a green patchwork quilt.

It did not take long to break up and peel back the sods and then dig out the newly levelled soil underneath it, which left Thorough-good wondering just how recently the ground had been prepared, such was the freshness of the work. Suddenly, a piece of tarpaulin sprang free, as Gregsy's shovel penetrated 2 feet beneath the surface.

"Bingo!" exclaimed the peterman. He dropped to his knees and began to scoop the broken soil away with cupped hands like some deranged archaeologist on the threshold of a major discovery of the ancients and before long the polythene began to be revealed in its entirety. Through its transparent folds, Jimmy Glavin's ghoulish corpse gradually apeared.

"It's Glavin all right, just where I buried the bawbag," Gregsy said and ripped away the insulating tape that unconvincingly semi-sealed the front of the polythene free, then pulled either side of the tarpaulin open.

Looking on in a mix of disgusted disbelief and anticipation, Thoroughgood and Emma almost stopped breathing as Gregsy, still cuffed, slipped his hands inside Glavin's anorak and began to rifle the inside pockets; but the excitement and anticipation that had shone on his face began to turn to frustration, anger and now disbelief as his search revealed precisely nothing. "I, I dinnae understand it, there's hee-haw here," the peterman exclaimed, shaking his head in utter disbelief.

Pulling his hands clear of the corpse, a nauseating whiff of decomposition filled the air, and Gregsy stared at Thoroughgood completely at a loss to explain why his search had come up empty.

"It should be here, a blue Sony tape recorder, right where I left it in Glavin's inside pocket … it cannae be anywhere else … somefin's bang no right …" said the peterman, his darting eyes already frantically searching the area either side of the corpse. Locating a shred of black polythene that had burst through the disturbed soil and was flickering in the breeze, Gregsy's paws quickly started to shovel the dirt away from around it.

As a bin liner slowly revealed itself Emma called from behind him: "What have you got there James … is it another body?" she asked.

But before he had even opened the refuse bag, Gregsy knew the answer to her question and as he clapped eyes on its glistening, gore-streaked contents he groaned in sickening recognition at his find, just before a hail of blood, shattered bone and grey matter exploded from his cranium; Gregsy pitched forward into the grave, embracing the corpse of the man he had murdered just a few weeks earlier.

As he recoiled in shock, Thoroughgood automatically looked up and swept the area around The Blood Acre. Twenty yards away, his Smith & Wesson levelled at them, stood O'Toole.

Thoroughgood jumped to his feet and stepped in front of the screaming Emma, providing a protective screen. "O'Toole, you maniac, what've you done?" he shouted.

Continuing to train his handgun their way, the DI now advanced at speed; yet he was also glancing around him almost as nervously as Thoroughgood and the demented workings of his face began to alert the young cop that all may not be what it seemed.

"Thoroughgood, you fuckin' smart arse, what have you got yourself mixed up in—" said O'Toole, but for the second time in a matter of minutes, a shot rang out and an exit wound in the DI's chest exploded, spraying a ruby plume of detritus through the air. Just as he staggered down to his knees, a third shot cracked out and a sickening sense of déjà vu swept over Thoroughgood and Emma as O'Toole's head exploded and he toppled into the pit in front of them.

Shielding Emma, his eyes again scanning the horizon, Thoroughgood shuffled towards the dyke, knowing that his defensive actions would be an exercise in futility if the shooter's trigger finger twitched again.

Yet as he did so, the flicker of flame that had illuminated the gloom in the distance behind O'Toole had drawn the cop's gaze to the dormer window of the old cottage at the north end of the graveyard.

Desperately dragging Emma over the dyke, Thoroughgood realised that whoever he was, the sniper had beaten him to the contents of The Blood Acre and had been lying in wait for both them and O'Toole.

And now was almost certainly coming for them to finish the job.

Some 200 yards away, inside the garden cottage a hand lovingly stroked the barrel of a Fusil à Répétition modèle F2 bolt-action sniper rifle.

Then a rough-hewn Glaswegian voice spoke: "But Jesus said, 'suffer little children, and forbid them not to come unto me: for of such is the kingdom of heaven.' Matthew, Chapter 19, verse 14."

"Good shot, mon ami!" replied his confrère.